KU-404-093

Three Blind-
Date Brides

JENNIE ADAMS

FIONA HARPER

MELISSA McCLONE

Northumberland County Council	
3 0132 02124175 2	
Askews & Holts	Aug-2012
AF	£5.99

MILLS
BOON

All the characters in this book have no existence outside the imagination of the author, and have no relation whatsoever to anyone bearing the same name or names. They are not even distantly inspired by any individual known or unknown to the author, and all the incidents are pure invention.

All Rights Reserved including the right of reproduction in whole or in part in any form. This edition is published by arrangement with Harlequin Enterprises II B.V./S.à.r.l. The text of this publication or any part thereof may not be reproduced or transmitted in any form or by any means, electronic or mechanical, including photocopying, recording, storage in an information retrieval system, or otherwise, without the written permission of the publisher.

This book is sold subject to the condition that it shall not, by way of trade or otherwise, be lent, resold, hired out or otherwise circulated without the prior consent of the publisher in any form of binding or cover other than that in which it is published and without a similar condition including this condition being imposed on the subsequent purchaser.

® and ™ are trademarks owned and used by the trademark owner and/or its licensee. Trademarks marked with ® are registered with the United Kingdom Patent Office and/or the Office for Harmonisation in the Internal Market and in other countries.

First published in Great Britain 2012
by Mills & Boon, an imprint of Harlequin (UK) Limited,
Eton House, 18-24 Paradise Road, Richmond, Surrey TW9 1SR

THREE BLIND-DATE BRIDES
© by Harlequin Enterprises II B.V./S.à.r.l 2012

Nine-to-Five Bride, Blind-Date Baby and *Dream Date with the Millionaire* were first published in Great Britain by Harlequin (UK) Limited.

Nine-to-Five Bride © Jennifer Ann Ryan 2009
Blind-Date Baby © Fiona Harper 2009
Dream Date with the Millionaire © Melissa Martinez McClone 2009

ISBN: 978 0 263 89700 5
ebook ISBN: 978 1 408 97066 9

05-0912

Printed and bound in Spain
by Blackprint CPI, Barcelona

NINE-TO-FIVE BRIDE

BY
JENNIE ADAMS

**Welcome to the www.blinddatebrides.com
member profile of:
Kangagirl (aka Marissa Warren)**

My ideal partner…

I'm a very ordinary girl looking for Mr Nice and Ordinary to date, with the possibility of forever and a family one day, if it's what we both want. You should be willing to respect my rights in a partnership of honesty, openness, affection and friendship that will create the strong foundation we need to be together and stay together. You should be gainfully employed, in a job that puts food on the table and pays the bills rather than one that is the core of your existence. Therefore Mr Tall, Dark and Driven need not apply!

My details…

- **Age:** 29 years young
- **I live:** in Sydney
- **Marital status**: single
- **Occupation**: secretary

You'll match if you…

- Are between 29 and 35 years old
- Either live in Sydney or want to live here
- Are also single, but with a child would be okay
- No corporate highfliers

Australian author **Jennie Adams** grew up in a rambling farmhouse surrounded by books and by people who loved reading them. She decided at a young age to be a writer, but it took many years and a lot of scenic detours before she sat down to pen her first romance novel. Jennie is married to her own real-life hero, and together they share a hers-and-theirs family of three adult children. Jennie has worked in a number of careers and voluntary positions, including as a transcription typist and a pre-school assistant. Jennie makes her home in a small inland city in New South Wales. In her leisure time she loves taking long walks, starting knitting projects that she rarely finishes, chatting with friends, going to the movies and new dining experiences. Jennie loves to hear from her readers and can be contacted via her website at www.jennieadams.net.

For Fiona Harper and Melissa McClone.
How much fun was this?
For Joanne Carr and Kimberley Young,
with thanks for making the www.blinddatebrides.com
trilogy a reality.
And to the special man in my life—I won't tell we
agreed on marriage on our first date if you don't!

CHAPTER ONE

'YOU want us to turn this smaller bridge into a clone of the historic Pyrmont Bridge. I'm sorry, but we can't do that for you. The sites simply don't compare.' The boss of the Sydney-based Morgan Construction, Building and Architecture braced his feet on the uninspiring bridge in question, drew a deep breath and blew it out as he addressed the middle-aged man at his side.

Rick Morgan's rich voice held an edge of command and control that shivered over Marissa Warren's senses. The three of them stood atop the small Sydney bridge while the Morgan's boss explained the company's stance on the refurbishment plans. Rick could bring about virtually any architectural feat, be it in refurbishment or new construction. What he wasn't prepared to do was break his own code of working standards.

A pity Marissa couldn't push away her equally unfeasible reactions to the man. She hadn't expected an attack of awareness of the company's big boss. The girls in the office swooned about Rick, but Marissa was no longer interested in hot corporate types. Been there, so over that.

It must be the sway factor of the bridge getting to her. Or the sea wind pressing hard against her back trying to disrupt her balance. Those must be responsible for the odd feelings coursing through her.

Anything other than genuine attraction to this corporate high-flyer who owned the large company that employed her. Since she'd started at Morgan's six months ago she hadn't said more than 'good morning' to the boss in passing and, frankly, close proximity to a man with power on his mind made her want to run in the other direction, as fast as her pink glow-in-the-dark joggers could take her.

It hadn't exactly worked out well for her the last time, had it? Tricked, taken advantage of and publicly dumped, all in the name of career advancement. Michael Unsworth's, to be precise.

Marissa tugged her gold blouse into place over the chocolate skirt and noted Rick's words on her steno pad. *Not noticing him.* Not the charisma, nor the stunning grey eyes fringed with thick black lashes. Certainly not the leashed sensuality that seemed an integral part of him. So totally not noticing any of that.

Anyway, she'd just recently finished telling her Blinddatebrides.com friends Grace and Dani, aka Englishcrumpet and Sanfrandani, about her utter commitment to finding her Mr Ordinary. Though she'd only known Dani and Grace over the Internet a matter of weeks, they were wonderful women and understood and encouraged Marissa's dating goals. She meant to find that Mr Ordinary, to prove to the world… Well, simply to prove she could control her own destiny, thanks very much.

'This bridge isn't a key thoroughfare, Cartwright. It doesn't impact on port access for large seafaring craft.' Rick's strong tanned hand gestured to emphasise his words. 'It isn't a Heritage listed structure and its refurbishment won't make it look like one. The work needs to be about strength, durability and safety in keeping with the established design. The company's initial assessment explained this.'

The bridge spanned two small juts of Sydney's coastline. It rested within the city's sprawling confines but was far from core harbour material. Here there were no stunning views. No

Sydney Harbour Bridge. No shell-shaped Opera House rising as though directly from the water.

Unlike Pyrmont, with its massive central swing span, this bridge was just a smallish, nondescript one tucked away on a commercial section of shore.

'You're not listening to what I want.' Cartwright's mouth tightened.

'I've listened. As did the Project Manager who liaised with you initially. The advice in his report was sound.' Overhead, a seagull offered a cry to the pale blue sky as it searched the ocean below for food.

Rick had a strong face to match his strong tone. Wide cheekbones and a firm square jaw that, even at nine-thirty in the morning, revealed a dark beard shadow beneath the skin. A tall vital man with thick shoulders and defined musculature beneath the perfectly cut charcoal suit and pale green shirt.

Marissa didn't want to be aware of him, but she couldn't seem to help it.

'We can make something truly stupendous of this area.' Cartwright repeated his mantra.

Again.

For about the tenth time, paying apparently no attention at all to Rick's explanation.

The company boss growled softly beneath his breath.

It was not a sexy growl!

Marissa inhaled the tang of sea air and Rick's citrusy aftershave cologne and stopped herself from closing her eyes in what would have been a completely inappropriate appreciative sigh.

Instead, she forced her attention to Cartwright's rounded face. Maybe she could help... 'Since you're limited with what you can do in terms of refurbishing this bridge, perhaps you could implement some onshore improvements to emphasise the dock area and make the most of that aspect of things?'

'My thoughts exactly, Marissa. Something more commercially viable.' Rick cast a quick glance her way, offering a small nod of approval. The quirk of his lips that went with that approval made her tummy flutter.

Okay, so the company boss could show appreciation as well as look good. He still fell under the *Tall, Dark and Aggressive about Success* category.

She reminded herself rather desperately that that definition was one hundred per cent not right for her. Despite what her headed-for-thirty-years-of-age and back in the dating pool hormones might suggest otherwise. What did they know, anyway?

Enough to make her join a dating site, and to recognise an appealing man when she saw one?

The first had been a sensible, well-considered decision, nothing more, and, as for the second…

'Not going there,' Marissa muttered towards the foaming sea and tossed her head of curly hair before she remembered the hard hat squashed over the top of it.

Fine, so the impact was lost a little. And she hadn't actually been thinking about emotions. She'd made her choices clinically. That was all she needed to remember. Marissa grimaced and shoved the hat out of her eyes.

'Are you all right?' Rick leaned his head close to hers. The grey of his eyes deepened with a combination of amusement and interest as his gaze roved over the hard hat, her face, the hair sticking out about her cheeks and neck.

'I'm fine, thank you.' He probably wondered why she'd tossed her head like that. 'It was nothing, really. I had a twitch.'

In the brain. It started when I looked into your eyes this morning as you said, 'Good, you're here,' in that deep, toe-curling voice and it hiccups back every time I look at you or listen to you.

'Er…a twitch that made my head nod and the hat fall forward.'

Toe-curling, *authoritative* voice, Marissa. Get it right if you're going to think it at all.

'I see.' Though his lips didn't move, Rick's eyes smiled.

Marissa stared at that charming expression and thought, *deadly*. The man was deadly to her senses.

'A central steel swing span—' Cartwright began again.

'Would require a whole new bridge, one far larger than this one and located in deeper water.' Rick raised a hand as though to push it through his hair—also covered by a hard hat, except in his case he looked good in it—and dropped it to his side again. 'As Hedley told you in his assessment.'

'Hedley isn't management level,' the man spluttered. 'He doesn't understand some of the committee members' vision for the project. We could have the bridge swing open and closed at certain times of the day—a ceremonial thing even if only smaller craft passed through. It could create a major tourist attraction.'

'But you don't have the funds or planning permission to make that kind of change,' Rick pointed out gently, 'nor the conditions or traffic to demand it.'

'I have influence where the approval is concerned.' Cartwright suddenly turned to glare in Marissa's direction. 'Are you getting all this, girly? I don't see that pen moving.'

'It's a stenographer's pencil,' Marissa corrected kindly while Rick's big body stiffened at her side. 'I've written down every new piece of information you've provided and, actually, I'm almost thirty. Not quite a "girly" any more.'

'*Miss Warren* is part of the Morgan's team. She is not—'

'Not at all perturbed,' Marissa inserted while a flow of gratified warmth filled her.

Rick drew a breath. His gaze locked with hers and the starch left him. His voice dipped about an octave as he murmured, 'Well, you really don't look…'

'That old?' She meant her response to sound cheerful, unconcerned. Instead, it came out with a breathless edge, the result of that considering gaze on her. Of the way he had championed her, despite never having worked directly with her until today.

And perhaps a little because of her need not to feel quite as ancient as she did in the face of her looming birthday. 'Thank you for thinking so.'

Thank you very, very much and you look appealing yourself. Very appealing.

Did hormones have voices? Whispery ones that piped up right when they were least welcome?

First chance we get, Marissa thought, those hormones and I are having a Come To Mama meeting and I'm telling them who's in charge of this show. Namely, me.

Stupid birthdays, anyway. They should be cancelled after twenty-five and never referred to again.

You'll have found Mr Right by your birthday and won't have time to notice that over a third of your estimated life span has passed you by while you wasted some of it on Michael Unsworth, the cheating, lying, using—

'Well. What was it we were saying?' Marissa forced a smile. She mustn't think of Michael, *or* of Rick Morgan's charismatic presence.

'We were discussing this bridge…' Prosaic words but Rick's gaze moved over her with a delicious consciousness before it was quickly masked.

He was attracted to her!

Her hormones cheered.

Marissa frowned.

He couldn't be attracted. At all. Why would he be?

A moment later he blinked that consciousness away and turned to stare at the other man. 'Unless you have something new to add to the discussion, Cartwright, perhaps we could wind this up.'

Focusing on work was a great idea, really. If her heart had already done a little flip-flop dance, well, that didn't matter. She would simply force all systems back into submission because control was the thing.

Control her destiny and it couldn't hurt—*control*—her, and that was exactly how she wanted things to be.

Rick cleared his throat. 'Mr Cartwright, your committee members will have my report before your eleven o'clock meeting this morning.'

'There's no need to send it to everyone. I'll deliver it at the meeting.' The man actually seemed to believe that Rick would agree to this.

'I assure you, it will be no trouble to see the report into the hands of the whole committee.' Deep voice. Steel-edged politeness.

Marissa had arrived at work this morning expecting to be stultifyingly bored with office filing for at least the next several days. Instead, Rick's secretary had propped himself up in her doorway and croaked out his request that she meet his boss on site so he could take himself off to the doctor.

Next minute Marissa had been whipping along in a taxi, and then she'd found Rick waiting for her at the bridge site like a knight in shining hard hat.

Well, not really a knight. No horse. But he'd listened patiently as she'd given a flurried explanation to go with her sudden appearance, then he'd said, 'Yes, I know. Shall we?' and had cupped her elbow to escort her onto the bridge.

That constituted contact, which was why she could blame this entire blip in her reaction to him on her senses, not her intellect.

Rick went on, 'The report will explain why your ideas won't work, and will agree with my assessor's initial report and recommend the committee works directly with him from now on. Had there not been a temp from downstairs manning my office the day you made your appointment, you'd have been informed that you should meet with the Project Manager today, not me.'

Having a temp make an inappropriate appointment for him explained how Rick had ended up wasting his time on this meeting. Marissa had wondered. Her attraction to him didn't explain anything, except her hormones apparently hadn't read her Blinddatebrides profile or her list of requirements in a prospective mate.

Date. Prospective date. And this man wasn't one. She expected all of her to take note.

'You'll be billed for this discussion. I hope your interactions with our company will remain amicable and be a little more focused in the future.' Having made it plain that the man's efforts to bypass the proper channels hadn't come free of charge, Rick nodded. 'Now, if you'll excuse us.'

Good. It was over. They could get back to the office and Marissa could forget this weird awareness of the boss and return to her real work. In this instance, taking care of the backlog of filing Gordon had left behind before he'd gone on holiday and, once that was done, a long list of non-urgent hack work he'd left for her.

Rick's firm fingers wrapped around her elbow.

Instant overload.

Nerve-endings. Senses. Her gaze flew to his. He was already watching her. His fingers tightened.

For a frozen heartbeat his gaze became very intent indeed. Then he shook his head and swept her away along the bridge and she started to breathe again and reminded herself of her focus.

Nice. Ordinary. Guy.

Someone to have babies with. If they wanted to. At some point when they decided they'd like that. No rush at all. Again, Marissa was the leader of this particular outfit, not her clock or her hormones or anything else.

She frowned. What did she mean, *clock*? As in ticking biological clock? How silly. She simply wanted someone steady and dependable and completely invested in building a solid relationship of trust, friendship and affection with her.

Sure, that might mean a family one day, but she didn't feel driven to have children. Just because she found herself noticing mothers with babies in supermarkets and shops and on the street…

No. The Big 3-0 didn't stand for B. A. B. Y.

Not at all.

It only stood for birthday-she-didn't-want-to-think-about. Hmph.

And just because she'd noticed the Morgan's boss…

'Tom explained he was unwell before he sent you out here to meet me?' Rick spoke the words as he steered her along. 'Did he give you his travel pack?'

'I met with Tom briefly at the office before his wife whisked him away to go to the doctor.' Marissa tapped the bag that slapped against her hip with each step.

Rick must be around six foot two inches tall. Much of it appeared to be strong, ground-eating legs, not that she wanted to think about his legs, or even his anatomy in general. 'And, yes, I have Tom's travel pack.'

The shoes that went so nicely with her chocolate-brown knee-length skirt were also shoved in the tote.

'You'll need it for dictation on the trip back to the office.' He hit the base of the bridge without slowing his pace, though he took care to make sure she could keep up.

As he walked forward he dropped his hold on her and drew out his mobile phone. The conversation when the number picked up brought an edge of concern to his face and deepened the grooves on either side of his firm, moulded lips.

Would those grooves crease appealingly when he smiled?

Not interested in the answer to that. Not interested in the lips that would form the smile, or the abandoned feeling in one particular elbow either.

'You'll recover, though?… What's the treatment?… Can Linda get some time off work? If she can't, I'll arrange nursing care for you.' He listened for a moment and some of the tension in his face eased. 'Okay. You've got it covered then, but if you think of anything you need, you let me know, and don't worry about work. I'll cope.'

He paused. His grey gaze examined her, frankly assessing her before he spoke again. 'It wasn't your fault I ended up at this meeting this morning, Tom. We agreed to put a temp in the chair that day and she apparently didn't know any better than to book me for this appointment instead of the Project Manager. Cartwright took advantage of that fact.'

The second pause lasted longer, or maybe it felt that way because his gaze stayed on her the whole time. 'Yes, I know and I suppose you're right. I'd had the same thought.' His tone softened. 'Now let Linda put you to bed, man. I'll check in with her later.'

Before Marissa could get all mushy over that obvious concern for his employee, or feel uneasy as a result of his focus on her, he closed the phone.

'Is Tom—?' She got that far with the question before he brought them to a halt beside a large slate-coloured four-wheel-drive car.

People called them *cars*. Marissa told herself this was a muscular extension of its owner. All strong lines and height and breadth and power. It was twice as tall as an ordinary car, and it should stand as a warning to her. There was no softness to be found here, no gentler side, just sheer strength.

Really? Because Rick had *seemed* quite considerate, as well as all those other things.

'Tom is ill with what appears to be a hard-hitting virus. Ross River fever, the doctor thinks.' Rick removed his hard hat and ran his hand through his hair for real. Thick dark hair with a glint or two of silver at the temples. He was thirty-seven years old, her boss Gordon had told her, with degrees in both civil engineering and architecture.

Rick had used those and other skills to forge his way to massive success consulting on structural refurbishment and undertaking new construction work. Bridges, buildings, roads, he'd covered all of it and now had a team of several hundred people working under him, just in the office side of his business alone.

That was what Marissa needed to remember. The word 'driven' probably didn't begin to describe him.

Driven. Willing to do anything to get what he wanted, no matter how that impacted on others? Like Michael Unsworth?

'Ross River fever can be quite debilitating while it lasts, can't it? Tom did look very unwell this morning.' Marissa had worried for the man until he'd assured her that his wife would soon be there to collect him. She didn't want her thoughts on Rick, and she pursued the conversation with that in mind. 'I hope Tom recovers quickly and fully.'

'Linda will make sure he rests, and I'll be keeping an eye on his progress…' He used the remote on his keyring to unlock his car. Even the movement of those strong, long-fingered hands appealed.

'I'm glad I could fill in for Tom this morning, though the meeting turned out to be a bit of a waste of time for you.' Marissa wrestled with the strap of her hard hat and finally got the thing off. Wrestled to get her thoughts into submission at the same time. A quick shake of her head took care of any hat hair possibility, though she knew that nothing would keep her curls down for long.

'I appreciated that you got yourself here quickly when Tom couldn't. Make sure you hand your taxi receipt in for re-imbursement.' He had his hand out, reaching to open the passenger door. It paused mid-stretch as his gaze locked onto her head and stark male awareness flared in the backs of his eyes. 'Your hair—'

'Is it a mess? I'm afraid I can't do a whole lot with it, though I do occasionally tie it back or put it up.' She uttered the words while she tried to come to terms with the expression in his eyes, with the reciprocal burst of interest it raised in her. Goosebumps tingled over her nape and down her arm. 'It's just that it takes ages and I was busy this morning,' she finished rather lamely while she fought not to notice those reactions.

'"Mess" wasn't really what I was thinking.' He murmured the admission as though against his will, and then, 'Let me have the hat.' His fingers brushed hers as he took it from her.

Warmth flowed back up her arm again from the brief contact.

Totally immune to him, are we? Doesn't look like it, and he definitely did *notice you just now. You saw it for yourself. Oh, shut up!*

He tossed the hats onto the back seat and ushered her towards the front one. 'Hop in. This was my third stop this morning. I have quite a bit of dictation for the trip back to the office. It's up to you whether you speak your notes into a recorder or write them down, but there are deals in progress, so we need to get moving.'

'I'm quite willing to be occupied.' *And you see?* The Morgan's boss *was* highly focused on his work, his success. All those things Michael had cared the most about, had used her to achieve. Marissa hopped, or rather, he boosted her up into the high cab of the car and she landed in the seat with a bit of a plop. It was a soft, comfortable, welcoming seat, contrasting with the strength of the vehicle itself.

Not that she thought Rick Morgan had a soft side to match his car. She couldn't let herself think that. He was off-limits to her in any case and she needed her hormones to accept that fact without any further pointless comparisons.

The manoeuvre had also left rather a lot of leg exposed and she quickly tugged the skirt back into place.

Rick's gaze locked onto that expanse of leg and he caught his breath. Blinked twice. And then he strode around the front of the vehicle with his shoulders thrown back and a shuttered expression on his face that made her more conscious of him than ever.

He couldn't want her. In fact he was probably wondering why on earth he had noticed her at all. She would seem like part of the furniture to him. Like a coffee table with sturdy blocks keeping it low to the ground. Well, women her height didn't have slender legs that went on for ever, did they? Not that she was comparing herself to a coffee table.

'I'll take written notes.' She didn't want to speak aloud in front of him for who knew how long, repeating everything he said. That would feel far too intim—*uncomfortable*. 'It'll be more efficient.'

'Then let's see what we can do about cementing the positive outcomes that are riding on this morning's earlier visits.' He set the car in motion while she prepared herself—a man with power and achievement on his mind.

Michael Unsworth had been all about those things too, in the most arrogant of ways, though it had taken her way too long to see that, to see beyond his surface charm. He'd led her on, taken credit for all her hard work for him as though he'd done it all himself and, when she'd called him on that, he'd dumped her, had claimed their secret engagement had never existed. She was more than over all that, of course. It had happened months ago and she'd told him what a snake he was at the time.

Yes. Totally moved on. Her ongoing tendency to occasionally blare raging *I don't need a man* style music in her apartment at night notwithstanding.

She happened to like the musical accompaniments to some of those particular songs, and if she truly felt that way she wouldn't be trying to find a man she liked on a dating site, would she?

And you don't think you're so keen to find a man because Michael dumped you and your birthday will be the anniversary of the day you believed you and he became 'secretly' engaged as well as making you officially 'old'? You're not out to prove something? Several somethings, in fact?

She was simply out to do something positive and proactive about her future. She didn't even care if she found a man before she turned thirty. The dating site was a way to look around. If nothing eventuated, no big deal.

And this awareness of her boss… Well, it would go away. He might be *somewhat* nice, but that didn't change his corporate status. She would ignore her consciousness of him until it disappeared.

'Yes.' She was ready, under control and safe from the temptation of a corporate boss with power on her mind. Marissa clutched her pencil and hoped that was true!

CHAPTER TWO

RICK turned his car into the traffic and started to dictate. First came the report for Cartwright's committee meeting. Then a bunch of short memos to be emailed to various department heads regarding the other projects he had visited this morning. Marissa's pencil flew across the pages while she remained utterly conscious of his presence at her side.

In the confines of the big car she registered each breath and movement as he managed the congested traffic conditions with ease. Maybe joining a dating site had raised her overall awareness of men in a general sense?

That might explain this sudden inconvenient fixation on Rick.

He paused, glanced at her. 'All right? Are you keeping up?'

'Yes.' She waved the hand with the pencil in it and didn't let on for a moment that it ached somewhat from the thorough workout. 'Gordon always dictates when we're out on site work.'

Which had been all of three or four times since she'd started with her middle-aged boss six months ago, and Gordon always paused to ponder between each sentence.

'Take this list down then, please.' Rick went on to give a prioritised outline of workaday items—phone calls to be made, documentation to be lifted from files and information to be gathered from other departments within the company.

He had crow's feet at the corners of his eyes. They crinkled when he scrunched his face in thought or gave that slight smile, and made him look even better. Gorgeous, with character.

Whereas Marissa had spent over a hundred dollars on a miracle fine line facial cream last week, an action that had puzzled the younger of her Blinddatebrides friends Dani, and made Grace laugh, albeit rather wryly.

When Rick wound up his dictation, she gestured at the steno pad now crammed with instructions. 'Someone's going to be busy. There's also a BlackBerry in the pack Tom gave me. Do you want me to read you the day's list?'

In case he'd missed something in the estimated ten hours of straight work he'd just hammered out for whoever got the job of replacing Tom in his absence? She pitied those girls in the general pool on the first floor. Maybe he'd take two of them. Not her problem, in any case.

After this trip, Marissa would take her fine line wrinkles and go back to Gordon's office.

Rick probably wouldn't be in a good mood about the first floor help, though, given his last temp from there had booked an appointment for him to go out on a matter someone else should have handled.

'Yes, check through and see what I've missed, would you?' He signalled, slowed and turned and she realised with a start that they were back at their North Sydney office building. The city pulsed with busyness around them before he took the car underground, but she could only focus on *his* busyness.

Note to self about go-getter busyness, Marissa: it is not an endearing or invigorating trait.

She quickly pulled the electronic organiser from Tom's travel pack in her tote. Scanned. Read. Tried not to acknowledge the burst of irrational disappointment that swept through her.

'There's a notation of "Julia" for twelve-thirty.' He wouldn't hear the slight uneven edge in her tone, would he? How silly to care that he was seeing someone. She should have realised that would be the case. It shouldn't matter to her that he was! 'That's the only thing listed that you haven't brought up.'

Of course the listing *could* be for any reason. Hairdresser appointment. An hour with his gym trainer. Or a pet schnauzer he walked faithfully once a day.

Dream on, Marissa.

'Ah, yes.' His face softened for a moment before he turned into his parking space and opened his door.

A go-getting corporate shark who had no business noticing the help if he was already involved. Probably with some sophisticated woman, maybe the daughter of a fellow businessman, or a corporate high-flyer herself. She'd be stunningly beautiful and *her* face cream would work like a charm, if she needed it at all.

You're being ridiculous. He barely noticed you in passing and he certainly didn't seem thrilled once he realised he had. Nor do you want to be thrilled or notice him.

Marissa released her seat belt, shoved the PDA back into her tote bag and drew out her work shoes.

With her head bent removing the joggers, she said in what she felt was a perfectly neutral tone, 'Feel free to go on ahead. I can either stop by the first floor general pool for you and ask them to send someone up, or bring the PDA and my notes to whoever you've chosen to replace Tom. You can pre-lock this monster so I just have to shut the door, I assume?'

'Thanks for the kind offer.' Rick watched as Marissa Warren pushed a second trim foot into a shapely shoe. She had beautiful ankles. And legs. And a sweetness in her face that had tugged unexpectedly at something deep inside him from the moment he'd seen her up close for the first time this morning.

He'd noticed her in the office, of course. He noticed all the staff. As owner and manager, it was part of his job to remain aware about who worked for him, though the company was so big nowadays and employed so many people that he didn't always have anything specific to do with some of the workers.

In any case Marissa was completely unsuitable as a woman he should notice, legs or not. He wasn't prepared to risk commitment and the failure that could go with it, and he didn't tangle with the kind of women who might want it. Marissa struck him as a woman who would want all sorts of pieces of a man that Rick might not have the ability to give. Not that he'd ever wanted to.

'I'll wait for you.'

She didn't realise yet there would be no parting. But this didn't have to be about anything beyond work requirements. And, ultimately, he didn't have a whole lot of better options.

'If you insist,' she muttered, and pushed her joggers into her tote bag.

Why he couldn't seem to take his gaze from her, he simply couldn't explain. Yet she'd drawn his attention from the moment she'd arrived at the bridge, that hard hat rammed down on her head like armour plating.

Most of the women in the office were either in their forties or fifties, married and/or otherwise committed, or giggling twenty-year-olds. Marissa didn't fit either of those groups. She didn't seem the type to giggle.

Maybe that explained this odd attraction to Gordon Slaymore's secretary.

Rick got out, closed his door, moved to her side and pulled hers open. 'Ready?'

'Yes. It was kind of you to wait, though unnecessary.' She stood at about five foot five inches in height with a compact body that curved in all the right places. Brown eyes sparkled one moment and seemed to guard secrets the next and that wealth of hair caressed her face and nape in all its curly wildness. Her nose was strong and straight, her mouth soft and inviting in a girl-next-door kind of way.

He shouldn't want to know about the guardedness or cheerfulness. Definitely needed to steer clear of the girl-next-door part. 'Let's go, then.'

'Right.' She would have got down without touching him. The intention to do so flared in her eyes.

Given the way he reacted the few times they'd touched, he should have allowed exactly that but some bizarre sense of perversity made him clasp her hand and help her. Then, because he didn't want to release his hold on her, wanted to stroke that hand with his fingertips, he dropped it altogether, closed the door and locked the vehicle.

He wanted to kiss her until they were both breathless from it, and when she joined him in the lift the urge to do that came very close to overwhelming him.

While he fought urges he usually had no difficulty controlling, Marissa reached out a small, capable-looking hand towards the panel. No doubt to press for the first floor and the help she thought he wanted.

Instead, he pushed the button that would take them directly to his floor, and thought how he would like to taste those softly pouting lips.

This wasn't happening. It *didn't* happen to him. He was no green youngster who reacted this way to a woman. He'd found her easy enough not to notice until now and he planned to go on not noticing her.

'Gordon's on holiday.' The abrupt announcement wasn't exactly his usual smooth delivery, but at least it got them back onto a business footing. 'You probably only had maintenance and catch-up work planned, you have some experience behind you and can keep up with my pace of dictation. I've decided it will be best if you assist me during Tom's sick leave.'

'You want *me*?' An expression rather close to horror flashed across her face before she quickly concealed it.

'I don't imagine I'll find anyone any better qualified and

as easily available as you are.' He'd meant to state the words in a calm, if decided way. Instead they almost sounded bewildered. And perhaps a little insulted. He had to admit that her reaction had been refreshingly honest and appeared to come straight from her heart. Emotional honesty hadn't exactly been abundant from some of the people in his life.

And just where had that unhelpful thought come from? A very old place!

After a moment she murmured, 'Well, I'm sure it won't be for long.'

The grudging acceptance wasn't exactly effusive and it left him wanting to…impress her with how amenable he could be as a boss.

'Gordon has four weeks off, doesn't he?' Rick pushed away his odd reaction and forced his attention to matters close to hand. 'I seem to recall that from a brief talk I had with him before he left. I'm sure that will allow more than enough time for Tom to recuperate and return. If not, we'll simply deal with it. You can make whatever arrangements are needed to replace yourself in Gordon's office. Put a temp in there and have the first floor supervisor monitor the temp's progress.'

'Yes, of course. I didn't meant to sound… Well, I was just surprised, that's all.'

Oh, she'd meant it, but he pushed that aside too.

'Then, if you have no other questions…?' He paused and she shook her head. 'Good. We'll just get on with it, then.'

With his unwelcome awareness of her firmly set aside and filed, he whisked her out of the lift and into the hub of his work.

He would simply rein in his odd response to her and they would get along just fine.

Expediency. It was all about what was best for the company.

CHAPTER THREE

To: Sanfrandani, Englishcrumpet
From: Kangagirl

I had to cancel the after-hours second drink with the bank clerk guy. Work issues. I've been roped in to work for the big boss for the next while. Totally out of my control and since I don't know how long things will be busy and the bank clerk might want to see other women in the meantime, I didn't ask him to reschedule. Still, it looks like there will be one or two perks with this temporary job. I peeked ahead in the BlackBerry and we have a special meeting scheduled for tomorrow, a group of Asian businessmen. We're taking them to an animal petting zoo.

From: Sanfrandani
Ooh. What sort of animals?

From: Englishcrumpet
Kangaroos? I've always wanted to see one of those. I hope the different work goes well for you, Marissa.

'What did his last servant die of? I wonder.' Marissa muttered as her fingers flew at lightning speed to produce yet another memo that needed to be rushed urgently to one of their departments.

She absolutely did *not* enjoy the pace and challenge of working in Rick's sumptuous office suite with its thick beige carpet and burnished gold walls and stunning view over Sydney Harbour. And its frenetic pace. Maybe this workload was why Tom had gone down with a virus.

Except Ross River virus wasn't something one contracted due to stress. And the company boss did *not* fascinate Marissa more and more with each breath she took. He wasn't tremendously adept at his work, and appealingly sexy as he went about it. He was…obsessed by it. Yes, that was it.

He'd probably prove to be a terrible boss, never giving the poor overworked secretary a second thought after that initial consideration. And *she'd* refused to look his way for at least the last five minutes, anyway, so there.

Rick dropped another pile of papers and three tapes into her tray. 'You're coping all right? Not feeling too pressured? I know there's a lot of work, but we can take things steadily.' His gaze caught and held hers with quiet sincerity.

Which rather shot holes in her thoughts about him. She was far better off viewing him as a workaholic quite prepared to take her down with him! 'I'm managing. Thank you.'

He lingered in front of her desk for a moment and his gaze moved from her hands to her face and hair before coming back to her eyes. For one still moment she couldn't seem to look away and he…didn't seem to be able to either. Then he cleared his throat. 'That report hit the right places before eleven a.m.?'

'Report…' Oh, yes. Right. Well, he'd proofed the thing just minutes ago and she'd sent it. Except…Marissa forced her gaze from him to the square-framed clock on the far wall of the office space and realised it was now twelve twenty-five.

'I faxed the report on time to each committee member. You must be due for your lunch appointment.' *She* must be due to remember he had that appointment, and what that meant. The man was not available. There was Julia in his life, not that Marissa imagined *herself* in Rick Morgan's life. Not in that way.

He doesn't have a photo of a woman on his desk.

Maybe he carries it in his wallet, or has it tattooed on his right biceps.

Oh, for crying out loud!

'We'll start again at one-thirty. Your meals can go on my account at the cafeteria while you're working for me, unless you prefer to eat elsewhere.' He simply announced this, in the same way any generous, thoughtful employer taking care of his employee would. 'If you need anything from your desk in Gordon's office get it as quickly as you can when you come back from your break.'

Right, and she was finished with fantasising about tattooed biceps too. *Julia. Remember Julia?*

'We're in for overtime, aren't we?' She asked it with an edge of desperation as she popped up out of her seat. The movement had nothing to do with feeling needed and energised and as though Rick wouldn't be able to function as well without her help. She wanted a lunch break, that was all.

She'd travelled the 'feeling needed' road already, hadn't she? The indispensable-secret-fiancée road until Michael Unsworth had no longer needed her slaving away on his behalf.

The smile on her face dissolved at the thought. She snagged her tote bag and headed for the office door. 'I will eat at the cafeteria. I often do, anyway. Have a lovely time with Julia.'

'Thank you.' He let her walk to the door before he spoke again. 'Could you bring me back two beef and salad rolls and a bottle of orange juice after your meal? I won't actually be eating lunch while I'm gone.'

Again, there could be a hundred reasons for that. Only one flashed through her mind, though, and to her mortification her face became red-hot as a barrage of uninvited images paraded through her clearly incorrectly functioning brain.

'Certainly.' She bolted through the door and promised herself she would dedicate her entire lunch break to locating and lassoing her common sense and control, and tying them down where they belonged. 'I'll see that the meal is waiting when you return.'

She did exactly that after eating a sensible salad lunch that wouldn't get her hips into trouble and she didn't think about her boss. Not once. Not at all. She was a professional and she didn't give a hoot what Rick did with his time.

Marissa followed up this thought by rushing from the building to the convenience store situated at the end of the block. It was perfectly normal to buy an entire six-pack of raspberry lemonade and just because that was her comfort drink of choice didn't mean anything. Bulk was cheaper.

With a huff Marissa turned from placing the drinks in the fridge in the suite's kitchenette beside the boss's lunch and OJ and made her way to Gordon's office.

There'd be a temp tomorrow. For today the general pool was a little short-staffed so the office was silent as she collected the framed photo of her Mum and Dad taken last year just after they'd downsized into their two-bedroom home in Milberry, and a small tray full of bits and pieces—nail files, amazing hand cream to go with the amazing face cream, breath mints.

She also picked up the laminate of cartoon cuttings she'd collated a few months ago—cheery ones, joky ones, sarcasm about pets and life and getting up in the mornings. It made an entertaining desktop addition and there was no significance to the fact that she had avoided any cartoons to do with ageing.

Everyone got a day older each time they rolled out of bed in the morning. That was life. It was certainly no big deal to her. And she'd left off cartoons about babies, children and families because…this was a laminate she'd wanted for work, and those things didn't fit into that world.

And the fact that you purchased a pair of baby-gauge knitting needles recently and two balls of baby-soft wool?

It had been an impulse buy. One of those things you did and then wondered why you had. Besides, she hadn't bought any knitting patterns to go with the wool and, if she did decide to use it, she'd knit herself a pair of socks or something.

She would!

Back in her new office, Marissa shoved the laminate onto the left half of the desk and quickly buried it beneath her in-tray and various piles of folders, typed letters and other work.

When her boss walked in and fell on the lunch she'd brought as though starved to death, Marissa kept on with her work and didn't spare him a glance. If she had a 'spare' anything, she would invest it thinking about which man she might date next off the Blinddatebrides website.

Silly name, really, because she wasn't desperate for marriage or anything like that. They'd had a special on and there were lots of nice everyday men out there, and her thirtieth birthday *wasn't looming*.

It was still weeks away, even if Mum had fallen eerily silent about it, the way she did when she got the idea to spring a surprise on her daughter. Marissa didn't want a surprise party—or any kind of party—and she hoped her Mum had understood that from her hints on the topic.

There was no big deal about wanting to find a man before she turned thirty anyway, and nor was Marissa's pride in a mess because she'd been duped and dumped.

She had her whole world in complete control, and she liked it just fine that way!

'Good afternoon, Rick Morgan's office, this is Marissa.'

Rick sat at his desk and listened as Marissa answered yet

another phone call and took a message. He'd told her he didn't want to be disturbed while he worked his way through the report that had been delivered.

Yet he hadn't managed to tune out his awareness of her as she beavered away at her desk.

Maybe it was the way her hands flew across the computer keys that had him glancing her way over and over. Or the fact that when she thought herself unobserved her interest in the materials she processed showed all over her expressive face.

Frowns and nods of approval came into play until she finally printed out each piece of work with an expression of satisfaction. Would she be as open and responsive—?

That wasn't something he needed to know, yet the thought was there, along with others. Rick finished reading the report and scooped up the signed letters that needed to be mailed.

'You like hard work, don't you.' It wasn't really a question but he set the signed letters down on the corner of her desk and waited for her to answer anyway. That was another problem he appeared to have developed. He couldn't seem to stop himself from getting up from his desk and finding a reason to visit hers.

Once there, his gaze seemed to have a will of its own, roving constantly over her face and hair, the nape of her neck, the hands that moved with such speed and efficiency over the computer keyboard. He wanted those hands on him.

No. He did *not* want Marissa Warren's hands on him. Yet there was something between them. It had been there from the moment they'd met at the bridge this morning and he'd let her come to the most predictable conclusion about Julia because of that.

Now he wanted to explain, wanted her to know he was free—but he wasn't, was he? Not to get involved with his temporary secretary, or any other woman who wanted more than a casual physical interlude with him. He'd made his choice about that.

'Do I like hard work?' Her gaze flipped up to his. Almost immediately she veiled the sparkle in her eyes. A shrug of one shoulder followed. 'I guess I like to think I'm as efficient as the next person and there seems a lot to be done in this office at the moment. Or perhaps it's always this busy?'

'Tom and I work hard, but there's more to contend with right now than is usual, even for us.' To move his gaze from her, he shifted it to a photo of an older couple that she'd added to her desk. The woman had curly hair, cut shorter. Her parents...

Was she an only child or did she, like him, have siblings? An intriguing-looking laminated sheet covered the left half of the desk. Much of it had work strewn on top but the bits he could see appeared to be cartoon cuttings.

Her foibles and family history shouldn't interest him. Another sign of trouble, and yet still he stood here, courting time with her when both their interests would be better served if he didn't.

'Will it be a problem for you to work longer hours for the next few days?' That was what he really needed to know. 'Is there someone at home who'll mind?'

Marissa's answer was only relevant to him in terms of how it impacted here.

Except his body stilled as he waited for her response, and that stillness had little to do with concerns about his working life.

'Tom has welcomed the longer hours because he and Linda are saving to buy a house.' The words left his mouth in an explanation he hadn't intended to give. 'He's used to my ways and knows his way around this office. He copes.'

'I can manage any work Tom would have done.' She spoke the words with her chin in the air. An answer, but not all the information he had wanted.

'I don't doubt that.' He wanted her to know he thought well of her. Wanted her to...think well of him. The last time he'd experienced this particular care about another's opinion of him, he'd been twenty years old and convinced he was in love, until the girl had started talking about the future—theirs—and he'd wanted to run a mile.

Just like his father, except Stephen Morgan was *in a family* and he did his running a little differently. Rick hadn't even tried for a less than overt approach. He'd got out of that relationship so fast he'd probably left the girl spinning and he'd avoided commitment ever since.

'I'm not…tied to any home responsibilities.' Marissa offered this information cautiously, as though she'd prefer not to have given it.

'Then I won't worry too much if I do have to ask you to work extra hours.' Rick stared into the warm brown eyes fixed unerringly on him and the moment stretched out, expanded to encompass not only the words they had exchanged but also what they weren't saying. The sparkle in the air between them. His awareness of her, hers of him, the denial of both of them.

Sexual attraction. That was all it was, but even so it wasn't wise and he *had* to realise that and move them past it. He drew a deep breath. 'It's clear you can cope with the workload. You've handled yourself very well so far today. I appreciate your efforts.'

'Th-thank you.' A pleased expression lifted the corners of her mouth and softened her eyes. 'I've simply done my job.'

Something about that softening brought back the urge he'd had earlier in the lift to kiss her senseless, and he lowered his tone of voice to a low rumble. 'So I've observed.'

'I can work whatever hours are needed. I'd just appreciate knowing so I can gear my social life accordingly.' She cleared her throat and couldn't quite seem to meet his gaze. 'I cancelled a drink after work today because I figured I wouldn't be out by five.'

Rick wanted to say there'd be no time whatsoever for her to spend on 'drinks'. Presumably with some man. He noted at the same time that she must be looking. Looking, but not seriously involved right now.

But women who looked and carried photos of their parents with them did want depth and permanency, and that kind of relationship was not on his agenda.

'I should get on, if that was all.' She reached for the pile of letters to be mailed, began to calmly fold them into the window envelopes she had waiting on her desk.

Dismissed by his temporary assistant. Rick gave a snort of amusement and reluctant admiration before he swung away. 'I'll be in my office and…er…I promise there won't be any more correspondence brought out for you to type today. I know your tray is still loaded.'

'No.' She didn't look up. 'You'll just hold it over for tomorrow so I won't get stressed out. I won't anyway, but that's okay. I understand the tactic. Gordon does the same thing.'

Now he'd been compared to a fifty-year-old.

Rick disappeared into his office, pushed the door closed so he wouldn't be tempted to listen to Marissa taking phone calls or watch her as she worked, and decided that it was very different working with her rather than Tom.

That explained his ongoing interest in her. He half convinced himself he believed this. Well, maybe a quarter. He immersed himself in his work.

At twenty minutes to six that evening Marissa stuck her head around his door. 'Your presence is requested at an emergency conference.'

He'd started to believe they might have nearly caught up on their workload. So much for that idea. 'Which department heads? What's the problem?'

She pushed the door open fully and read a spiel of information from her steno pad.

Rick gave a mild curse. 'Where? Have they assembled already?'

'Conference Room Two, and yes.' She had her tote bag on her shoulder and a determined glint in her eyes. Her computer was shut down and her desk cleared. Whatever work she had remaining she had tidied away. 'I assume you'll want us to join them immediately. If it ends quickly, we can come back.'

He got to his feet. 'I'll secure my office.'

She swept in beside him while he sorted files and locked them away. 'Anything on screen that needs to be saved before I shut this down?'

'No. Nothing, but I can do that.' He locked the final cabinet and swung round.

She'd clicked out of applications as he spoke and she stood there now, bent at the waist, leaning in to press the button on the back of the computer.

Rick's senses kicked him hard. She would have to possess the most appealing bottom to go with those equally devastating legs, wouldn't she? And he would have to notice it instead of being completely unaware of her, as he needed to be. He didn't want to notice her, or be impressed or intrigued by her or find her different or interesting or highly attractive!

If he'd thought it would help, he'd replace her with someone from another department but no other personal secretary had a boss on holiday. He certainly wasn't about to subject himself to some child from the general pool again. And, for goodness' sake, he could control this.

He always controlled the way he reacted to women. There was no reason why this situation should be any different. In fact, because she worked for him and he never, ever, mixed work with his social interactions that way, it should be easier still.

Yes, and it's been dead easy so far, hasn't it?

'Let's move.' He hid a grimace in his chin. 'Here's hoping the meeting doesn't go on too long.'

CHAPTER FOUR

MARISSA followed Rick along the corridor and tried not to look at the breadth of his shoulders, the shape of the back of his head or…other parts of him.

Not to mention the man was seriously compelling as a go-getter businessman…but what was she thinking? The terms 'go-getter', 'businessman' and 'compelling' were mutually exclusive in her vocabulary!

And just because he'd been kind to his secretary and had phoned in again to check on the man and declared he wanted to be told if anything—*anything*—needed to be done for Tom while he was recuperating, just because he'd treated Marissa herself with the utmost consideration he could manage within the demands of his work…

She still wanted a *nice ordinary guy*—hello? Fine, so maybe Rick did have a degree of niceness. His career outlook made him totally out of bounds for her.

Maybe he's a total playboy, she thought with a hint of desperation, remembering the Julia lunch date that hadn't involved lunch. A cad, a womaniser, a toad on a lily pad on a pond full of scum.

You don't think you're judging him ever so slightly on Michael Unsworth's record without getting to know the man first? Without even knowing just who this Julia is to him?

No. She didn't think that, and she wasn't grasping at mental straws to keep her hormones under control either. Rick Morgan wasn't for her. She'd road-tested one corporate man and decided that brand didn't suit her, and that was all there was to it.

'Sit here beside me.' He held the chair for her while the six men in the room glanced their way. 'You know what to do with the notes.'

She nodded to acknowledge the others' presence and Rick's words, and tried not to notice the brush of his hand against her back as he pushed her chair in for her.

The boss simply had nice manners, and so did a lot of accountants and shop assistants.

Butchers and bakers and candlestick-makers.

Marissa jabbed her pencil onto the page and locked her gaze onto its tip. 'I'm ready.'

To get the meeting over with. To go home for the day and log onto Blinddatebrides.com and read at least ten new profiles, answer any invitations she'd received and be really positive about them. And she had been positive to this point. It wasn't her fault if no spark of true interest had happened when she'd met any of her dates so far.

Unlike the spark that immediately happened when she'd met Rick Morgan.

Not a helpful thought!

The meeting went beyond long.

'So we find a way to meet the changes to the fire safety code without compromising on design integrity.' Rick referred to a skyscraper monstrosity the company was building on the city's shoreline. 'We'll simply present our clients with choices that surpass what they wanted initially.'

He raised several possibilities. While general discussion ensued, Marissa snatched at the momentary respite in note-taking. She should have eaten something more substantial than a salad for her lunch. Instead, she drew one of two bottles of raspberry lemonade from her tote bag and consumed half of it in a series of swallows. She'd planned to take both bottles in her bag home but at least it gave her an energy burst.

The conference moved on. Marissa consumed the rest of the drink, continued her work. Wished she could get up and walk around. Her right foot wanted to go to sleep. Another sign of impending old age?

There is no old age occurring here!

'It seems to me Phil's presented you with a workable resolution to the issue with the reservoir, Fred.' Rick caught the stare of the man at the other end of the oval table.

Marissa vaguely noted that Rick's beard shadow had really grown in now. Did he shave twice a day? Would he have a mat of dark hair on his chest as well? Her skin tingled in response to the thought.

What was wrong with her? She needed to focus *away* from the man, not so solidly on him that she noticed almost everything about him and wondered about the rest!

Rick's face showed no sign of fatigue, though the grooves on either side of his mouth did seem a little deeper.

It wasn't fair that men just developed character while women fought gravity. Women wrinkled sooner, got older faster. And people had coined entire sayings around the thirtieth birthday. *It's all downhill after thirty…*

'If you don't want to accept the plans,' Rick went on, 'I need to hear a good reason for that. Otherwise, I think we can move onto the next issue.'

Marissa nodded in silent agreement.

Just then Rick glanced her way and their gazes locked before his dropped to her mouth. He stilled and a single swift blast of awareness swept over his face and, very, very briefly, he lost his concentration and stopped speaking.

It was only for a second and probably no one else would

have thought anything of it, but in that single moment she had all of his attention—an overwhelming degree of attention, as though he could *only* focus on her. And, right down to her marrow, she responded with a depth of warmth and interest, curiosity and compulsion that…stunned her.

A moment later his face smoothed of all expression and he carried on with the meeting, and Marissa did her best to pull herself together.

Her lungs chose to function again after all, and she sucked in a deep breath and couldn't—simply couldn't—think about the strength of the response he'd drawn from her just then.

A burst of note-taking followed and when it ended she gulped down the second bottle of lemonade and tapped her foot incessantly. It was almost a relief to focus on her exhaustion and discomfort.

'Anything else?' Rick sent the words down the length of the table. He wanted the conference over with. It was eight p.m. and his secretary was wilting, her fluffy hair sticking out in odd places and the pink lip-gloss, that made him think of snatching kisses, all but chewed off.

Her shoulders were curved, her left elbow propped on the table while she pushed the pencil across the page with grim determination with her other hand.

He had the oddest desire to protect her from the workload he had inflicted on her—even while he'd noted her pleasure in it. He had the oddest desire for her, period. It had stopped his concentration earlier, had simply shut down all channels until he'd pulled his attention forcibly away from her. No person had had the power to disrupt his thoughts so thoroughly before.

It was more than simply a blast of lust, Morgan. Maybe you should admit that to yourself.

Yet what else could it have been? He didn't experience any other feelings. Just look at the way he'd run the one and only time he'd linked up with a woman who wanted more from him. More than his father could give, more than Rick knew if he could give. At least he chose to go forward honestly, not let anyone down…

Around the table, people scooped up folders and files.

Rick nodded. 'Then that's a wrap. Anything else, get it to me in writing tomorrow.'

The room cleared while Marissa continued to write. In the end, he reached out and stilled her hand by placing his over it. Gently, because for some reason she drew that response from him whether he wanted it to be so or not.

Touching her was a mistake. Her skin was warm, soft, and the urge inside him to caress more of it was unexpectedly potent.

Wouldn't his youngest sister gloat about this fixation of his? Faith had tried to convince him to fall for the 'right kind' of woman for years, to take the leap into emotional oblivion and surrender and believe he'd like it.

What was he thinking, anyway? This was all completely irrelevant. He'd done the not-getting-involved-life-alone mental adjustment years before and he hadn't changed his mind.

He never would. He'd seen too much, thanks to his father.

There were no *emotions* involved in desiring Marissa Warren. Just some unexplained stupidity. 'We're done here. Let's put you into a taxi so you can get home. Unless you drove to work?' He removed the steno pad and pencil from her grip, pushed them into his briefcase on the table and took her elbow to help her up. A simple courtesy, nothing more.

'I should type the notes while they're fresh. No, I didn't drive. I hire a Mini from a neighbour when I go to Milberry to see Mum and Dad. It's heaps cheaper than owning my own car and I don't often need to drive.' The words stopped abruptly as she came fully to her feet and swayed.

'Marissa? Are you okay?' He pushed her chair out of the way with his thigh and caught her beneath both elbows even as he registered the personal snippets about her. Registered and wanted to know more, and cursed himself for his curiosity.

'Sorry.' She caught her breath. 'I feel a bit light-headed.' Her body sagged into his hold. For a moment her forehead rested against his chest and all that curly hair was there beneath his chin.

It came naturally to curve his body around hers. He simply did it without thinking. She felt good in his arms, smelled sweetly of gardenias and some other floral scent. He wanted to press his face into her hair and against her skin and inhale until he held the scent of her inside him.

Total insanity, and he had no idea where it had come from. It must be too long since he'd taken a woman to his bed. He had focused more and more on work over recent months.

'Take some deep breaths.' The instruction was to Marissa, though he could do with it himself. 'You won't faint on me, will you?'

'No, I just need a minute.' Her breasts brushed his chest as she drew a series of breaths.

His whole body was sensitised, his vaunted self-control rocked. He wanted to take her there and then, but he also wanted to cup her head in his hand, tenderly brush her hair from her brow.

Why was she faint, anyway? Lack of food? Was she ill?

'I stood up too fast and I shouldn't have had two bottles of drink in a row like that on an empty stomach. I think I gave myself a sugar overload.' Her fingers curled around his forearms.

'You should take better care of yourself.' The admonition skated far too close to a proprietorial concern. 'I shouldn't have had you work so late without food either.'

'It's my responsibility to eat enough.' She muttered something about thighs and coffee tables.

Rick gave in and raised his hand, stroking his fingers over the soft skin of her jaw. Simply to lift her face, he told himself, to search her eyes, see if she had recovered sufficiently.

Long lashes lifted to reveal brown eyes that slowly came into focus and filled with belated acknowledgement of their nearness.

Perhaps it was the late hour, the silence of the room or the many hours of work that had gone before that momentarily shorted out his brain, because he lowered his head, his lips intent on reaching hers, something inside him determined to make a connection.

She took a deep steadying breath and straightened away from him and the welcome he had glimpsed in her eyes was replaced with the rejection he should have instigated within himself.

The sense of loss startled him and his hands dropped away from her more slowly than they should have. None of this made sense. None of his reactions to her. They shouldn't even exist because he'd told himself to shut down any awareness.

'I'm sorry. I'm fine now.' She held out her hand for her notes and pencil. So she could keep working and truly faint?

'I'll keep these for you for tomorrow.' He closed the brief-case and guided her towards the door. He simply wanted to ensure his employee was okay. This had only truly been geared towards that.

Aggravatingly off-kilter, Rick took Marissa straight to street level and left the building at her side.

'Hand this taxi receipt to accounting so they can reimburse you as well,' he instructed as he flagged a taxi forward from the rank. 'Are you able to start at eight tomorrow? I realise that's early and today has exhausted you but, as well as our regular workload, there's a visit scheduled to a petting zoo. An early lunch for business discussions, and then the zoo itself…'

'I saw that in the BlackBerry.' Her chin hiked into the air and her brown eyes flashed. 'I'll be here at a quarter to eight so I can meet with the supervisor and brief one of the early shift temps on the work required in Gordon's office before we do whatever work we can and then leave. You don't need to make any allowances for me.'

Rather than making him feel bad for asking for another long day out of her, her expression of determination went straight to his groin—a reaction he needed as little as all the others. Perhaps he should have remained in the building and done some laps in the top floor swimming pool before he went home. Like a few hundred or so.

'Then thank you for your willingness to put in the hours.' Rick helped her into the taxi. He would *not* respond to her in such a confusing way again. It was intolerable and unacceptable and he was locking it down right now.

Just like your father would?

And he could leave his family life out of it. That had nothing to do with anything.

'I'll see you tomorrow.' He turned his back and strode away, promising himself he would leave all thoughts of her behind him.

'That's great. Keep smiling. You all look wonderful. Your families will love these photos.' Marissa had two cameras dangling from her left arm by their straps and another one in her hands. At her side Rick held three more.

They were at the brand-new Sydney animal petting zoo and their group of Hong Kong businessmen guests were one hundred per cent enchanted. She and Rick snapped pictures as fast as they could.

She'd made a vow to herself last night when she'd stepped into her sensible apartment in an equally sensible building in a suburb not far from her work.

Actually she'd made it online to Grace and Dani, since they were her Blinddatebrides buddies and, as well as enjoying their long-distance friendship, Marissa felt accountable to them for her dating efforts. It was good to make herself accountable so she would do as she should—find a nice, ordinary, no-surprises man to fall in love with.

Which meant she needed to forget all about being ultra aware of the boss—okay, so she hadn't admitted that part to Dani and Grace.

Rick is interestingly older, though, a mature man with lots of layers. Intriguing, complex.

Someone a mature, well-rounded, thirty-year-old woman might find appealing? Not that she was about to become mature. That made her sound positively ancient and, really, she was just beginning her life.

'How are the photos coming?' Though Rick's question was calm and sensible, the expression in his eyes as he glanced at her still held remnants of yesterday evening's interest.

Marissa's pulse fluttered. 'I'm almost done. Every digital camera is different but I think the shots I'm getting will be fine.'

'Good. That's good.' Rick gestured to the businessmen. 'Perhaps a group shot of all of you?'

He made the suggestion in the deep, even tone he'd used when Marissa had stepped into his office suite this morning and found him already immersed in a deluge of paperwork at his desk. A tone that said they were all about business. But his gaze had contradicted that.

The man had probably invented the term 'confusion'. For anyone near him, that was. And she hadn't wanted him to kiss her last night. She'd simply lost her focus for a moment.

'Hold the pose, gentlemen.' She forced a wide smile as she changed cameras again. 'I need another two photos yet.'

Ozzie the koala didn't seem to mind being held and oohed and aahed over. He sat quietly, his keeper at the side looking on. Ozzie looked utterly adorable with his thick fur and blunt nose and fluffy ears, though his claws were sharp and strong, made for climbing the eucalyptus trees he fed from.

Fortunately the koala was tame and well-behaved. If Marissa could tame her hormones around her boss in the same way, that would be helpful. She took a moment and tried not to *think of* Rick's presence close beside her, or the fact that more than simply her chemical composition seemed interested in him.

She had to see him as her boss and nothing else, and with that in mind, she switched her attention to work. 'Here's hoping this visit ends in a successful outcome.'

'The team seemed pleased with our talks. They'll meet with at least two other major companies before they leave Sydney and then there'll be a period of time before they make a decision, but I'm hopeful.' Rick lowered the final camera and turned his gaze to their visitors.

He smiled towards the group. 'That's the last photo.'

Mr Qi spoke quietly to the keeper and then gestured them over. 'We'd like one of our hosts with Ozzie. Miss Warren will hold him, please.'

To refuse in such circumstances would be out of the question. Instead, Marissa pasted a smile on her face and came forward to hand over her share of the cameras. She drew one long uneasy breath as Rick approached her.

His head bent close to hers. 'Are you okay with this? All the animals here are trained to sit placidly.'

'That's not…' She refused to admit the thought that being close to the boss, not the furry animal's manners concerned her. 'I've never held a koala but I'm not worried he'll hurt me. I just hadn't expected them to ask for this.'

'Sometimes we overlook our own tourist attractions,' he murmured and his gaze roved over her. For all the world as though he felt *he'd* overlooked *her*?

Well, she wasn't much to notice today, in any case. She wore a drab navy cardigan buttoned to the neck over a soft white blouse. A long, ordinary, unadorned navy skirt completed the outfit, so there wasn't a whole lot worth looking at.

Covered from neck to calves in the most unappealing outfit

she had? And mostly as a deterrent to herself? To help her not to think about her boss? Who, her?

'Keep the cardigan on while you hold him.'

His comment didn't make a lot of sense, but she gave a small nod to indicate her acquiescence before she turned to face their guests.

They all waited expectantly with cameras poised.

'This will be a thrill for me. Thank you for the opportunity.' It cost nothing to be positive, right? At least Rick hadn't realised the real reason for her unease.

That depressing, confusing, annoying, irritating and wholly aggravating thought disappeared when the keeper put the koala into her arms and another feeling altogether swept through her.

Ozzie cuddled into her like a baby, a warm soft weight with one arm draped over hers and his head turned to the side beneath her chin. Her arms closed around his warmth and a wealth of completely unexpected emotions clogged her throat before her thought processes could catch up with her reaction.

For one long aching moment as Rick stepped behind her, put his arm about her shoulders and she looked up into those intense grey eyes, she longed for the completion of a child. A baby to love and nurture, care for and protect, and the feelings that she'd suppressed over recent months—even longer—all tore through her.

She hadn't impulse-bought that baby wool to make socks for herself. A part of her had reached from way deep down inside for something she wanted, had tried to ignore—how could she want such a thing? It was so foolish to long for something that might never happen for her.

It took two to produce a baby—two willing people and a whole lot of thought and commitment and other things. She should only allow herself hopes and dreams and goals that she knew she could achieve. She certainly did not want to have her boss's baby. It would be absolutely beyond the point of ridiculousness to imagine such a thing.

Even so, Rick's eyes locked with hers and something deep flickered in his expression, something more than curiosity or simply a man noticing a woman.

Maybe he'd read all those thoughts in her face before she'd been able to mask them? Panic threatened until she assured herself he couldn't possibly have done so. She hadn't realised they were even there until they'd hit her so unexpectedly. Why would he realise such things about her?

'All right?' His gaze was steady as he looked at her, and she managed a shaky breath before the tension fell back enough so that their surroundings came into focus again and she felt in control of herself once more.

'Yes, thanks.' She let her fingers stroke over the koala's soft fur, let herself come back together. 'He's unexpectedly light for his size.'

'A wombat would be far heavier to hold—the compact steamroller of Australian wildlife.' Rick's quip helped ease the moment, they both smiled at long last, and then they smiled for the cameras.

When the photo session ended Rick's arm seemed to linger a moment before he dropped it, but he strode purposefully forward and with due ceremony invited the men to enjoy another hour at the zoo. 'I asked the keepers to save a surprise, and we hope you'll enjoy the opportunity to feed some wombats and kangaroos and other animals while you think over our lunch discussion. There'll be coffee and cake waiting at the restaurant for you when you're finished.'

He left them with smiles and bows and swept Marissa away, who had now pulled herself together. That reaction earlier… It was just some crazy thing that had happened.

She removed her cardigan, rolled it into a ball and wiped her hands on it and warily acknowledged that perhaps biological ticking and the Big 3-0 did appear to have somewhat of an association inside her after all. What to do about that was the question.

When they climbed into Rick's big car, she set the cardigan on the floor behind her seat.

'They smell a bit, don't they?' Rick watched Marissa dispose of her cardigan and tried not to think of that moment back there when she'd first taken the koala into her arms and seemed so surprised and devastated, and he'd wanted to hold *her*, just scoop her up and take her somewhere and cuddle and comfort her.

'Yes, Ozzie smelled of eucalyptus and warm furry animal.' She buckled her seat belt and sat very primly in the seat, her back stiff enough to suggest that she didn't want to delve too deeply into her reaction to holding the animal. 'His coat was a little oily. Thanks for the hint to keep my cardigan on.'

She'd seemed empty somehow, and he'd wanted to give her what was missing, but his response had been on an instinctive level he couldn't begin to fathom. Well, it didn't matter anyway because she was his secretary, nothing more, and since that was exactly how he wanted things to be… 'You're welcome.'

He glanced at her. She was dressed conservatively, but the prissy white blouse just made her hair look fluffier and made him think all the more about the curves hidden away beneath the shirt's modest exterior.

So much for his vow not to think about her as an attractive woman after having his arms around her for those brief moments last night.

'You seemed well prepared for the koala experience.' Her voice held a deliberate calm and good cheer. 'Have you—'

'Held one? Yes. Once.' It hadn't left any notable impact on him, unlike watching her experience today.

Perhaps his instincts towards Marissa weren't entirely dissimilar to those he felt towards his sisters and nieces—a certain protectiveness that rose up because his father had failed to be there for them.

Rick tried to stop the thoughts there. Stephen Morgan was a decent enough man.

Except to Darla, and unless any kind of genuine emotional commitment was required of him. Then Stephen simply dropped the ball as he always had.

Rick forced the thoughts aside. There was nothing he could do about any of that, no way to change a man who inherently wouldn't change. No way to know if Rick himself would be as bad or worse than his father in the same circumstances.

'We often take our overseas business contacts places like this.' It didn't matter what he'd felt for Marissa—or thought he'd felt. By choice he wouldn't act on any response to her, and that was as much for her good as anything else. 'They have a good time and happy businesspeople are more inclined to want to make deals. Those deals mean money and building the business.'

He relaxed into this assertion. It felt comfortable. Familiar. Safe.

When Marissa turned her head to face him, her gaze was curiously flat. 'You're a corporate high-flyer and success means everything to you. I understand.'

She made it sound abhorrent. Why? And success wasn't *everything* to him.

No? That's not what you've been telling yourself and the world for a very long time now.

He did not need to suggest she got to know him better to see other facets of him—all the facets of him. Instead, he agreed with her. 'Success *is* very important to me. You're quite right.'

CHAPTER FIVE

MARISSA hadn't meant to offend Rick. Surely she hadn't? And he *was* a great deal like Michael Unsworth, only more so. She didn't hold that against him, but she had the right to protect herself by remembering the fact.

She didn't want to think about Michael. It was best if she didn't think about *Rick* in any light other than as her employer. And she certainly didn't want to dwell on that hormonal whammy that had hit her back at the petting zoo.

If she wanted something to cuddle, she probably needed a kitten or something.

Do you hear me, hormones and non-existent clock? This is my destiny and I choose what I want and need and don't need.

She refused to be dictated to on the topic by any internal systems. With that thought in mind, she worked hard for the rest of the day, and cursed the stubborn part of her that insisted on admiring Rick's business acumen as she came to see more and more of it in play. Couldn't she ignore that at least?

Maybe she should simply admit it. She liked his drive and determination. With a frown, she shoved another file away in the room dedicated to that purpose just off their suite's reception room.

More files were slapped home. Not because she was fed up with herself. She was simply being efficient.

Yes. Sure. That was the truth of it. A pity she didn't seem capable of the same single-mindedness when it came to finding Mr Right through Blinddatebrides.com. She'd yet to initiate any kind of invitation to a man, had cancelled that second drink yesterday, and hadn't looked at those ten profiles as she'd told herself she would. She'd been bored by all the candidates she'd met so far.

Grace had dated a man straight up on joining the site, even if she had panicked about it at the time.

Dani remained tight-lipped so far about dates but she sure seemed to have her head together about the whole process, right down to the site's efficiency and how it all worked. Why couldn't Marissa follow *her* plan there, and stop fixating on the boss?

Marissa had logged on in her tea break, anyway. It wasn't her fault she'd run out of time before she could do more than read some of the contact messages.

Shove, shuffle, push.

'I'll be on the top level for the next hour.' Rick spoke from the doorway in a tone that didn't reveal even the smallest amount of any kind of sensual anticipation he surely should feel in the face of yet another 'meeting' with the mysterious Julia, who seemed to have a place reserved for her almost daily in his diary.

That was something Marissa had discovered today as she'd scanned ahead further in the BlackBerry to try to gauge the kind of workload they might have ahead of them.

Well, good on him for seeing this Julia. With such a knowledge foremost in her thoughts, Marissa simply wouldn't look at him as an available man, which was *all to the good*.

It was just as well the woman didn't mind being slotted in like a visit to the dentist or a board meeting or teleconference, though.

Marissa shoved two more files away and forced herself to face him. 'You won't mind if I take a short break myself? I'll just talk on the Internet with friends. There's nothing in the diary—'

Marissa broke off a little uneasily, but Rick wasn't to know those friends were on an Internet dating site with her. Not that she cared who knew she had a subscription to a dating website. She could do what she liked. It was her life and just because she hadn't even told her parents she'd joined Blinddatebrides.com didn't mean she felt uncomfortable about it or anything.

Grace and Dani knew she wanted to find a nice man. Marissa had been very open with them really.

Her online friends were signed up to the dating site, of course, so Marissa hadn't exactly been exposing deep secrets by admitting she wanted to meet some men. And she hadn't told Grace and Dani everything about herself by any means. She certainly hadn't told them her plan to clinically vet those men until she found one she was prepared to fall in love with.

Well, that was her business, and it mightn't even happen and her vetting ideas made a lot of sense.

'Please do take a break.' Rick turned. 'I sought you out to suggest that.'

A moment later, after delivering that piece of thoughtfulness, he was gone.

Marissa appreciated the reprieve from close contact with him. That was what made her feel all mushy and approving, not only his consideration for her. She told herself this as she logged onto Blinddatebrides.com and scrolled through the messages she'd skimmed earlier. This time she made herself read them and follow through to look at profiles.

And she set her fingers to the keyboard and replied that she would be delighted—*delighted*—to arrange something with Tony, 32, computer software. Perhaps lunch tomorrow?

Marissa got off the site without checking for instant messages from Grace or Dani. She wasn't avoiding them. She just felt guilty about giving herself the time when she should be working, even if Rick was on the top floor of the building with Julia doing she didn't want to think about what.

When the fax machine made its warming-up sound, Marissa left her desk with a rather desperate alacrity. She'd struggled to concentrate on her typing despite her determination to plough through as much work as possible before Rick got back.

She snatched up the first page of the fax and skimmed it, and then read it more carefully while two more pages emerged from the machine. If the large 'urgent' stamp on the top of the first page hadn't been clue enough, the contents were, drat it all to pieces. She'd hoped for something to distract her thoughts, but not this way.

'I'll ring his mobile phone and tell him he needs to get back here. It's not my problem there's an emergency and I'll be interrupting...whatever.' She walked to her desk and pressed the speed dial for his mobile number, only to return the phone to its cradle when the thing rang from on top of his desk in the next room.

What now? Try another department head? Which one? The contents of the fax covered material from all the departments.

'Right, so there's no choice. It's marked for his attention specifically, and it's urgent.' Marissa snatched the door key from her purse and pushed it into her pocket. If she could have thought of any other way to handle this, she'd have taken it.

The trip to the top level went by far too fast. She'd never been up here before. There seemed to be a large atrium surrounded by rooms behind closed doors.

Rick's workaday lair? A place to come when he wanted privacy without leaving the building?

She'd crossed half the cavernous expanse of tiled floor flanked with tall banks of potted ornamental trees, the fax clutched in a death grip in her hand, before she realised the sounds of splashing weren't from an indoor fountain.

Marissa's gaze lifted and the view in front of her cleared just in time for her to see strong arms lift a little girl out of the water and pass her to a dark-haired woman who stood beside…a swimming pool.

Rick was in the pool, his wide shoulders and thick arms exposed and water dripping from his face and down his chest.

Just the right amount of dark hair there.

What on earth is going on here?

Child. Woman. Rick in the pool and not a sensual indicator to be detected in the room.

And finally this thought:

That's what the swimming roster that circulates by email means, the slots for before work each day.

She'd only seen the email twice, and had thought the staff took turns booking some *other* swimming facilities.

Marissa's steps faltered to a stop.

'Thank you, Unca Rick.' The little girl waited impatiently while the woman removed her flotation devices, only to immediately lean fearlessly over the edge of the pool, arms extended, to the man who was Marissa's boss—in a very different guise right now.

He was a specimen of male beauty and Marissa couldn't take her gaze from him. The child would have tumbled back in if the woman hadn't held onto her arm. If Rick hadn't immediately caught her by the tiny waist. Big gentle hands keeping her from harm.

The little girl planted a kiss on Rick's cheek and his arms came around her, his hands gently patting her back before he set her on her feet again beside the pool.

'You're welcome.' Oh, the soft deepness of his voice.

Marissa's abdomen clenched in a reaction she wholly did not want to admit was happening. She hadn't joined Blinddatebrides.com to find Mr Virile and Able to Produce Strong Children, nor Mr Gentle and Sweet With Said Children. She certainly wasn't looking for those traits in the man before her.

'The next time *you'll* put your head all the way under the water, okay, Julia?' His smile was gentle, encouraging and, to Marissa, quite devastating. 'Fishes do that all the time.'

Julia…

The woman smiled and turned her head and the likeness between all three of them clicked it all fully into place.

This child was Julia—a sweet little girl about four or five years old with a shock of dark hair flattened wet against the back of her head and still dry in the front. The woman beside the pool was Rick's sister. The entire scene was so far removed from what Marissa had expected, she couldn't seem to find her breath or get her legs to move.

Or perhaps that was simply the impact of so much raw sensual appeal concentrated in the man in front of her, and the crazy twisting of reactions inside her.

And Rick wasn't involved.

Now she thought about it, hadn't Gordon said when she'd first started here that Rick was a solitary man and seemed to keep his dating low-key and…transitory?

And hello, that wouldn't exactly make him a candidate for a relationship. Plus Marissa didn't want to have one with him. He might be in a swimming pool, but the term 'corporate shark' still meant more than a boss doing laps in chlorine-scented water.

Oh, but he hadn't looked like a boss or a shark when he'd held his niece so tenderly in his arms. Marissa clenched her teeth because she *was not going down this track and that was that!*

Maybe she made a sound because Rick's head turned and his expression closed as though she'd caught him at something he hadn't wanted her to see.

Why would he feel that way about giving a swimming lesson to his niece? Not only that, but surely he'd guessed what Marissa thought about 'Julia' and yet he hadn't said a word.

'I'm sorry for barging in.' Sorry and quite annoyed by his

hidden depths, whether that made her unreasonable or not. 'I have an urgent fax and I thought—' She'd thought he'd be behind one of those closed doors beyond the pool with a lover. 'Er…I didn't realise there was a swimming pool up here.'

'It's not a problem. We've taken enough of Rick's time away from his work anyway.' The woman smiled as she wrapped her daughter in a towel and gathered her into her arms. 'I'm Faith, by the way. Rick's youngest sister.'

'Marissa.' She sought the comfortable communication skills that should have flowed naturally. 'Marissa Warren. I'm filling in while Rick's secretary, Tom, is on sick leave.'

'Ah, I see. For a while?' The other woman glanced at Rick and her eyes seemed to gleam. 'That should make for an interesting change.'

'It's not for all that long.' Rick cleared his throat. 'Didn't you say you needed to be going, Faith?'

His sister's mouth softened. 'Yes. There's a chance we might get a call from Russell tonight if things with his unit go as planned. I don't want to miss that. I asked Mum and Dad if they'd like to come over, speak with him and then watch you-know-who while I finish the call. The deployments are hard and he doesn't have his parents around, but Mum and Dad were too busy.'

Something in Rick's face seemed to tighten with… sadness? Some kind of regret for his sister? A measure of long-standing anger? 'What time? Do you want me to phone conference in from the office?'

'No, that's okay.' Faith lifted her daughter higher into her arms. 'Julia and I will be fine on our own but I appreciate the offer.'

They left after that and Marissa faced the company's boss where he stood in the water. No tattoo on the right biceps. Just muscles that seemed to invite the stroke of questing fingers. Marissa wanted to stay annoyed at him for concealing the truth about Julia from her. Instead, she could only see his kindness to his sister and niece, meshed with the appeal of a great deal of male sensuality.

Somehow *this* Rick was even deeper and more difficult to try to ignore. 'Your niece and sister seem lovely. It's…er…it's kind of you to give the little girl swimming lessons.'

'I'm a skilled diver and for some reason Julia feels safer in the water with a man.' His closed expression warned her off the topic, yet families were all about being there for each other, right?

Why would he mind her knowing he'd been there for his sister and niece?

Before she could consider possible answers, he climbed from the pool. In the brief time it took him to walk to the nearby lounger, snatch up a towel and wrap it around his hips, her concentration fled completely.

'I always try to swim here every day anyway.' His gaze swept, heavy-lidded and resistantly aware, over her. 'For the exercise.'

'You look very fit. Exceptionally fit, really. Quite muscularly fit.' Heat washed over her from her toes to the top of her head as she acknowledged that saying so might not have been particularly prudent. And why was he looking at her that way? He was the half-naked one.

Board shorts and a towel. The man is perfectly adequately covered. This was quite true. The problem was that the board shorts had clung, hadn't they? And the towel still left a lot of skin on display. His waist was trim and his shoulders were stunning.

'Your hair wasn't wet yesterday.' The blurted words were an accusation, as though, if his hair had been wet and she'd worked out he'd been swimming, she would have felt more prepared for the sight of him this way. 'And you didn't smell like chlorine. I have a really good nose for that sort of thing.'

'Today's the first day Julia's allowed me to put my head under the water, and I shower afterwards.' His hair fell in a dripping mass over one side of his forehead and was pushed back from the other.

Spiked lashes blinked away the droplets of water that clung to them. 'I want her to like swimming so I have to accommodate her fears. With her father away, she needs someone…'

'I…er…it must be difficult for your sister, having a husband in the armed forces and unable to do the daddy things at times.' Did the words even make sense? How could she concentrate, with every ounce of her so aware of the sight of him this way?

Not only that, but her hormones insisted on pointing out that Rick had seemed quite appealing indeed in the daddy role. Well, uncle, but it was the same general kind of thing.

Not really.

Yes, really.

She had to get over this idea of wanting a baby!

She had *not* thought that in association with Rick, anyway. She'd merely had a brief moment of considering how, in a bygone time, as in at *the dawn of time*, women may have reacted to strong men by wanting to…um…mate with them.

Which Marissa did not want to do—at all, whatsoever—with her boss.

It seemed expedient to get out of here. But she couldn't quite recall how to bring that about. 'Um…well…'

'Yes?' Rick's gaze locked with Marissa's. He felt worked up and overwrought for no reason he could explain. Other than to name the reason 'Marissa' or, at the least, 'his reaction to Marissa'. That was something he didn't want to do.

Her fingers tightened around the papers in her hands. 'The fax.'

'Let me see what it says.' He took the pages from her, careful not to touch her. Bent his head to read while she finally looked everywhere but at him.

The knowledge of that belated restraint absurdly made him want her all the more. 'I'll need the files on this from the Civil

Engineering department. Go straight there, will you? See if you can catch someone before they close for the day but tell him or her they don't need to hang around. This is something I'll have to address myself.'

'I'll go right now.' With relief evident in every line of her body and expression on her face, Marissa took the fax, wheeled about and escaped with it.

Rick watched her go. She seemed more than glad to get away from him now. Which was, of course, exactly as he wanted things to be…

CHAPTER SIX

From: Englishcrumpet
Just let Tony down gently.

From: Sanfrandani
Better to tell the man so he knows where he stands.

From: Kangagirl
I know you're both right. I don't want to hurt his feelings, that's all. Tony is a really nice guy. Maybe I shouldn't have met with him twice so close together. We had lunch the day after I found my boss giving his niece a swimming lesson on the top floor of our work building, and then we had dinner tonight. If I'd given myself more time between...

From: Englishcrumpet
Do you really think seeing Tony this Saturday or next would have made any difference? What exactly did you say was wrong with him, anyway?

From: Sanfrandani
No spark, wasn't it?

From: Kangagirl
Yes, and that's enough about me and my evening. Tell me about your dating efforts.

'This is a very tall building.' The words passed through Marissa's lips despite herself as they travelled up the outside of the building-in-progress in a cage lift.

It was Monday morning. She'd survived the disappointment of yet again finding 'no spark' during that second date with Tony, had also survived an entire week of working for Rick Morgan.

Had survived by the skin of her self-control, actually, and, really scarily tall buildings should be the least of her concerns.

For the real challenge, try genuinely not noticing the boss who'd taken her to the scary tall building in the first place, rather than merely pretending not to notice him. He superimposed himself on the Blinddatebrides men's profile pictures when she viewed them, took over her brain space during her dating efforts. Marissa felt a spark all right—towards completely the wrong man!

Her fingers tightened their death grip on the handrail inside the cage. 'And the lift is very fast.'

Dizzyingly so now she'd made the mistake of watching things whizz past. She'd thought that might save her from looking at Rick.

'We're quite secure, despite the fact you can see everything around you.' He took her elbow to help her off as the lift stopped. Held on while she came to terms with the height. Held on and her skin tingled while his expression deepened because of their nearness. 'Don't worry.' His voice seemed to come from deep in his chest as he placed his body between hers and the outside of the construction so she only saw him. 'I've got you. I won't let anything happen to you.'

She'd been half okay until he said that. Now she had to add chivalry to his list of attributes.

'Thank you, but I'm sure I'll be quite fine now.' She forced herself to step away from him, did her best to ignore the ache that doing so left behind.

Rick's hand dropped slowly to his side as though he too hadn't been ready to lose that contact.

Had touching her jolted him the same way? The answer was in the lock of his muscles, the tightness of his jaw and the way his lids lowered as his gaze drifted from her eyes to her mouth.

Then suddenly he turned to greet the site manager and the construction boss led them over every inch of the building.

Marissa composed herself and gave the tour her determined attention. This was a genuine meeting, the kind that should happen, not the sort where a man went on about turning a bridge into something completely made-over when that simply wasn't possible.

She took pages of notes of specifications that Rick would expect her to incorporate when he worked on his department memos after the visit and decided she was okay with this. She had it all under control now. All she needed to do was keep her attention on her work, not look at her boss any more than she had to and not think about him at all.

Yes. And that worked really well when they were in constant communication at point blank range, didn't it?

'Overall, the project looks good at this stage.' Rick nodded his approval as they finished their discussion at ground level almost an hour later.

'I'm happy enough with things so far.' The site boss pushed his hard hat back off his head. 'But we have two more days of work, maximum, before we need that shipment of materials from the Melbourne supplier. If we don't get it by then, we're stalled and that's going to cost us in time and wages.'

'And you think the reason for the delay is related to under-lying union issues at their end?' Rick nodded. 'Let me look into this. I'll see if I can get things moving for you. Do you have a copy of the order?'

'Right here.' The site boss removed it from his clipboard.

Rick took it, glanced at it and passed it to Marissa. 'At least you won't have to note all this down.'

Their fingers brushed. His words brushed across her senses at the same time. Just words, but his gaze searched her face, took her in as though he didn't realise he was doing it. As though he couldn't stop himself from doing it.

'I hope we can get back to the office soon.' She needed the security of her desk and at least some semblance of routine. She needed Tom to get better fast and come back to work so she could hide in Gordon's office.

More than that, she needed to stamp the words 'dating website' on her forehead so she remembered what she was supposed to be doing.

Not *supposed* to. *Wanted* to. *Must do. Was doing!* 'So I can get to work on this transcribing.'

They made their way back to work with Rick dictating on the way. Once at the office, Marissa worked on his department memos and, because they were so pushed for time, they ate lunch at their desks. The busy afternoon that followed should-n't have allowed time to feel anything but the strain of hours of hard work, and yet she felt a great deal of *other* strain.

Marissa wished that strain away as she made yet another phone call for her boss. 'This is Marissa Warren. I'm filling in as Rick Morgan's secretary and need you to supply me with a list of names of all the people who've worked on the Chartrel project.' She clasped the phone against her ear and smelled Rick's scent on it from when he'd taken a call at her desk minutes earlier.

Marissa closed her eyes and inhaled before she could stop

herself. When she lifted her lids again, Rick's gaze rested on her from the other room, deep grey eyes honed on her.

She forced her attention back to her work, buried herself in it. Maybe she should never emerge again. That might fix things. When Rick came to her desk an hour later, she knew it hadn't fixed anything at all.

'I need you to take these to the departments personally, Marissa.' He held out several signed memos. 'I know we're busy, but I want you to wait for their responses.'

'All right.' She agreed without hesitation. Eager to please him. No. She wasn't overly compliant or willing to go the extra mile. She certainly didn't think they were equals in this and would both be rewarded at the end. The roles were clear. Hers and his. This wasn't the same as the past.

Rick wasn't using her to try to make himself look bigger or better.

Maybe not, but he was still using her in his own way. He'd swept her into working for him without giving her a choice.

Your employment contract states: 'and other duties as required'. He didn't ask you to do anything you're not obliged to do.

Fine. The man had every right to commandeer her. He was still too similar to Michael—all business orientation and focused on his work goals. Marissa held the thought up like a shield, and added another. She wanted to find a safe man, an ordinary man, and yes, okay, maybe she did want to get married and fulfil the promise of the Blinddatebrides.com website.

She *was* almost thirty. Surely a desire for genuine commitment was acceptable at that age? Her mother had been married a decade by then, with a child—what if Marissa could only have one baby, like Mum had?

Didn't it make sense that Marissa might be thinking of getting started on that? That was nothing more than a logistics thing.

She wheeled about. 'When I get back, I'll do something about the explosion out here that was once my...that is...Tom's desk.'

Not her desk.

Tom's desk.

Tom's chair.

She was keeping it all warm for *Tom* and nothing more. On this fortifying reminder, she left. Graciously and calmly, as befitted someone totally in control of her life, her hopes, her dreams and herself.

By the middle of the afternoon it was raining—a drenching fall that obscured the skyline and turned the water in the harbour choppy. Marissa stared at the dismal view before she turned back to the photocopier.

'Deep breath,' she muttered. This was an irritation, after all, not a major problem. She eased open the three side doors on the machine, the one at the back, and pulled out both paper drawers and hit the spring catch on the feed cover so she could see in there as well.

Paper jams happened and, yes, there would now be pages missing from the report and she'd have to figure out what she'd lost, but that was *fine*.

The printer had needed a new ink cartridge an hour ago. One of the computer applications had quit mid-keystroke and she'd lost a few minutes of work. The phone continued to ring hot and there'd been more people from other departments through the door today than in the entirety of last week. She had enough typing sitting on her desk to take her the rest of the day by itself.

Rick was also busy. He was deep in phone talks about some crisis or another right now and it was clear from the content of the several tapes he'd asked her to work on 'urgently' that he was handling the equivalent of photocopier breakdown times about a thousand from *his* desk.

The corporate shark was doing his thing with a great deal

of style today, controlling his world, working through problems, making it all come together despite the difficulties and…thriving on it and being cheerful about it as he went along. Marissa did not find this at all stimulating, and it did not show her a different side of her boss, making it exponentially more difficult for her to keep viewing him as a corporate danger zone.

'Let's go. We're finished with this for today.' The day had felt interminable to Rick. From that trip up the building construction, when he'd wanted to protect Marissa, keep her safe, never let anything happen to her, through the rainy afternoon and on into this evening, Rick had struggled with his attraction to her.

She was amazing, the way she got down to work without a word of complaint, no matter what was thrown at her. And he…found that too appealing about her.

Maybe that explained this current madness, because not only was he determined to take her out of the office and feed her, he had no intention of letting her refuse. He took her bag from the desk drawer and pressed it into her hands, and drew her out of her chair.

Well, it was no big deal. Marissa deserved a reward for working so hard. As her boss, he wanted to give her that reward. He'd done the same for Tom countless times.

But this wasn't Tom and, the moment Rick touched Marissa, desire buzzed through his system and threatened to overwhelm him. Well, he would control that desire by the force of his will—maybe he needed to show himself he could do that.

'Wait. What are you doing? I have work up on the computer and I'm nowhere near finished.' She dug her shoes into the carpet, her eyes wide and startled as surprise and uncertainty and the same fire he fought in his bloodstream all bloomed in her gaze.

'We're going to eat and then go to our respective homes to

get some rest.' That sounded suitably businesslike. A pity he ruined it by adding, 'The office can wait until tomorrow.'

Not only had he not intended to downplay the importance of his work, but his voice had mellowed as his gaze roved over her, over the hair sticking out from the times she'd whipped the transcription headset on and off, and bent over the photocopier cursing.

She had trousers on today. Pale tan trousers and a black cashmere top that hugged her curves, and soft leather lace-up shoes she hadn't needed to change for their fieldwork.

Though the clothing screamed 'comfortable' and 'sensible' it also lovingly displayed every curve. He'd believed himself beyond reacting to those curves now.

Fooled yourself, you mean.

Well, it was too late to back out of this dinner now. Instead, he scooped everything on her desk into the tray and locked it away while she gasped. Then he shut down her computer and hustled her to the door.

'We're eating.' As colleagues. An hour in her company outside of working hours might take care of his inexplicable interest in her in any case. What did he know of her, after all, personally? She might bore him to tears. He might do the same to her. 'Don't argue. There are shadows under your eyes. And if there's too much work for you we'll farm some out to the general staff.'

This was not an option that had ever occurred to him before. That it did now shocked him into a silence that lasted the entire ride in the lift to the underground parking area.

As he helped her into his big car, she spoke.

'I'm not overwhelmed by the workload and it's kind of you to want to feed me but I assure you I'm not faint or anything.' She turned her head to face him. 'I've taken care to eat snacks regularly since that incident the first day.'

'I know.' He'd been watching, had checked on her though

she wouldn't have realised he was doing it. And, because that knowledge of himself made him feel exposed, he reiterated, 'This is not a kindness. It's a reward for efforts rendered, for both of us, that's all. And I'm pleased to hear it about the workload because, in truth, I don't really like the idea of handing work out of my office.'

They passed the rest of the trip in silence. He figured it was just as well since the words coming out of his mouth didn't seem to be much under his control.

When they arrived at the restaurant, Rick settled Marissa at the table in the same way he seemed to manage everything. With care and courtesy and without any hint of being the user and taker Michael Unsworth was.

'Thank you.' How could Marissa keep up her shield against her boss when he behaved this way? Right now she didn't want to, and that was a dangerous attitude. 'I've finally managed to take a breath for the first time today. I guess…I'm glad you thought of this, of us catching a quick meal on the way home.'

Marissa toyed with her water glass and tried not to think how nice it *was* to be seated opposite Rick in the tiny restaurant tucked away in a side street only about a ten minute drive from his offices.

Bilbie's @ Eighty-Eight sported just a handful of dining tables, spaced far apart and lit individually with a fat red candle on a chipped saucer in the centre of each.

Rain stung the darkened windows and the street lights and car headlights blurred out there, but inside all was quiet and calm.

Well, except for the tension she felt as she finally lifted her gaze and looked into Rick's eyes. Because it was a tension that had nothing to do with residual work stresses, that had an intimacy to it that just wouldn't seem to leave them.

Despite Rick's assertion this was nothing more than a reward for hard work. Despite her need to be attracted to someone other than him.

The latter wasn't working out very well right now.

So why hadn't she declined this meal with him?

Good manners. It might have seemed churlish if she'd refused.

Sure, Marissa. That's what it is.

Rick tore a piece of dense crusty bread from the loaf and dipped it in the herbed dressing and held it out to her. 'It would take as long for you to go home and prepare something for your dinner.'

'Thank you. I didn't realise what I was missing. Here. With this restaurant. It's…a nice setting. You know, for colleagues to visit briefly on a one-off basis. I don't find it romantic at all. I'm sure you don't either. Overall, I'd say the place is homely.' She popped the bread in her mouth before she could say anything else.

The taste and texture of the food enticed a soft sigh from her. The sight of his intent expression as he watched her did the same again. 'The bread…the…er…the bread is delicious.'

'The décor could do with a facelift.' In the candlelight the grey of his eyes darkened as his gaze focused on her. His lashes cast shadows over the strong slash of his cheeks. 'I don't particularly like the colour red either. I prefer autumn tones, like your—' He frowned. 'Like the season.'

Like her hair and the clothing she chose to wear most often? Marissa felt warmed despite herself.

Was she so foolish that she couldn't avoid falling for this kind of man again? For her ex-fiancé's kind of man? Because Rick *was* corporate to the core. He wouldn't care about building a family or doing any of the things she wanted…

'Feta on warm salad.' A waiter deposited the entrées and whisked a bottle of white wine forward, poured and left the rest of the bottle on the table. Disappeared again.

Rick drew a deep breath. 'Eat.' He gestured to the food,

lifted his fork and seemed determined to back the tension off. Back it right off and keep it backed off.

Marissa wanted that too. To assist in that endeavour, she said a little desperately, 'You said you're a skilled diver. Is that something you've done for long?'

Small talk. Surely if she smothered them in small talk it would have the desired effect?

'I started diving in my twenties after my sister Darla… For leisure.' He sipped his wine and something in his face seemed to close up. 'I've dived coastal reefs and other places but nowadays I mostly work locally on some endangered species projects.'

'Your niece really is in good hands with her swimming lessons, then.' A flash of that day, of him bare-chested and off-centre as he'd made up excuses for those swimming lessons, did something warm and tingly to her insides. It softened her emotions and made it difficult to remember him as the high-flying boss, a man very much out of her emotional league.

'Your family—'

'I'd rather hear about you.' He didn't bark the words, but the closed door was clear just the same. 'About your interests. We probably don't have a lot in common.'

No. They probably didn't, and she should appreciate that he wanted them both to accept that.

Rick let his gaze slide to his hands for a moment as he asked, 'So. What are your hobbies?'

What hadn't she tried might be easier to answer. But here was her chance to bore him rigid.

Marissa realised they'd eaten their way through the food and she hadn't even noticed. Well, she was focused now.

'I've tried motorcycle riding. I was eighteen and had a boyfriend at the Milberry further education college that year. He had tattoos and really long hair.' Was that enough boredom factor? 'I also tried my hand as a jillaroo on an outback station for twelve months but I guess that's a career, not a hobby. Does it count as a hobby if you just tested it out to see how it fit?'

She'd missed her parents a lot during that twelve months. And she was fighting to try to be boring. This wasn't supposed to be a cheerful reminiscence session.

His eyes gleamed with interest that he probably didn't want to feel either. 'I can't imagine you roping calves or whatever girl station hands do.'

Maybe if she went on some more he'd reach that stage of boredom they both wanted.

'I *can* ride a horse, though I'd only had pony club lessons before I went outback.' Her parents had found the money to give her those childhood lessons. They'd been filled with pride the first time she'd taken her little borrowed pony once around the walking ring all by herself. 'The jillaroo thing didn't really work out. I found I didn't like dust and big open spaces all that much.'

Instead of questioning her lack of intrepidity or yawning, he laughed. A deep, rich sound that rippled over her skin and made her catch her breath, and made him look years younger even as his laugh faded abruptly.

Their main courses arrived. Fillet of sole for her on a bed of spiced lentil mash, salmon steak for him with green beans and wild rice.

Marissa though he might leave the discussion there, or change the topic. Or simply let the silence grow as its own demonstration of his complete lack of interest in the minutiae of her life.

Instead, he caught her glance again and said, almost desperately, 'What else have you done with your time?'

'I went through a craft phase that lasted several years.' Surely he would find that very ordinary. She sipped her wine and a part of her registered the wonderful fruity tartness against her tongue before she went on. 'I crocheted a throw rug, made one patchwork quilt—a very small one. Tried out bag beading and made a tissue box cover, created my own calendar out of photos.'

Bought baby wool and hid it in the bottom drawer of my dresser, even though I know it's there and there's a part of me that wants to get it out and buy a knitting pattern for tiny little booties and work out how to make them.

Why did she have to feel this way? Why did she suddenly want all these things with an ever-increasing fierceness? Was it just because she was soon to turn thirty? Well, whatever the reason, it was highly inconvenient and she wished she didn't feel this way, and it was really not conducive to her peace of mind to have such thoughts in Rick's presence!

'And you've made a laminated desk cover of cartoons. I glanced at some of them. You've gathered some good material.' Though his words were bland, the look in his eyes was anything but.

'I've tried out a lot of different things. I'm not like that about work, though,' she hastened to add. 'I'm perfectly happy at Morgan's and hope to stay with the company for a very long time.'

'You've worked with us about six months, haven't you?' As easily as the conversation had rambled through her hobbies, it shifted to ground she didn't want to visit. 'What about before that? There's a stretch of time between those early things and now.' And now he looked interested in quite a different way.

Marissa tried not to let her body stiffen but she so didn't want to answer his question. She shouldn't have let the conversation head in this direction at all. 'I worked as a secretary in marketing for a number of years before…before I moved into my lovely position working for Gordon. I also like my apartment here better than the old one.'

There were no memories of her stupidity within its

walls. Michael had never lived with her, but he'd spent time in her home.

Well, a complete break had been in order, and why was she thinking about that when she'd deliberately pushed it out of her mind straight after it had happened? Had learned the lesson and moved right along.

Had she? Or was she defensive on more than one front and trying to patch over the problems by finding a special man she could hand-pick at her own discretion? That question rose up just to add something else to her broodiness and worries about ageing, as if they weren't big enough problems by themselves.

Her mouth tightened. 'And Morgan's is a great company to work for. Anyway, you don't want to hear that boring stuff about me.' She waved a hand.

'Maybe I do.' His intent gaze questioned her. 'What made you leave your previous position? Was it a career choice or something more personal?'

She tightened her lips and shook her head, forcing a soft laugh from between teeth inclined to clench together. 'It was time for a change of pace for me, that's all. Now it's your turn. Have you ever learned to crochet or knit, or maybe taken cooking lessons?' Maybe those questions would shut him down?

'Funny. No. None of those.' For a moment it seemed he would pursue the topic of her career choices but in the end he let it go and moved on. 'I'm not much of a cook, to be honest.' And then he said, 'My eldest niece is taking lessons. She's sixteen and a combination of teenage angst one minute and little girl vulnerability the next. Darla, my other sister, is a good mother to her. The best.'

And then he speared a piece of bean with his fork and chewed it and fell silent and stayed that way until the meal ended.

Eventually he lifted the wine bottle. 'Another glass?'

'No, thank you. I've had enough.' She wished she could blame the wine for the slow slide away of the barriers she needed to keep in place in his company.

Instead of controlling her attraction, she longed to ask more about his family, despite his tendency to guard any words about them.

'Coffee, then.' Rick signalled and a waiter magically appeared.

She drew a breath. 'Yes, coffee would be nice.' Maybe that would sober her thoughts, though she'd had very little to drink.

The beverages arrived. His gaze narrowed on her. 'You're lost in thought.'

Not thoughts he'd want to know. She forced a smile. 'I *should* be thinking. About work tomorrow.' About the fact that they were boss and employee and this evening had been a reward to her as his employee. Nothing more. 'The rain seems to have stopped.'

'Yes.' He turned his gaze to the windows, almost as though he knew she needed a reprieve from his attention.

They finished their drinks in silence.

'I'll take you home.' He placed some notes inside the leather account folder and got to his feet.

Outside the restaurant, he ushered her into his car and waited for her address. When she gave it, he put the car into motion. She wanted to make easy conversation and lighten the mood but no words would come. Then they were outside her apartment building and she turned to face him.

'Thank you for feeding me dinner.' *Will you kiss me goodnight? Do I want you to?* 'It wasn't necessary.' And she mustn't want any such thing. Naturally *he* wouldn't want it!

'Your cheeks are flushed. Even in this poor light I can see.' He murmured the words as though he couldn't stop them. 'It's like watching roses bloom. I took you to dinner to prove we have nothing in common but work, and yet…' He threw his door open, climbed out of the vehicle.

He did want her still. Despite everything.

The warmth in Marissa's cheeks doubled and her heart rate kicked into overdrive, even as she sought some other explanation for her conclusion. It *had to be* the wine.

She mustn't be attracted to him, or to his layers. Yet she struggled to remember all the valid reasons why not.

His hand went to the small of her back to lead her inside. 'Ready?'

CHAPTER SEVEN

'WELL, here we are, right at my door,' Marissa babbled as she opened said door, and then appalled herself by adding, 'Would you care to—?'

'For a moment.' He stepped in after her, and then there they were, facing each other in her small living room.

Her fourth floor apartment was functional and neat. A lamp glowed from a corner table. She flicked a switch on the wall and the room came fully into focus—the lounge suite in a dark chocolate colour with a crushed velvet finish, her crocheted throw rug folded neatly at one end.

Prints on the walls and a kitchen cluttered full of gaily coloured canisters and racks of spices completed the picture. 'It's nothing special,' she said, 'but I've tried to make it a home.'

'You succeeded.' His gaze went to the lounge and returned to her face, and a desire he had fought—they had both fought—burned in his eyes.

'Well, thank you again.' She shifted beside him. Wanted him to stay. Forced herself not to offer coffee, late night TV, late night Marissa…

'Goodnight. I shouldn't have come in.' His gaze tracked through her home again.

'Yes. Goodnight. You should…go.'

The muscle of his upper arm brushed the curve of her

shoulder as he turned. He made a choked sound and his fingers grasped her wrist.

'We mustn't—' But she lifted her head as his lowered and then his mouth was on hers.

He tasted of coffee and wine and Rick—a wonderful, fulfilling taste that she lost herself in. So totally lost herself…

Rick's stomach muscles clenched as he fought the urge—almost the *need*—to crush Marissa close. He didn't *need*. He made choices.

Like this one? What was he doing?

Marissa made a soft sound in her throat and her hand lifted to his biceps, and then his shoulder, over his shirt. He wanted her hand on his skin. Somewhere. Anywhere. To warm him…

When she finally stroked her fingers over the cord of his neck and up to the edge of his jaw, he pressed in to her touch. As though he couldn't survive without it. The feeling was shocking, almost unmanning, and yet still he kissed her, pressed nearer, kept going.

Rick caught her hand as it dropped away from his face. Caught it between their bodies with his and held it to his chest. Felt eased somewhere deep inside as he did this.

He meant to control this. It was only desire. It had to be—he could still prove it. Somehow. If he merely kissed her again, tasted her again and then…

The *and then* part didn't happen. Not in the way he intended. Not *Goodbye* and *Glad you enjoyed the dinner* and *That was nothing out of the ordinary*.

Instead, he should ask what the hell he was doing kissing her in the first place.

Even that question couldn't get through. Not with his lips fused to hers, their bodies a breath apart. It should have—it needed to. A part of Rick acknowledged that. He kissed her again anyway. Kissed her and drew her against his chest and wondered if he was stark, staring crazy as his heart thundered and his arms ached to keep her within their clasp.

Marissa didn't know what to do. She'd let this get out of her control and she didn't know how to bring it back. Rick's kiss, his touch, his arms around her all combined not only to swamp her senses but also to overwhelm her in too many other ways.

His hold felt like a haven, his touch what she had needed and waited for. Her emotions were involved in this kiss, and she couldn't let them be. She had to protect herself. He didn't even want to desire her, and she was determined to have no feelings for him. She *didn't* have feelings for him. Right? *Right?*

She gasped and drew sharply back. Her hands dropped from him.

He released her in the same instant, and stared at her as though he couldn't believe what he'd done. As though his actions astounded him. As though he'd *felt* them in the same deep places she had?

Don't fool yourself, Marissa.

His jaw locked tight. 'I showed a weakness of character by doing that. I apologise.' He stepped back from her and the warmth of his eyes returned to a stark, flat grey.

Marissa wanted to take consolation in the fact that he looked as though he had run a marathon, looked as torn and stunned and taken aback as she felt, but he'd soon recovered his voice, hadn't he? And his self-control. She had to do the same.

'This mustn't be repeated. I'll never participate again—'

'I don't mix work with pleasure, or pleasure with emotional commitment. I don't *do* emotional commitment.' He spoke the words at the same time, and then looked at her sharply. 'What do you mean—?'

'Nothing.' She cut her hand through the air. Best to simply deal with this moment, and do so once and for all.

He *was* corporate. He *didn't* feel more than physical interest in her. She had somehow managed to embellish this encounter as if she believed his response to her ran deeper, and his words right now made that absolutely clear. *No commitment.*

She wanted to ask *Why not?* Instead, she forced out the words that had to be said.

'There was an attraction between us and we both gave in to it for a brief moment.' That should put it into perspective. 'It was a mistake and now it's over and done with. I'm sure we'll both very quickly forget it.'

'I'm sure you're right,' he agreed and left.

From: Kangagirl:
I was dumped very publicly by my fiancé in an office environment where we worked together. Now I'm up to my neck in one again. An office situation and lots of hard work, I mean, not anything else because I wouldn't be that silly. I feel pressured, that's all.

From: Englishcrumpet
What's your ex-fiancé's name and where can we find him in case we want to let him know what we think of him? The dirt bag!

From: Sanfrandani
Marissa. Do you still have feelings for the guy?

From: Kangagirl
No. I couldn't possibly have!

But Marissa hadn't been thinking of Michael Unsworth when she'd given her half desperate answer to her friends when they'd discussed last night's dinner. She'd been thinking of Rick. She placed several more loose letters and memos onto the pin inside the file on her desk and told herself not to think back to that kiss at all.

She needed to forget her boss in that way altogether and get back to her dating plans.

No distractions. Especially no Tall, Dark and Delicious distractions.

Tall, Out of Bounds and Emotionally Blockaded, she amended. All the things she could never accept. Except the tall part.

And *she* wasn't emotionally blockaded. She was cautious. A whole different matter.

Rick's mobile phone beeped out a message on his desk.

Marissa forced her attention to her work. What she really needed was for Tom to get better and come back so she could go back to working for Gordon, and stop thinking about Rick.

The fax machine whirred. Marissa got up at the same time that Rick left his desk. They met in front of the machine and hers was the hand that reached first for the sheet of paper that emerged.

'I'll take that. I think it'll be for me.' He reached out his hand.

'Certainly. Here you go.' She passed the fax to him, couldn't help but see the image of a head and shoulders that filled the space. A cheeky smile that belied the wounded expression in dark eyes. Arched brows and thick dark hair and a bit too much make-up on the face, if the black and white image was anything to go by. The girl looked about sixteen. His older niece?

Curiosity slid in sideways to assail her before she could stop it.

The office phone rang. With the fax clasped in his hand, Rick strode to her desk and answered it. 'Rick Morgan.' A pause. 'What's going on, Kirri?'

There was silence as he listened to whatever response he got and Marissa realised she was in the middle of the room, a party to a private conversation—something Rick wouldn't want her to overhear, if his reaction when she'd seen him with his other niece was any indication.

Marissa scooped a pile of files from the corner of her desk and headed for the file room. Rick's words followed her, as did that faxed image with the wounded eyes.

'You're as beautiful as ever, Kirri. You have lovely blue eyes and a killer smile and you're sweet on the inside where it counts most of all. And so is your mother. You know that, Kirrilea.' His tone was both gentle and fierce. *Not* exactly emotionally blockaded right now!

He drew a breath and Marissa glanced out of the file room at him—just a really brief glimpse—but that one moment showed he was holding back some kind of deep inner anger, wanting to comfort his niece and not let her hear that anger in him, all at the same time. 'Next time don't ask Grandad something like that, okay? Ask me, instead.'

Another pause while Marissa started to push folders away and tried hard not to listen, not to wonder about this grandfather who wouldn't tell a teenager she looked lovely, about her boss's family altogether. Rick had said, 'Ask me.'

She bit her lip. He must have plenty of commitment capability, because he seemed to have it for his nieces, his sisters…

There were other things that week. A call from his mother. Final swimming lessons with his niece and the tinge of colour on the tips of his ears as he'd asked if Marissa might manage to make a certificate, perhaps with an image of a fish on it. Something to state that Julia had passed her first unofficial swimming class.

Marissa navigated each glimpse into his layers with the promise to herself that she wouldn't let them intrigue her. That she didn't want to help him unlock his inner ability to commit—she didn't even know if he truly possessed such a thing. *He* clearly believed he didn't. That she didn't think of his kiss constantly and wake in the middle of the night wondering what it would be like if they *did* live at the dawn of time, if she had chosen him.

Tick, tock, tick, tock.

No. No tick-tocking. No Big 3-0 depressive, subconscious birthday countdown, no biological rumblings at all, and no re-membering kisses. No, no, no!

On Thursday, while Rick dictated straight over Marissa's shoulder to finalise a memo he didn't have time to even place first on a tape, a woman rushed through the door and zeroed her gaze onto him.

'I'm sorry. I'm probably interrupting, but something's happened and I don't have to take the chance because I know I committed to hostess duties for you tonight, Rick, and I'd never let you down, but I just wondered…'

The woman was thin, with a determined air about her, and she sported a feminine version of Rick's nose and jaw. She flipped straight brown hair over her shoulder and for a moment Marissa saw eyes very like the ones in that faxed photograph.

Marissa's interest—curiosity—spiked.

Anyone would be curious, she justified, and hated her weakness where her boss was concerned.

'What's happened, Darla?' Rick strode around the desk, clasped the woman's elbows. 'Is Kirrilea all right? Did our fath—'

'Kirri's fine, and Dad is his typical self. There's no point wishing he'll change because he's made it clear he won't, but I won't have him upsetting my daughter—' She broke off. 'I told Kirri to send you the fax. I hope you didn't mind.'

'I didn't.' He chopped a hand through the air as though to dismiss the very idea. 'Tell me what's brought you here.'

Marissa printed the memo Rick had dictated. 'If Rick can sign this I'll put the phone on answering service and hand-deliver the memo. That way you won't be disturbed while I'm gone.' She would get out of their way and try not to think about his complexities. Or her ever-growing conviction that he had emotional commitment aplenty for his sisters and nieces and therefore why wouldn't he have the capacity for that in any other relationship?

'I'm so sorry. I'm Darla.' The woman stuck out her hand, shook Marissa's firmly. 'Forgive my rudeness. I was a little excited.'

Marissa liked Darla's honesty and her determined smile, the strength she sensed in her and, most of all, her clear affection for her brother.

'I'm Marissa. The borrowed secretary. Very transitory. And it's no problem.' Nor were the callisthenics of her brainwaves. Marissa would get those under control as of now. 'Please, excuse me.'

She took the signed memo, dealt with the phone, left them and delivered the memo.

Should she dawdle back to give them more time? It probably wasn't necessary. Rick would have taken his sister into his office.

He hadn't. They stood exactly where Marissa had left them. Darla was talking fast while Rick nodded.

Marissa's steps slowed as both heads turned her way. 'Um…'

Darla spoke first. 'Would you truly not mind the overtime, Marissa? Rick says you might be prepared to help him out, but I don't want to ask if it will cause any problems.'

Rick leaned a hand against the edge of Marissa's desk. Tension showed in the line of his shoulders and yet, when he looked at his sister, all Marissa could see was affection and…pride?

'My sister has the chance to meet with the central management team in charge of her real estate brokerage.' Rick's gaze met Marissa's and held. 'There may be a promotion in the offing…if you'd be prepared to hostess a business dinner at my home tonight.'

CHAPTER EIGHT

'OF COURSE. I'll be happy to hostess the event.' Marissa spoke the words while panic did its best to get a grip on her.

The business dinner at Rick's home had been noted in the BlackBerry. Everything went in there and, indeed, Marissa had prepared Rick some information so he could be fully informed before the evening. She'd thought that would be the extent of her involvement. The idea of spending a night working at Rick's side, in his home, in a whole other setting to the office, where she would see even more parts of him…well, it unnerved her even while her hormones set up a cheering section about it.

Marissa spoke to the other woman. 'If Rick feels I could be of assistance, I…I'm sure I can cope with hostessing the event.'

Somehow. Maybe. If she managed to get a grip on herself and her thoughts about her boss between now and then. Marissa tried to keep the hope out of her tone as she added, 'That is, if there's no one else more suitable, maybe someone else in the family who could take your place?'

'There isn't,' Rick said, squashing that hope quite flat.

A smile broke over Darla's face. 'Oh, thank you!'

The woman impulsively threw her arms around Marissa and then turned to her brother and hugged him. He cupped her head so tenderly in his hand as he hugged her back. A fierce well of protectiveness crossed his face before they separated.

Layers. How many more could he possibly have? Now Marissa's hormones had given up the cheer squad routine and brought out the tissues, going all emotional on her right when she didn't need that to happen.

'It's settled then.' Rick drew his wallet from his pocket and pulled out some notes, frowned when his sister opened her mouth. 'I know you like good luck charms. Buy one to wear tonight.' He gestured to the silver bracelet on her wrist. 'You'll find room for it on there somewhere. And get something for Kirrilea—a trinket. And tell her my secretary very kindly laminated that faxed page and I have it on my desk where I can enjoy it.'

Darla's fingers closed over the money and his hand, and a sheen of moisture came to her eyes before she blinked and turned away. 'God, I wish our father had half… Well…' She smiled with a fierce determination that quickly became the real thing as she turned once again to Marissa. 'Thank you. I hope I'll have good news after tonight but, even if not, I appreciate the chance to attend the meeting.'

She rushed out of the office at the same frenetic pace she'd entered it.

'If her speed is anything to go by, she probably does the work of five people and very much deserves a promotion.' Marissa made the observation lightly when she didn't feel light at all. But she would be okay tonight. *She would.*

'I know she deserves it.' He murmured the words without appearing to think about them.

There'd been no wedding band on Darla's finger, no mention of a man in the proceedings and an impression that Darla was alone and turned to her brother for emotional support.

Alone with a sixteen-year-old daughter. Darla hardly looked old enough. And Marissa now wanted to clutch at straws, even though something told her that would be futile.

'Did you really need me to help you tonight, or did you just want Darla to feel free to chase this job promotion?'

Rick's eyelashes veiled his expression as he answered. 'There's no one else suitable at such short notice.'

'Right, then I guess that will be fine.' She would simply maintain her professionalism and make it fine. She could do that. All it would require was a little concentration, a lot of focus and maybe some tranquilliser for the hormone squad!

A phone call came in then. Marissa thought she recognised the voice, but couldn't place it. When she asked for a name, the caller paused for a heartbeat before saying, 'Just put me through. I'm returning his call.'

Marissa connected the call.

Rick rose from his desk and closed his door after he answered the call. Super-secret business, apparently.

Marissa got on with her work.

Whatever, anyway. She had more important things to think about. Like tonight!

'I think Carl Fritzer is deliberately goading you on the topic of environmental issues.' Marissa directed the comment to Rick and then nodded her thanks to the catering guru as she accepted a platter of artfully arranged biscotti and small handmade chocolates.

The evening was more over than started now, and the three of them stood in the kitchen of Rick's penthouse apartment. It was a large and lush place—four bedrooms at least and functional in all the nicest ways but, for tonight, Rick had taken everyone outside to the rooftop terrace.

Marissa had fought with herself every step since she'd arrived. She didn't want to be delighted by his home, nor constantly and utterly aware of him in it. Didn't want to note that his midnight-blue shirt and black trousers made him look even more Tall, Mysterious and Compelling. She still wanted Ordinary, darn it. She did!

'I truly don't understand why Mr Fritzer would do that.' *Focus on work, Marissa.* 'What difference does it make to any possible business dealings between our company and his?' The stamp of ownership she put on her statement was a whole new problem. Since when had it been the 'Marissa and Rick team'?

Remember what happened to the 'Michael and Marissa' so-called 'team'? Well, you should!

Marissa forced herself to go on. 'Morgan's follows all the codes to the letter and, in a lot of cases, goes a lot further than most companies in its efforts towards environmental friendliness.'

'The man seems to consider a bit of goading as good entertainment value, but I noticed his colleagues don't seem to share his enthusiasm for the topic.' When Rick shrugged, his shirt clung to his broad shoulders, outlined the strength of the muscles beneath the cloth.

There was something different in him tonight when he looked at her, too. She couldn't pin it down, but he seemed to be weighing her up, or searching for something. He was perhaps softer towards her? More attentive? Interested in a different way?

Some of his examination seemed—she didn't know—almost empathetic or something? But that made no sense.

What if he *was* beginning to think of her in a deeper way? Given her determination to steer utterly clear of even noticing him, the thought shouldn't please her, yet she felt a reciprocal softening towards him.

'There may be something Fritzer is hiding about his own dealings or standards.' Rick's gaze caressed her face and neck as he went on. Did he realise he was doing that? 'I'll have a team investigate that possibility before I commit us to any work with the company. I can find out anything I need to know before they get to the stage of an acceptance of our offer of services.'

He hesitated and a combination of unease and knowledge, awareness and that same empathy flared in his eyes again. For a moment Marissa thought he would reach for her, right there in front of the caterer…

'Is that coffee? Just what's needed.' One of the female business delegates strolled inside. 'Can I help with anything?'

'I think we have it under control.' A frown crossed Rick's face before he lifted the tray of coffees.

Disappointment surged through Marissa and she told herself not to be foolish, forced her attention to the drinks Rick held on the tray.

The lattes bore everything from starfish shapes to mini Harbour Bridges in the foam tops. He thanked the caterer. 'The rest we can manage for ourselves, if you're happy to let yourself out?'

The young man scooped up a backpack from the corner of the kitchen. 'Cheers. It was a pleasure to help you, as always.' He strode to the apartment's front door and left.

They returned to the West Australian business delegation of men and women where they sat in big squashy outdoor chairs grouped around low tables.

Rick's apartment and exclusive terrace took up the entire top level of the building. The formal outdoor dining area seated up to twenty people. They'd eaten there with city views all around them and the lush foliage of the rooftop garden behind them. The sight and scent of flowers and plants and shrubs filled the area. Roses and mint, hardy native shrubs mixed with hydrangeas and mat-rush and Easter cactus.

His home was truly gorgeous and Marissa couldn't help but appreciate the beauty. He wore his wealth very comfortably here. He'd seemed pleased when she'd first arrived and admired his apartment and surroundings.

It was also a large enough home, and secure enough, that a small family could thrive quite nicely here if necessary. A house with a full garden would be better, of course, but children could enjoy the terrace garden, or be taken to play in the large park right across the road from the building…

Oh, what was she thinking? She had to focus on the business of the evening, not fantasies that were becoming more and more difficult to quash.

'Well, it's a lovely evening for a business function and this is the perfect setting for it.' She caught Rick's eye and gestured with her hand, but all that did was draw their attention to the fact that darkness had now fallen and, beyond the well-lit terrace, the city lights, Lavender Bay, the Harbour Bridge, and buildings of all shapes and sizes glittered before them.

The setting was romantic. Her hormones had recognised this immediately, even if Marissa had been busy trying not to notice the fact.

Why couldn't she stop viewing her employer in this way? Stop herself from developing a deeper and deeper interest in him when she knew that doing so was utterly futile? Was it because she felt she knew Rick better now? Somehow, she'd started to trust him as she'd watched him care for his sisters and nieces and saw his business dealings, which were far more frank than Michael Unsworth's behaviour had been in the workplace, or out of it.

'Well, here's the coffee, everyone,' she called. 'Actually, it's coffee *art*, with thanks to our now departed caterer.' She pushed the memories of Michael away and tried not to think about her shifting feelings towards her boss. Rick was much more difficult to dismiss than thoughts of Michael, and that knowledge was not comforting.

Rick didn't want any kind of emotional commitment. He hadn't said why, but he'd made that fact clear. She suspected it had to do with his father, or his family life generally, but what did it matter in the end? Her boss didn't want *her*. Maybe she should simply be grateful he was being honest about that. She started to hand out the drinks.

Rick watched Marissa hostess the small group, chatting as she went, and he thought about her use of the term 'we,' as though she felt as invested in the company as he did. He couldn't forget kissing her, nor reconcile himself to the shift inside him that had somehow been different from anything he had experienced before.

She looked beautiful tonight, all soft curves beneath the golden dress, her hair up and her nape tantalisingly bare. He wanted to press his lips to that soft skin, to somehow pay homage to her.

Thoughts battered at him. She looked right here—in his home. He wanted to keep her here. And other thoughts—of taking her to his bedroom, closing the door on the world and staying there with her until he knew all of her, understood all of her and she'd given all of herself to him. How could he want that when he would never give her the same in return?

Maybe he didn't want it. Not really. Couldn't this all be about lust and the confusion of feeling this way towards a woman he was working with and coming to admire in a working environment?

The business talk moved on. Fritzer goaded a little more, and Rick ignored it. He sat at Marissa's side, his arm stretched across the back of her chair in a gesture he knew was possessive, but he couldn't make himself stop it. He needed to be near her, close enough to touch even if he didn't.

Yes. He was in trouble, but he could control it. He must be able to do at least that.

Over coffee, talk turned to what the city had to offer.

One of the women leaned forward. 'We have half of tomorrow before we leave. I'm wondering what to do with the time.'

'There's plenty on offer in terms of entertainment, shopping, whatever you like, really.' Rick stretched out his legs, stared at the neat crease in the dark trousers. Imagined the gold of Marissa's dress against the fabric.

All roads led back to it. The fact that he wanted Marissa— still wanted her.

'You might consider the new animal petting zoo.' Marissa spoke the words to the other woman. Her gaze met Rick's and a delicate flush rose in her cheeks as she seemed to wish she hadn't raised the topic.

She went on, waved her hand. 'Holding a koala is a unique experience.'

And then he remembered *that* moment, the trembling of her shoulders and the rush of protective instinct that had coursed through him, had tapped into instincts he'd been ignoring ever since that moment.

'The koalas smell of eucalyptus oil, don't they, Marissa?' *Keep it light. That's all it can be.* 'Did you manage to wash the scent out of that cardigan?'

'I did get the cardigan clean, and I imagine our overseas visitors probably made good use of a dry-cleaner's after that visit.' Marissa lowered her gaze to her coffee cup. 'We've had some interesting moments during my brief time filling in as your assistant.'

Maybe she wanted to remind them both that this wouldn't last. That soon she would go back to her regular job and he wouldn't see more of her than a glimpse in a corridor from time to time. Maybe he should be glad she wanted to remind him of that.

Instead, a kaleidoscope of images and moments spent with her bombarded his mind and his senses. Marissa with a hard hat squashed over her curly hair that day on the bridge. Presenting him with a laminated certificate for his niece for completing her swimming lessons. Cursing at the photocopier beneath her breath when she thought he couldn't hear her.

He wanted Tom back on his feet but the thought of Marissa easing back to the periphery of his working life didn't sit well with him.

'We should go.'

'Yes, it's been a productive evening.'

'We'll take a vote with the full group and you'll hear from us.'

One by one their guests stood. It took another few minutes for Rick to see them completely out and away.

When Rick closed the door finally on the guests, Marissa moved to the terrace to collect the empty cups and return them to the kitchen. She turned as he joined her.

'I'll get the biscotti tray.' And then she needed to leave, to forget this glimpse into yet another side to her boss.

'Leave it for now.' He poured two glasses of liqueur, passed one to her and led her to the edge of the terrace with his hand on her arm.

'I guess we deserve five minutes to celebrate this evening's hard work. To enjoy the view now it's quiet and there's time to focus on it.' She couldn't help the observation that followed. 'Somehow I'd expected your apartment to be all chrome and black and sharp lines with the view carefully shut outside through long planes of plate glass. The terrace entertainment area surprised me. It's lovely.'

'I'm pleased you like it.' His gaze darkened on her, again seemed to search inside her.

Would he be as pleased to know she'd imagined it being a home to a family? No. He wouldn't, would he? She lifted the glass and inhaled the aroma of the drink. 'I smell spices and tea and rum. And vanilla?'

'It's Voyant Chai Cream. I think you'll like it.' He watched her over the rim of his glass as they sipped.

'Very smooth.' She sipped again. Savoured. Tried hard not to think about the war going on inside her body that shouldn't be going on at all, and especially not where Rick was concerned.

For the first time in her life Marissa was subjected to forces of her own nature, her own hidden needs, which she had never even considered she might struggle to control. She couldn't seem to stop herself from associating some of those desires with her boss. She forced her attention back to the drink in her hand. 'It's delicious.'

'Yes.' The single word seemed to wrap around her, be meant for her. All he did was match her sip for sip before he finally set his glass down, tucked his hands in his pockets and looked out over the harbour, and yet she felt his desire for her as though he'd spoken it aloud.

'It was a good night, don't you think?' He glanced at her, the heat in his eyes partially concealed, but very much there. Talked business as they should be doing. 'Despite that bit of goading, I expect they'll sign with us for their project.'

'It was—yes. I believe it was a successful evening.' She set her glass down with trembling fingers.

The softness of the city night cast his face in clarity and shadows. Just like the man. She had to pull herself together, to play this out the safe way, to keep her focus on their working relationship and not these odd, nebulous things she wanted that she didn't even know if she could ever have.

She should put herself to sleep or something until she'd passed her birthday, get it behind her so she could realise it hadn't changed anything, that she was the same inside and she didn't have to pine for a family of her own.

'In part, that success is thanks to you.' He let his gaze roam over her face. 'I think you captured all of them.' His hands fell to his sides. She thought he murmured, 'You captivated me.'

A long beat of silence followed as she fought with herself.

Finally she spoke. 'I should go. Tomorrow is another working day.' Maybe if she reminded herself of that she wouldn't respond to him quite so much.

Marissa moved away from the view, from the sparkle of city lights. They stepped inside and she collected her bag from the kitchen. 'I'll get the doorman to organise me a cab straight off the rank downstairs.'

'I'll take you down.'

'There's no need.' She drew a breath as they paused before his door. 'Goodnight, Rick. I'm glad I could help. I hope your sister gets the job promotion. I got the impression it would mean a lot if she did.'

'Darla deserves the break. She's worked hard for that company for many years, first as a part-timer and working up to full-time once Kirrilea started school.'

'You're proud of her. Of your niece, too.' She faced him before the closed door, searched his eyes.

'They're easy people to be proud of.' Rick reached past her to open the door. His fingers wrapped around the doorknob.

And the tension wrapped right around them, too.

'Back away from me, Marissa. Tell me not to mess with a perfectly good working relationship. Tell me not to mess with you.'

'You've been different tonight.' She whispered the words and he braced his feet and drew her into the V of his body.

Her hand lifted to his chest and he kissed her. Pressed his mouth to hers and his body to hers, and pleasure and a feeling rightness swept through her.

'More.' He whispered the word.

Marissa lost herself so thoroughly in Rick's kiss, lost senses and feelings and responses and, yes, emotions, in him. When his lips left hers to trail over her ear to the sensitive cord of her neck, she closed her eyes and let the feel of his body against hers, his hands cupping her head, her shoulders so sweetly, sweep through her.

Could a man's touch communicate straight to the heart of not only a woman's senses, but also her soul? It seemed so.

She clasped her hands on his shoulders, curled her fingers around his upper arms and held on. When he skirted his hands up from her waist, over her back, to where her shoulders were bared by the wide cowl neck of the dress, she shivered.

A strained, needy sound passed through his lips. It was the last thing she consciously registered for long moments as they stood by his door, their bodies tightly entwined, her resistance and grand plans in shambles. Her bag lay at her feet. She had no idea when it had landed there.

'Say my name.' The words were harsh and possessive, demanding and enervating. 'I want to hear it. I don't want you to be thinking of him—'

What did he mean? A chill rushed over her skin and all through her body. She wrenched away from him. 'What do you know? What have you heard? About that fake engagement I believed was real? About Michael—'

'Ah, I didn't mean to say that.' He pushed a hand through his hair. 'I had to know why you left your last job, Marissa.' His eyes were dark and turbulent. 'The information about your personal life—I didn't ask for it, I stopped the man when I realised where he was headed with the conversation but by then it was too late.'

'Right. I see. So you phoned my old company to investigate why I left, and you found out things about me at that time.' If his gaze softened into pity she would die right there, and now it all made sense. This. This was the empathy he'd displayed earlier.

'Without meaning to find those things out, yes.' He seemed to search for words.

Apology. Regret.

Yes, she heard them in his tone but, most of all, she heard that he knew of that embarrassment. He now probably thought she was desperate and on a manhunt. What if he thought she'd set out to hunt *him*? Mortification, shame and anger crashed through her. She clutched at the anger because the others were too awful to bear.

'That call. I knew I recognised the voice.' And Rick had closed his office door and talked about her. 'I don't care if you say it was business.' Her voice shook. 'I'd started to trust you. I can't believe I did. What did the man tell you? That Michael Unsworth made a fool of me? What does that have to do with my good record at Morgan's?'

'Nothing. I didn't want that information. I didn't ask for it.' He reached for her hand but she drew back.

He went on in a low voice, 'I'm sorry he hurt you, Marissa.'

'Well, don't be sorry because I am totally over the way Michael treated me. I learned from it and I moved on. Was that what this kiss was about? Pity? Tell me!'

He drew a harsh breath into his lungs. 'You know better than that. I want you in my bed and I have from the first day I had you up on that excuse for a bridge with me. Maybe you should pity *me*, because I can't seem to get that desire for you out of my system, no matter what I do.'

Rick's admission stunned Marissa into silence. More, perhaps, because of the flash of something deeper than desire that burned for a moment in his gaze before he masked it.

Oh, will you listen to yourself, Marissa? Do you want to fall for Mr Corporate a second time?

Rick had just *proved* his ruthlessness to her!

But he'd also apologised and seemed as though he meant it.

She scooped her bag from the floor. 'I just want us to work together and get along and I want to follow my well thought out plans for my life in peace. Is that so much to want?'

'It isn't. It isn't too much to want.' He took a step towards her as she wrenched open the door. 'Marissa—'

But she didn't wait to hear what he might have said.

She left.

CHAPTER NINE

To: Sanfrandani, Englishcrumpet
From: Kangagirl
One last thing to tell you both. I spoke to Mum on the phone early this morning. We had a good talk and I let her know I'd rather spend a weekend with her and Dad a bit down the track after my birthday, that I'm really busy at the moment and don't want a party of any kind.

From: Englishcrumpet
I'm sure your mum will understand.

From: Sanfrandani
You can throw a big party when you're ready.

From: Englishcrumpet
Or not.

From: Kangagirl
People make a big deal out of the thirtieth birthday, but really, it's just another day on the calendar. I probably won't even think much about it at all.

Grace had instant messaged a little after that, a message Marissa caught on her way out the door to go to work. She'd asked whether Marissa was in denial about her thirtieth birthday.

Marissa hadn't had time to respond. And right now she was focused on other things. Rick Morgan things, to be precise. Work things. Marissa barrelled along the corridor towards Rick's suite of offices.

Anyway, she had to come to terms with that looming birthday. It wasn't denial to say it wasn't significant, it was the power of positive statement. Say it enough times and she'd come to believe it.

If she could apply the same outlook to her relationship with Rick—her *working only* relationship—that would be a great help.

As a mature professional, she could work with Rick until his secretary returned. She only had to survive that long and then she could forget him, forget what he knew about her. All she needed to do was hold her head up and he'd soon realise he had no reason to pity her.

Dani and Grace had blamed last night's kiss on too much alcohol or maybe an overload of successful business-related feeling when Marissa had calmly and casually discussed the topic with them via two separate Instant Message sessions last night and this morning—before she'd sent that later message about Mum and avoiding a birthday party.

You mean when you buzzed them, desperate for some support because you were scared stiff you'd let yourself fall for the boss only to find out he'd invaded your privacy?

She had *not* fallen for the boss, nor did she intend to. And he *had* invaded her privacy.

He's head of a multi-million dollar company and you've been working directly for him, handling some very sensitive material. He exercised his right to enquire about your past em-

ployment and he said he only *wanted to know about that. You know the department head who spoke to him is a big gossip.*

Marissa had worked out the identity of the caller, of course. It had only taken the jolt of discovering that Rick had gone after the information for her to remember the owner of that somehow familiar voice.

Okay, fine, there was that. But she still didn't have to like it or feel comfortable. Rick *did* know her secret.

Perhaps he hadn't acted inappropriately, and he had seemed to truly regret the outcome. And she knew one of his secrets. That he wanted to make love to her, had desired her from Day One.

That knowledge did not thrill or tempt her. She couldn't let it!

Her initial IM sessions with Dani and Grace hadn't been the result of a desperate buzzing, either. More of a, *Hello, if you're there a talk might be nice but no problem if you're not* kind of buzzing. An, *I don't need help or anything. Just felt like chatting* sort of buzzing.

They were all friends. Grace had already confessed that she was concerned about her daughter Daisy going off on her gap year backpacking around Europe and Dani had admitted she had financial pressures and was worried about paying off her student loans from college and graduate school.

Marissa had owed it to them to contribute her share to the confidence stakes, and so she had admitted that she might be having a teensy tiny issue with awareness of her boss. Nothing dramatic. Certainly nothing to worry about. She could put it to rights.

Grace had been the voice of reason, had encouraged Marissa not to blame Rick too much for his accidental knowledge of her past. Dani had been a little silent on the subject, but certainly sympathetic. They'd swapped mailing addresses and phone numbers after their chats, and Marissa had visited the early opening post shop this morning and sent them both some gifts.

Chocolate. Australian chocolate, to be exact, because chocolate lifted your spirits and gave you confidence.

Because her friends might enjoy it, and Marissa did not need courage to face Rick again, even if she had eaten a chocolate bar this morning while mailing the others. All in all, she was dealing very well with her life right now.

She hadn't even thought about that knitting idea for the past couple of days. Not really. Other than to look at the wool, wondering about the exact blend of lemon and pink and blue of the variegated strands…

Marissa shoved open the door to the office suite.

'Good morning, Rick.' She spoke his name in a firm, even, totally in control and not at all kissed senseless or embarrassed or overwrought tone as she crossed the office space at a fast clip.

Stride in. Purposefully get to work. Keep it impersonal and he would soon see she was not at all carrying any scars from the past.

No? So why did you let that past dictate the kind of man you want in your future?

Because she'd learned from her mistake!

'Thank you, Collins. I appreciate you bringing that to my attention.' Rick's voice was pitched in a businesslike tone that had absolutely nothing to do with Marissa's greeting or, indeed, with her at all.

Because he wasn't alone, was he? How unprofessional of her to just storm in and start yammering away without even looking. Well, she'd only said good morning, but even so…

Concentrate, Marissa. If professionalism at all times is going to be your motto, you might start with attention to detail. Such as—who might be with your boss when you enter the office.

She hurried to her desk as Rick and the other man headed out of Rick's room. Right. Marissa set about sorting her in-tray's contents into 'Get it done early', 'Can wait until later this morning' and 'Yeah, sure she'd really get to this today. Not!' piles on her desk. The laminate covered in cartoons quickly disappeared beneath the piles of work. She wasn't in the mood to be amused anyway.

Rick saw his visitor out. The man gave Marissa a nod in passing. And then Rick turned to her and yanked at his tie and a wealth of regret showed in his eyes as he seemed to search for words.

'About last night…' He cleared his throat. 'About my investigating why you'd left your last position, I mean…'

'I overreacted.'

Please accept that as the truth, and please don't bring up the kiss that led to that discussion.

'My reaction was silly because that piece of past history is exactly that. I've moved on. I'm dating, at least casually, again—looking for a nice, ordinary guy. Let's just forget all of it. That's what I'd like the most at this point.'

If her request rang hollow, she hoped he didn't note it. And if his gaze remained as dark and uncertain as before, she couldn't let herself think about that. Professionalism at all times. She couldn't let there be anything else.

Rick's gaze searched hers before he nodded and murmured, 'I'm pleased you're prepared to forget it.' He didn't *look* pleased, but really, what would she know?

The next couple of hours passed in a flurry of the usual busyness. Rick worked on, but he had a hard time concentrating. He wanted to go out to Marissa, tell her again that he was truly sorry, somehow make up for the way he'd invaded her privacy. He didn't want to think of her 'dating casually' and how possessive and inappropriate was that?

'I was wondering, after everything, if Darla got the promotion? I meant to ask earlier but I…got distracted.' Marissa asked the question from his office doorway, and he looked up into brown eyes that had melted for him last night, had filled with warmth and delightful response before he'd ruined it all with his thoughtless words.

Ruined what couldn't be allowed to happen anyway. Maybe he should just be grateful that something had put a stop to where that kiss had been headed. And forget about her 'dating' plans. 'Darla got the promotion. I'm taking her and Kirri out during Kirri's school lunch break today to celebrate.'

'I'm really happy for her. Please pass on my congratulations to your sister when you see her.' Marissa turned away and went back to her desk and her work.

That was as it should be, right?

So why did Rick feel so empty inside, as though he'd almost grasped something special in his hands, only to have it slip away after all?

What was the matter with him? He pushed himself back into his work and tried not to think beyond it.

Marissa observed her boss's concentration on his work and tried her best to emulate it. She didn't want to think. About his complex family. About him at all.

The hours came and went and, late in the afternoon, after a quiet lull of concentrating solely on her work uninterrupted, the phone rang. She took the call, put it through to Rick. 'You have a call on line one. It's Tom.'

Rick murmured his thanks and she went on with her work.

'Tom.' His voice softened. 'How are you?'

Another phone line rang. As she reached for it, Rick said, 'Just rest and do whatever the doctor tells you, Tom. If it's another two weeks, so be it. Marissa—Marissa's holding the fort well enough in your absence.'

Marissa tuned out Rick's voice and answered the second call. 'Marissa Warren.'

'Marissa, it's Dad.' His voice was strained as he went on.

'Mum's in the hospital, love, with quite bad abdominal pain. They're doing tests right now and they're going to send her for an ultrasound before they—' He cleared his throat. 'To see what's wrong.'

'I'll come straight away, Dad. Is Aunty Jean—?' Panic flooded through her and she couldn't remember what she'd been going to ask.

'Yes, Jean's on her way.' Her father drew a breath. 'She should be here in another hour.'

'Good. That's good.' Marissa had to get to Milberry. It was her only thought as she clutched the phone tighter in her hand. 'You can't use your cellphone inside the hospital, I know, but you'll phone my cell once Mum's back from the tests, let me know if there's anything—?'

Marissa was in trouble. Rick ended his call with Tom and reached her desk before he realised he'd moved. As she raised her eyes and locked onto his, something deep inside him clenched.

'If there needs to be an operation they might move her to a larger hospital in another town.' Marissa paused and listened again. 'Yes, I understand we don't know enough at this stage. I'll just set off, Dad. You're right. That's all I can do for now. I love you. When you see Mum again, tell her I love her and I'm on my way.'

The moment she replaced the phone, Rick spoke.

'What do you need?' Whatever it was, he would get it for her, do it for her. The decision was instinctive. He didn't want to examine the significance of it, could only worry for the woman in front of him. 'Where's your mother? Let me know the fastest way you can be at her side and I'll make it happen.'

Marissa was already on her feet, her hand in the drawer to retrieve her bag when she stopped, looked up at him. She blinked hard and her mouth worked. 'Mum was rushed to hospital in all this pain.'

'What happened to her, sweetheart?' The endearment slipped out, perhaps as unnoticed by its recipient as it was unplanned by him.

Her brown eyes darkened. 'I only know it was abdominal pain. The ambulance had to get her from the newsagent's while Dad came back in from his work on one of the roadworks crews outside of town. Dad only got to see her for a second before they took her away, and they wouldn't tell him much. I have to get to Milberry. I need the Mini.'

'The car you hire from your neighbour.' He remembered her muttering something about that, the day she'd felt faint after their crisis meeting.

It felt so long ago, and a Mini wasn't the vehicle to get her out of the city and to her family with any kind of speed or comfort.

Rick caught her wrist between his fingers, rubbed his thumb across the soft skin. Hoped the touch offered some comfort, and silently acknowledged that a part of him wanted the right to more, whether that meant his emotions were involved in her, or not.

He couldn't worry about any of that now. 'Do any flights go to the township? I only know of it vaguely. It's rather off the beaten path, isn't it? How far is it by road? I can charter a plane for you if there's an airstrip…'

'There are no flights, no airstrip. Milberry doesn't have an airport. It's a reasonable sized town but there's nothing much around it.' Marissa stared at the mess on her desk as though she didn't know what to do with it, and then she stared at him as though she wasn't quite sure what to do with his offer either. 'It'll take me almost three hours in the Mini. Mum's been at the hospital about an hour already, I think.'

'I'll take you myself—'

'I forgot. My neighbour left Sydney this morning with the Mini.' She broke off and said in confusion, 'You'll take me?'

'My car will be faster than a Mini, faster than you having to hire something.' He wanted to beg her to let him do this for her. Instead, he made it a statement and silently urged her to simply agree with it. 'We can leave straight away.'

Confusion clouded her worried brown eyes. 'You can't… I can't ask…'

'I can, and I'm not asking you to ask.' *He* needed permission. Needed to be allowed, wanted to draw her into his arms and promise her everything would be all right, that he would fix everything for her. 'Give me one minute and we're out of here.'

He used that minute to get on the phone and instruct one of the senior staff to come in and pack the office up for them and secure everything.

His borrowed secretary was in trouble. He could help her and he'd chosen to do so. That didn't have to be any big thing, and his relief as Marissa put herself in his hands and allowed him to usher her from the building was simply that of a man who had got his way.

He told himself all this, but the intensity he felt inside didn't lessen.

In moments he had Marissa out of the office building, into his ground-eating vehicle and away. A glance showed that her face hadn't regained any colour. She was also utterly silent. 'Tell me the route.'

She gave him the directions and fell silent again.

Rick clenched his hands around the wheel and got them clear of the city. Once he had, he murmured her name and reached for her hand. He curled his fingers around hers and she cast a glance his way.

'Move into the middle seat so we can talk while I drive.' He tugged on her hand. 'You're going to tell me everything your father said, the name of the hospital your mother is in and all you know about her situation.'

She obeyed him without question, and that told him, more clearly than anything else, the extent of her concern for her mother.

Once he had her shoulder pressed against his arm, her body close enough to feel her warmth and know she could feel his warmth, Rick relaxed marginally.

'Talk, Marissa.' He stroked his fingers over hers, registered the tremble that spoke of her tension.

'Dad said they were sending her for an ultrasound of the abdominal area.' She drew a deep breath. 'There's a small imaging facility in Milberry that does that sort of thing and they were opening it up for her. I guess the place must close at five. That would have meant another ambulance trip, though a short one.

'Dad wanted to go with them but the nursing staff said no. I suppose they needed to focus on finding out what…what needed to be done after the tests.' Her breath hitched as she ended this speech.

Rick squeezed her hand, drew it onto his thigh and curled his fingers over hers. 'There are lots of things that can cause pain that are not life-threatening. If it was her appendix, for example, an operation should set it to rights.'

She nodded. 'Maybe that's what it is.'

'How old is your mother? Has she enjoyed good health until now?'

'She's fifty. She never gets sick. Not like this. Neither of them do.' Suddenly the fingers beneath his curled with tension. 'What if…'

'What if we ring the hospital and ask if there's any news?' He inserted the question gently.

Marissa tugged her bag from the floor by its strap. Her fingers were curled beneath Rick's, against his strong thigh.

She couldn't seem to make herself let go or shift away. She didn't want to leave the comfort of that press of warmth against her shoulder and arm.

Rick *wasn't* Michael Unsworth. He wasn't anything like her ex-fiancé. That knowledge was probably even more cause for worry, but right now she only had room to worry about Mum.

She lifted her phone. A moment later she had the hospital on the line.

'It's Marissa Warren. My mother…' she cleared her throat '…my mother, Matilda Warren, arrived by ambulance with abdominal pain. I'd like to know how she is.'

'Your mother is still under examination,' the woman on the end of the line said briskly. 'She's had several tests done and Doctor is with her now. We'll know more in a little while. Are you on your way to see her, dear? There might be more news if you leave it another half hour or so…'

'We're only about another hour away now.' Rick murmured the words.

She glanced at him, realised she'd ended the call and simply sat there with the phone in her hand.

'I've taken it for granted that they're there, in good health…' She trailed off.

'Then keep believing in that good health. And if she needs anything that I can arrange or help with, to be airlifted to a different hospital in a private helicopter or anything…'

'I hope she won't need that, but I appreciate your words.' She swallowed hard and her fingers flexed beneath his as she registered just how much his concern meant to her.

She couldn't think about that now, couldn't see his actions as a sign of his ability to care, or commit. 'We'll lose phone reception for a while about half an hour out of Milberry. I may not get to hear the test results until we're close to town.' Her gaze tracked over him despite herself. 'There's an area that doesn't pick up very well.'

'You should make any other calls now before we lose reception.'

'Yes, I'd better do that.' How did Rick feel about holding her hand? Had he simply wanted to offer comfort? It felt somehow deeper than that, and he was so determined to help her, anything she might need…

He glanced her way. 'Did you want to try your father again?'

'No. Dad won't have his phone on inside the hospital, but I'd like to send a message to one of my friends.' She toyed with her phone. 'Yes, I think Grace would be out of bed by now, or at least close to it.'

She'd also arranged a drink after work with a man from the dating site. Marissa looked up his number in her phone listings—just as well she'd put it in there—and sent a quick message explaining her situation. Doing that made her aware, finally, of how close she was pressed to Rick's side, how much she'd been leaning on him, physically and emotionally.

'I'm sorry. I'm not usually so…needy.' She moved away to the passenger seat.

'You weren't.' He cast a glance at her that revealed warmth and caring in the depths of his eyes. 'There's nothing wrong with leaning on someone else sometimes.'

Marissa's phone gave a number of beeps and she quickly glanced at it. 'Two messages.'

She checked the first message. 'This one's from my friend Grace in London, well, an Internet friend, actually. She says, "Be strong, sweetie, and hugs and prayers for your mum. Grace xx." Grace has a nineteen-year-old daughter and has lived a complete different life to me in so many ways, yet I feel a connection with her. Knowing her is kind of like having a fun older sister.'

'What about the other message?'

She didn't really want to tell him about the man she'd planned to meet for a drink. Why had she bothered anyway? The thought rolled over her, and she did her best to push it away. Right now wasn't the time to try to figure out whether she was wasting her time on the dating site, whether her reasons for joining were even right…

Marissa opened the message reluctantly, and then relaxed. 'This is from another of my Internet friends, Dani. Grace must have forwarded my message to her. I didn't want to wake Dani.' She read the second message out. '"Sending prayers. Call me if you need 2. Any time!!!"'

'Where does Dani live? Is she an older woman like Grace?'

'San Francisco, and no. She's younger than I am and more ambitious in certain ways. Well, perhaps not *more ambitious*, but highly focused in her working life particularly, I think. Dani is at the start of her career and she's studied hard and really wants to have a great job. At the moment she's working in some dead end position she doesn't like to talk about and hoping something better will come along.'

'Do you have sisters or brothers, Marissa?'

He'd probably asked to keep her mind occupied. Marissa wanted to open up to him anyway. As she recognised that, she stared out of the window at the scenery flashing by.

Grassy paddocks on either side of the road interspersed with native gum and paper-bark trees. Hills undulated as far as the eye could see and gave a sense of quiet and open space very different from the teeming life of the city.

They weren't too far from Milberry now. What would he think of her home town?

'No sisters or brothers. I'm an only child. Maybe that's why I want…' She broke off, cleared her throat. 'Mum and Dad only ever had me, but Mum made sure I had lots of chances to play with other children, to get the social interaction I needed. What about you? Just the two sisters?'

'Yes. I'm the eldest. Darla's in the middle, and Faith is the youngest.'

And his sisters had married, made families, but Rick hadn't.

Minutes passed. Marissa clutched her phone and willed it to ring.

'There's the ten kilometre sign.' She stiffened in her seat and, as though their nearness had brought it about, her phone finally complied with a ring tone. With a gasp, she fumbled for it and quickly answered.

'Yes. Yes. Okay. All right. I can't wait to see her.'

While Marissa paused to listen to her caller, Rick slowed at the outskirts of the township.

'We'll see you soon, Dad.' She ended the call and sat forward to give Rick directions.

CHAPTER TEN

'WE'RE to go straight to Mum and Dad's unit. I don't know what to think!' Marissa's words tumbled out in a rush, concern warring with threads of relief she couldn't truly believe. Not yet. 'They've let Mum go home with my Aunty Jean to watch over her. Aunty's a registered nurse.'

'How could they release her so quickly after such pain?' Rick put the question that was filling her thoughts into words. 'What was the diagnosis? Is this a decent hospital we're talking about? If not, we'll get her admitted somewhere else.'

'Apparently a cyst ruptured on one of Mum's ovaries. She is still in some discomfort but it's not severe now. They say she just needs to rest with the appropriate medication. Once they were certain of the diagnosis they let her go.'

Marissa drew a quick breath. 'It is a good hospital, the staff are reliable and Aunty Jean wouldn't let them release her unless she was confident Mum was up to that. Even so, I need to see her. If I look at her, I'll know—'

'How do we get to your parents' home?' He gestured ahead of them. 'Let's get you there so you can see for yourself.'

'If you follow this road it will take you straight through the main street of the town.' He understood what she needed and that…warmed her. 'After the Region's Own Bank building you turn left and Mum and Dad's unit is in the second street on the right.'

His gaze glanced left and right as he followed the directions she'd given him.

Many of the homes were red brick or weatherboard with corrugated iron roofs. Just about every front garden had rose bushes or camellias, a front fence with a wrought iron gate with an old-fashioned curlicue scroll design on top, and a mailbox on the right-hand gatepost.

There were vintage cars interspersed with sedans and utility trucks in the main street.

A rally weekend, Marissa realised vaguely, and sat forward in her seat again as they neared the turn to her parents' home.

'That's their place.' She pointed. 'The small pale brick one with the red sedan and green station wagon parked out front.'

Rick followed Marissa's directions and parked on the street behind the other two cars. He studied the workmanship of the square building design, with its regulation small porch, front window awnings and slightly curved pathway from the front fence to that porch, but his thoughts were focused on the woman at his side.

He'd expected Marissa to leap from the vehicle before he'd even parked it properly. Instead, at the last minute, she turned to face him.

Her eyes were wide, her expression a combination of concern and chagrin. 'I haven't thanked you for dropping everything to get me here the way you did and for your kindness during the trip. It…well… I hope Mum truly is a lot better, though I'm still concerned for her, and I appreciate—'

'I know you do, and there's no need to say anything.' Maybe she was hesitating at the last moment out of fear of what she would find. If so, the sooner she saw her Mum the better. He opened his door and came to her side to help her out.

With her hand clasped in his as he helped her down, he

admitted, 'I wanted to bring you.' He'd needed to, in the same way he'd needed to fix things for Darla over the years, for Faith.

No. Not the same. This was different.

Yes. It's more than those urges have ever been.

He didn't want to think that. Their gazes met and held for a brief moment and something flared between them. She did fly up the path then, and rapped on the door even as it opened from inside.

Rick followed more slowly and watched as a man with thinning grey-streaked dark hair pulled Marissa into his arms and held her tight. The comfort given and exchanged in their hug caught at something inside Rick and his chest hurt as he acknowledged the deep closeness playing out in front of him.

'Dad, this is the boss of Morgan's, Rick Morgan. I told you and Mum I'm working for him while his secretary is on sick leave and Gordon is on holiday.' Marissa rushed the words out and then her voice softened. 'Rick, please meet my father, Abraham Warren, but he prefers Abe.'

Did Marissa's face soften on *his* name? It had seemed to and while something inside Rick took the thought in a stranglehold and refused to let it go, heat rode the back of his neck as he shook the older man's hand and murmured a greeting.

He was concerned. He needed Marissa to see her mother and feel assured that the woman would be okay. It wasn't anything else. Certainly not some misguided and misplaced hope that Marissa's father would approve—*like*—him.

'Thank you for bringing Marissa to us.' Abe stepped back. If he noticed anything odd in Rick's demeanour, he didn't show it.

Rick wished he had some of the same self-control.

Abe went on, 'Come inside, both of you. Marissa, Mum's fretting that you rushed to get here, but she's also bursting to see you. Maybe she'll settle down and rest once she has.'

The combination of protectiveness and residual worry in the man's tone said it all.

The small unit had a living area filled with a two-seater couch and several chairs. A kitchen backed onto the area and there were rooms packed tightly together off a hallway to the right.

Bedroom, bedroom, bathroom, Rick guessed. The laundry room would be at the back behind the kitchen. A woman emerged through an open door and smiled at Marissa. Hugged her briskly and stepped aside. 'Go on and see your mum. A rupture is nasty and it can be very dangerous but your mum's going to be just fine and I'm staying two nights to watch her in any case. It only took me two hours to get here from Tuckwell. I left quickly when your dad phoned.'

Marissa stepped through the door and disappeared. A moment later Rick heard a soft sob quickly stifled, followed by a rush of low words. Marissa's voice and another one—older, soothing and being soothed. He wanted to burst into the room, do something. *Hold Marissa and never let anything upset her again.*

Instead, he stood in the middle of the living room, fists clenched as he forgot all about the two people waiting there, watching him. Then he turned to Marissa's father. 'Your wife truly is well enough to leave the hospital? Marissa was worried.'

'Yes, and Jean will help me keep an eye on her.' Abe examined Rick with shrewd eyes that seemed to have realised something about his guest. Maybe that Rick had eyes only for his daughter.

Rick ran a hand through his hair. 'It's been an uneasy few hours. Far more so for you, I'm sure.'

Abe stared hard at him for a long moment before he spoke again. 'Very true. Now, how long have you and my daughter—'

'Well, it must be time for a cup of tea.' The nurse cleared her throat rather noisily. 'How about I put the kettle on, Abe? I'm sure Tilda would enjoy a cup about now. We probably all could do with one.'

On her way past Rick, she gestured towards one of the squashy cloth-covered lounge chairs. 'Why don't you have a seat? And I'm Jean, Tilda's sister, though I'm sure you've worked that out.

'We can make our way through the introductions properly in a minute and you can tell us how the vintage car festival seems to be shaping up, how many of the cars you saw as you drove in.' She glanced at Abe and her gaze seemed to warn him off launching a more personal inquisition. 'It's one of Milberry's special weekends, you know.'

Rick had given away more of an interest in his borrowed secretary than he should have. At the moment he couldn't raise much concern for the fact. Marissa had needed to get here. Rick had needed to smooth a path for her and he'd go on smoothing one for as long as he felt it was needed.

'I'm afraid I didn't take much notice of the traffic on the way in.' Rick took a seat as ordered and put his hands on his spread knees. He gave himself time to look around this room owned by the people who had raised Marissa. There were photos of her everywhere.

Marissa as a baby, toddler, child and teenager and more recent ones.

'Her hair was always curly.' He murmured the words, took the cup that Jean offered, nodded his thanks. Cleared his throat. 'It is rather noticeable. Her hair.'

'Yes.' Jean slipped into the other room to deliver the tea to Marissa's mum.

That left Rick and Marissa's father. 'There won't be any lingering effects from the illness, I hope?'

The older man rubbed a work-worn hand over his tanned jaw. 'She's exhausted now and they've given her some medication to deal with the after-effects but they say in a few days she won't even know it's happened. I'm just grateful...' He swallowed and took a deep breath. 'Now, if I can just get her to rest properly until she really is all better I'll be satisfied. We could both get a bit of leave from our work—'

'Rick, will you come in and meet Mum before she tries to have a nap?' Marissa asked from the doorway of her mother's room, and Rick rose immediately to his feet.

He caught her hand in his briefly at the door. Then he searched her face and noted the slight redness around her eyes. Asked in a low voice, 'Will she mind me seeing her when she's not a hundred per cent?'

'Probably.' Marissa's smile held relief and gratitude and a wealth of affection for the woman Rick had yet to meet. 'But her curiosity about my boss will overrule that.'

He didn't feel like a boss right now. The expression in Marissa's eyes as she looked at him, the way she'd curled her fingers around his hand—those hadn't seemed very business-like either.

They stepped into the bedroom together. There were no chairs. It wasn't a hospital room, but the room shared by two people who'd loved each other and lived together for many years. A framed wedding photo hung on the wall at the foot of the bed. Knick-knacks sat cheek by jowl on a dresser with a man's watch and a well-worn hat.

Rick imagined sharing such a room with Marissa. The idea was alien and stunning all at once. He turned to the woman in the bed. 'I'm very sorry to know you've been unwell, Mrs Warren.'

Marissa stepped past him, went to her mother and caught her hand in hers, pressed it to her face and kissed the back of it before she eased down gently to sit on the bed beside her mum. 'Yes, you're not allowed to pull a stunt like that again, Mum. You scared me silly.'

'I'll try not to.' Tilda Warren shifted slightly in the bed and, though her face bore the marks of the strain and discomfort she'd experienced, she looked enough like Marissa that Rick couldn't help but like her on sight.

She smiled at Rick. 'Thank you for bringing Marissa to us.

I won't pretend I'm not glad to see her. The last few hours were a bit frightening and I'm glad to see my girl.'

'And now you're going to rest and hopefully go to sleep.' Marissa fussed a little and then, with obvious reluctance and an equal amount of determination, prepared to leave the room. 'I'll look in on you later, even if you've gone to sleep. Just to be sure…'

'Thank you, love.' Tilda sighed. 'I admit I feel rather wiped out and I think I probably will sleep, at least for a while. They gave me painkillers. You'll need some dinner, though, and—'

'And we can take care of that by ourselves,' Marissa interrupted with a loving smile, and they left the room together.

The depth of the relief Rick felt surprised him. That Marissa's mother would be okay; that nothing had happened that would cause Marissa a lot of long-term unhappiness.

When Marissa stared rather blankly at the contents of the fridge, he asked if there were any restaurants or take-away food places in the town. 'You've all had a stressful time. Let me at least pick up something for dinner.'

He did that, managing it without stepping on Abe's toes. Abe sat with his wife even after sleep claimed her before he finally emerged and spent some time talking quietly with his daughter while his sister-in-law got up and down at intervals to look in on Marissa's mum.

They spoke in hushed tones of nothing much. Abe asked a little about Rick's business. Jean asked about his roots, and Rick admitted he'd never lived outside the city, that his sisters and nieces were there. His gaze tracked Marissa's every movement. He had a plan for how he might do something for her mother as well…

Mum truly would be okay. Marissa looked in on her one last time and finally started to believe it. As she acknowledged this, some of the things she'd pushed aside in her haste to get here filtered through at last, and she frowned for a whole other set of reasons.

She stood and collected her bag from where she must have dumped it beside a lounge chair when she'd first come into the house. 'You'll be all right through the night, Aunty?'

'Absolutely, and Abe can handle me creeping in and out of the room a few times to see to meds and things tonight.' Jean rose to her feet as well. 'It means turning you out of the spare room, though. There's only a single in there with the sewing machine.'

Marissa glanced towards Rick. He'd also got to his feet and stood watching her. In truth his gaze had rarely left her since they'd arrived, and she felt ridiculously warmed and…comforted by that knowledge. 'If Rick doesn't mind, we'll find a couple of rooms in one of the motels for the night. I'd like to visit Mum again tomorrow morning and then I know we'll have to leave.'

Jean patted her arm. 'Your dad will look after her and she'll stay quieter if there aren't too many people here to distract her from that. You know what she's like. She was already saying she wanted to get out of bed and start organising things.'

They were all on their feet now, and Rick gestured towards the second bedroom in the house. 'Do you keep anything here, Marissa? Maybe you should gather a change of clothes and some nightwear and a toothbrush before we go.'

'You won't get any rooms.' The words came from Abe as he slapped a hand against his thigh. 'I forgot about the impact of the vintage car festival. All the motels are fully booked, or so it said in the paper this morning.'

'And Rick has no spare clothes, not even a toothbrush.' Marissa turned his way. 'I'm sorry. I didn't give that a thought when we left Sydney. I do have a few things here, but you—'

Rick shrugged his broad shoulders. 'I'll make do, and maybe we can go to a motel in a nearby town?'

'The nearest town large enough is mine, and it's a two-hour drive away.' Jean pointed this out with a frown. 'You'd both be most welcome to stay at my place but it's a long way.'

At that moment a soft knock sounded on the front door. Her father opened it.

It was Mrs Brill from the end of the street, a busy woman with five children and a truck-driver husband. She had a casserole in one hand and a key in the other.

She held out the casserole. 'This is for dinner tomorrow night, and I saw the extra cars outside and wondered about accommodation. I've got the converted garage with a sofa bed that pulls out and a camp-bed I bought at a garage sale for the second room in there.'

'That would be really helpful. We were just wondering how best to work that out.' Jean spoke the words in her brisk, no-nonsense way. She took the casserole and handed it to Marissa, who carried it through to the kitchen.

By the time Marissa returned, matters were decided—Mrs Brill had left to start the short walk back to her home and Rick held the key to the converted garage.

CHAPTER ELEVEN

MARISSA gathered her things into a carryall. Her father bundled some more things in on top for Rick to use and, with a murmured word of thanks, Rick drove them the short distance to the end of the street.

He pulled to a stop before an unpretentious home with a large front garden and larger back garden. Mrs Brill had walked ahead of them and took them straight through to the back, where the garage sat surrounded by a swing set and a collection of children's toys and bikes and other things.

'Thank you. This is very kind.' Marissa managed to choke out the words without looking at Rick at all. Mrs Brill *was* kind, and Marissa appreciated the hospitality. She just couldn't imagine her multi-millionaire boss, with his city central penthouse apartment with all mod cons, here.

'You're welcome, love. You even have your own shower and loo.' Their hostess disappeared with a wave.

Rick unlocked the converted garage, flipped the light switch and they stepped inside.

The room had a square of someone's old carpet slung over a concrete floor, unlined walls covered in dartboards and fishing paraphernalia, and a sofa that converted. A pile of bedding and two bath towels sat waiting on it.

A door to the right opened into a second room.

Marissa bit her lip. 'It's probably not what you're used to, but it was very good of Mrs Brill.'

'It's fine, and it was very generous of her.' Rick set the bag down on the floor and tossed a can of deodorant in on top that he'd taken from the glove compartment of his car.

'I don't know what Dad's put in the bag for you.' For no clear reason, Marissa's face heated and she looked everywhere but into Rick's eyes.

She hadn't thought too much about their accommodation until now, and was realising that it could feel a little awkward for a whole other lot of reasons.

The moment the thought rose so did her consciousness of him.

'Toothbrush, disposable razor, a pair of boxer shorts still in their wrapping, T-shirt, and the ugliest pair of long john style pyjamas I've ever seen.' Rick's tone deepened as he spoke those last words, as his gaze met with hers and held.

'Dad usually wears a T-shirt and boxers to bed. Maybe he wasn't thinking straight.' She spoke the words with a hint of confusion, felt far more as her senses began to respond to Rick's nearness, to the intensity that had risen in his gaze.

'He's your father. He was thinking perfectly.' Rick turned abruptly towards the second room. 'I'd better set up the camp-bed so we can both get some sleep. Mrs Brill said it hasn't been used since she bought it.'

Marissa's face heated even more as she recalled some of Dad's questions to Rick, about his work, his prospects. Surely her father hadn't viewed Rick as a possible boyfriend or something?

You've kissed the man and you are *still attracted to him. Maybe Dad noticed that.*

'You don't have to… I wouldn't want you to think, or feel you need to…'

'You really are tempting when you blush like that.' He spoke the words in a hungry tone of gravel and midnight. 'God knows I'm trying not to notice, Marissa, but I think you know what I am thinking, and for all that those thoughts appear to have me by the throat right now, they can't do either of us any good.'

'You're…you're right. I'll take the camp-bed. It won't be very large and you'll probably only have a sleeping bag for it, and a pillow. No doubt Mrs Brill left a pillow.' The words babbled out of her as they stepped into the second room together. 'See, there's a pillow there.'

'I thought I'd driven you away, you know—lost your approval and good regard when I made the mistake of looking into your working history.' The softening of his tone seemed to sit uneasily with him, yet his gaze revealed how that thought had bothered him.

Rick's jaw clenched as he stared at the pile of canvas and wood and springs and hooks. 'I didn't need to do that, Marissa. I knew it but I went after the information anyway because I felt you were holding something back from me. It's too late to undo it but I want you to know I very much regret the incident.'

'I believe you.' She couldn't raise any anger. Not in the face of his regret, and all he had done for her since.

He's not Michael Unsworth. You can't continue to compare the two. Rick is a far better man in so many ways.

It was a dangerous conclusion, even as she admitted the truth of it. Rick's layers were beginning to make too much sense, appeal too much. She had to remember he still wanted nothing to do with the kind of relationship she hoped one day to find. He didn't want commitment.

Since that seemed to be all she wanted lately, with a side order of Family and Babies and Not Feeling Old When She Turned Thirty thrown in, it would be a very good thing if she could stop being so attracted to her boss.

He drew a breath. 'I'm glad you've forgiven me. Now, let's see about this camp-bed.'

'It looks rather old. So does the sleeping bag.' She eyed both dubiously and returned her gaze to the bed. 'I'm guessing there probably isn't an instruction manual for putting that together.'

Rick glanced at her. One brief, intent, aware glance as the walls of the room seemed to close in on them. He rubbed a hand over the back of his neck. 'I'm sure I can figure it out, and you won't be sleeping on it. I will.'

He tossed the pillow and sleeping bag aside, crouched down and started to assemble the bed. In fact, he had it put together minutes later.

Marissa smiled despite herself. 'I should have known you'd do that with the same precision you do everything.'

With a slight smile he picked up the sleeping bag, unzipped it and laid it flat over the surface of the bed, then leaned down to press the centre with his hand. 'See? It looks quite comfy. I'm sure it'll be fine.'

He turned to reach for the pillow. As he did, the bed snapped down in the middle and up at both ends. Wood crunched and splintered. Springs twanged and bits and pieces flew in all directions.

'What—?' Rick pulled her back, his shoulder turned to protect her from anything that might fly through the air.

Seconds later it was all over, and so was the bed. Marissa stared at the splintered old wood, bits of torn canvas, the sleeping bag tangled within it all, and springs that had irrevocably sprung. 'Oh, my. That was rather dramatic, wasn't it? It made matchsticks out of some of it.'

'Dramatic? The thing could have taken out your eye. And how I'll explain this to your Mrs Brill—' Rick broke off with a disgusted manly snort of outrage and offence. 'I'm *certain* I put the bed together correctly.'

'Oh, I'm sure you did. It just…cracked under the pressure.' A laugh burst from her. She just couldn't help it. 'Your face! This isn't a corporate implosion, you know.'

'I'll arrange for a new bed to replace it.' He growled the words and kicked one of the larger pieces of wood with his foot. 'Maybe we can get rid of the evidence before morning.'

'That—' Another laugh choked out of her. 'We could bury the evidence in the garden.' Her grin spread. 'Shovels at twenty paces. I won't tell if you don't.'

His brows snapped down and he glared at her and she laughed all the harder until she had to lean over with her arms wrapped around her tummy.

'I don't see anything the least bit amusing about this.' His lips twitched. He kicked another piece of wood out of the way.

A moment later he started to laugh as well. His deep chuckles filled the air.

Marissa grinned at him and sucked up lungfuls of air and then, to her mortification, tears welled in the backs of her eyes. She blinked them back, turned away so he wouldn't see while she fought for control.

'Hey. It's okay.' Gentle arms came around her, turned her into his chest. 'Your Mum's all right. Your aunt said she'll be almost as good as new tomorrow.'

'How did you know?' The moment he reached for her she'd wrapped her arms around him. Now she lifted her head, gave it a rueful shake even as her body wanted so very much to press to his and never move away. 'I don't know where that came from. I thought I'd settled down after I saw for myself she was okay. And *I'm* fine now, aside from feeling silly again.'

'You could never be silly.' He closed his eyes and kissed the tip of her nose and then he just…held onto her.

She could have stayed there for ever—in his arms, giving and receiving comfort and closeness.

But she wanted more. Her body wanted to meld to his, curves to angles, softness to strength.

'I mustn't…' He murmured the words and set her away from him.

He retrieved the sleeping bag then, and shook it. Splinters of wood rained onto the floor. Many more of them stuck like porcupine quills to the sleeping bag's thin, lumpy lining.

'I'll sleep on the floor.' His voice rumbled the words. 'Why don't you take a shower and I'll make up the other bed for you before I wash? You'll want to be up early in the morning to see your mum again.'

'Thanks.' Their prosaic words did nothing to cover the tension that had risen between them. 'I…I guess I will have a quick shower.' She'd raided the room at the unit for a pair of comfy pyjama bottoms she'd had about a hundred years, a spaghetti-strap stretchy top and loose jumper and old jeans and a shirt to wear for tomorrow, toiletries and spare panties.

Marissa bundled up what she needed and disappeared into the bathroom that had obviously been somebody's DIY project. She couldn't let Rick sleep on the floor with splinters sticking all through that sleeping bag, but she needed to pull herself together a little before they had that discussion.

Rick showered while she sent text messages to Dani and Grace and let them know that Mum was going to be okay, though she planned to keep a closer eye on her parents' health from now on!

When Rick came out of the bathroom, Marissa was already in the bed, the jumper discarded, and had brought the pillow from the other room and placed it beside hers. Action seemed the best way to address the issue.

Rick's gaze roved over her face and shoulders and snapped back to her eyes. 'Is this a good idea?'

She'd glanced at him, just once, before she too focused her attention solely on *his* face. That single moment had revealed his broad tanned chest, narrow hips and thighs encased in dark boxers, long bare legs. 'We have to be sensible.'

The comment referred to him sleeping in the bed, not on the floor, but could have referred equally to her runaway thoughts right now. She wanted Rick to climb into the bed, wrap his arms around her and make love to her. She wanted it with her senses, and with deeper emotions. She wanted it for herself, not only because her hormones were giving her trouble. She was afraid to look deeper into all the other reasons she wanted it.

'I'll use the sleeping bag. I shook it out.' He said the words even as his gaze devoured her and tenderness formed in that gaze. 'If not on the floor, then I'll sleep on top of the bedcovers.'

'The sleeping bag is prickled right through with splinters still. I checked.' That tenderness somehow helped her to regain some of her equilibrium. She gestured as calmly as she could to the space beside her. 'It's roomy enough. We'll stick to our sides. I just want to sleep and forget the stress of worrying about Mum during that trip.'

It was the right thing to say.

He relaxed a little at last, murmured, 'I guess if there's no choice, there's no choice.' He turned the light off, plunged the room into darkness and she heard him pad across the carpeted floor towards her.

One last bout of nerves got her then.

'You didn't wear Dad's pyjamas. Not that you should have. No doubt you thought they were quite hideous and it's not as though he should try to intimidate you or imply anything about the two of us or try to circumvent certain behaviour.' Each word tumbled after the other. 'Not that we intend to indulge in such behaviour.'

The bed dipped as he sat on the edge. 'I…er…I don't usually sleep in any… No, I didn't wear the pyjamas.' A rustling sound followed as he settled into the bed right beside her. All that naked skin on his upper torso and…

His weight rolled her into the middle. Their bodies brushed before she quickly pulled herself back to her side.

'Sorry.'

'My fault.' He inhaled. Stilled. Finally murmured into the darkness, 'You smell the same. Of flowers.'

They were facing each other in the darkness. She knew it from the direction of his words and she thrilled to that small knowledge even when she shouldn't have.

'I…er…yes. The perfume…I keep some of the perfume in my bag.' If she leaned forward a little, would they touch? Would he wrap his arms around her and kiss her?

Don't think about it, Marissa. You're being sensible now, remember?

'I hope the smell isn't bothering you.'

'No.' His voice dipped to a low, dark tone. 'It's not bothering me.'

For a moment, silence reigned and then he said painfully, 'I don't want to hurt you. What your parents have with each other, what you deserve to have, I can't go there. Relationships for me…don't go there. Because of my family, the example of my father. I'm not assuming, or suggesting anything…'

'It's fine. It's always best to say what you're thinking, make it all clear.' And he had, and it was hard to hear it—hard when they lay so close together and her body longed for the touch of his.

A part of her still wanted his touch now, and a part of her wondered if it would be so bad. If she gave in to her desire for him, even though there could be no future in it. Just one time, to make love with him—with due care and responsibility—so she could at least have that experience, that memory of him.

But that was all it would be, because he wasn't Mr Right For Her. All else aside, he didn't match her criteria. He was still Mr Corporate. 'Um…well…we should go to sleep.'

'Yes. We definitely should sleep.' Rick wanted Marissa so much he ached all over from it. The way she'd been with her parents this evening had caught at something inside him, had deepened his feelings towards her in ways he hadn't been able to fathom or control. It was why he'd pushed her away with his words.

'*You* should try to sleep, anyway.' He doubted he would do the same with her so close.

His leg brushed against hers as he repositioned himself in the bed and he registered a long length of flannelette.

The ugliest and most unromantic nightwear in the world for women. Wasn't that what they said? She had apparently covered herself from belly to ankle in the stuff. Her shoulders had been bare, with just a thin strap indicating some kind of fitted top.

Images of running his hands over her legs and thighs over that thick cloth invaded his brain anyway. He felt far from repelled right now.

He forced his attention to other things. To the reason they'd come here. Maybe, if he focused on that, he would find the control and distance he needed to endure this night without reaching for her, without reaching for all he wanted *from* her and *with* her that he must not take. 'Are you okay now, Marissa? About your mother?'

'Yes. I cross-questioned her about what had happened until she probably wanted me to shut up, but I needed to know she truly would be all right.' Marissa's breath caressed his face as she sighed into the darkness.

Did she realise exactly how close they were? That their heads were turned intimately towards each other?

'Mum said I didn't need to rush here, that she didn't expect that.'

'She wanted to see you, though. Your father told me he was glad you'd come so quickly.' *Her* family held a strong bond for each other.

He didn't have that with his parents. And he didn't know *how* to have it with a woman. Marissa was right to want someone who didn't come with a bunch of complications attached.

You could figure it out. You could risk it.

He stilled, and then he clamped down on the thoughts and an unexpected well of anger towards his father rose up instead.

No. Rick would never risk short-changing a family the way Dad had, and that meant not risking his own family, period.

'Mum was worried about missing shifts at the newsagent's. Silly thing.' Marissa fell silent and Rick thought she might finally try to go to sleep, or at least pretend to, as he would.

Then she spoke again in a low tone of admission. 'It scared me to see Mum vulnerable. My parents have always been strong and I've never thought about losing them. I should do more to show how much I appreciate them.'

'What would you do? They seem happy, and proud of you. I looked at the pictures of you in their living room.' Had looked— had wanted to touch each one. Had wondered if she had a child, would it have her hair? Those expressive brown eyes?

'Some of those pictures are awful.' Despite the words, a smile filled her tone.

He'd planned to bring this up in the morning, but, 'What about sending your parents on a holiday? I've done it for my sisters occasionally.' He drew a breath, wished he could see her face to know if she would allow him to do this for her, to give her this.

He'd been thinking of it since Abe had said he wished he could ensure his wife rested properly. 'I have a holiday home on the Queensland coast that's vacant right now, just sitting there doing nothing. They could spend a week there. Your father mentioned he'd like to take her away, that they could both get holiday. He wants to make sure she spends proper time resting up. In truth, I'd appreciate having someone there to check the place is being looked after properly under the caretaking arrangements I've made for it.'

In the face of her silence, because he didn't know what she was thinking, he added, 'It's easy to reach. They could fly direct from the nearest airport.' He considered trying to sell her on the local attractions. Made himself stop speaking and wait for her answer.

'I'm sure they'd love it. I'll talk to Dad and I'll buy them plane tickets.' Her hand reached through the darkness, found his upper arm and tracked down it until she found his hand and gripped it. 'Thank you for thinking of it, Rick. That will be perfect for them, and it's very generous of you.'

He couldn't prevent himself from lifting their joined hands, kissing her fingers, pressing that hand against his chest and drawing a deep breath as he held it there. 'You're welcome. I'm happy to do it, and they'll be helping me at the same time.'

His heart had started to thump. Just because he had her hand pressed to his chest. Just because…he wanted her so very much.

'Try to sleep.' He rasped the words past an inexplicable ache in his throat, releasing his grip on her hand one finger at a time because he couldn't manage more. 'I traded cellphone numbers with your father and obviously they have yours. If they need you they'll call, but I don't think that'll happen, and your mum will probably be happier if you seem well-rested when she sees you tomorrow.'

'Goodnight, Rick.' Marissa didn't expect to sleep. She lay there absorbing the slight musty smell of the room and Rick's far nicer scent of soap and deodorant and warm man beside her. Thought about her mum and dad and what Rick had done for her today, and about his family and his limitations…

How ironic that she now wanted Mr Tall, Dark and Aggressive About Success and he'd made it clear he could never be right for her.

Rick woke to the tenderest feeling deep inside, and realised he had Marissa clutched in his arms like the most precious of bundles. His face was pressed into her hair and her softness seemed to melt into him.

His arms locked and for a long, still moment he couldn't let go as his heart began to hammer and emotion swamped him. A cold sweat broke out on his brow.

'Rick,' she murmured. Her eyelids fluttered up to reveal sleepy eyes and something deep inside him shifted and parted and tried very hard to let her in.

Panic welled inside him and he eased his hold on her and moved away.

'Is it morning?' Her lips were soft, so kissable, her face flushed from sleep.

Heat flared in his body then, but even that couldn't fully wipe out his earlier feelings of…what?

He didn't know, only felt the ache still, that had seemed to insist that if he held her close enough he could somehow assuage that emptiness.

'It's early, but yes, it's morning.' He rolled to the side of the bed, swung his legs over and sat with his back to her. Tried for coherence—he who always had control of himself and now felt he had very little of any. 'We should take our showers. Maybe once we're both through it'll be a reasonable enough time to visit your mother. I'll leave a cheque for Mrs Brill to pay for the broken bed in the other room.'

Rick retrieved his clothes from the carryall and shut himself in the bathroom. Perhaps a blast of cold water would straighten out the confusion of his mind—and settle his senses!

CHAPTER TWELVE

'IT's good that your mother seemed much better this morning, and I'm glad she and your father let us talk them into taking that holiday.' Rick's hands tightened slightly around the steering wheel as he spoke. 'You're happy with how long you stayed, the amount of time you had with her?'

He wore her father's T-shirt loose over his suit trousers and looked a little rumpled and delicious and appealing and, beneath that, tense. He'd been that way since they'd woken this morning with their arms around each other.

In that first moment, before she'd remembered his words of warning to her last night, Marissa had hoped he might kiss her. The desire had been there in his gaze, but with other emotions she hadn't fully understood. He'd seemed almost uncertain for a moment, somehow shocked and uneasy at the same time.

After that he'd withdrawn physically from holding her. She'd remembered why that was the only sensible course of action. He still seemed withdrawn.

Except when your eyes meet because, in the first instant when that happens, you have all his attention and there's warmth amongst that attention. Warmth and desire and...

No. There was no *and*—there couldn't be. She had to keep her imagination and all the hopes it wanted to raise under control.

'I hope you didn't mind hanging around for hours again. I

would have liked to stay longer but it will be easier for Dad to get Mum to rest if I'm not there, and then, when she's recovered enough, he'll whip her away for that week at the beach. They'll probably go on Tuesday, if she continues to feel better.' Perhaps, if they discussed this kind of thing, he would eventually relax?

And you, Marissa?

She admitted she had formed a bond inside herself to him somehow in the past day and night, despite everything. To wake held in his arms had felt safe and right and wonderful. It had seemed to tell her in physical action of a great deal of his care and she had wanted—

She'd wanted to give that care back to him in the same way, and that knowledge terrified her because Rick had simply been holding her. If he'd felt something, perhaps it was empathy because she'd been afraid for her mum. And Marissa couldn't let herself feel a great deal more for him.

You're sure you don't already feel those things?

Uneasy, she shifted in her seat. These feelings surpassed even the confusing and disconcerting ones of longing for a baby, of feeling so broody and so resistant to the idea of turning thirty and being alone.

'I'm just pleased Mum seems so much better. And I really do appreciate what you did to take me to her.'

'I hope she doesn't go through anything like that again.' He drew out to overtake a slow-moving truck, and smoothly returned them to their lane.

They'd left Milberry after brunch at Mum and Dad's unit. Marissa had missed her computer access this morning. She'd come to rely on checking in for instant chat messages from Grace and Dani. How would she get on now with her plan to find Mr Right on the dating site when her thoughts centred so much on Mr Couldn't Be Right?

What would Dani and Grace think of this morning's events?

Nothing, because I'm not going to tell them. Marissa focused her stare out of the window without really looking at anything they passed. Grace and Dani were her friends. They meant a lot to her and she *liked* confiding in them but she had to sort these feelings out about Rick for herself.

Sort them and then leave them behind. Her chest hurt at the thought but she wasn't falling for him. She liked him, appreciated him.

He was not someone she could love.

And you, Marissa? You're completely straightforward? You're not carrying around any emotional complications?

She didn't have any family troubles. And she refused to consider any memories of fiancé troubles. She was over all that.

As he drew his car to a stop outside Marissa's apartment building, weariness tugged at Rick. He turned his head, noted the shadows beneath Marissa's eyes. 'Let's see you up to your place.'

'Come up with me.' Marissa made the request in a soft tone edged with concern. 'I want you to drink some coffee before you go any further. It's been a big weekend and…we woke very early this morning.'

Even this obscure reference to those moments in a borrowed garage tugged at him. At his senses, he assured himself. Only in that way. He wanted her still. Enough that he couldn't get the thought of making love with her out of his mind.

This was true, but he also couldn't get the thought of *holding* her out of his mind. Holding her and never letting go. He'd warned her off, but now *he* didn't want to be warned off, even though that was the only option for Stephen Morgan's son. Was this what Faith had meant and what he'd said he wouldn't do? Was he poised on the edge of that dive into emotional oblivion?

If so, he didn't like the feeling, and he could not allow himself to take that leap. Even the thought of that being a possibility terrified him.

Just as his father must have felt terrified, and had thus drawn back?

It wasn't the same.

Maybe it was exactly the same. Did that even matter? His instinct told him he mustn't—couldn't—want Marissa so deeply, so for her sake. Yes, for her sake he had to shut those feelings down.

'Coffee's ready. It's only instant, I'm afraid, but I didn't want you to have to wait too long for it.' Marissa carried the drinks into her small living room, only to find Rick sprawled out on her sofa, his chin on his chest. Spiky lashes formed crescents on strong male cheeks. He'd lain right back so his feet dangled off the end of the third cushion. He was fast asleep.

He looked younger, exhausted, and somehow vulnerable this way. Her heart ached as she stared at him. Feelings she hadn't meant to allow welled inside her, wanted to be set free.

How could this one man have found his way into such hidden parts of her so easily and so quickly? The mega-boss man. She had judged him by Michael's standards when she shouldn't have. Rick cared for his sisters and his nieces, was capable of acts of kindness.

He had also stepped outside her perception of acceptable boundaries when he'd investigated her; he wasn't right for Marissa.

Because he didn't have enough to give to a relationship. Because he would always have a ruthless edge—the part of him that had made him a success in business, even if he'd gone about achieving that success by more acceptable means than Michael. What if he turned that edge on her? Hurt her with it, as Michael had hurt her?

Marissa set aside the coffee, covered Rick with her one and only patchwork quilt from her handicraft phase and went into her bedroom with her laptop computer. It was time to sign onto Blinddatebrides.com and do something proactive about the *real* future she needed to seek.

To: Englishcrumpet, Sanfrandani
From Kangagirl
Did you know you can tell how old a woman is by what happens when she pinches the skin of the back of her hand between her fingers?

From: Englishcrumpet
Thanks a lot, Marissa. Now I feel really depressed.

From: Sanfrandani
I don't get it. Is that one of those English/Australian jokes?

From: Kangagirl
If the skin goes back quickly, you're not old.

From: Englishcrumpet
Sigh.

From: Sanfrandani
Oh. Well, my skin seems okay, and…er…duty calls. I have to say goodbye for now. TTYL.
Sanfrandani has signed out.

From: Englishcrumpet
What's going on, Marissa? I'm getting the same vibe I get when Daisy is holding something back from me.

From: Kangagirl
It's nothing. Actually, it's something. I thought I could sign on to Blinddatebrides.com and find Mr Nice, Ordinary and Unthreatening. I thought I could vet candidates and

find one to match my criteria and magically make us fall in love with each other or something. That I could keep myself safe from getting hurt that way. My thirtieth birthday is getting closer and I don't want to get old, I'm starting to wonder if I'm scared I'll never have a chance to have a baby, and I think—I think I might have sort of half slightly started to fall for my boss.

From: Englishcrumpet
Oh, Marissa.

From: Kangagirl
I don't know—maybe I should quit my Blinddatebrides subscription. I'm not sure I can keep looking for a man on the site any more.

From: Englishcrumpet
You must have had an exhausting time of it. Why don't you have a rest and worry about your Blinddatebrides plans and all the rest of this later? Maybe this will all look better when you're not so tired. One thing I know is Dani and I won't want to lose your friendship!

From: Kangagirl
I don't think I could cope with losing either of you. I am tired. I think I'll close my eyes for a little while. Over and out for now from Australia.

'I phoned Mum earlier. I thought she might have wanted to hear how Russell was doing,' Faith said to Rick as she walked with him to his car.

It was mid-afternoon on Sunday. Julia was taking a nap inside Faith and Russell's house, and Rick had just eaten lunch with his sister.

'Marissa said it must be hard for you, having Russell away.' The comment simply came out of him, in the same way so many thoughts of Marissa got past his defences.

And yesterday Rick had fallen asleep on Marissa's couch, only to wake hours later and discover her asleep on her bed, her laptop in power saver mode beside her.

Rick had wanted to kiss her awake and make love to her. More than he'd wanted anything in a long time. He'd wavered, had reached for her, but then he'd touched the laptop control pad and a website had shown on the screen.

Blinddatebrides.com. We pride ourselves on our success stories.

There were pictures of brides and grooms smiling into each other's eyes as though they'd found the whole world there. Marissa had been logged in. There'd been an IM chat still sitting in the corner of the screen. He hadn't read it, but it was clear she was a member of the site. Quite possibly the friends she'd mentioned, Grace and Dani, were also on the site.

Rick had walked away and kept walking because that was the right thing to do. The only thing he was able to do. He wished he could stop thinking about her, but that didn't seem to be possible, no matter how much he wanted it.

'She seems really nice, Rick.' His sister touched his arm. 'Why don't you—?'

'That won't happen for me.' The words were harsher than he intended. 'I'm sorry, but you know that's not in my plans.'

'I know you like to tell people you're too old and set in your ways and that the company owns you and any other excuse that feels reasonable at the time.' Faith spoke the words in a low tone. 'I don't think it's the truth. You don't want to be like our father, so you hold yourself back.'

Rick chopped a hand through the air. 'I don't want this conversation with you.'

'Well, too bad, because maybe it's time we had it!' She

drew a harsh breath. 'Do you think I don't see what he's like, Rick? Do you think it doesn't bother me every day to know our father treats you and me and my husband and my daughter better than he does Darla or Kirrilea simply because Darla had the bad luck to do something that made him uncomfortable, that put pressure on him which he refused to face up to?'

'He loves everyone in the family.' But their father only loved to a degree, didn't he? It might seem as though Stephen had perfectly normal feelings towards some of his children, his grandchildren, but the reality was that it seemed that way because they hadn't pushed him outside his emotional comfort zone. 'If it came down to it, he'd ignore all our needs…'

'Of course he would.' Faith swung to face him. 'If he knew Russell came home from active duty the last two times and cried in my arms for hours, he'd cringe away from it. When Julia gets older and starts to test her boundaries like Kirri's doing now he'll draw back from her too, and the thought of that kills me. If I decided to do something to totally shake him up—'

'That's enough.' For the first time in his life, Rick shut his sister up. 'This conversation is finished. Just leave it, all right?'

Faith's expression froze and then she reached past him to yank his car door open. 'Maybe I've been wrong to believe you're better. To think you could have something with a woman like Marissa. Maybe it's best if you don't.' She stepped back. 'You acted just like him right now.'

Rick drove half a kilometre down the road before he pulled over and used his mobile to phone Faith's house. 'I'm sorry. I didn't mean any of that.'

'I didn't either! I had the phone in my hand to ring you.' Her breath shook as she inhaled. 'You're not like him, Rick. I should never have said it. You've always been there for Darla and me, and our daughters. You're the complete opposite of Dad. Please don't ever believe otherwise.'

Rick reassured his sister and ended the call. But Faith's

initial words had been right. He was *exactly* like Stephen Morgan. He'd already proved it once before and left a woman broken-hearted.

CHAPTER THIRTEEN

'I WOULD have taken you out, Darla.' Rick needed to pull his head together, to figure out why he'd lost control when he'd talked with Faith.

Well, Marissa didn't want him anyway, so why was he worrying about it?

Because Marissa is the reason you became so upset?

And, instead of working out anything, he was hosting a family gathering.

His sister toasted him with the gourmet sandwich in her hand and shook her head. 'I didn't want you to take me out. Not this time. This mightn't be anything amazing, but the celebration is on my tab and I want it that way.'

'It's all great.' He meant that. He just hoped she got what she needed from this.

Because Darla had invited them all, and Kirri was at her side and Stephen stood in the corner making polite noises and Rick was so tense he thought he might lose it if anything went wrong for his sister today.

'The sandwiches are fabulous, Darla. Do you mind if I ask which caterer you used?' Marissa asked from beside him.

From the moment Darla had phoned to ask if they could do this today, Marissa had got right behind his sister's plans.

Right now, she couldn't have said anything better if she'd

known. Darla grinned and Kirrilea ducked her head with a pleased flush.

Marissa's eyes widened and she laid her hand on his niece's arm. 'It was you? I'm so impressed. Will you tell me what the combination is that has sun-dried tomatoes and cottage cheese and that delicious tangy flavour?'

She'd hit it off with his sisters beautifully—liked Darla on an instinctive level that showed in every word she spoke to her, made Kirri feel great and enjoyed Julia's childish chatter.

If the knowledge of that made Rick possessive about her, maybe he was. If each time he looked at her he wanted to drag her out of there and to the nearest bed and hold her and make love to her, that fact didn't seem any easier to change either.

Rick's mouth tightened and, since there was one thing he *could* do right now that would be utterly appropriate, he forced himself to leave Marissa's side and went round the room charging glasses, moving back to stand beside his sister.

He turned to face Darla and cleared his throat. 'I think a speech is in order. Particularly as you and Kirri have spoiled us all so nicely with food and drink.'

His free hand reached for Darla's. 'You've come a long way from the part-time real estate receptionist who took rental payments over the counter three days a week. You've worked your way up through the ranks and your promotion is well deserved.

'I'm even more proud of what a fabulous parent you are to a very special, wonderful daughter.' The words of pride and love poured out of him and somehow eased him. 'I love you, Darla. I couldn't be more proud of you in all the ways there are.'

'Thank you, Rick. Those words mean the world to me.' Darla smiled through suddenly bright eyes as a still silence descended over the room.

Marissa felt the thrum of heartache mixed with the deep emotion between sister and brother.

So much hurt, and now that she'd observed Stephen Morgan in action, she believed she understood. Rick's father was a pleasant man. He cared for his family. That was quite clear. But he wanted to care only on his terms. Any time things drifted to any kind of emotional ground, he closed himself off from it.

Even in the simple act of his youngest granddaughter running to him for a cuddle. He had patted her head but he hadn't picked her up. That meting out of a measured amount of affection was so sad, and how difficult he'd made it for his family.

She smiled at Darla with determined good cheer. 'Congratulations. I hope the job promotion is all you want it to be.'

Faith hugged her sister and got a bit tearful. Hugged Rick and got equally tearful.

Rick's mother gave her daughter a peck on the cheek and a smile, and their father cleared his throat and declared it must be time they all left. It was only a brief lunch, after all. He'd reached the door, his wife close behind him, when Darla's mouth firmed and she reclaimed Rick's hand.

'That lovely speech deserves one in return, and in fact I chose to do this here because I wanted to say a few words and I felt this was the right place for them.' She turned her gaze to Rick and her heart was in her eyes so clearly that Marissa caught her breath.

Their parents hesitated in the doorway, but Darla didn't seem to care whether they stayed or left.

Rick started to shake his head, but Darla simply set a jaw very like her brother's and went on.

'Without you, Rick, without your financial support and your encouragement and your unconditional love, I don't know if I could have done any of this.' She swallowed hard. 'You were there when my beautiful girl was born. You'd have come into the labour suite if I'd let you. Instead, they told me you paced non-stop outside until it was over.'

Her gaze skimmed her daughter's down-bent head and returned to her brother. 'Thanks to your financial support, I could be at home with my baby and eventually get my career and my finances on track.'

Rick's Adam's apple bobbed. 'I did very little—'

'You helped me get where I am today, and you helped me know I didn't have to be scared or feel alone or deserted.' Darla's voice cracked. 'You loved my daughter from the day she was born and you've loved me from the day I was born, and I love you and I just…need to say that today.'

She hugged her brother and Rick held her in a tight embrace. His shoulders were taut, his eyes closed as though against such pain. Love for his sister filled every plane and angle of his face.

Marissa took a step towards them before she could stop herself. She needed to hold Rick. To assure him he'd done enough for his sister, that he could…love?

But they drew apart then and after a moment Kirrilea stuck her arm through her mum's and glanced beyond her to the couple near the door.

Her eyes were far too mature for her face as she said, 'Grandad, you probably have golf or something, so don't feel you and Grandma have to stay. We're fine here.'

The older couple left with brief farewells, acting as though nothing were amiss and there'd been no outpouring of emotion in the room just moments before. As though they hadn't been dismissed, if politely. As though they weren't lacking—

'Darla—'

'Don't worry about it, Rick.' Darla squeezed her daughter's shoulders. 'Wise heads on young shoulders, huh? I think we're really okay here. This was a good thing. It was. And it's time for us to head out.'

It was time for Marissa to remember, too, that Rick being able to love his sisters didn't mean he could commit his heart elsewhere. Why was she even thinking this, anyway? *Her* heart was far from involved.

A few minutes later, everyone had left.

'It's time to get back to work.' Rick's preoccupation was clear as he murmured the words, later on, back at the office, but he settled behind his desk and drew a folder of reading material in front of him.

Marissa might even have managed to set aside her reactions and thoughts about him if she hadn't stepped into his office to leave some letters for signature and seen that he'd tacked the laminate of his niece to the wall by his window where it competed with the view of the harbour. Where he would look at it at least a hundred times a day.

And she admitted it. She wanted to ask a thousand questions and tell him she understood so much more about him now and she wanted him to see all he had inside to give. All he had already given.

Rick had dropped everything to rush her to her mother, but he'd also done all he could to allow Tom a comfortable and worry-free recovery. He had been *kind*. That wasn't the same as a romantic commitment.

Marissa got down to work. She wished she could shut her thoughts down altogether.

'Our Hong Kong businessmen called while you were in the filing room,' Rick said from the doorway of his office half an hour later. He looked rumpled and somehow determined and resigned and intense all at once. 'Tom phoned minutes before them.' His voice turned to a harsh, low rumble. 'He'll be back in the office on Wednesday.'

'That's two days away. I thought he was taking longer.' The whispered words fell from her lips as the shock of that knowledge passed through her. Just two more days and she would cease to see Rick all day every day, work closely with him. Would cease to feel a close part of his life, even if that closeness was only in her…heart?

In her thoughts, in the fact that they had drawn together out of necessity for a short time! Marissa stiffened her spine and tried hard to hide her shock and the dismay she didn't want to admit.

'Well, that's great. Tom must feel a lot better. I'll do my best to leave everything in good order for him, and Gordon is due back on Monday, anyway. I'd been wondering how that would work out.'

Rick ran his fingers through his hair. 'Yes. It will be convenient for…everyone.'

He would be rid of her, wouldn't have to fight his attraction to her any more. Wasn't that what he had wanted from the start? To *not* want her?

'We leave for Hong Kong tomorrow after lunch.' His jaw clenched. 'It will be a two-night stay. They'll tell us with due formality they've chosen to do business with us and, though they could have done that over the phone or with a contract in the mail, it's due process for them, and important we acknowledge the gesture and respond as they expect.'

'And, because I participated in the initial dealings here, they want me along?' Did *Rick* want her presence there, or did he wish he didn't have to take her with him? 'I've never visited Hong Kong and, though my passport is current, I can invent a reason not to attend if you don't want—'

'I want you to come.' His gaze touched over her hair, each facial feature, dwelt on her mouth and came back to her eyes. 'I'd like to show you some of the sights, take you shopping.'

He wanted to give her a last huzzah before it all ended? The knowledge somehow hurt and wrapped around her heart, all at once.

Marissa tipped up her chin. 'I'd like the chance to visit Hong Kong, see a few of the sights and my presence is expected. I don't want to let the businessmen down.'

It seemed business was all they had left now.

Rick sent Marissa to bed straight off the plane the first night in Hong Kong. He knocked on her hotel room door the next morning and realised how much he wanted this time with her.

His plans, his way of showing her—what? A good time in a place she'd never visited before? So he could say goodbye this way and not look back afterwards? His body burned with the need to be near hers. His emotions burned for her in ways he had never expected or experienced.

Something had happened that day when Darla had brought their family's relationships to the fore and Kirri had dealt with her grandfather with a teenage combination of kindness and something close to pity. Rick had felt as though, finally, an issue that had hovered over all of them had been addressed.

Quietly and without any particular fanfare, but that exchange with his sister had loosened something tight way down inside him.

Rick hadn't realised how the situation had festered, even while he'd believed he had pushed it all aside.

But you're still like your father.

He didn't want to be like Stephen, but he'd already proved he was. Marissa didn't deserve that. She needed someone tender, gentle, and completely committed to her. Someone who would *know* his ability to meet all her needs.

'Good morning. These rooms are great. I have the most amazing view of Victoria Harbour and the city.' Marissa stood framed in the doorway of her room.

A fierce determination seizes him. For today he planned to spoil her and indulge her and enjoy her. He would have *that much.*

And then she could go back to Gordon's office and to her search for a man?

Her gaze rushed over him like a warm breath and ducked away again, and all his senses fired to life despite himself. No. He still didn't want her searching for a man, but he chose to push that thought away for now.

'All the colour and activity I glimpsed last night really is as stunning as I thought.' She touched her hair self-consciously, smoothed her hands over cream trousers, and skimmed the buttons of her brown long-sleeved blouse.

Nervous. She was nervous.

You could try speaking instead of standing here eating her up with your eyes.

She'd said the view was stunning.

'It is a great view.' But he meant the one in front of him right now. 'We have a spending budget for today,' he ventured, and wondered if she'd believe him if he said their business-men hosts had provided it.

'Work-related expenditure? Tax deductibles?' She raised a hand to her hair again and he wished he could pull the ribbon from it and let it loose.

Instead, he took her arm, led her away from the room. 'Not all of it, no, but I'll be very disappointed if you don't join me and enjoy the day. We're going to visit a temple, see an outdoor Chinese opera, shop, ride in a rickshaw.'

'It sounds magical.' Did her voice hold a touch of wistfulness?

Rick forced a smile. 'We don't meet our hosts until this evening. They've planned a pre-dinner cocktail cruise on a junk so we can see the light show. The pace here is frenetic and the volume of people can take you by surprise so stay close to me and tell me if you need a time-out if I don't create one for you soon enough, okay?'

* * *

Rick took Marissa through all the things he'd promised. A wiry man pedalled them along the street in a rickshaw with a gaily coloured top. When they'd taken in the awe of a Buddhist temple and the outdoor opera and so much bustling activity in the markets that Marissa felt dizzy with it, Rick hustled her into an opulent boutique hotel restaurant tucked away between towering buildings.

'This afternoon we'll shop.' He made the announcement as they ate food he'd chosen from a confusingly long list of Cantonese dishes—small servings of prawn and pork dumpling, steamed bean curd with salted fish sauce and other stunningly flavoured foods they interspersed with sips of tea.

'I've already bought some things.' She gestured to the goodies bundled at their feet. 'For Mum and Dad.'

'This afternoon I want you to buy for yourself. Pretty things. Whatever takes your fancy.' He lowered his eyes as though he couldn't quite meet hers as he admitted this.

The desire to burrow her fingers through the hair at his nape rushed through her. When their eyes locked she saw a sharp ache in him before he blinked it away.

'Rick…' She wanted him to open himself to her, to let her in totally. 'I can't let you buy me—'

'Yes. You can. If you don't, I'll only add the money to your pay.' His stare compelled her, almost implored her. 'Don't think too much, Marissa. Just agree. It would please me.'

Her hand tightened in her lap. How could she deny him when he asked her this way?

When he seemed to need this so much?

Just as he'd needed Darla to let him do something to help make her attempt at a business promotion successful. No. Not like that, because he *loved* Darla. This was *kindness*, nothing more.

'Then I guess we really are going shopping.'

They finished their meal and he ushered her to her feet. He arranged for their packages to be returned to their hotel for them, and he took her shopping.

Patiently and with absolute pleasure as she delighted herself in the most sumptuous retail experience she would perhaps encounter in her life. She wouldn't spend much. Just one or two things to please them both.

'What about this shop?' Rick drew her attention to a store full of exquisite silk garments and she knew she wouldn't be able to walk out of the place empty-handed. She stopped short. 'Oh, no.'

'Yes. Pick something to wear tonight. There must an outfit here you'd like.' He turned her to the displays of clothing.

She found the dress almost straight away. A simple cream sheath with a lovely watermark effect in the fabric. It was sleeveless, with a high traditional collar and exquisitely fitted bodice covered in tiny hand-sewn pearls. Her fingers reached for it, stopped just shy of touching as she imagined how much it might cost.

'Try it on,' he growled before he spoke in Cantonese to the shop assistant nearest them.

Moments later, tucked into the privacy of a changing room, Marissa lifted her arms and allowed the dress to glide over her head and settle against her curves.

The rustle of the fabric was almost sinful—whisper-soft and sleek—and the dress fitted as though made for her. She had to have it, wanted to wear it. For him.

No. Because it was beautiful, lovely.

While Marissa tried the dress on, Rick bought a shawl to go with it and arranged for it to be delivered to the hotel. A cream and brown confection that reminded him of her skin and her hair and her deep, expressive eyes.

When she emerged from the changing room with her face flushed a delicate pink and the dress clutched carefully in her hands, a surge of possessive heat rose inside him. He wanted to lavish gifts on her for the rest of his days, dress her in beautiful things and then strip those things away from her body and make love to her slowly and thoroughly and never have to stop.

And afterwards he wanted to hold her, cradled in his arms. None of which could ever happen.

'Did it fit?' Even to his ears, his voice was low and rough, sensual and far too intense. He'd brought her here to say goodbye, but he'd intended to control that leave-taking, not have to fight himself all the way.

'Yes. Yes, it fitted.' She swallowed, looked as though she didn't know whether to run or come closer.

It was too much. His fingers reached for her wrist and the warmth of her soft skin. He circled the fragile bones and inhaled slowly. Her pulse fluttered beneath his thumb.

'The…er…the shoes I've packed will go nicely with the dress.' She lifted her other hand, dropped it before she touched him. 'And it really is—'

'Beautiful.' But not as beautiful as Marissa. He released her reluctantly, completed the transaction for her and then rubbed a hand over the back of his neck.

'There's a jewellery store beside this one. I'd like to pick up something for my sisters and nieces.' And he would like to buy Marissa all kinds of necklaces and bracelets.

'I might like a scarf or something from here before I go.' She glanced around her. 'Out of my own money. I'll meet you in the jewellery store in a few minutes.'

Dismissed again, very nicely, and despite himself he couldn't help the tug of a smile as he remembered other times she had dispatched him.

Rick left her to it.

His body tingled with awareness as he walked out of the store, and with an odd ache because he didn't like separating from her. He could say it was because he needed her close for her sake. She couldn't speak the language. But he practised his Cantonese to keep the skills. It often wasn't needed, and she was more than capable of keeping herself safe without him.

The jewellery store was top end, and had every conceivable gift item. Rick's gaze shifted to the display of engagement rings. What kind of ring had Michael Unsworth given Marissa, if any?

His brows drew down. At the same time his gaze landed on a ring that would be perfect for her. A rare amber stone set against rich brown tiger's eye and surrounded by diamonds. It would match her eyes and hair. He wanted to buy it for her. Dear God, he wanted to—

Rick turned away from the display with a stifled sound of shock and rejection and…disbelief.

And then she was there beside him, a small store bag clutched to her side with the top pinched tightly together so there was no chance he would glimpse inside it.

Her gaze went to the displays of jewellery, though not the engagement rings. 'I wonder if I could find something for Dani and Grace. I think it's just as well we'll need to leave here soon. This sort of retail therapy is rather addictive.' She glanced up at him then, and her face stilled. 'Are you—?'

'I'm fine. I'll…help you look.'

She cast one or two uncertain glances his way as they browsed, but eventually he must have pulled himself together enough that she stopped wondering what was wrong with him.

Rick didn't know the answer to that. He helped her choose gifts for her friends and, when he purchased items for his sisters and nieces and mother, added a jewelled headband for Marissa. He was under control again. He couldn't be anything else, could he?

'The "Symphony of Lights" is aptly named.' Marissa breathed the words and felt her senses come alive from all directions.

They were aboard an authentic junk on Victoria Harbour. Mr Qi had explained the meaning behind the themes but she'd got stuck on 'awakening' for she feared she had awakened to Rick and she didn't know what to do about it.

Rick stood behind her on the deck of the junk. To their left, bright orange sails caught the sea breeze with startling efficiency as they moved through the water. Rick's legs were braced. His hands held her lightly under her elbows and, if she leaned back just a little, she could pretend he held her as a lover would.

The war of emotion and delight and wonder and sensation battered at her from without and within, snatched her breath. All because of a powerful man in a business city that provided the perfect backdrop for all the things about him she had sworn she would never like, and now found she…liked too much.

A fringed end of brown silk shawl brushed over her wrist and she stroked her fingers over the delicate fabric. 'You shouldn't have bought me this.' But she was glad he had. Her delight when she'd stepped into her room and found it on the bed had rippled through her.

She wore the jewelled band in her hair as well, felt rather like a princess in all her finery.

'The shawl matches the colour of your eyes. I couldn't resist it.' Maybe he didn't intend her to hear the low words, but she did, and she shivered in his hold.

After the light show they returned to land and ate in a traditional restaurant overlooking the harbour. Rick looked stunning in a dark suit and starched white shirt, the gold and onyx cuff-links at his wrists flashing occasionally when he gestured with the hands that had cupped her elbows with warmth and sweet tenderness during the light show.

His tie was burgundy silk. She'd bought it and had pushed it into his hands at the end of their shopping trip, and she liked to see it on him. Felt far too possessive about him.

Now, his gaze strayed to her continuously and his fingers idly stroked that tie as he talked business with their hosts until Marissa struggled to breathe normally, her heart and body awash with longing for him.

She'd fallen in love. She finally let the truth of it rise from deep in her heart, as soft as the whisper of silk against her skin, as frightening and devastating as the meaning of life.

Mr Qi had talked about the themes behind the light show while blue and red and green and yellow and pink light reflected off the water. Marissa had taken in the show but it was Rick's nearness at her back that had made her feel awakened. Now she longed for partnership and celebration with Rick but he didn't want that. He didn't want any of that with her.

She swallowed back the emotion that clogged her throat and dropped her gaze lest Rick see what was in her eyes.

'Thank you for organising for us to see the light show and for this wonderful evening.' Marissa addressed her words to Mr Qi, to all their hosts, tried to smile and seem natural as she praised the city, its beauty, the temples and age-old religions and staggering strength of the Hong Kong business world.

'We are pleased you've enjoyed our city.' Mr Qi turned to Rick. 'And pleased to create a business bond with Morgan's for our Australian building investments.' In his flawless English Mr Qi went on to outline the group's decision.

Rick murmured words of appreciation.

Two more hours passed before they finally wrapped up the evening. By then every nerve in Marissa's body was stretched tight. She hadn't set out to love Rick—couldn't believe she'd allowed it to happen—but she did and she didn't know what to do about it. She wanted a family with him. Wanted *his* babies. Wanted him to tell her that thirty wasn't so old and that he thought she was beautiful and always would think that, even when she was very old indeed…

When they got back to Australia she'd return to Gordon's

office. Would Rick remember her? Think about her? Or quickly forget her and go back to a brief nod as he swept by, his thoughts centred on his work and not the woman who had helped him with it for a short time?

They left with handshakes and bows and the assurance of a deal large enough and lucrative enough to raise Rick's business profile more than ever. At the last moment Mr Qi presented Rick with an embossed envelope. 'Perhaps you might like these.'

Rick thanked him, tucked the envelope inside his inner jacket pocket and then they were away. He took her back across the harbour. It was like crossing a big river and, before she was ready for it, they were inside their Kowloon hotel once again.

Rick took Marissa to her room in silence, so attracted to her in the lovely dress and all the more to the softness in her eyes and the guarded vulnerability there. He held her shawl. It had slipped from her shoulders as they'd crossed the harbour and he'd taken it into his hands, the soft fabric warmed from her body.

She paused outside her room. Turned to face him. 'Thank you for a wonderful day, for the gifts.' Her hand rose to touch the jewelled band that held her curls off her face.

His hand lifted to her shoulder, captured a lock of her hair and pressed it between thumb and finger, because he couldn't stand not touching her, yet it only made him want her more. 'I'm glad you wore your hair down tonight. It's you. So vital and alive and free.'

If she knew how much he wanted to bury his face in that mass of curls, to inhale the essence of her and hold her and somehow wrap her around him and inside him…

'I don't ever look sleek and neat as a pin, no matter how hard I try.' Her lips tilted in a soft attempt at a smile.

'You look…' Holdable. Kissable. 'It's you. I hope you never change.'

'It won't matter. Soon you won't even notice me. You'll go back to passing me in the corridors with a nod—'

'No.' He didn't know if he could ever dismiss her from his thoughts. Rick tugged her into his arms before he knew his own intention, took the possibility of other words from her mouth with his lips.

As his arms closed about her and her mouth warmed beneath his, he fought his demons and didn't know any more whether he had lost or won, only that he needed her.

How could holding her be such torment? How could he let her go?

She drew back with a gasp. A pulse fluttered at the base of her throat. Her eyes were wide and uncertain, filled with desire and…anguish.

'Marissa—'

'Wh-what did Mr Qi give you before we left?' Her words were an attempt to draw back from the brink.

He blinked and struggled with harsh stark feelings that tore at him. Why had he thought he could bring her here and not want to make love with her? That he could give her the sights and sounds of Hong Kong and not want her for himself?

He tugged the envelope from his pocket and flipped it open. There were photos. Two of them, taken at the petting zoo. Mr Qi had had the digital images made into prints for them. In the first photo Marissa had the koala in her arms. She smiled and, behind her, Rick smiled for the cameras. He stared unblinkingly at that first photo for a moment before he tilted it forward.

The one behind it made him catch his breath because in this photo her heart was in her eyes. The wounds she'd sustained when her fiancé had dumped her, her need to know she could connect in a meaningful way again and have it work out for her. The ache in her as she'd held that bundle of fur in her arms. Her tender feelings for the man in the picture.

He was that man, and he wanted those feelings from her even as he recognised the expression in his eyes in the picture. Longing, hunger. He'd thought it wouldn't show. Hadn't realised the strength of those feelings, even then. The thought of making love to her, of giving her something she wanted and thus locking her irrevocably to him in the process, rushed him, shocked him. Even as he admitted he'd known all along that longing for a child had been part of her reaction that day.

'A couple of prints from the petting zoo.' He cleared his throat, turned the envelope so she could see the top print, and then tucked the small packet back into his pocket.

His desire to kiss her, possess her, tore at him and he backed away from it and from her because if he touched her at all he wouldn't stop. 'It's late and we have a long flight ahead of us to get home tomorrow.'

'To get back to work and our usual tasks. In my case, anyway. You'll just go on as before, but with Tom.' Marissa almost asked Rick to stay. The words trembled on the tip of her tongue but, before she could find the courage to say them, or the sanity to stop herself, he took the decision from her.

'Goodnight.' There was a bite in his voice that was self-derision and intensity and longing and refusal wrapped into one. His room was across from hers. He entered and closed the door with a soft click that seemed far too final.

She sagged for a harsh, struggling moment before she let herself into her own room, and with a sound wrenched from her, fell back against the door. Her spine welcomed the hard surface, the chill inanimateness of it, while her heart railed at her, told her to go to him—

She tugged the jewelled decoration from her hair, set is on the bedside table. Thought of Rick in that room across the hall, so close. Took a stumbling step towards the door.

The rap from the other side made her heart slam in her chest. She lunged for the doorknob and wrenched the door open and knew, *knew in her heart that if there was any way she could keep him with her, even just for the one night, she would.* All thoughts of self-preservation were gone, lost to her, because if she could only love him once then she wanted to.

He held her shawl crushed inside a white-knuckled fist. He didn't even pretend it was the reason. 'Tell me no, Marissa. Tell it to me right now.'

She drew a shaken breath. Her fingers wrapped around his strong hair-roughened wrist. 'I need you tonight, Rick. Here and now. I'm only prepared to tell you that.'

CHAPTER FOURTEEN

RICK crossed the threshold of Marissa's room without any awareness that he had moved. He only felt her body in his arms as the door clicked locked behind him and his mouth came down over hers.

It wasn't an easy kiss, or a soft one. He covered her lips with his and took every part of her that she would give. Possessed and suckled and stroked until his blood bubbled in his veins and his body shook and his emotions roiled and he didn't know how to quiet them, how to assuage them.

'I want this.' She sighed the words into the crook of his neck and pressed her lips to his skin there.

He buried his free hand in her hair, lodged it deep in the wild curliness as he tipped up her head to give him the access he wanted to her mouth. Her chin and face and neck.

The need for her turned molten, raged through him and made his knees quake and his heart stutter with—

Not longing. Not a need so deep it was unfathomable. He could not acknowledge that, be at the mercy of that. Yet his hand in her hair gentled to reverent pressure as he brought her head forward and let himself have the softness of her, the sweetness of her as their lips touched, brushed, in the gentle kiss he should have given her to start with.

He tossed the shawl onto the bed behind them, a splash of brown against the soft golden tone of the quilt.

Let him please her, wring everything from this time with her—for both of them. Let him at least have that, give her that. It was a supplication and a hope and a determination as Rick gave himself—all of him that he could—to the woman in his arms.

Stroking hands over her hair and the skin of her arms. Whisper-soft kisses to soothe the startled sensitivity of her lips where he had kissed her.

Where Marissa had ached from Rick's focused plundering of her senses, her heart melted in the face of his gentleness. The man, the layers, the complexities. Maybe no person would ever truly know all of him and, despite the ache in her heart for him and for the knowledge that he didn't share her feelings, he felt something.

He gave her something. Perhaps more of himself than Michael had ever given.

The thought surfaced and she pushed it away because Michael was a shadow. A piece of the past.

Rick was real and here in her arms and if her heart broke tomorrow and went on breaking she would have to find a way to survive it somehow because she couldn't end this. She would not deny herself this.

So she would give him her heart in her touch and the haven of her arms, just this one time. It was madness and insanity and the essence of a need so deep she couldn't fathom it. She faced it and chose it.

'I want to feel your warmth.' She needed that.

Her hands pushed his jacket off broad shoulders, down muscular arms, flung it across the chair behind him. With shaking fingertips she traced the hard heat of his chest, touched the silk tie.

'I'm glad you wore this.' The sight of it on him had raised proprietorial instincts she hadn't known she had.

The primitive emotions warned her how far she had fallen. She didn't want to know. Not now. Not yet.

'I'm glad you wore the dress and shawl.' His words were a low growl as her fingers worked the tie out from beneath his collar.

His hands roved restlessly up and down her arms. She sensed both urgency and his restraint, the war of the two inside him. The tie disappeared and the flat of his hand pressed into her back between her shoulders, pressed her forward until their bodies locked once more.

'You bought them for me.' Clothes he had wanted her to have. Clothes she had wanted to wear for him.

'And you put them on with those dainty high heeled shoes and all I could think about all night was touching you, your beautiful legs wrapping around me, welcoming me.' He made a harsh sound and stroked his thumbs over the points of her jaw. 'Since that day when I lifted you into my car I've thought about your legs—'

He kissed her and praised her and murmured all the ways he wanted to show her how beautiful he thought her, and Marissa forgot about coffee table analogies and fear and what would happen tomorrow, and lost herself in him.

Rick's hands shifted to the back of her dress and his gaze was intent on hers as he set her skin free inch by inch until cool air touched her back and warm fingers skimmed over her spine.

This was really happening and she made the choice to take everything, give everything that could be shared, to awaken and celebrate in this moment, with him.

'I need your hands on me.' He lifted her hand to his mouth, kissed her fingers and placed them against his chest over the fabric of his shirt. 'On my skin. Over my heart. Please, Marissa.'

The gravelly plea curled around her heart. He must feel something for her. His rough plea suggested he did, his gaze echoed it. Need. He did need her somehow.

She stepped back and his arms dropped to his sides. Spiky lashes swept down as his gaze locked on her mouth, roved her body with possessive intent and with awe.

She released the buttons on his shirt one by one. Feasted with her fingertips upon the skin stretched tight across his muscled chest, let the abrasion of dark curly hair fill her senses. One cuff-link came away. The other. He shrugged the shirt off his shoulders and flung it away, wrapped her in arms that felt as though they could shelter her for ever.

Then Marissa's breath caught on a stifled sound of longing that came not only from her senses but also from deep in her soul and heart.

He tipped up her chin and searched her eyes and emotions warred in his gaze before he crushed her close, his hands flat against her back as he pushed clothing away. 'Say my name. I need to hear it.'

'Only you, Rick.' She had no room in her heart or her senses for any other. 'I only want to think of you, of this— this moment.'

His arms trembled as he laid her on the bed. He reached into the pocket of his trousers, laid a small foil packet on the night-stand beside her and bowed his head as though fighting with himself somehow.

Marissa let her gaze encompass that gesture and swallowed hard. 'I thought you might have to raid the supplies in the bathroom.'

She could tell him she was on the pill, that she'd stayed on it since Michael, but she didn't want to bring the other man's name into the room. It would feel like sacrilege.

Rick knelt on the floor at her side, stroked skin too tight and too hot and stripped away the layers until she was naked before him—and naked emotionally—and she shuddered with vulnerable need and would have covered herself.

'Don't.' He spoke that single hoarse word and his arms closed around her. He buried his face against her heart and shuddered, a strong man on his knees and emotionally vulnerable to her. Right now, that was who he was, as vulnerable as her.

She clasped his shoulders and tugged. 'Come to me. Please, Rick.'

Rick shed the rest of his clothes and joined Marissa, drew her into the hold of his arms and against his body, and they touched in so many places finally.

He was drowning in Marissa's arms, in an overload of wrenching feeling that welled up from somewhere deep inside. His hands shook as he ran them over her face, caressed her neck and shoulders and the dip of her waist.

A convulsive swallow made him aware of the tightness in his throat as he buried his gaze in soft brown eyes blurred with warmth and longing.

'This night.' He spoke the words, a benediction and a warning and a promise. 'For this night you're mine.'

'And you're mine.' Her arms bound him to her. 'For tonight *you're mine.*'

He hadn't known anything of pleasure. Not until now and it swamped his senses, poured over him and through him and her fierce words were right at the centre of it.

When she opened herself to him, his heart filled with aching wonder and stark desperation. He loved her with his body and his touch and his senses, with everything within him he still didn't fully understand and when it ended, he kissed her and, cradled her in his arms and didn't want to leave her.

Eventually he forced himself to release her. He padded to the bathroom, and returned to her side and climbed back into the bed. His arms tightened around her and he couldn't prevent the tight sigh of sound that escaped as he buried his face in her hair.

He didn't know how to handle the overload of feeling, the possessiveness that rose up, the wild thoughts of finding ways to make Marissa stay with him, to keep her at his side. The temptation to take her again without benefit of any package…

'You were all I needed,' she whispered as she drifted into sleep. 'In the end, you were all of it anyway. I hadn't realised…'

And she'd been all to him, despite those temptations. He held her until she slept and he stayed at her side, his arms around her, and felt the hours slide away one after another until there were too many gone and he felt panicky and lost and somehow shattered because she *had* been all, but she was wrong that he'd been enough for her.

He rose from the bed then, quietly retrieved and donned his clothes.

Brushed his fingers over the shawl abandoned at the foot of the bed and took the memory of her hair spread across the pillow, her soft mouth and the touch and taste of her with him as he left the room.

As he backed away emotionally, just as his father had done for as long as Rick could remember. Wasn't that what he was doing?

You don't want to hurt her. The way your father has hurt Kirri and your sisters and would have hurt your mother if she didn't choose to push it all away.

It was sound reasoning.

Why did it leave him so hollow inside?

To: Sanfrandani, Englishcrumpet
From Kangagirl
So much has happened in such a short space of time, I don't know where to start. Well, I guess it doesn't matter where I start. The ending is still the same. I fell in love with Rick and he doesn't feel the same way but I don't want you to worry about me because I'll get over it. Tomorrow when I go to work I'll be back in Gordon's office.

Rick's secretary will be back, you see, so he won't need

me any more, and my boss will be back, so it all works out. I'm glad, really. And it's my birthday on Friday. I've entertained a lot of nonsense thoughts about turning thirty. As though the day means anything, really.

And I bought you both a little something in Hong Kong. You can expect a small package each in the mail in the next week or two, depending on the vagaries of the postal service at either end…

To: Englishcrumpet
From: Sanfrandani
I'm worried about Marissa. She's so generous, thinking about us when it's clear her heart is breaking. I don't know how to help her. I wish she hadn't fallen for this guy. That's twice in a row that she's loved and ended up devastated, and this time it seems even worse for her. It doesn't seem fair!

To: Sanfrandani
From: Englishcrumpet
All we can do is be there for her. I wonder if she could have avoided this? Love seems to survive even the greatest resistance sometimes, whether it's welcome or not.

CHAPTER FIFTEEN

'MARISSA. I didn't expect to see you here.'

The male voice was familiar. Marissa looked up into Michael Unsworth's bland, suave face and blinked her eyes. He had to be a mirage. Fate wouldn't be so cruel as to do this to her just days short of her birthday, when she already felt miserable and depressed and…heartbroken for a man who simply didn't want to love her or even keep her in his life. Not his personal life, not his close working life.

Rick Morgan was that man. Not this echo of the past.

But here Michael stood, right in the middle of the coffee shop she'd slipped away to for lunch. 'Michael. Excuse me. I'm late getting back to work.'

It was only the barest of white lies. She looked at the man and she felt nothing but a distanced dislike because of his shabby past behaviour. Rick had her heart. There was no room for any other. Not in any way.

'Er…look, Marissa, I didn't intend for you to find out this way.' Michael's voice oozed sympathy but the feeling didn't reach his eyes. 'Especially so close to your…er…well…to your birthday. I promise you if I'd known you'd be anywhere near this place—'

'I can't imagine why you would be concerned about seeing me near my birthday or any other time, and the last time I checked, people could eat where they liked.' Marissa didn't want to revisit his earlier birthday promise to her—that they would be secretly engaged and eventually get married and love each other for ever.

How could she have been so foolish as to even think she'd fallen for him anyway? He wasn't half the man Rick was.

And how could you be so foolish as to love Rick, who told you he would never commit to you?

'Who is this, Michael? A friend of yours?' A woman drew level with them.

Several things registered with Marissa in that moment. The woman was Jane McCullough, the daughter of Michael's company boss. The two of them were clearly together. And Jane was pregnant.

The feelings Marissa had thought she had under control about having a child made themselves known again then. 'You… You're expecting a baby.' Her voice wobbled. 'Congratulations.'

And Jane was much younger than thirty. Probably no more than twenty-five…

'Marissa, this is my fiancée, Jane McCullough.' Michael inserted the words with a hint of warning in his tone.

What did he think she would do? Tear out the other woman's eyes because she had him and Marissa didn't, because she was starting the family Marissa now knew she would never, ever have? If she couldn't have that with Rick, she would never want it with anyone.

'We've met in passing, though I don't know if Jane would remember her father introducing us.' Marissa offered a polite nod to the woman. A smile was beyond her right now. 'I hope you're keeping well.'

I hope Michael is true to you, truer than he ever was to me.

Jane frowned as she apparently considered the significance of Marissa's past involvement with Michael.

And Marissa excused herself a second time and walked away. The only good thing she could think of as she stepped back into the Morgan company building was that at least she'd eaten a wholesome sandwich and even a piece of fruit for her lunch. 'There'll be no fainting on the job today.'

Rick would be proud, but it wasn't about Rick any more. Hadn't been since they'd got off the plane days ago and he'd finally faced her fully.

'If the protection fails and there's a baby, I'll take care of you. I expect you to let me know.'

That was what he had said, the only words about the night they'd shared, the most wonderful experience of her life and she'd thought it had meant something special to him as well. In her heart she still believed it had, but just not enough. He'd looked at her then with such anguish in his eyes, but ultimately he'd turned away.

They'd spoken since. Awkward words when she'd bumped into him on her floor, when he'd dropped by Gordon's office to speak to him, and twice when Rick had visited the company's cafeteria at the same time she had.

She didn't remember seeing that much of him before she'd started working for him. Maybe he'd been there but she hadn't truly noticed. Now she noticed everything, longed for each glimpse of him. How could she go on day after day this way? Seeing him, speaking briefly with him while their gazes locked and she fought all her longing for him and needed him so much she kept thinking she saw the same longing in him?

It had to end. The torture had to end but she didn't know how to make that happen.

'Marissa.' Rick stepped into the lift behind the woman he couldn't get out of his mind. 'I thought I might see you at the cafeteria today.' He'd been looking, going places she might be…

'I went out instead.' Her low words were guarded.

He stood beside her and felt helpless. And then she raised her hand to press the button for her floor, as she had done that very first day, and all the moments they had shared since then washed through him and he realised…

He'd fallen in love with her. The ache in his chest couldn't be anything else. The need to be near her any way he could…

'You…er…where are you going? You haven't pressed for a floor.' Her mouth softened to a vulnerable line as she looked at him for one brief moment, seemed to take in every feature as though she needed to commit him to her memory as much as he needed to be with her.

I'm going to whatever floor keeps me with you in here the longest.

'Er…the top floor. Swimming.' In truth, he hadn't been up there for ages. He'd lost interest in most of the things he routinely did, had only kept going with his work because it made the time pass. *He loved her.* Where did he go with that? He, who hadn't believed he could…

Marissa pressed the button for the top floor and the floor she shared with Gordon, and her hand dropped to her side. He wanted to capture her fingers in his and never let go. He wanted a chance with her. His heart leaped into his throat and stayed there. Words pushed past anyway. 'Please, will you—'

Ding.

The lift stopped, the doors slid open. She glanced at him and a choked sound came from her throat. 'I have to go. I have to get back to work. I can't—' She stepped out of the lift and was gone.

But maybe not completely gone from him? As the lift doors closed and he felt as though his heart had stayed behind on that other floor with her, Rick pondered that emotional leap.

He wasn't like his father. How could he be when this love in his chest, this need for Marissa, filled all of him? He just hadn't known what love was—the real, strong, all-encompassing love of a man for only one woman.

Was it too late? He didn't know, but he understood now what he had to do…

Her birthday was almost over. Well, the working part of it was over at least. For the first time, Marissa had contemplated calling in and pretending she was sick so she wouldn't have to go to work today.

But she'd gone to work and she'd got through the day without even a glimpse of the company boss, and now all she had to do was manage the birthday dinner her parents had sprung on her after all.

Marissa left her apartment and climbed into the taxi her mother had arranged for her. She even managed a slight smile as she thought how much Mum must have enjoyed putting together this 'little surprise', complete with an 'undisclosed destination' for this taxi ride.

Hopefully the driver knew where he was taking her!

Well, Marissa would enjoy the night if it killed her. She owed her parents that much.

Eighty-eight storeys above ground level, Rick waited in a restaurant in Sydney's Centrepoint Tower building. The tables faced panels of glass that gave a moving panoramic view of the harbour and city.

Rick only had eyes for the woman who followed the waitress towards the table set for eight. Marissa wore the silk dress bought in Hong Kong, the shawl spread across her shoulders. Her face held determination and unhappiness she was working very hard to mask, and surprise. That last was the result of believing her parents had sprung a birthday event on her after all, no doubt, and of that 'surprise' leading her here.

He'd begged for her parents' co-operation to make tonight happen, had laid himself bare to get it, and after a thorough grilling from Abe and a gentler one from Tilda, they'd come through for him. Tilda had admitted that Marissa had made it clear she didn't want to celebrate this birthday, that the date itself had unpleasant memories for her, thanks to her ex-fiancé, and, on top of that, her daughter didn't seem to be coping very well with the idea of turning thirty.

To Rick, Marissa's age was perfect. *She* was perfect. He'd chosen this restaurant because he wanted to lay all of the city at her feet. Maybe that was whimsical, but he'd gone with his heart. Now he had to convince Marissa of his love, and convince her to let him love her and prove those thoughts to her. If she would let him. If she could find something in her heart for him.

Would her smile fade and utter rejection replace it when she noticed him? Had he left it too late and lost her, if he ever truly had a chance with her in the first place? His fingers moved to the outline of the ring in his pocket and for a long moment his breath froze in his chest and he thought his lungs might give out and he'd end up on the floor.

He knew the precise moment she spotted him, noted his presence, instead of her parents.

In fact, Abe and Tilda were here, waiting beyond them tucked away near the bar with Rick's sisters and nieces. Close enough to know the significance of this meeting, far enough away not to overhear any softly spoken words and not to distract Marissa during these first moments.

Marissa's step hitched. Unease bloomed in her too-pale face. Her gaze shifted to the empty seats at the table and came back to him, and she started to turn away.

'Please don't leave without hearing me out. When you've done that, if need be, I'll be the one to go.' His heart hammered as he stepped forward.

'I don't understand. I was supposed to meet Mum and Dad. How… Why…?'

'I asked them to help me arrange this. I phoned your father and talked him into this because I realized…I had to do this…' There were no smooth words and his throat tightened and an inexplicable rush of emotion swamped him.

'You're so beautiful tonight.' So beautiful it squeezed his heart just to look at her. 'I'll always remember how you looked in that dress the first night you wore it.' And afterwards, as he'd stripped it away from her and they'd joined in the most intimate way possible.

Why hadn't he realised then that he loved her? That his *heart* needed her? Why hadn't he come home to her then?

'I want you to go. My parents must be on their way and I don't want them to know how I feel…' She stopped the words.

They stood beside the end of the table, and instinctively he caught her hands in his. There were diners all around them, people enjoying the wonder and pleasure of the night as though dining in the sky itself.

He could only see the woman before him and he spoke in a low tone filled with the emotion inside him because he couldn't hold back the words. He didn't want to. She had to have all of them, all of this, he'd finally realised. 'I thought if I stayed away from you that would be best for you.'

To tell her with her parents and his sisters waiting was the only way he could think of to let her know he meant this. That he would risk everything.

Rick took a deep breath. 'I told myself you would find someone better, someone who didn't have the issues behind him that I do. But I love you, Marissa, with all my heart and mind and soul. I didn't understand what it meant when I made love with you that night and didn't ever want to let you go, but I know now.'

A soft sound came from her throat and she swallowed

hard. 'Don't do this to me, Rick. Don't say things like this to me when you can't mean them.'

'I mean them. I mean all of it.' He drew her forward. His arms ached to hold her and for a moment the ruthless side of his nature goaded him to simply pull her into his embrace and try to get what he wanted through a connection they had already proved, but he wouldn't do that.

Because she deserved all of it, even if at the end she turned him away.

'You made it clear you wouldn't love me, that you only wanted that one night. That you wanted to be single. Because of your family history.' Marissa didn't know what to do. She wanted to turn away, to rush out of this glittery setting that spread all of Sydney at her feet but, with Rick's hands on hers, she couldn't move at all.

She couldn't make herself break even this tenuous hold, and she couldn't stop the hope that rose in her heart. 'You don't have to feel sorry for me or think because I'm turning thirt—'

'I'm seven years older, Marissa. You might consider that too old, I don't know. I don't care about either of our ages because I only want you, and I swear I'll make you forget your ex-fiancé.' His words were tortured but determined. 'If you'll just give me the chance, say you'll stay with me, maybe one day you'll learn to love me, to want me.

'I know what I told you, that I couldn't commit. You understood why I believed that, but I was wrong. I know this because you have all my heart. Every part of it.'

It was the most humbling and loving of speeches and her hands squeezed his as she felt the eyes of people around on them, but she could only see Rick, only look into deep grey eyes that couldn't seem to shift their gaze from her.

'If you're worried I'll be pregnant, I'm sure I won't be. You took care of me.'

Could Rick truly love her? Oh, Marissa wanted to believe it, but how could it be true?

'It's not about a possible pregnancy, though I want my baby growing inside you.' He uttered the words in a low tone filled with need. 'I want lots of babies with you, as many as will make you happy and I want them for myself too. I want you working at my side or at least close by every day and I want us to go home to the same bed at night. Most of all, I just want the chance to love you.'

'Oh, Rick. I want those things with you.' They would be a dream come true, better than any plan she could have conjured up and tried to set into motion through Blinddatebrides.com. He didn't know about that, about exactly how she'd gone about her dating efforts.

'I don't want to hold back any more. Not from you. Not ever from you.' His hand rose to cup her face, to skim over her hair, as he seemed to search for words. Finally he spoke them, his gaze never wavering from hers. 'I've spent a lifetime pushing down the fact that my family isn't perfect, that my father couldn't meet certain emotional needs. I thought I couldn't do any better.

'What I didn't realise is I *did* fill the gaps he left. Darla helped me see that, and I don't have to feel guilty for acknowledging how he is.'

Marissa's heart ached for him. 'No. You're not to blame for any of that.'

'I want to follow the example of *your* father, and love with all my heart. I want to love *you* that way, Marissa, if you'll let me.' His gaze seemed to worship every part of her as his hands rose to stroke her arms, to gently cup them in strong palms. 'Years ago I thought I was in love, but the feelings… weren't real. Not like what I feel for you. I backed away, and I thought I did it because I was like my father, but I know now that wasn't it. I didn't love her because she wasn't you, because I could only love you. I was waiting for you.'

His mouth softened and his eyes softened and all his love for her welled into the air between them until she had to believe it, couldn't deny it any longer.

'Oh, Rick.' Marissa's breath caught. She clasped his arms where he held her, wrapped her hands around thick muscle covered in the constraint of cloth and remembered those strong arms holding her as he'd gently led her to paradise. 'You truly love me?'

'Yes.' His voice dropped to a low whisper. 'Yes, if you'll let me, I will love you for the rest of my life and I swear I'll never let you down or leave you wondering or wishing I'd given you more, opened to you more. You'll have all of me, Marissa, the good and the bad, if you'll take me.'

The sounds around them seemed to fade to nothing as she stared into his eyes. Outside, the city lights winked and seemed to tell her the time had come. That this *was* the real thing and somehow, magically, it had come to her, despite her fears and her foolish worry about getting older and her joining a dating site so she could hand pick her fate, as though that were possible.

'I want to agree,' she whispered and his hands tightened and his muscles seemed to lock as he stood before her, waiting. 'But there are things you don't know about me. About what I've been doing, what I've wanted out of life and how I went about trying to get those things.'

'Like looking on a dating website?' He didn't seem the least surprised, or concerned. 'That day you fell asleep in your apartment and I fell asleep on your sofa, I came into your room and saw the site on your laptop. When I realised how much I love you I thought about joining up and trying to woo you from there, but I didn't want to wait that long to tell you how I felt. Once I realised how much I love you—'

'I was going to hand pick a man exactly right for me.' The

words burst out of her—a confession, an admission of the ignorance of her plans. 'I thought if I made my choice clinically I'd be able to guard myself, not get hurt.'

His fingers stroked up and down her arms while his gaze lingered on each feature of her face and finally came back to look deep into her eyes. 'I'm not perfect. I'm far from it, but I love you with all my heart and I'm hoping that will count for something. And I won't put my career before you. I want you to know that because I think your ex-fiancé did that.' He made it a vow as his hands lifted until his fingers were in her hair. 'I'll make whatever changes are needed so that can never happen because you will always be first with me. Over and above everything.'

How her heart soared then and, even as it did, she knew she had to be equally honest. 'It was foolish of me to believe I could find love the way I planned to.

'I looked at the pictures of happy couples and I wanted that too because I'd been used and humiliated. I thought my heart had been broken but I didn't love him. Not the way I love you. I could never love anyone the way I love you and I realise now that you can't choose love. It comes to you. It finds you.'

'It found me the day I looked at a woman with a hard hat squashed down over her curls and a sparkle in her eyes.' He drew her hand to his chest, pressed it over his heart where she could absorb the deep beat.

A beat that told her how much he meant this. 'It stuck around as she called the photocopier names and rushed to be at her mother's side and lay in my arms in a bed in a borrowed garage and a bed in a sumptuous hotel room on the other side of the world. I bought the clothes because I didn't want you to forget me, but I can't forget you.'

He clasped her hands in his and there, in front of the entire restaurant, he drew something bright and glittery from his pocket, held it between his fingertips and went down on one knee. 'Please say you'll marry me, Marissa. Give us a chance. Let me give you all the things you've been longing for.'

'I want to marry you, spend my life with you.' Her heart hitched as his fingers tightened over hers, and one final confession poured out of her. 'I bought baby wool. To knit booties. I really do want a baby and I don't think that's something that's going to go away. But I want a baby…with you, not with anyone else.'

His fingers wrapped so hard around hers, he almost crushed them. 'That's…I want that more than I can tell you.'

'Oh, Rick.' And she let go of the last foolish fear, the pride that had led her to try to find Mr Right in all the wrong ways when he had been there in front of her all the time. 'I love you with all my heart.' The words came *straight from* her heart.

His fingers trembled as he wrapped them around hers. The mouth that was usually firm and commanding wobbled a little too as he held the ring at the tip of her finger and looked into her eyes as though seeking her permission. She swallowed hard and, through a sheen of tears, looked at the exquisite ring.

'I asked Mr Qi to get it for me.' Rick cleared his throat. 'Actually, I talked him into flying it out here personally with a whole bunch of paperwork from the jeweller's and other stuff to make sure it could be delivered straight to me. I spotted it that day we were there…'

He'd gone to all this trouble for her. To make this special for her. A birthday to remember, so different from that other one. Her voice was a whisper of love and need as she said finally, 'Then I think I'd like to wear it now, if you truly do want this.'

'I do.' He slid the ring home, a perfect fit and the perfect symbol of all he felt for her.

And then, as she tugged on his hand, he got to his feet and crushed her into his arms and she felt his deep shudder of relief and longing as he pressed his face into her neck and murmured her name over and over.

'Thank you, my darling.' His fingers found their way through her hair to her nape. 'Thank you for putting your trust in me.'

'I love you, Rick.' Her hands touched his arms, his shoulders. 'I love you so much.'

He kissed her then, in front of the diners and the waiters and all of Sydney outside the sparkling windows.

When they finally broke apart, pleased laughter and murmurs of 'Hear, hear!' and 'How lovely!' broke out around them.

Rick drew Marissa around then, and she gasped.

Mum and Dad, Darla and Faith and Kirrilea and little Julia all stood there. They smiled, grinned. Her Mum and Darla and Faith had tears in their eyes.

Marissa's gaze flew to Rick's. 'You asked me in front of all of them. You went down on your knees in front of not only the strangers in this room, but in front of your family and mine. If I'd said no—'

'I wanted you to have your proposal in front of everyone so you'd know I meant it, that I would put my heart on the line for you.' A wealth of determination and love and understanding and hope shone in his eyes. 'Especially in front of the people that matter the most to both of us.'

His parents weren't among that number. Had he asked them to come, only to have them turn him down?

'It doesn't matter, Marissa.' He seemed to read her thoughts. *'You're here.'*

'And *most* of our family are here.' His and hers—and they would share that family.

Marissa promised herself there and then that she would weave Rick into *her* family, with Mum and Dad and Aunty Jean and the others, and she would work equally as hard to be part of his family, with his sisters and his nieces and, yes, his parents, who cared to a degree but also had their faults.

She wrapped her arms around his shoulders and drew his head down and kissed him fiercely, and when they broke apart and he told her she certainly knew how to pick her moments, she laughed and linked their arms together.

'I'm picking *every moment* for us, from now until forever.' And Marissa raised her voice and told the man she loved, 'Because you're my Mr Absolutely Right and you always will be, and I want the world to know I love you exactly as you are. I don't want *you* to change in any way.'

There were hugs all around and eventually they sat down to dine and celebrate a birthday that had turned out to be a milestone for a very different reason.

Marissa looked at Rick's ring on her finger and thought of being with him, of going home with him day after day. Old? One day she hoped to be. With Rick, and their children around them.

As their family spoke among themselves and the meals were brought out, Rick touched the shawl at her shoulders and bent his dark head to hers. 'I'm going to marry you with a big wedding and all the trimmings and all of Sydney looking on. I hope you're ready for that.'

'Maybe not *all* of Sydney. That would be rather a crowd.' But her smile broke through. 'I do want the world to know I'm yours, and you're mine, and I'd like to share our joy with as many people as we can.' She fell silent. 'A big wedding would take a lot of planning, though, and it would mean we'd have to wait months for it.'

'I'll put a team onto the matter. One of those wedding planner teams.' It was his turn to fall silent, but not for long. 'Everything has to be perfect for you but if I keep a close enough eye on it all…'

A glint of corporate determination filled his gaze.

She watched the plans click over and his expression become more and more focused and her heart melted for him all over again.

'You'll move in with me before then, won't you? Now that I have you, I don't want to let you go.' He hesitated. 'Or I can move in with you. Anywhere you want; I just want us to be together. I want to wake up every day with you at my side, make love to you until I've shown you how much I love you, how much you mean to me.'

A lifetime of togetherness. Her heart filled and she twined her fingers with his, simply because she could. 'Then I think maybe we should start on that plan as soon as possible and I would like to live in your apartment, at least at first. Later we might want a…different location.'

'For our children.' The possessive words wrapped her in desire and warmth and promise. 'For when *our* family of two becomes three or more.' He lowered his voice again. 'I want to make love to you quite desperately right now, Marissa Warren.'

The first opportunity they got, after the cake and the good wishes, they slipped away.

And later, as Marissa lay in Rick's arms and he told her again how much he loved her, she gasped.

He rose up on one elbow and looked into her eyes. 'What is it?'

'I've just realised I have a little explaining to do to my Blinddatebrides.com friends. At least my subscription has a few months left to run, so I can keep using the IM facility to chat with them, and I can check out profiles for them.'

Rick barely flinched before he relaxed again. 'I'll help you, if you like. Just so long as you take *your* profile off the "available" listings.'

'The only man I want to be available to is you.' She kissed him and they lost themselves again.

And, a very long time later, Marissa murmured, 'I wonder which of my online friends—Dani or Grace—will be next to find *her* Mr Right on Blinddatebrides.com?'

* * * * *

BLIND-DATE BABY

BY
FIONA HARPER

Welcome to the www.blinddatebrides.com member profile of:
Englishcrumpet (aka Grace Marlowe)

My ideal partner...

Young at heart, just like I am. No cardigan-wearers, please! My teenage daughter has just flown the nest and it's high time I remembered what it's like to be young, free and single. I'd be lying if I said I was looking for a soul mate—true love like that only happens once in a lifetime, and I've been there, done that, worn the black veil... But I'm looking for someone to share my life with. Preferably someone who loves rock music and cold Chinese takeaway!

My details...

- **Age:** thirty-ten (think about it!)
- **I live:** in London
- **Marital status**: widow
- **Occupation**: growing old disgracefully

You'll match if you...

- Are young at heart
- Are London-based
- Are unattached
- Want to join me

As a child, **Fiona Harper** was constantly teased for either having her nose in a book, or living in a dream world. Things haven't changed much since then, but at least in writing she's found a use for her runaway imagination. After studying dance at university, Fiona worked as a dancer, teacher and choreographer, before trading in that career for video-editing and production. When she became a mother she cut back on her working hours to spend time with her children, and when her littlest one started pre-school she found a few spare moments to rediscover an old but not forgotten love—writing.

Fiona lives in London, but her other favourite places to be are the Highlands of Scotland, and the Kent countryside on a summer's afternoon. She loves cooking good food and anything cinnamon-flavoured. Of course she still can't keep away from a good book, or a good movie—especially romances—but only if she's stocked up with tissues, because she knows she will need them by the end, be it happy or sad. Her favourite things in the world are her wonderful husband, who has learned to decipher her incoherent ramblings, and her two daughters.

To my editor, Kimberley Young,
who urged me to dig deeper—
somewhere else—and I found unexpected treasure.
And to Jennie Adams and Melissa McClone—
even the (very) early morning IM chats were a blast!

CHAPTER ONE

GRACE MARLOWE and six o'clock in the morning weren't normally on speaking terms. But here she was, standing in the middle of her darkened kitchen, the clock ticking in time with her heartbeat. Pearly light seeped between the slats of the blind, draining all colour from her funky little kitchen. She wrinkled her nose. Everything was grey, even the lime green mugs and the pink toaster. This truly was a repulsive time of day.

What was she doing here? Right about now she should be mumbling incoherently in her sleep, her left foot tucked over the top of the duvet to keep it nice and cool.

In a sudden flurry of movement she turned and headed towards a cupboard—any cupboard—and opened the door. It didn't matter which one. She just needed to be doing something. Because she refused to think about why her little flat seemed like a gaping black hole this morning.

Bags of dried pasta and tins of tomato soup stared blankly at her from inside the cupboard. She shut the door carefully and tried the next one. Five boxes of breakfast cereal sat in a row, waiting for her to choose one of them. She closed that door too.

The kettle was within easy reach and she absent-mindedly flicked the switch. It roared into life, unnaturally loud in the pre-dawn stillness. She really must get around to de-scaling it some time soon. It boiled so violently when limescale had furred up the insides. The curse of London hard water…

Grace blinked. Just for a few seconds she'd forgotten to be miserable and lonely. That was good, wasn't it?

She reached for her favourite mug, the oversized baby-pink one with the words 'Hot Mama' spelled out in crimson glitter. A present from Daisy last Mother's Day. Daisy shared Grace's love of kitsch and had known her 'hot mama' would appreciate the sentiment of the slogan and the garish colours.

Daisy had given the mug to her with a twinkle in her eye that had made Grace chuckle, pleased to see proof that her daughter had inherited her sarcastic genes. But when the laughter had subsided, she'd mourned. No more pigtails and scraped knees. Daisy was all grown up and ready to fly the nest.

In fact, she'd already flown.

It was Mother's Day again in a couple of weeks and, for the first time ever, she wouldn't spend it doing something totally fabulous with Daisy. Last year they'd gone to the ice rink and had spent the whole afternoon falling on their bottoms. Then they'd eaten a Chinese takeaway so huge it had gone down in family history as 'the one that could never be surpassed'. But this year Daisy would be in Paris or Romania or Prague. She was going to be away for a whole year. And after backpacking there was university…

Grace hugged the mug to her chest. She missed her daughter already and she'd only been gone eighteen hours. How completely pathetic.

She dropped the mug to the counter with a clunk and stood there, her arms folded and her brows pinched together. Come on, Grace! You're supposed to be the cool one, remember? The mum that all Daisy's friends wished was theirs. The mum who had once worn fishnets and thigh-high boots to parents' evening. The mum who had dressed up as Santa, complete with beard and pot-belly, when little Joseph Stevenson's dad had been too hungover to play the role. The fact that it had been Grace's tequila that had caused the hangover in the first place was neither here nor there…

But Grace didn't feel cool. For the first time in nineteen years she felt old and lonely. And not just wandering-round-not-knowing-what-to-do lonely. There was an ache deep inside her that could only have been caused by someone sneaking into the flat in the middle of the night, carving a huge chunk off her soul and stealing it away. She had a funny feeling that chunk might currently be sleeping in a youth hostel in Montmartre, but she couldn't be entirely sure.

She made the tea and forced herself to turn the light under the cooker hood on. Sitting here in the dark would only give the impression that she was depressed, she thought as she slumped into a chair and lay her head on the table. Steam curled from the mug in front of her and she watched it rise gracefully on unseen currents and drift away. Eventually, she peeled her face from the table top and reached for the mug to take a sip.

Yuck! She stuck the tip of her tongue between her lips and grimaced. What the heck was wrong with her tea this morning? Looking into the mug gave her a pretty big clue. No teabag. Lukewarm water with milk in it was really not her thing.

Sighing, she hauled herself up from the table and crossed to the cupboard where the teabags lived. She reached inside and pulled out the Earl Grey. As she did so, a small pink envelope fell out of the cupboard and fluttered onto the floor.

Teabags forgotten, she bent to retrieve it and stood for a long moment looking at the familiar rounded scrawl that simply read 'Mum'. She smiled. Ever since she'd been able to write, Daisy had had a habit of making her cards and notes, leaving them in unexpected places. Over the years the inde-cipherable crayon drawings had been gradually replaced by scribbled messages in a neat, even hand, but the flush of joy

Grace felt at seeing each one had remained the same. She greedily tore open the envelope and began to read.

> *Dear Mum,*
> *Please, please, please don't be angry with me for this…*

Grace frowned. She knew it! Daisy had borrowed her favourite David Bowie T-shirt last week, and she'd warned her daughter not to get any thoughts about 'accidentally' packing it in her rucksack. Little rascal. A smile turned up one corner of her mouth and she carried on reading.

> *…but I've got you a little going-away present. I know how much you sacrificed to bring me up on your own, and now it's time for you to have some fun.*

Grace stopped reading. A burning sensation tickled her nose and the backs of her eyes. She took another sip of hot water, shuddered and pulled herself together.

No one could have asked for a better daughter. And, somehow, Grace felt that God had blessed her with Daisy to make up for Rob being snatched away from her after such a short time together. Killed by a landmine on active duty in Iraq at the age of twenty-three. Where was the justice in that? He hadn't even lived to see Daisy take her first steps or hear her say 'Dadda'.

Grace sucked in a breath, overcome by the sudden urge to cry, but she shook her head, refusing to give in. She had Daisy. She had to focus on Daisy. Because Daisy had been the reason the sun had kept rising and setting for the last eighteen years.

She looked round the kitchen. Although she knew it was stupid to think so, it was easy to imagine the sun just wouldn't bother to put in an appearance today.

Come on, Grace! Stop wallowing!

She looked again at the letter in her hands. Daisy didn't have to thank her for everything she'd done. It had been her job and her joy. Being a widow at twenty-two had been hard, yes, but every time she looked into those beautiful brown eyes she'd known a big piece of Rob had lived on.

But I know you, Mum. I know you'll talk about moving on or getting a hobby, or finally buying your own coffee shop so you can boss everyone else around instead of being bossed…I also know you'll do absolutely nothing about it. So I've taken the liberty of giving you a little nudge and I make no apologies for what I've done. You need this, Mum. Don't you dare try and wriggle out of it!

Grace's colourful language as she read the rest of the letter shattered the greyness of the pre-dawn kitchen once and for all.

'She did *what*?'

She stared in disbelief at the pink sheets clutched in her hands. 'You did *what*?' she yelled in the direction of Daisy's bedroom, even though her daughter had had the good sense to put a few hundred miles and a large body of water between them before she'd dropped the bombshell. Very good thinking. Because, right at this moment, Daisy would have been lucky to see another sunrise if she'd been within strangling distance.

Grace stared at the letter once again, then threw it down on the kitchen table. Despite what Daisy said, there had to be some way to get out of this.

Noah padded across the cream rug in his study, absent-mindedly rubbing his damp spiky hair with a towel. Even though he had already had his morning run it was still dark outside. And quiet. But he didn't mind quiet. This was his favourite time of day. The time where ideas could brew and grow and take shape.

He turned his computer on. While he'd been running he'd worked out how to make the villain of his current novel even more dastardly. His editor would be pleased. The latest in his series of psychological spy thrillers was doing so well, the publishers were pushing to have the next one in as soon as possible.

He carefully folded the towel and hung it over the back of a chair before sitting at his desk and checking his emails. His inbox rapidly filled but, instead of clicking on the top message, he took a little detour, clicking an email link and arriving at a web page he was very careful not to visit when his PA was around. He logged into the site and opened up a page he had marked as a 'favourite' last Monday.

Grace hit the switch in Daisy's room and blinked and squinted in the harsh yellow light. Maybe purple hadn't been the way to go with the colour scheme. It was giving her a headache.

Daisy's baby-pink laptop was on the desk and Grace picked it up and sat on the bed, one foot hooked underneath the other thigh, and settled the machine in the triangle of her legs. The ancient laptop chugged and whirred when she pressed the power button. While she waited for it to boot up, Grace inspected her fingernails and resisted the temptation to pick off some of the electric blue polish. Finally, she opened the web browser and typed in the address Daisy had printed carefully in the PS of her letter.

Blinddatebrides.com! What *had* her daughter been thinking? The thought of going on a date, blind or otherwise, was bad enough—but marriage? Been there, done that, worn the black veil…

A companionable coffee or dinner would be okay. She could probably live through that. While the page loaded, Grace's mind wandered. Blind-date brides? How did that work? You turned up at the restaurant and…what?

Random images stampeded through her mind—wedding

dresses made out of co-ordinating tablecloth linen…gold rings as napkin holders…waiters who were really undercover ministers, waiting to pounce at any hint of an 'I do'…

Goose pimples broke out on her legs and worked their way up her body until the fine hairs on her arms raised. She shook her head. Okay, Daisy had undeniably inherited her impulsive genes, but even she wouldn't subject her own mother to that kind of humiliation. Not unless she was present and in the possession of a video camera.

She winced as she typed in the username Daisy had invented to create an account. Frankly, it just added insult to injury. *Englishcrumpet?* Classy. Hadn't Daisy seen enough old *Carry On…* films to know that *crumpet* would attract all the wrong sorts of guys? The sort who always seemed slightly sweaty and tried to peer down your cleavage when they thought you weren't looking. Grace practically had to force her fingers to punch it out on the keyboard.

She logged on to the site and headed straight for the customer service section, bypassing minimalist cartoons of hearts, confetti and kissing stick figures. There had to be a number she could call and yell at someone about identity theft and being made to go on dates you really didn't want to go on. It all looked deceptively easy. She clicked on a friendly-looking button that said 'Contact us'.

Great. 'Customer service teams are available to help you from nine a.m. to six p.m., Monday to Friday,' she read aloud. 'What good is that at—' she checked the display on Daisy's alarm clock '—six twenty-five on a Saturday morning? Most normal people go on dates at the weekend! Fat lot of good you are!' she said to the smiley-face cartoon on the web page, obviously designed to calm and reassure distressed customers. All it made Grace want to do was frisbee the stupid laptop across the room.

Then she spotted another button: 'Email us'.

She stopped scowling and rubbed her finger across the mouse pad to click on the link. Email would work. Not as direct as yelling, but she could use lots of capitals instead. A new window popped up: 'Thank you for spending time letting us know how we can make Blinddatebrides.com better. A customer service representative will respond to your message within twenty-four hours…'

But the date was in less than fourteen hours! Grace was sorely tempted to revisit the whole 'frisbee' idea.

It was far too early in the day to start reading any kind of small print they might have stashed away in the deep recesses of this website. She needed help. Now. She dragged the mouse pointer to a sidebar button that read: 'Chatrooms,' spied a chat headed up 'New to Blinddatebrides.com' and typed, *'HELP!'* Might as well not beat about the bush.

For an instant, her little plea for salvation blinked alone on the page. It was six-thirty in the morning, for goodness' sake! Who in their right mind was going to be trawling for dates at this time of day? Only the utterly desperate—which summed her up quite nicely at the moment, actually.

Then a miracle happened.

Sanfrandani: What's up?

Grace looked around the room. Was this person talking— erm, typing—to her? There was only one thing for it. Grace flexed her fingers and began to type.

Englishcrumpet: I'm new to this.
Kangagirl: Hi, Englishcrumpet! Don't worry, we're all new in this chatroom! How can we help?
Englishcrumpet: Oh! There's two of you! Are you up at the crack of dawn panicking about a date too?

Sanfrandani: LOL! It's almost my bedtime! The 'Sanfran' in Sanfrandani stands for San Francisco.
Kangagirl: And I'm just about to head home from work here in Sydney.
Englishcrumpet: Australia?!
Kangagirl: That's right! Didn't you know this was a global site when you signed up?
Englishcrumpet: I didn't know anything about this site until fifteen minutes ago! That's the problem. Someone else joined on my behalf.
Sanfrandani: How are you finding the site so far?
Englishcrumpet: Well, I found two kind souls willing to help a sister in need, so it can't be all bad.

Grace scratched the tip of her chin with a fingernail. She'd jumped to one conclusion already. Might as well make sure she had her facts straight before she carried on.

Englishcrumpet: You are a girl, right, Sanfrandani?
Sanfrandani: Yes! Believe me, if you saw me, you'd know I was a girl.

In through the nose, out through the mouth…Grace took a deep breath and dived right in.

Englishcrumpet: I just found out I have a date with someone from this site tonight!
Kangagirl: Good on you, girl!
Englishcrumpet: But I don't want to go on a date! I want to know how to get out of it!
Sanfrandani: Do you have his email address?
Englishcrumpet: No.
Kangagirl: What about his username? Then you could contact him through his profile page.

Englishcrumpet: I don't know that either!
Sanfrandani: Okay, Crumpet, what do *you know?*

Grace didn't need the pink page from Daisy's letter to relay the next bit of information. Every time she closed her eyes, the words floated in front of her face. She dropped her lids right then and—hey presto!

Englishcrumpet: The note says: Barruci's, Vinehurst High Street. 8 o'clock.
Kangagirl: Nice place?
Englishcrumpet: Erm…I think so. A bit out of my league. I tend to prefer the Hong Kong Garden takeaway if I'm spoiling myself.
Kangagirl: LOL!
Sanfrandani: Why don't you want to go on a date with this guy? The matching system at this site is supposed to be really good. He might just be your type.
Englishcrumpet: Have your dates been perfect matches so far?
Kangagirl: Not bad. On paper they should have been perfect, but just no…you know…
Sanfrandani: So why not go?

Grace's shoulders sagged. There were a million and five reasons why she should stay in, watch bad Saturday night TV and treat herself to a takeaway—especially now she'd mentioned it and was craving roast pork chow mein. What she wouldn't do for a leftover tub of it cold from the fridge right now.

She wasn't going to go. No matter how perfect *on paper* her mystery date might be. It had been years since she'd been on a first date. Of course, after Rob had died, she hadn't even been able to conceive loving anyone else for quite a few years—and she'd had Daisy to bring up. Looking after a toddler on your own was pretty time-consuming.

And later, when she'd thought about dating again…well, a widow just had too much baggage for men her age. It had been a relief when she'd decided to give up trying. None of them had even started to measure up to Rob, anyway. Love like that only happened once in a lifetime.

There was an insistent ping from the laptop.

Kangagirl: Crumpet? Are you still there?
Englishcrumpet: Yes. I'm here.
Sanfrandani: So why not give this guy a try? You can come back tomorrow and share all the gossip with us!
Englishcrumpet: I don't really want to go out with anyone at the moment. I'm a widow.

There was a pause for a few seconds. The usual reaction. People didn't know how to handle it when she told them. Grace sat back, propping herself against the pillows, and waited for the inevitable hasty retreat. These girls would politely excuse themselves and find someone more fun to chat with.

Kangagirl: I'm so sorry, Crumpet. Hugs.
Sanfrandani: Me too. Even if you don't go on the date, come back tomorrow and chat, okay? It's going to take time.

Okay. Now she felt like a real heel. These were perfectly nice women and she was making it sound as if it was all recent history. Had she really been alone that long? She looked round the purple room. Last time she'd been on a first date, there had been teddies on the bed and pony posters on the walls. Now there were shaggy cushions and one of the walls was covered in wallpaper that boasted stylised purple flowers on a silver background.

Englishcrumpet: Actually, my husband died quite some time ago. But what I said is true. I don't really want to go on a date, but I can't leave the poor man sitting there on his own—that would be too cruel. Oh, I'm going to kill my daughter for this when she returns from backpacking!

Kangagirl: Your daughter set you up?!

Sanfrandani: LOL! What's her taste in men like?

Englishcrumpet: Her taste in men is fine—for a nineteen-year-old. I'm just not sure what sort of man she'd choose for her mother!

Kangagirl: I think you should go. He could be cute!

Sanfrandani: What's the worst that could happen? You have a nice meal, chat a little. In a couple of hours it'll all be over and you never have to see him again if you don't want to. At least you'd have got back out there. Next time you could pick someone for yourself. Think about it.

Grace slid the laptop off her legs and left it on the duvet. Her right foot was all tingly from having been sat on for so long and she gave it a shake and stood up to get the blood moving again. Daisy's dressing table stood a few feet away and she walked over to skim her fingertips over the curled edges of one of the photographs tucked into the rim of the mirror.

Daisy smiled back at her, her long dark hair ruffled by the wind, her eyes bright with mischief and easy confidence. Her gaze left the photograph and wandered until she met her own eyes in the mirror and she started. People said that she and Daisy looked more like sisters, rather than mother and daughter, but Grace could always see so much of Rob in her daughter. Just for a moment she was stunned by the similarity between her own reflection and the photograph. Apart from the eye colour, it was as if she were looking at herself in a time warp.

Yes, there were fine lines and wrinkles round her eyes now, and her once slender build had more curves, but she still looked closer to thirty than forty. What a pity that inside her head she was closer to being twenty-one. Being Daisy's buddy had kept her thinking and feeling like that.

What would happen now Daisy was gone—only due to pop in and out of her life in between travels and university courses? Would she turn grey overnight? And it wasn't just her hair she was worried about. She could imagine her skin taking on a dull grey pallor, her eyes becoming glassy. Would she wake up one day and discover an overwhelming urge to wear baggy home-knitted cardigans?

Come on, Grace! Snap out of it.

She twisted to check out her rear end and fluffed her hair with her fingers. She smiled. Even through the striped cotton of her pyjama bottoms, she could tell her derrière could stop traffic in the right pair of jeans. She was way too young to hide it beneath baggy cardigans. She did a little wiggle, just to prove herself right. Her reflection enjoyed the joke and laughed along with her.

See? She was still the same old game-for-anything Grace.

She picked the photograph of Daisy out of the mirror frame and studied it closely. One corner of her mouth lifted. That child was a chip off the old block, no doubt about it. This stunt with the dating agency was just the sort of crazy thing she would have pulled at nineteen. Why was she getting in such a lather about one silly date?

You never have to see him again if you don't want to.

It was time she saw a little more sparkle in her own baby-blues.

She jumped back onto the bed, grabbed the laptop and typed in a frenzy, before she could change her mind.

Englishcrumpet: Okay, girls. I'll do it. I'm going on the date.

After making a quick character sketch for his Ukrainian villain and jotting down some related plot ideas, Noah checked his emails again. He'd better get a move on, though. His PA would be here in twenty minutes and he really ought to finish getting dressed.

Yes, it was Saturday, but he had a big crime writers' conference coming up soon in New York and they needed to go through the final travel arrangements and double-check that the notes for his seminar were all ready to go. Last job would be to proofread his keynote speech for the opening luncheon.

He shook his head, hardly able to believe that this was how his life had turned out.

It seemed he was always travelling, always speaking here and there. Everybody wanted to know what the secret of his success was, as if there were some ingredient other than a modicum of talent and pure hard graft. Living the life of a best-selling author had its great points, but there was a downside he hadn't expected. For a start, he spent far too much time on publicity and promotion and struggled to find time to scribble more than a few words some days. Just as well his army background had taught him discipline and how to be cool under pressure.

And then there were the women.

His friend Harry thought he was crackers to complain about the women, moaning that he'd settle for just one per cent of the female attention Noah seemed to generate.

Oh, Noah had certainly enjoyed glamorous women making a beeline for him in the early days, when his books had first reached the top of the charts. The women had laughed and smiled and hung on his every word, marvelling at how clever and handsome he was and how he was just like a hero in one of his own novels. But after five years it was definitely getting a little tired. He was starting to feel like that guy in the movie who woke up and discovered the previous day was repeating itself. Only, in Noah's case, it seemed to be the previous cocktail party repeating itself.

Okay, the colour of the skimpy dresses and the hair extensions changed. But that was as far as it went. He'd even stopped being surprised how so many stick-thin women professed to love martial arts or were totally fascinated by the cold war. One woman had even spent an hour telling him in great detail exactly how she could strip down an AK47, a hungry glint in her eyes the whole time.

After all his experiences, he could really write a convincing portrait of a glamour vixen who'd do anything to bag herself a rich and successful husband so she could bask in his glory and ride the celebrity merry-go-round for ever. Maybe he'd put such a character in his next book. And maybe he'd have the merry-go-round explode…

Compatibility started with sharing some interests, but it had to go deeper than that, surely. And it had to be a genuine interest, not facts and figures cribbed up on before a date. That was why his new pet project had come in handy. He'd read an article about this website in a Sunday magazine and had been intrigued with the possibility of being able to remain almost anonymous.

He flipped back onto the web page he'd minimised earlier. Blinddatebrides.com.

If Martine, his PA, knew he'd been surfing on such a site, she'd have fainted.

But what was so surprising about him wanting to find a wife? He was of marriageable age, financially very secure and he had a huge house all to himself. It was just crying out for a wife. And he was fed up going everywhere on his own, being the odd one out at friends' parties, always having to duck into the bathroom to avoid the glamour vixens at the writing 'do's'. Securing a wife would have the added bonus of being the ultimate deterrent.

He wasn't asking for the moon. At forty-one, he was old enough not to fall for all that love-at-first-sight, finding-your-soulmate nonsense. He didn't believe that his soul had another half floating around somewhere, desperately looking to re-attach itself. That sounded like a gruesome scene from one of his novels rather than romantic, anyway.

What he needed was a partner in life. Writing could be a lonely business. He spent days on end on his own, not speaking to anyone, travelling alone. It would be nice to have someone other than a part-time PA in the house. Someone to share a meal and glass of wine with at the end of the day. Someone to bounce ideas off or moan to about the latest deadline. And, if there was a little chemistry there, so much the better.

He'd been on three dates with Blinddatebrides.com so far and all had been unmitigated disasters. The women had been nice in their own way, he supposed, just not suitable at all. He was on the verge of downgrading his expectations in the short-term and just looking for a date-buddy, someone who wouldn't mind attending functions with him to keep the vixens at bay. Even the stupid computer at Blinddatebrides.com—or the trained hamsters, or whatever they used to match people up—should be able to cope with something as simple as that.

Although the match suggestions from Blinddatebrides.com had seemed fine when he'd checked out the profiles, when he'd met the women in person…well, that was where it had all gone wrong.

Hopefully, tonight's choice would buck the trend. He leaned forward to focus on the pixelated little picture on her profile. Local businesswoman. Age forty. And the picture was intriguing. Dark glossy hair. Stunning blue eyes and the smallest of smiles that hinted at both intelligence and mischief. Not his usual sort, but he'd kept coming back to this profile even after he'd discounted it. And if there was one thing he'd learned from all these years accessing his creative right brain, it was that sometimes you had to ignore the facts and go with your gut.

'Coo-ee!' Martine's voice echoed round his empty kitchen. She'd obviously just let herself in. He reached for the mouse and had just closed the window as she walked through the study door.

'What was that?' she said, eyes fixed on the monitor.

He'd hired her for her razor-sharp instincts, but sometimes he wished he owned a remote control so he could switch them off.

'Nothing for you to poke your nose about in,' he said with a grin and handed her a stack of travel documents.

CHAPTER TWO

THE girl standing behind the reservations desk glanced up at him. It was the same girl as last week. He remembered the neat little bun she wore at the nape of her neck and how he'd wondered if it hurt to scrape one's hair into something that tight. Just like last week, she didn't seem to be in a particularly good mood. A raised eyebrow was all the welcome he got. Good. His attempt at going incognito was working.

'Smith,' he said, returning her look. 'Table for two. Eight o'clock.'

She blinked, then deigned to check the reservations book. 'This way, sir.'

She took off at a brisk pace.

'Has my…dinner companion…arrived yet?'

The girl didn't even turn to answer. The little bun wobbled back and forth as she shook her head. If Barruci's didn't have the finest wine list in this corner of London, he'd have boycotted the place weeks ago. But it was the best little restaurant in the suburb of Vinehurst, right on the fringes of London's urban sprawl. A few minutes' drive to the south and it was all countryside. Vinehurst had probably once been an idyllic little village, with its narrow cobbled high street, a Norman church and an old-fashioned cricket pitch that was still used every Sunday. Somehow, during the last century, as

London had spread, it hadn't swallowed up Vinehurst, as it had similar hamlets and towns. There was a distinct absence of grey concrete and high-rise buildings, as if the city had just flowed round the village, leaving a little bubble of rural charm behind. It was a great place for a first date.

At eight o'clock on the dot, a woman walked into the restaurant.

It was her.

The dark wavy hair was coiled behind her head somehow and she wore a neat black coat, fitted at the waist. Even though he was too far away to tell if her eyes were really the same colour as her profile photograph, they drew his attention—bright and alert, scanning the room beneath quirkily arched brows. He watched as her gaze flitted from one table to the next, pausing for a split-second on the men, then moving on when she saw they weren't alone.

Noah put down the menu he'd been perusing and sat up straighter, giving no indication that his heart was beating just a little bit faster. Could the hamsters at Blinddatebrides.com finally have got it right?

Finally, the woman leaned over and whispered something to a waitress. The girl nodded and waited as the woman stopped to remove her coat. There was a collective pause as every man in the place held his breath for a heartbeat, then pretended to resume conversation with their friends, wives or girlfriends. In reality, they were tracking the woman's progress across the room. Even the ones who were far too young for her.

Under the respectable coat was a stunning dress. The same shade and sheen as a peacock's body. The scoop neck wasn't even close to being indecent, but somehow it didn't need to be. It teased very nicely while it sat there, revealing not even a hint of cleavage. The hem was short and the legs, the legs…

Well, the legs hadn't been visible in the Blinddatebrides.com photo, but they were very nice indeed. Too nice, maybe. Maybe she was a vixen incognito. He loosened his tie slightly and tried to smile as she followed the waitress through the maze of tables, leaving a trail of wistful male eyes in her wake. The smile felt forced and he abandoned it. He didn't do small talk; he did conversation. And he didn't do overly effusive greetings these days, even in the presence of such fine legs.

When the waitress pulled out the chair opposite him for her, he stood and offered his hand. 'Noah…Smith.' A necessary diversion from the truth if he was to gauge if his dates really liked him for his personality rather than his bank balance. Sometimes he wished he'd had enough sense to use a pen name, but the lure of seeing 'Noah Frost' stamped in square letters across the front of a book jacket had been too great after all the years of rejections.

'Hello,' she said, shaking his hand, then quickly pulling hers away again. 'You've got really nice teeth.'

He opened his mouth to say, *All the better to eat you with,* but managed to stop himself. Instead, he just kept quiet and motioned for her to sit down. He did the same.

'Nice teeth?' he said, smiling again. 'Do you want to check my hooves to see if I'm good stock too?'

She blushed ever so slightly and the mischievous little smile from the profile photograph made an appearance.

'Grace Marlowe—blind-date virgin…' She clapped a hand over her mouth. It looked as if she were trying to wipe a cheeky smile away as she dragged her hand over her lips and let it fall. It didn't work. The grin popped back into place as if nothing had happened.

'That came out all wrong. What I meant was…this will be my first time.'

She closed her eyes and bit her lip. Without opening her lids, she kept speaking. 'I'm making it worse, aren't I— digging myself an even deeper hole?'

Noah stared at her. This wasn't how the other dates had

started. Where was the murmured conversation, the polite questioning as to jobs and musical tastes?

'It's only because I'm more of a blind-date veteran that I'm not in there with a matching shovel.'

She opened one eye. 'You're nice, Mr Smith. And chivalrous to a lady in distress.' The other eye popped open and she tipped her head to one side. 'How come you've had so many first dates if you're such a nice guy? What's wrong with you?'

Now it was his turn to laugh. His male pride really ought to be dented. None of his other dates had been so blunt. But none of his other dates had been quite so interesting.

'This is only the fourth date I've been on.'

'In how long?'

He shrugged. 'A month?'

'That's a lot of ladies who passed you by, Noah. Tell me why I shouldn't follow the crowd.'

Despite the fact that he was known for his cool, unruffled demeanour, he found himself laughing again.

'I've got nice teeth?'

'There is that,' she said, her eyes twinkling. And they really were that blue. She looked at the tablecloth and scratched at a catch in the linen. 'Sorry about the teeth thing. I was a little nervous, and when I'm nervous I tend to say the first thing that pops into my head.'

Although it seemed to get her into trouble, he found it quite endearing. And refreshing. The more successful he'd become, the more people second-guessed their every word around him. Getting an honest reaction—rather than one that had been carefully edited before it left a person's mouth—was a wonderful novelty.

'Shall we order?'

She breathed out a sigh, making a little round shape with her mouth. 'That would be lovely.'

He opened the large, unwieldy menu and scanned it, even

though he was pretty sure he was going to start with the carpaccio of beef and follow it with the scallops.

'We can discuss my many faults over the appetisers,' he said, completely deadpan.

The bright eyes appeared above the menu, laughing at him. Noah smiled to himself and paid careful attention. You could tell a lot about a person from what food they ordered. She chose the beef too. Another good sign.

No. Not a sign—he didn't believe in signs. Just an indicator of compatibility.

She let him choose the wine and, by the time he'd narrowed the choices down to match their courses, their appetisers had arrived.

'So, what do you do, Grace?'

She looked up from her salad—not by raising her head, but by looking at him through her lashes. A flicker of emotion passed across her face and she popped a piece of avocado in her mouth. Didn't she want to tell him what she did for a living? It couldn't be as bad as last Saturday's date. A pet psychologist, for goodness' sake!

When Grace finished chewing, she mumbled, 'I'm a barrister.'

Not quite what he'd expected. He wondered if she'd be too tied down to her job to think about travelling with him. That might be a deal-breaker.

'How about you? What do you do for a living?'

He opened his mouth and closed it again. Time to learn from past mistakes. The moment he mentioned thrillers and novel-writing, the game was normally up. Noah wasn't a particularly common name and people tended to guess the connection, even if he used his totally imaginative Noah Smith alias. And he didn't want Grace to go all giggly and stupid like some women did.

'You do have a job at the moment, don't you?' Grace said.

'Of course I do. I'm a writer.'

To his relief, Grace looked pleasantly unimpressed. 'What kind of writer?'

He shrugged. 'I write about military stuff. Quite boring, actually.' Another little detour.

Grace dabbed her mouth with her napkin. 'Are you pulling my leg?'

Rats. She could tell he was fudging the issue. Just as well he hadn't decided to be an actor instead of a novelist. At least his characters were convincing, even if he wasn't.

'No,' he said with his best poker face.

Grace looked at him long and hard. Had she guessed his secret? If she had, she wasn't smiling and going all gooey, which was unusual.

'So, tell me about your other dates,' she said, her eyes never leaving his face. 'What went wrong?'

'Nothing.' He took a deep breath and let his face relax out of his smile. 'But it's a serious business, finding a wife. I'm not going to trot off down the aisle with just anyone.'

She put her knife and fork down and stared at her salad for a few seconds. 'You're really looking for a wife on an Internet dating site?'

Why did his dates seem to find that so hard to believe? After all, the site in question was Blinddatebrides.com. It kind of gave the game away.

'Aren't you looking for a husband?'

Grace shook her head hard to loosen her hairdo a little.

'What are you looking for, then? Love? A soulmate?'

She dropped her chin and gave him an *Are you serious?* look from under her lashes.

Good. She didn't believe in those things either.

'I'm glad we're on the same wavelength,' he said before taking a sip of wine.

Grace pursed her lips. 'It's not that I don't believe in those things. Just that I'm not expecting to find them at Blinddatebrides.com. Nor do I want to. I mean, the whole Romeo and Juliet, all-consuming passion thing really only works for teenagers, don't you think?'

He raised his eyebrows in what he hoped was a non-committal way. He wasn't sure what this 'in love' thing was. Oh, he'd thought he'd found it once, but it had turned out to be a case of mistaken identity. What people sang about in love songs or wept over at the cinema wasn't real. It was all an illusion—one he bought into about as much as he had the chick with the AK47.

His parents didn't do all that hearts and flowers nonsense and they had been perfectly happy for almost fifty years. If it could work for them, it could work for him.

The evening passed quickly. Too quickly.

As Noah dug into his dessert, he decided he'd seen enough of Grace to know she wasn't what Harry termed a 'WAG wannabe' in disguise—definitely not a gold-digger! There was a recital at one of the local arts centres next week that he'd planned on going to, and he was going to ask Grace if she'd like to go with him.

He cleared his throat. 'Grace?'

She looked up at him, a chocolate-dipped spoon half in her mouth. Slowly, and while Noah's mouth began to water, she pulled it out, sucking the last of the rich brown mousse off.

'Do you want some?' she asked, eyebrows raised, mouth slightly smudged with chocolate. Noah meant to shake his head, but it didn't seem to want to move.

'Uh-huh,' he heard himself say.

'It is rather divine,' she said, her eyes doing her trademark sparkle.

'Uh-huh.'

Great. He'd won awards for his command of the English language and all he could do at present was grunt like a caveman. He watched as she carefully dipped the long spoon into her dessert and pulled out a bulging dollop of creamy chocolate mousse.

As she fed him the mousse, she unconsciously licked her lips. Noah felt a kick of desire so hard it almost rocked him out of his chair. His voice was horribly hoarse when he opened his mouth to speak. 'Grace…?'

'Yes.'

'Um…' Just like that, his brain emptied. Words circled round, but the ability to string them into coherent sentences had just vanished. He grabbed at a few of the nearest phrases in desperation. 'Concerts!' he blurted. 'Do you like live music?'

Grace's face lit up. 'I *love* live music!'

It was only as his heart rate started to slow, pounding heavily in his temples, that he realised it had been racing for the last couple of minutes. He swallowed, which really wasn't a good idea, because he tasted the chocolate mousse again and his pulse did a U-turn.

'In fact, I was only at a concert a few days ago,' Grace said, before turning her attention back to her dessert.

'Really?'

She nodded and swallowed. 'I saw this great band up in London recently—The Hover Cats—have you heard of them?'

He shook his head.

'I don't expect many of your colleagues share your passion, do they?'

She looked puzzled. 'Why not? I know jazz and easy listening are popular in cafés, but that's not all we listen to. Aren't you being just a little bit narrow-minded?'

For the second time that evening, Noah felt as if he were under interrogation. 'But I thought you said you were a—'

'A barista,' she said, folding her arms. 'I work in The Coffee Bean further up the High Street.'

If she'd jumped up on the table and started doing the can-

can, Noah couldn't have been more shocked. She had such
potential. And all at once he was intrigued, as he often was
when he met someone who defied his expectations. What had
led her to make those choices? Grace had the personality and
energy to do anything she wanted. His brain whirred off, analysing her as if she were a character in a book.

She'd been sitting in silence as he'd absorbed the information, but now she flicked a glance at the door and started
talking very fast. 'Talking of coffee, I don't really feel like
having one—busman's holiday and all that. Do you mind if
we call it a night?'

She reached for her handbag and started to push back her
seat. For the first time all evening, the confidence, the pizzazz
drained away. She glanced at him for a mere moment as she
smoothed down her skirt and he saw a look of both hardness
and vulnerability on her face.

'Grace, I'm sorry. In no way do I—' He reached for her
hand. 'Don't go.'

She shook her head. 'You know what, Noah. This really
isn't going to work out. I think I should just leave.' And, with
that, she nimbly eased herself out of her chair and headed for
the coat rack.

Known for his command of the English language? Hah.

Well, if Grace was leaving, so was he. He pulled his wallet
out of his pocket, left more than enough twenty pound notes
on the table to cover the bill and darted after her.

Grace didn't even remember putting her coat on. It was only
as the chilly night air hit her face that her brain whirred into
action. Without making a conscious decision, she turned right
and hurried down Vinehurst High Street as fast as the stupid
high heels she'd stolen out the bottom of Daisy's wardrobe
would let her.

'Grace!'

She bit the tip of her tongue between her teeth, shook her head and just kept walking. Every time she told people what she did for a living she got the same reaction, the same look. The one that said, why wasn't she busy saving lives on the operating table or running a million-pound Internet business she'd started in her front room like other women of her generation?

Because she hadn't been prepared to sacrifice time with Daisy to build a career, that was why. Daisy had already lost one parent and she didn't need the other to become a dim and distant memory while childminders did all the hands-on stuff. So Grace had taken a job that let her fit her hours round the school day and didn't require evening shifts.

The owner of the coffee shop was Aunt Caroline—or Caz, as she liked to be called. She was really Rob's aunt, but had welcomed Grace into the family with open arms and had been a lifesaver when he'd died, taking Grace under her wing and letting her rent the upstairs flat. Grace's parents had moved to the West Country when she'd got married and there had been no one close by to turn to. Her parents had begged her to move in with them, but she'd refused—too young, foolish and independent at the time to realise what a gift it might have been. But Rob was buried in the churchyard here and she hadn't been able to wrench herself away, leave him behind.

She became aware of someone following her and picked up speed. She shouldn't be made to feel ashamed of her job. She made the best pastries in the area. And, even if she hadn't, she didn't want to apologise for her work.

She could hear heavy, pounding footsteps behind her now. Just for a while, she'd thought she'd been having a decent conversation with someone who didn't assume she had an IQ of twenty because she baked and served coffee for a living. And he'd been nice to her…But only because he'd misheard her and thought she was something she wasn't.

'Grace!'

He was right behind her now. She stopped and turned round, hardening herself, putting on that sassy front she used with difficult customers at The Coffee Bean. 'Mr Smith.'

'Grace, you got me all wrong! I don't care if you work in a coffee shop or a lawyer's office. I don't want the night to end this way, do you?'

No, she didn't. Adult company, a little bit of sophistication, had been nice. And she'd thought Noah had been gorgeous too, right up until the end. But he'd come after her. That was quite nice. To be exact, he'd run after her. And they had been having fun.

She started walking again. 'What if I worked as a litter picker? Would you still have come after me?'

His features shifted and changed. When they'd been sitting down in the restaurant, she hadn't noticed how tall he was. Now, she had to tilt her head up to get a look in his eyes.

They were the most beautiful colour. Green. Not the emerald-green of story books, but a cool, glassy green that verged on grey. Even so, their paleness didn't detract from their intensity. When he looked at her she felt as if she had one hundred per cent of his attention, as if she were the only thing in his field of focus. But now they didn't seem focused, they seemed puzzled.

'Of course, I'd have come after you. I came out for a nice dinner and ended up chewing my own size twelve shoes. I needed to apologise.'

He wasn't taking the bait, playing her little game, but his honesty won her over. She didn't have time for slimy men who oozed the right things. She'd settle for Noah Smith and his no-nonsense words—even if they were occasionally muffled by his shoe leather. Had he really said size *twelves*…?

He fell into step beside her. 'So, are we okay? Do you want to go somewhere for coff—a drink?'

She smiled. 'How about if I was a sewage worker? Would you want to have a drink with me then?'

There was a tiny break in the rhythm of his steps. 'Only if I was allowed to wear a peg on my nose.'

Her tense jaw muscles relaxed and a smile she'd been anchoring down sprung up. Finally, he'd joined her game. She grabbed his hand and speeded up. 'Come on. I know the perfect place.'

Noah had no choice but to follow Grace as her shoes measured out rapid little steps. Even in heels, she only just reached past his shoulders and he didn't have to do more than stroll to keep up.

The sky glowed a murky pink, reflecting the street lamps of a vast city. Typical for a spring night in England, an icy splosh of rain hit the top of his head, not even deflected by his hair. If he and Grace didn't hurry up, they were about to get soaked. Just as he opened his mouth to ask where they were going, she dragged him into a doorway.

Out of the wind whistling down the High Street, the air was surprisingly close. Grace was only inches away, smiling up at him cheekily. He took a deep breath. It didn't matter that the rain was now falling out of the sky and his right arm, out of the cover of the small doorway, was getting wet. All that mattered was the slight shine cast on her lips by the street lamp on the other side of the road. He couldn't stop looking at them. The smile faded from her face and she regarded him with wide eyes.

The sound of the rain slapping against the pavement seemed to grow and intensify until it filled his ears. He knew he was about to lean forward and kiss her. Not that he'd made a decision; somehow he just knew. And there was nothing he could do to stop himself.

Just as his muscles prepared themselves for movement, he

heard a jangle of keys and suddenly Grace was gone. He looked in confusion at the open door and listened to her heels track their way across the darkened shop. Attempting to follow was a bad idea, he discovered, sending a chair flying and leaving himself with a throbbing shin.

'Hang on a moment,' Grace said from somewhere in the darkness.

A few seconds later a light went on above a counter on the other side of the room. As his eyes adjusted to the blackness, a thunderclap rumbled a few miles away. Grace skirted round the tables and closed the door. She didn't say anything as she moved past him; it was only as she was walking away back to the counter that she spoke.

'This place serves the best coffee in the whole of South East London.'

Now he noticed his surroundings. The place almost resembled an auction room with its assorted wooden tables and chairs—no two matching. Large velvet-covered sofas occupied one corner and big canvases of abstract art and pictures of coffee beans hung on the walls.

'The best?'

Now Grace was more than ten feet away and standing behind the safety of a counter she seemed to have regained her usual chatty manner. 'Absolutely. And I know that because I make it. What will you have?'

'Espresso,' he said without thinking. 'Double.'

'Coming right up. Make yourself at home.' He moved towards one of the low armchairs near the counter and sat down as Grace began banging things and turning knobs. A minute or so later she joined him with two cups of steaming espresso. The smell of freshly ground coffee filled the air like a fog. They sat and sipped their drinks in silence.

Grace hadn't switched any extra lights on and they were sitting on the fringes of the yellow glow from the counter.

Even in this artificial twilight she seemed brighter and bolder and more alive than just about anyone he knew.

'So, Noah…How does a guy like you end up listed on an Internet dating site? If you don't mind me saying, I wouldn't have thought it was…you know…your thing, or that you needed help in that department.'

Noah considered what she'd said for a moment, then smiled.

'I decided that meeting people via the Internet was as good a way as any. It's all down to chance, really. You meet someone in a bar, or at work, or wherever…Why not the Internet? Joining a site with a matching service should help take some of the guesswork out of it.'

Grace rolled her eyes. 'You make it all sound so romantic!'

Romance. What was that, anyway? He, like most men, had thought it meant flowers and chocolates and candlelit dinners. That much he could manage. In the five years he'd been with Sara, the one woman he'd thought of marrying without the help of a dating site, she'd tried to explain that romance was more about connecting with someone on a deeper level, about seeing into someone's soul. He'd nodded and looked thoughtful and, although he'd tried hard to understand, he'd had the funny feeling he'd missed the point. Even though he'd *connected* to the best of his abilities she'd still walked away, telling him it wasn't enough. The truly tragic thing was that he honestly didn't know what he could have done differently.

Noah stared out of the plate glass window at the front of the shop. It was raining hard now, fat drops bouncing off the road and swirling down the gutters. That kind of romance was the last place to start if you wanted a successful relationship.

When he looked back at Grace that cheeky eyebrow rose again. How could she say so much with one small twitch of a muscle?

'Don't you believe in fate, in destiny?' she asked.

Noah didn't even have to stop and think about that one. 'No.'

'So it's all just down to random events and chemical reactions, then?'

'Well, partly…at least, I think that's what sexual attraction boils down to, but we're not just talking about that. Choosing someone to spend your life with is about more than chemistry, surely? Why? Do you believe in fate?'

Grace put her cup down and looked at the ceiling. 'I don't know…It's comforting to think that love isn't just some random genetic thing. Where's the magic in that?'

Uh-oh. If she was looking for magic, she was barking up the wrong tree. He didn't do magic any more than he did romance. Loyalty, honesty, sheer bloody-mindedness—he had those things in spades, but there wasn't any fairy dust involved. It was just the way he was made. Time to get things back on firmer ground. Time to return to facts and figures and things a man could quantify.

'Why did you join Blinddatebrides.com?'

Grace looked at the ceiling and shook her head. 'Actually, I'd never heard of the site before this morning. Someone else joined on my behalf and I'm going to kill her when I get my hands…' She bit her lip and grimaced. 'Sorry. That didn't sound the way I meant it to. I didn't want to imply that I regret meeting you.'

'Of course you didn't.'

He liked the way she didn't filter her words.

'Maybe I'll let her off with dunking her in the old horse trough on the common…Now that I've discovered having a blind date isn't quite as horrendous as I anticipated.'

The corner of his mouth twitched. 'I'm flattered. Me having such fine teeth, and all. You will tell your friend about the teeth, won't you?'

Grace put down her coffee cup. 'Oh, it wasn't a friend who set me up. It was my daughter.'

His stomach plummeted just that little bit further. He hadn't even considered that Grace might have children. She just looked too…And he was useless with kids. His friends' kids only tolerated him when he visited because, on occasion, he could be coaxed into letting them ride on his shoulders. Any attempts at communication just fell flat. They would stare at him with their mouths open as if he were an alien life form. No, Noah and kids just didn't mix.

'You have a daughter?' he asked, consciously trying to keep his tone light.

She nodded. 'Daisy. Nineteen—the age when she thinks Mama doesn't know best any more and is doing her best to organise my life to her liking.'

See? Nineteen was better. He might be able to manage children—well, young adults—at that age.

'So, you're divorced?'

She shook her head. 'Widowed.' Her hand flew up. 'Don't give me the look!'

He blinked. What look?

'It was a long time ago. I was barely more than a teenager when I got married and not much older when I found myself on my own again.' She gave him a fierce look, one that dared him to feel sorry for her.

'How did he die?'

Grace went very quiet. Was he tasting his own shoe polish again?

'Thank you for asking. Most people just…you know… change the subject.' She tipped her chin up and looked straight at him. 'Rob was a soldier. He was killed in the first Gulf War.'

Noah nodded. 'I served in Iraq myself.'

She pressed her lips together and gave him a watery smile. He didn't have the words to describe what happened next; he just felt a bolt of recognition joining them together in silent understanding. So many friends hadn't made it home. And he'd seen so many wives fall apart. But here was Grace, not letting the world defeat her. She'd worked hard to bring her daughter up on her own. It couldn't have been easy. And he'd bet she was a really good mother, one who had strived to be both mother and father to her daughter. If only every child were so lucky. He almost felt jealous of the absent Daisy.

This was getting far too emotional for him, pulling on loose threads of things he'd firmly locked away in his subconscious. Grace wasn't looking for the same kind of relationship he was. She didn't want to get married and, if she did, she wanted magic. His instincts told him it was time to retreat and let them both breathe out.

'Well, Grace…' He swallowed the last of his espresso and stood up. 'I think I'd better be going.' He shrugged. 'Can I call you a cab or give you a lift somewhere?'

She shook her head. 'No need. I am home. I live in the flat upstairs.'

Well, he hadn't been expecting that. It kind of left him with nowhere to go.

'It's been nice…'

A small smile curved her lips. 'Yes it has.'

The words *See you again some time?* were ready on the tip of his tongue. He swallowed them. But once they were gone he had nothing else to say, so he walked to the door, aware of her following close behind him. When they reached it, she flicked a couple of catches and turned the handle, oddly silent.

Before he crossed the threshold into the damp night he turned to look at her. 'It was lovely to meet you, Grace.'

'So you already said.'

He took a step backwards beyond the shelter of the doorway and the rain hit him in multiple wet stabs. He shuddered. For an instant, rational thought hadn't come into it—

he was only aware of his body's physical response to the drop in temperature, the cold water running down his skin.

Grace stood in the doorway, in front of one of the angled panes of glass, her eyes large and round. All the laughter had left them now, but they were focused intently on him.

'Bye, Noah,' she said, and looked down at the floor.

Suddenly, he was moving. He took two long steps until he was standing in front of her and, without stopping to explain or analyse, he placed a hand either side of her head on the window and leaned in close. Her lips parted and she sank back against the pane and jerkily took in some air.

And then he kissed Grace the way he'd wanted to all evening.

CHAPTER THREE

GRACE clung to Noah for support. She had to. If she released the lapels of his jacket, she'd be in serious danger of sliding down the glass and landing in a heap at his feet.

It had been quite a long time since she'd been kissed. Perhaps the memories were a little fuzzy, but she didn't think she remembered it being this good. Every part of her seemed to be going gooey. And he wasn't even using his hands. They were still pressed against the glass as he towered over her and it was merely the brushing, teasing, coaxing of his lips that was making her feel this way.

She'd never been kissed like this before. Never.

And with that thought an icy chill ran through her.

Surely Rob's kisses had excited her like this? He *had* to come top of her list. He was Daisy's father, her soulmate, her grand passion. Anyone else would only ever be second place. But when she thought of him, she could remember youthful exuberance, raw need, but never this devastating skill that was threatening to…

Her fingers unclenched and she laid her palms flat against Noah's chest, intending to apply gentle pressure as a signal that she wanted him to stop. But she didn't stop him. Noah chose that moment to run his tongue along her lip and she moaned gently, reached behind his neck with both hands and pulled him closer.

When Noah's hands finally moved off the window and started stroking the tingling skin of her neck, her cheeks, that little hollow at the base of her throat, she stopped thinking altogether. And she had no idea how long they'd been necking in the doorway like teenagers when he finally pulled away.

She was shaking—literally quivering—as he stood there looking down at her with his pale eyes. His thumb was still tracing the line of her cheekbone. Just that alone made the skin behind her ears sizzle.

This was so *not* what she'd been expecting on her first date. The chat rooms on Blinddatebrides.com that afternoon had been full of stories of nerdy guys and boring evenings, lots of jokes about kissing frogs. After getting her head around Daisy's whole madcap plan, that was what she'd been anticipating. She'd been expecting to feel a sense of relief that the ordeal was over, to chalk it up to experience and carry on with her life. She certainly hadn't been expecting to feel *this*.

'Grace?'

Even his whisper was sexy. Low and growly. She tried not to shiver more than she already was doing.

'I'd really like to see you again.'

Her body was telling her to yell *yes*, drag him back into the coffee shop and make use of one of those squashy sofas. And just that thought alone was enough to throw a bucket of cold water all over her. She didn't *do* one-night stands, or necking in doorways. She did *soulmates* and *love at first sight*—with marriage and baby rapidly following. This wasn't for her. Blinddatebrides.com wasn't for her.

She wriggled out of Noah's arms and retreated behind the door, using it as a shield as she held it half-closed. 'I'm sorry, Noah. I just don't think that's a good idea.' And before she could talk herself out of it, she shut the door, flipped the catches and walked through the shop without looking back.

* * *

Noah stared at Grace as she disappeared into the barely lit café. In the gloom, she became a dark grey blob, then, suddenly, the interior of The Coffee Bean was plunged into darkness.

He just kept on staring, even though he was now staring at his own reflection in the glass. The one woman he'd found who'd really caught his interest had just given him the brush-off. He couldn't remember the last time that had happened in the previous five years. The irony of it hit him so hard he started to chuckle.

Aware that the pubs were emptying and people were starting to fill the High Street, he pulled himself together. Men who stood and laughed at their reflections in shop windows were likely to be carted down to the local police station to sleep it off.

He looked himself in the eyes.

Well done, Mr Best-selling Author. You've finally found the secret to repelling women: be interested.

The narrow flight of stairs that led up to her flat seemed especially steep this evening. Grace opened the door at the top and, once she'd taken her coat off, she looked down at herself. Who was she kidding? In Daisy's prom dress and Daisy's shoes, she looked like someone playing dressing-up.

Sophisticated? I don't think so!

She stripped the clothes and the stockings off right where she stood and marched into the bedroom to find her pyjamas. Once dressed in her striped three-quarter length trousers and vest top, she stood, hands on her hips, and glared round her room. It was cluttered with lotions and potions, clothes borrowed from Daisy and clothes Daisy had returned.

There was no point trying to go to sleep. Not going to happen. She fetched Daisy's laptop and took it into the sitting room, where she collapsed onto the sofa with it. Once it had booted up, she logged into Blinddatebrides.com.

Blinddatebrides.com is running 12 chat rooms, 36 private Instant Messaging conferences, and 4233 members are online. Chat with your dating prospects now!

Grace clicked on the 'New to the site' chatroom where she'd found Kangagirl and Sanfrandani earlier on, but none of the names listed in the conversation were theirs. She shook her head. It had to be midday in Australia and she had absolutely no idea what time it would be on the west coast of America. Sanfrandani was probably fast asleep.

She was about to turn the blasted machine off when it beeped at her and a little window popped up.

Kangagirl is inviting you to a private IM conference. Click OK to accept the invitation.

Grace didn't hesitate. Another window popped up.

Kangagirl: You're back! Tell us how it went!
Englishcrumpet: Us?
Sanfrandani: I'm here too!
Englishcrumpet: Shouldn't you be in bed?
Sanfrandani: LOL! Only if I want to get fired. It's three o'clock in the afternoon!
Englishcrumpet: Oh.
Kangagirl: So…
Sanfrandani: Yes! Juicy details please!

Juicy details indeed. There *were* no juicy details. It had just been a kiss.

Yeah, right. And caramel moccachino was just plain coffee.

Englishcrumpet: We had dinner and coffee and then he left.
Sanfrandani: The question is: are you going to see him again?
Englishcrumpet: I don't think so.
Kangagirl: Didn't he ask?

Grace's fingers hovered above the keys. It was so tempting just to type *no* and save herself all the post-mortems. But these girls had been really helpful when she'd needed them this morning and she just couldn't lie to them.

Englishcrumpet: He asked. I said no.
Kangagirl: What was he like?
Sanfrandani: Big fat loser?

Grace shook her head. That would have been so much easier. She'd been out to a beautiful restaurant with a charming, cultured man, who kissed like a dream, and she'd done a runner? How did she explain that without seeming stark raving bonkers?

Englishcrumpet: I don't think we were a good match. He was too...
Kangagirl: Boring?
Sanfrandani: Old?
Kangagirl: Weird?
Sanfrandani: Big-headed?
Kangagirl: Come on, Englishcrumpet! Help us out here!
She blew out a breath. None of those descriptions applied to Noah. How did she put it into words?

Englishcrumpet: He was too much of a 'grown-up'.

Too much of a lot of things, but that was all she could put her finger on right now.

Kangagirl: And you—if you don't mind me asking—are the grand old age of…?
Sanfrandani: Kangagirl! You can't ask that!
Kangagirl: I'm Australian. It's practically my birthright to be blunt.
Englishcrumpet: I'm…thirty-ten.
Kangagirl: Huh?
Englishcrumpet: Think of 30 and add 10. I refuse to use the 'f' word.
Sanfrandani: Crumpet, you're a hoot!
Kangagirl: What was he, then? A senior citizen?
Englishcrumpet: It was more about lifestyle than about age. I hang out with my daughter and her teenage friends. So I like takeaways and bad horror movies and reading Cosmo. *He was a foodie, into opera and military history books.*
Kangagirl: Not your cup of tea, Crumpet?
Englishcrumpet: Very funny!
Sanfrandani: So…your search for true love hit a road bump?

Grace typed the next reply so fast she surprised herself.

Englishcrumpet: I'm not looking for true love.
For a few seconds, nothing happened. The cursor just blinked at her.

Sanfrandani: Don't believe in it?
Kangagirl: You're on the wrong website, then!
Englishcrumpet: I do believe in true love, it's just…

How did she explain? She knew true love existed, because she'd had it with Rob.

Englishcrumpet: I just don't think you can have that kind of connection twice in a lifetime.
Sanfrandani: I see.
Kangagirl: Oh. Hugs, Englishcrumpet.

Rob had been her other half. How could anyone else take his place? And she didn't know if she could settle for less. Even if she was lonely sometimes. Even if, secretly, in a dark place where she didn't even want to admit it to herself, she was a little bit jealous of the easy companionship Daisy had had with her last serious boyfriend.

Sanfrandani: How about dating with the idea of finding someone to share your life with? Even if it's not the meant-to-be-in-the-stars kind of love?

Grace sat back in the sofa and stared at the screen. Sanfrandani had a point. Just because it wasn't going to be the same as she'd had with Rob, it didn't mean she couldn't find a different kind of happiness with someone else. That was what Noah had been talking about, hadn't he? Could she see herself making that kind of mature, adult decision about a relationship?

Englishcrumpet: I don't know. Maybe.

The Coffee Bean was virtually empty, as it normally was on a Sunday morning before the shoppers were out in full force. It was Grace's ritual to treat herself to breakfast down here just one day a week—any more than that and she'd be the size of a house. Around ten-thirty, she crawled down the stairs from her flat, propped herself against the counter and yawned so hard she thought her jaw might dislocate.

Caz was resplendent this morning in a lurid Paisley kaftan, her silver-blonde hair caught into a loose bun that looked as if it might disintegrate under its own weight at any second. The owner truly was as original as her kooky little café.

Caz looked her up and down. 'Either you've had a really terrible night or a *really* good one. Which was it?'

That was the point. Grace wasn't quite sure. Whichever it had been, insomnia had come as part of the package.

'A tall skinny latte with two shots, please.'

Caz winked at her. 'Say no more. Coming right up.'

Grace yawned again and looked round the café. It was a charming place, full of interesting knick-knacks. Old enamel jugs sat on random tables, filled with daffodils. Old road signs and mirrors covered the walls. Best of all was the ornate Victorian mahogany counter, still with some of the original etched glass, that filled one side of the café and the black and white tiled floor—a reminder of its former life as a butchers. The Coffee Bean always smelled of something comforting. The locals loved it but, with two new coffee houses on the High Street—both international chains—they were feeling the pinch.

But the buying public obviously were dull enough to enjoy the same old plastic-wrapped nonsense in whatever town they were in. The same menu of coffees. The Coffee Bean was unique, with an ever-changing menu and warm staff who really loved their jobs. But, unfortunately, that didn't stop the profit margins falling and the costs going up.

Caroline handed Grace her coffee and returned to frowning over some printed-off spreadsheets.

'How are this week's figures?'

Caz shuffled the papers and tucked them under the till.

'Come on, Caz. I'm family. And I'm supposed to be your assistant manageress. Even if you keep the happy, smiley face for the other staff, put me in the picture.'

The other woman shook her head. 'It doesn't matter what we do. Java Express is running promotion after promotion.'

She shrugged. 'If things don't pick up, we'll be out of business in three months.'

Grace put her coffee down, marched around the counter and flung her arms round Caz, ignoring the overpowering scent of lavender and the flakes of dandruff liberally salting her shoulders. There was no way she was going to let The Coffee Bean close. It was like a member of the Marlowe family.

She'd first met Rob here, when he'd had a Saturday job with his aunt. A couple of years later, when her dad had consented to let her start dating, it had been the venue for her first date. Caz had even made their wedding cake.

Daisy had slept in her pram near the back door on many occasions as a baby. The customers had spent many an hour when she was a toddler admiring her drawings and sneaking her bits of cake. Later, when she'd been older, she'd done her homework on the little table in the corner every night. The regulars all loved her and had insisted on trying to help her, even if they'd always come up with different answers for her questions and spent more time arguing with each other than actually being any use with equations or the dates of famous battles.

Too many happy memories. And now Daisy and Rob were gone and The Coffee Bean and her memories were all she had left. She wasn't going to let them be hoovered up by a big corporation without a fight.

'We'll find a way. I'll create a new cake—one so spectacular it'll stop people in the street and force them to dive in and buy some.'

Caz patted her on the arm and pulled away. 'Amazing as your creations are, my flower, I don't think they're a match for Java Express's "buy one get one free"s on just about everything.' She shook her head. 'Trouble is, nobody wants to pay for quality any more. They want everything for half the price it was last year.'

'I've got my savings. Only a few thousand, but still…'

Caz folded her arms and shook her head. 'No way. You've

been saving for long enough to open your own shop. I can't take that away from you.'

'But I could be a partner in *this* shop, couldn't I? You offered that to me once.'

Caz's eyes became glassy. 'Bless you, Grace, but no. We both know the chance of saving The Coffee Bean is slim, and you might need that money for university fees for Daisy. I can't let you plug a hole in a sinking ship and lose your nest egg in the process.'

'I want to, Caz. You know how much this place means to me.'

'Sorry, Grace. Can't let you do it.'

Grace gave Caz a rueful smile and rubbed her arm. 'I'll try to find a way to make you, you know.'

Caz chuckled. 'I know you will. But I've had a good twenty years longer at perfecting my stubbornness.'

Grace opened her mouth to argue, but at that moment the old-fashioned bell on the café door jingled and both women turned to look at who had just walked in.

'Oh, my goodness!' Grace put her hands over her mouth.

She couldn't even see the delivery boy behind the largest bunch of flowers in the history of the universe.

His voice came out muffled from behind all the greenery. 'Grace Marlowe?'

Grace let out a squeak.

'Over there,' Caz said, gesticulating first towards Grace and then to one of the free tables. The boy carefully lowered the bouquet and stumbled free of the foliage.

Grace couldn't take her eyes off the huge bunch of flowers as she squiggled her name on the boy's clipboard. Nothing as unimaginative and predictable as lilies or roses. These were large architectural flowers—some of which she couldn't even put a name to—framed with angular leaves and rapier-sharp grasses. And the smell…

'Someone really did have a good night last night, didn't

they?' Caz was standing back behind the counter, her arms folded across her ample chest. 'Go on, then. Look at the card.'

Grace didn't need to look at the card. No one had sent her flowers in a long time. Even Rob had only managed a bunch of petrol station roses on the night he'd proposed. One of the heads had fallen off, but he'd been nineteen and she'd been eighteen and, at the time, they'd been the most beautiful things she'd ever seen. Of course, they paled in comparison to Noah's bouquet. Somehow, she wished he had sent her lilies. It would have been easier to dismiss them, easier to put Rob's eleven roses and one sad stalk in first place.

She scowled as she searched for the card amongst the tissue paper and sharp grasses.

> *To Grace,*
> *Thank you for an unforgettable evening.*
> *Noah.*

Grace blew out a breath. She didn't like this warm feeling spreading through her bones. How was she supposed to forget that kiss with these flowers stinking out her flat for the next week? Two weeks, probably. They came from one of the most expensive florists in town and looked like the sort of blooms that didn't need gallons of water.

She picked up the bouquet and rustled over to Caz. 'Here, you have them,' she said and dumped them on the counter.

Caz just folded her arms tighter and shook her head. Grace shoved them an inch or two closer.

'Go on. They're far too posh for me. They'll look out of place in my little flat. Have them for the café.'

Caz just raised her eyebrows.

'You're impossible,' Grace said and flounced off to find some scissors and spare jugs. When she returned she hauled the bouquet onto one of the larger tables and set about slicing through the cellophane and trimming the stems.

'Evict the daffodils from my jugs and I'll dock your pay.'

Grace turned and stared at Caz open-mouthed. 'You wouldn't.'

Caz just blinked.

'I'll take you to Industrial Tribunal,' Grace added, picking up a large green thing and trying to work out if it was a flower or just an ornate leaf.

'Fine,' came the reply. 'Do it. But by the time it gets sorted, I'll probably be out of business and you will get an award of big fat zero.'

Grace's eyes became slits. 'Like I said—impossible!'

'It's high time you let a man buy you flowers. So, sorry, you're stuck with them.'

Well, she'd see about that.

The computer whirred and, after a few seconds, pinged cheerfully at Noah. He looked up from his Sunday crossword and scanned the list of emails that had just arrived in his inbox.

A stab of guilt hit him as he spotted one from his mother, inviting him to Sunday lunch the following week. It had been a while since he'd made the trip to the coast. In his opinion, relationships with parents were best conducted from afar—another reason he was pleased his mother was now quite the silver surfer, even if his father refused flatly to go near the PC.

His fingers hovered over the keyboard as he tried to work out if he had a good excuse to duck out of travelling out of London to Folkstone next weekend. Eventually, he groaned and tapped out an acceptance.

He loved his parents, of course he did, but the house they'd owned for the last half century always seemed so bleak, despite the old-fashioned, over-cluttered décor. When he pictured that house in his mind's eye, nothing happened. No memories flooded his head. No jovial family dinners. No warm hugs to match the warm milk at bedtime.

His mother was one of those jolly-hockey-stick sorts who was much more likely to tell a child to pick himself up and stop making a fuss than kiss it better. But at least he saw a sparkle of warmth in her eyes occasionally. His father had been fossilised at birth.

Noah had thought that following him into the army might have elicited some longed-for approval. Noah had been wrong. The old man had hardly raised an eyebrow and had huffed something about how it would 'finally make a man of him'. His current success with his books produced only the odd snort, even though on one visit Noah had found one of his hardbacks hidden under his father's armchair with a corner folded down to keep his place.

He sighed. It didn't take one of his hunches to tell him that Grace wouldn't ration the affection and fun for her daughter, as if saving them for a rainy day that never came.

Finding that his hand had automatically returned to his mouse, he made use of it. There were a number of emails from Blinddatebrides.com and he clicked on one, wondering if one was from her.

Another match suggestion. He tried to get excited about the honey highlights and the perfect smile, about the capable-looking professional woman whose profile seemed to match his every requirement for a wife. But, when he imagined her sitting across the table from him at dinner, she refused to look like her picture. Her hair darkened. Her smile became mis-chievous. One eyebrow arched high.

Oh, dear. He knew what this meant.

He'd learned long ago that he was the sort of person who had hunches. Not just run-of-the-mill inklings, but powerful, knock-the-breath-out-of-you hunches. It had started when he'd been a teenager and had always been able to guess the

plot lines of all his favourite TV programmes. Even the fiendishly clever detective shows. Sometimes, with very little
visible evidence, he just knew how things were going to turn
out—in life and on the screen.

Over the years, he'd learned to follow his hunches, hone
his skills. His agent told him his ability to create rich and
twisting plots that surprised and satisfied was the main reason
his books were so successful. Sometimes his hunches were
so strong, so deep-seated, they dug in and refused to let go,
even when those around him questioned his sanity. When his
subconscious went all Rottweiler on him, there was normally
a good reason for it. He just didn't always know what that
reason was until much, much later.

And his inner Rottweiler had decided it liked the look of
Grace Marlowe.

Frankly, he couldn't blame it.

That was it then. No point in fighting it. He could pretend
to himself he would test the waters, see how things went, but
if he was brutally honest he knew how this would all end. How
it must end.

Grace Marlowe would be his blind-date bride.

Shaking his head at how sensible that sounded, how right
he felt about it, he flicked down to the next email on the list
and opened it up.

Englishcrumpet has sent you the following message:

Dear Noah,
Thank you for the lovely dinner and for the beautiful
flowers. I'm sorry if I gave you the wrong impression,
but I'm not interested in another date and I want to be
clear about that. Right now, friendship is all I'm looking
for and all I can offer you.
Best wishes, Grace.

Noah folded his arms and stared at Grace's message. This was going to make the whole 'getting married to Grace' thing interesting. He smiled to himself. He liked interesting.

Friendship? Well, he'd see about that.

Vinehurst had always been a picturesque corner of London, but it had suffered a difficult period recently, with the small shops like grocers, butchers, ironmongers going out of business as trade moved to the supermarkets and out-of-town retail parks. For a while, many of the little shops on the High Street had been empty, or taken over by cut-price operations selling electrical goods or cheap toys. But in the last ten years the area had undergone a regeneration, with many of the more affluent Londoners looking for more affordable housing away from central London's rocketing property prices.

Not surprising, as it had wonderful properties, from charming terraced cottages to grand Victorian villas. He'd seen the potential well before it had become fashionable. That was another hunch that had worked out for him. Friends had told him he was mad to buy the old manor house 'out in the middle of nowhere'. It was actually right on the edge of the city where it finally ran out of steam and let the fields and woodland remain undeveloped. Those same friends had moaned it was on the 'wrong' side of London. Why didn't he try Buckinghamshire? Or Gloucestershire? The right sort of people lived in Gloucestershire.

But he hadn't wanted to try Buckinghamshire. He'd had a 'feeling' about Vinehurst. It had excellent transport links to London, an airport nearby for light aircraft and his house had doubled in value in the four years since he'd bought it, thank you very much.

He stuffed his hands in his pockets and hunched into his collar as he walked up the street. A woman passing in the opposite direction caught his eye. She was young and pretty, with long blonde hair, and was pushing a toddler in a pushchair. But her undoubted prettiness wasn't what caused him to do a double take. It was the hothouse flower tucked behind her ear. Last night's rain had left dampness in the air and the wind was slicing its way up the street. He'd be surprised if the bloom didn't wilt in a matter of seconds.

He shook his head and carried on striding up the slight hill towards The Coffee Bean. No matter. People could do whatever they liked with their flowers. It didn't bother…

An old man with a flat cap nodded at him as they passed on the narrow pavement. Noah stopped in his tracks and swivelled round to look at him. In the buttonhole of his dirty grey overcoat was the most stunning orchid.

Something tickled at the back of his brain. There was a connection here. There had to be.

He was almost at the café now and, as he paused to let a couple of middle-aged women out of the door, he noticed they were also carrying a couple of exotic flowers each. What the…?

Once inside, he spotted Grace, sitting at a table close to the counter and carefully passing out flowers—his flowers—to every customer as they collected their drinks and wandered off to find a table.

He walked to the front of the queue and stood there, waiting for her to finish fiddling about with the remains of the bouquet he'd sent her. He knew the exact moment she sensed his presence because she went quite still.

Noah smoothed his face into the dictionary definition of 'calm and collected'.

Grace swore and jumped up.

'Noah! What are you…? I mean, why…?'

He blinked and nodded towards the foliage in front of her. 'More to the point, what are *you* doing?'

Grace bit her thumbnail. 'Sharing the love?' she said hopefully.

It was impossible to hold his mask of composure in the face of such genuine mortification. He smiled and Grace exhaled visibly.

She looked quite different from the night before—no dress, no heels, no clipped-up hairdo. Just jeans, a cute little wrap-around jumper in soft, soft blue and her hair swinging loose around her shoulders. She didn't look at all like the polished woman he'd imagined he'd end up with when he'd signed up to Blinddatebrides.com. She did, however, look completely adorable.

Grace stood up and hurriedly gathered the left-over bits of stalks and leaves into the tissue and cellophane on the table and threw them in a bin somewhere behind the counter. When she returned, she flicked her hair forward to cover her eyes.

'I sent you an email,' she said, twisting her thumb in the grip of her other hand.

'I know. I read it.'

Confusion clouded her features. 'Then why are you here? What do you want?'

Another one of those hunches slammed into him. If he pushed the issue now, she'd never agree to a second date. He knew that as certainly as he'd known the answer to three down on the crossword this morning. If he was going to find his perfect wife, he would have to plan this like one of his plots, set things up. He would need to be patient. Just as well he was very good at being patient when he'd set his mind on something.

'What I really want,' he said, watching her eyes widen, 'is an espresso and a piece of that divine-looking chocolate torte.'

'Erm…okay.' Grace forgot entirely that she wasn't actually rostered to work that morning and skipped behind the counter to get Noah's coffee and cake. Caz was suspiciously silent and

Grace felt her beady eyes on her as she carefully levered a slice of her famous torte onto a clean plate. She shoved the cake in his direction, holding the plate at arm's length.

'There you go. Take a seat.' She nodded at the half-empty café. 'I'll bring your coffee over when it's ready.'

She messed around at the coffee machine far longer than necessary. Why was he here? Didn't he believe her when she said she wasn't going to see him again? And how dared he look all sleek in his black jeans, his dark hair all wind-blown and sexy? It just wasn't fair that a man of his age should be twice as good-looking in the daylight.

When she'd done absolutely everything she could think of to delay giving Noah his coffee—save drinking it herself—she took a deep breath and walked over to where he was sitting. He'd chosen a slightly dilapidated floral armchair and, although she suspected that leather and clean lines were more his style, he looked totally at home in the higgledy-piggledy coffee shop.

'Here.' She placed the cup on the table to avoid accidentally brushing fingers with him, then slumped into an adjacent chair.

'Well, that's me sorted,' he said, wrapping his long fingers around the little cup. 'Now, Grace Marlowe, what is it that you want?'

Grace had no idea.

But she did know what she *didn't* want. She didn't want to be sitting here noticing his fingers, because that led to noticing his wrists and the muscular forearms that were just visible where he'd pushed his sleeves up. How did a man have beautiful wrists? Just looking at them made her fizz inside. And fizzing led to something else she didn't want—doubting her decision to say no to a second date.

Slowly, she became aware that the ridge of her thumbnail was between her teeth and she pulled it away. Bad habit. She hooked the offending digit in the loop of her jeans and took a sudden interest in the glass display case on the other side of the room.

What did she want?

Better focus on that, because getting up and wandering off to choose something to eat would give her an excuse to avoid this awkward silence. She sneaked a look at Noah. He didn't seem to be finding it awkward at all. The torte was half-finished and he was sipping his coffee. If only she could match his serenity.

A croissant would be nice.

Something plain to settle her stomach. She pushed her weight down onto her feet and began to stand but, before she got fully vertical, a plate holding a pain au chocolat appeared before her.

'Thought you might need this,' Caz said and plonked a large black coffee down too. And then she sauntered off, looking as innocent as the day she was born. Grace knew better.

What Grace had *wanted* was to get away from Noah for a few moments, to allow her heart rate to return to normal, to get far enough away to block her view of his wrists. She definitely hadn't *needed* Caz's pain au chocolat—or her so-called help. Just as she hadn't needed to feel all heart-fluttery about Noah last night. It was a conspiracy.

'Grace? What do you want?' he said softly.

Grace poked her finger into her pastry, scooped up a chunk of brittle, bitter dark chocolate and sucked it off her finger. 'This'll do.'

Noah didn't display his fine teeth again, but she saw a glint of humour in his eyes. 'Not for breakfast. What do you want out of life?'

She pulled a face. 'That's a bit deep and philosophical for a Sunday morning, isn't it?'

He shook his head and loaded his fork with more torte. 'I'd say it was a perfect Sunday morning type of question.' She watched him in silence as he ate his cake, having no choice but to notice his fingers, his lips. He had very nice lips. And didn't she know how nice those lips could feel!

She deleted that thought. She couldn't feel that way again. Shouldn't be able to. That part of her soul had been a one-shot deal and she'd used it up on Rob.

'Okay then. Tell me about your daughter.'

That was easy. She knew what Daisy wanted. 'She's back-packing for a year before starting university up north. In fact, she's probably eating a very similar breakfast to mine in Paris, right this very second.'

Grace stared hard at her pain au chocolat, wishing it had magical powers and could transport her to a city with the best, most ostentatious patisseries in the world. What she wouldn't give to gaze in wonder upon shelves stacked high with gorgeous rainbow-coloured macaroons, tartes and choux buns.

'I wish I was in Paris too,' she whispered to herself, just for a moment forgetting the hunk of charm and cool sitting next to her.

'Well, that's an answer. Grace wants to travel.'

'Huh?' She looked up to find he had leaned in a little closer. What was he doing? Compiling a list?

'Now your nest is empty, you want to see the world?'

She nodded. 'That would be lovely, but I have to be content to just do it in my dreams. I'm…er…not really in a position to just jet off to some far-flung place on a whim.'

She took in the cut of Noah's coat, his effortless style. Everything about him screamed money. He obviously didn't have to worry about university fees or saving for his own little shop one day.

'This cake is fabulous,' he said before finishing the last mouthful.

There wasn't a smudge of chocolate on him. Not even a crumb had dared to land on his charcoal pullover. Grace licked a spot of stickiness off her fingers, then wiped them on her jeans.

'Who's your supplier?'

For a moment, Grace couldn't work out what he was

asking. Then she blushed. The way she'd blushed at fourteen years old when she'd walked past The Coffee Bean and Rob had winked at her. The heat started in her neck and just kept on climbing.

'I am. I mean… I made it.'

For the first time since she'd met him—less than twenty-four hours ago, but it seemed a lot longer—Noah looked something other than cool. 'You did?'

She nodded, blushing hard enough now to match the icing on the finger buns in the display case.

'You have a real talent. Where did you learn to bake like this?'

Coming from Noah, a man who seemed to be a connoisseur of virtually everything, that meant something.

'I was at the end of a catering course at Westminster College when I had Daisy,' she said, looking at the crumbs on Noah's plate and wondering if you could read the patterns in the same way that gypsies read tea leaves. 'I had an idea I'd like to become a pastry chef.'

But long hours, early starts, the sheer hard graft that went along with working in a professional kitchen, had not been compatible with motherhood—especially single motherhood.

After Rob had died she'd been desperate. Twenty-year-old newlyweds didn't think about saving and life insurance. The army pension helped, but it had still been a struggle. Thank goodness Caz had come to her rescue. It had seemed like an answer to prayer. Not only had she had a roof over her head and a job, but a whole host of coffee shop employees virtually fighting each other to babysit Daisy. And she'd been able to bake. Okay, she hadn't finished her course, but she'd borrowed books from the library and even done a few adult education classes. At least working in The Coffee Bean had allowed her to indulge in her passion.

She bit into her pain au chocolat. The dark sweetness soothed her, as always.

'One day, I'm going to open my own patisserie,' she said quietly. She didn't know when or how, she just knew she would do it. But, instead of getting closer to her goal, her dream seemed to be disappearing into the distance like the retreating tide on the river Thames. And once the tide was gone, all that was left was mud. With every step, in every direction, she found herself stuck, held fast by the dark, sticky circumstances of life.

She looked up to find Noah regarding her, his grey-green eyes strangely intense. Suddenly, she realised there was another bullet point to add to the list of things she didn't want.

She didn't want to sit here feeling so comfortable in his presence that she drifted off, let her guard down, spilled her secrets at his feet.

'I have to go.' She stood up and jammed her hands into her jeans pockets. 'And I meant what I said, Noah. The flowers are lovely but—'

He reached up and tugged one hand out of her pocket. Just the feel of those long fingers wrapped around hers stole the words right out of her mouth. He tugged her down again and she sat with a bump.

'Don't look so scared, Grace,' he said and released her hand. 'I'm not about to stalk you, but I really enjoy spending time with you. If friendship is all you are offering, then I accept.'

Grace was speechless. That was what she'd said, but that wasn't what she'd meant. Not really. But as Noah slipped his long dark coat on, said his farewells and walked out of The Coffee Bean, she couldn't think of a single countermove. Automatically, she cleared his plate and walked over to the counter, where she handed it over to Caz. With nothing left to do in the café she opened the back door, navigated the narrow passageway there and climbed the stairs to her flat.

Down below, Caz stared hard at the dirty plate, twisting it

this way and that in the light. And, when she was satisfied she'd looked long and hard enough, she smiled to herself and brushed the crumbs into the bin.

CHAPTER FOUR

GRACE smiled as she opened Noah's latest email. Once you got through that ever-smooth façade, he could be really insightful and funny. Finding a message from him in her inbox always brightened her day. And he'd been true to his word. In the last six weeks she hadn't felt stalked, not one little bit. She was glad of his friendship. She still missed Daisy like crazy but it was Noah, along with the girls from Blinddatebrides.com, who kept her going.

Grace smiled as she hit the 'send' button on her email. She'd thought she'd be horribly lonely without Daisy around but, after that day she'd stumbled into the chat room and sent out a distress call, she'd been in constant contact with Dani from San Francisco and Kangagirl, really Marissa from Sydney.

She wasn't quite sure what had caused them to bond so firmly. They had very different jobs and lifestyles, but they just 'got' each other. And having two neutral ears to share her dating worries with had been a godsend.

She flipped the laptop closed and padded off to the kitchen in search of a snack. There were another two hours to kill until her scheduled chat with Marissa and Dani at midnight. A strange time of day to get sociable but, considering that Marissa was thirteen hours ahead and Dani was eight hours behind, live chats had to take place at either midnight or six o'clock in the morning. And the girls knew how she felt about six o'clock in the morning.

It actually seemed a little bit sad that her best friends lived on different continents and she'd never met them face to face. She didn't know how they liked their coffee or what their voices sounded like, but maybe that was a good thing. Yes, there was a lot of banter, but when that died down they weren't afraid to be honest with each other. They'd got to know each other so much better over the Internet than if they'd met up and done small talk over coffee.

Sadder still had been the realisation that the greater part of Grace's socialising up until now had involved Daisy and a group of friends. They were cool kids, but she doubted they wanted a forty-year—a *mature* woman hanging around now Daisy was overseas.

Grace raided the biscuit barrel and sat down with a glass of milk at the kitchen table—a great little find from a junk shop. It was pure nineteen-fifties Americana, complete with chrome legs and trim and a speckled Formica top.

As Grace munched, she began to frown. She hardly ever just sat in her kitchen and had a really good look around. There was something about it. Something she just couldn't put her finger on. It reminded her of…

Oh, God. It reminded her of student accommodation.

Suddenly she was on her feet, walking through her flat looking at everything with unfettered eyes.

She realised with horror that her approach to decorating hadn't changed much since she'd married Rob. Oh, the colours and the prints and the bad flat-pack furniture had changed, but the essential philosophy—cheap, bright and fun—was exactly the same. Shouldn't there be at least one set of nesting tables in her living room? Where were the dinky ornaments, bought with a completely straight face and displayed with pride on the doily-topped mantle?

Okay, maybe she was taking this a bit too far, but Noah was her age and she'd bet he didn't have a stick of flat-pack furniture in his house. With relief, she reckoned he probably didn't have any doilies or nesting tables either, but she'd bet his place still looked…well…grown-up.

She turned into her bedroom and surveyed the turquoise and fuchsia Indian-inspired bedding. She loved it, loved the bright colours and sparkly embroidery, but nothing about it said 'mature and sophisticated'. Should it? Did she want it to?

She was standing next to the end of the bed and dropped onto it, staring at herself in a long mirror on the wall. They were more lines on her face than there had been twenty years ago—was that really all that had changed? When Daisy had been at home, all this noise and colour had seemed fun, had seemed right. Now, it jarred.

She was living in a time warp.

The urge to bury her face in her hands was irresistible, so she didn't bother to resist it. She was going to end up like Mrs Sims who came into The Coffee Bean, wasn't she? Mrs Sims, who at eighty still wore bobby socks, white plimsolls and a skirt that was just crying out to have a poodle appliquéd onto it.

She stood up and wandered into the living room and flicked the telly on. After channel surfing for a few minutes, she stopped at one of her all-time favourite movies—an eighties high school, coming-of-age flick. It didn't matter that she'd missed the first twenty minutes, she practically knew the lines by heart, anyway. It would fill the time nicely until her chat with Marissa and Dani and stop her thinking of poodles and figurines that were a nightmare to dust.

Blinddatebrides.com is running 12 chat rooms, 41 private IM conferences, and 4955 members are online. Private Instant Messaging conference between Englishcrumpet, Sanfrandani and Kangagirl:

Englishcrumpet: Come on, Dani. Entertain us with your dating disasters! I can't ask Marissa because she's disgustingly about-to-be-wed and full of the joys of love.
Sanfrandani: Oh, you know…Same old, same old.
Englishcrumpet: But that's just it, Dani! We don't know. You're always so vague.
Kangagirl: It's time to spill the beans.
Englishcrumpet: Look, I told you about my dating bellyflop! Don't try and divert the conversation, Dani. Tell me you've had your fair share of no-hopers.
Sanfrandani: I've had my fair share of no-hopers.
Kangagirl: And…details, please?
Sanfrandani: And your one date wasn't a total washout, Grace. Has the mysterious Noah popped into the coffee shop any time recently?
Englishcrumpet: Yes, he has. In fact, he's got into the habit of appearing at The Coffee Bean pretty regularly—for coffee and something sweet, he says.
Kangagirl: Awwwww. What does he do again? Not many men have time to lounge around in coffee shops in the middle of the day.
Englishcrumpet: He doesn't lounge*—he brings his laptop and sits there alternately talking to himself, typing and staring into space. He writes stuff.*
Sanfrandani: What kind of stuff?
Englishcrumpet: Oh, I don't know. Military stuff. Spy stuff.
Sanfrandani: And his name is Noah?
Englishcrumpet: Duh! Yes!
Sanfrandani: Have you looked for his stuff in a bookstore?
Englishcrumpet: No. Do you think I should?
Sanfrandani: Yeah, I really do.
Englishcrumpet: Anyway, that's irrelevant. I just want to stress (looking at no one in particular, Marissa) that Noah and I are just friends.

Kangagirl: Just good friends. Now where have I heard that before?

Englishcrumpet: We are good friends now. But I'm starved of girl-type gossip since Daisy's been gone. Come on, girls! Give me something juicy!

Sanfrandani: I might gossip a bit more if I could get a word in edgewise sometimes.

Englishcrumpet: Sorry! Look, you really don't have to talk if you don't want to, Dani. I realise some people aren't as happy to witter on about themselves as I am.

Kangagirl: Noah doesn't seem to mind.

Englishcrumpet: Seriously, Marissa, there's nothing going on. I know you want to believe that everyone is going to fall in love as quickly and completely as you did with Rick, but I'm not looking for that. I just like the fact that Noah doesn't see me as 'Daisy's mum'. I'm just Grace with him.

Kangagirl: You can't blame a girl for trying to matchmake.

Englishcrumpet: Wanna bet?

Englishcrumpet: Can I ask you girls something?

Sanfrandani: Sure.

Kangagirl: Go ahead.

Englishcrumpet: I'm not mutton dressed as lamb, am I?

Sanfrandani: Cookery questions? Is that some strange 'olde English' recipe?

Englishcrumpet: No, I mean...do I act too young?

Kangagirl: You're fun, Grace! Don't change that.

Sanfrandani: You know we love you just the way you are.

How did she explain this? It wasn't about being fun. It went deeper than that—in ways she didn't really understand. In lieu of precise thinking, she did the best she could:

Englishcrumpet: I know this sounds weird, but I think it's time for me to come of age.

Noah tried to doze in his first-class seat, but there was too much turbulence and, after five minutes of nodding off then being jolted awake, he gave up and asked a flight attendant for a coffee. When it arrived he wished he hadn't bothered. It just made him homesick for cobbled streets and wild flowers in enamel jugs.

It made him think about Grace.

He seemed to be doing a lot of that recently. Especially when he was away from home. He missed going into The Coffee Bean, missed the waft of butter and cinnamon and ground coffee as he opened the glazed front door and heard the bell jangle.

He and Grace had got into a routine when he wasn't travelling. He would turn up at the café around mid-morning, after he'd made a dent in his word count goal for the day. It was a great incentive. Suddenly, he was twice as prolific as he had previously been. Grace would just bring him an espresso and whatever cake or muffin she thought he might enjoy. They were always outstanding. He had no doubts that she could have worked at any of the top restaurants in London if she'd finished training.

While he privately lamented her missed opportunities, he also applauded her choices. She'd sacrificed all of that to bring up her daughter. There were many parents who just didn't get that. The more he knew Grace, the more he was certain his hunch about her was right. She was an amazing woman, possessing all the qualities he could want in a wife. And if he could gift-wrap a patisserie for her and deliver it to her doorstep, he would. She deserved it.

But he was just a friend. And friends didn't do that kind of thing.

He took another sip of the aeroplane coffee, grimaced and set it to one side. Might as well take his mind off the rest of the journey by sorting out chapter seventeen. Somehow it had gone off course, and the pace had slowed to zero. He opened up his laptop and took a quick look at his emails before he started working. A few had arrived while he'd been sitting in the terminal in Stuttgart and he hadn't had a chance to read them yet.

There was one from Grace, wishing him a nice time in Germany and recounting a funny Coffee Bean anecdote. He decided in that moment that, when he saw her next, he was going to pull her to one side and tell her who he really was. He trusted her completely. And she definitely wasn't out to marry him for his money. She wasn't out to marry him at all. What a pity.

The next email was a reminder from his agent.

Oh, hell. He'd forgotten all about that.

Next week was the British Book Awards and he'd get way too much stick if he didn't put in an appearance, especially as his latest cold war story had been shortlisted for Best Thriller. Too much of a PR opportunity for his publishers not to nag him senseless about it.

He'd been trawling Blinddatebrides.com for a suitable 'date-buddy', but he'd been so busy that he hadn't actually got past the looking-at-profiles stage. Which meant another ceremony which he would have to treat like a military operation if he was going to keep one step ahead of the glamour vixens. It was all so very tiring.

Could he schedule a date this week before the ceremony? And wasn't it a bit fast to ask someone he'd only just met to come with him? When he was his alter ego, Noah Smith, women were pleasant and interested, but they were hardly stalker material. What if, when he revealed his secret in a big *ta-dah* moment, his date turned all bunny-boiler on him? A week just wasn't long enough to test the waters.

His inner Rottweiler whined and barked.

Yes, yes, there was Grace. But she didn't want a relationship. She just wanted…

He didn't need a wife for next Thursday. He just needed a date. Someone to stand by his side, charm the socks off everyone and deflect the Mrs Frost wannabes.

Grace would be perfect. But would she do it? If he asked her nicely?

During her break, Grace took a journey next door to the book shop. She waved at the man behind the counter, who wore a home-knitted waistcoat every day of the year, even on a glorious April day like today.

'Morning, Martin. How are things going?'

Martin shook his head. 'What with all the posh shops opening up round here, the landlord wants to raise the rent. It's not right—all these newcomers pricing the locals out of business. I was only just surviving competing with all those online booksellers as it was.'

'Will you fight it?'

The old man sighed. 'No point. The lease is up for renewal next month and I don't have the cash for all the solicitor's fees. If my son had wanted to take it on, I'd think about it, but it's only me now and my wife'll kill me if I don't retire in two years' time.'

A defiant look crossed Grace's face. 'Well, I'm spending all my book money here until you go, and I'm going to tell everyone who comes into the coffee shop to do the same. We'll give you a good send-off and a wodge of money for your retirement.'

Martin went a little red and pretended to attend to a stray thread in his waistcoat. 'Thanks, love. Now, what were you looking for?'

'Military history,' said Grace, feeling a little flutter in her tummy as the words left her mouth.

* * *

Now, where would Grace be on a fine morning like this, if she wasn't in The Coffee Bean? Noah peered through the window. Caz waved madly at him and motioned for him to come in.

She was a character in her own right, that one. Today, she was dressed head to foot in white and rhinestones, from her bejewelled flip-flops to her floaty skirt and the scarf in her hair. If she stepped outside into the sunshine, she was likely to blind someone.

He opened the door and wandered up to the counter, eyeing up the display case. There was a new pink thing in there, with raspberries and white chocolate, and he was itching to taste it. Who cared that he'd had to double the length of his morning runs to make sure his trousers didn't get too tight?

'She's just popped next door,' Caz said, not even pretending to beat around the bush.

Caz knew. Noah knew she knew. They both smiled at each other.

'Fine. Could I have a coffee and some of that raspberry thing while I'm waiting?'

Caz just winked at him.

Martin's military section was completely out of proportion to the size of his shop, Grace thought as she ran her index finger along the spines on yet another shelf. Mind you, he looked the sort to enjoy making up intricate model aircraft kits, so perhaps it was a passion.

She couldn't find a Noah Smith anywhere. But this was a little book shop on a small suburban high street. Perhaps she'd have to go further afield. Perhaps she'd have to use the Internet to find his titles, even if she ordered the actual book from Martin.

Two women walked into the shop as she emerged from behind the shelves and headed for Martin's counter.

'Have you got number four in the *Frozen Spies* series?' one asked. 'The latest is in the window, but my son has just got into them and wants to read them in order.'

'Let me go and look, madam,' Martin said and scurried off.

Madam. So quaint. And Grace would lay money on the fact that whatever franchise bought this little shop wouldn't have staff that said anything but, *Huh?*

'Did you see him on telly the other week—on that Friday night chat show?' the second woman said while she rummaged in her handbag for something.

'Who?'

'The author of *Frozen Spies*.' She nudged her friend and did a wink that didn't quite work. 'Wouldn't mind a little bit of undercover action with him myself, if you know what I mean.'

Grace stifled a smile as Martin returned with a book and placed it on the counter. 'Here we go! *Wasteland. Frozen Spies* number four.'

The book-buying woman picked it up and checked out the photo on the back as Martin rang it into the cash register— nothing so newfangled as a bar code scanner in this shop, thank you very much.

'Ooh, yes,' she said, winking at her friend. 'I see what you mean! Come to Mama!'

And the pair of them collapsed into giggles like a pair of fifteen-year-olds. Unfortunately, Martin's prehistoric till was playing up and it looked as if Grace would have a long wait if she wanted to quiz him about military books. She waved at him over the top of the giggling duo's heads and mouthed, 'I'll be back later.'

With a scone, probably. Martin looked as if he could do with a little cheering up.

Out of curiosity, she looked for the book the woman had been talking about as she walked past the window. There was a large display of a dramatic-looking hardback, the jacket in shades of silver and blue and grey.

Silent Tundra by Noah Frost.

Grace ran back into the shop and dived into the window display.

Noah choked on the raspberry thing when he saw Grace striding into The Coffee Bean with his latest book clasped in her hand. She spotted him sitting in his usual spot and he could have sworn he'd seen a wave of static electricity run up her body and leave her hair standing just a little on end.

Part of him was truly worried about what she was going to say; part of him was triumphant at this totally unique reaction to his identity.

'Oh! Mr *Smith*. So lovely to see you!'

He tried to swallow the mouthful of pink raspberry mousse stuff and just made himself cough again. Grace whacked him on the back. With the book. He really should try and write thinner ones.

He swallowed hard and managed to clear his mouth of food. His voice came out hoarse and raspy. 'Grace! I can explain…'

'I bet you can! But I don't want any more of your lies.'

'Grace—' the voice was low and authorative, and coming from the woman in white with her hands on her hips '—you are creating a scene in my coffee shop.'

Grace shut her mouth and looked around. Noah counted at least twenty pairs of eyes staring at them. Not even a teaspoon clinked.

'Sorry, Caz.'

'Now, go and have a walk and calm down. Listen to what the man has to say.'

'I—'

'Go,' Caz said and nodded at the door.

Grace stalked out of the shop with the book tucked under her folded arms. Noah followed her. She waved his book at him. 'I have to give this back to Martin. I didn't pay for it.'

He just nodded and caught up with her. He could wait a few minutes if he got the chance to explain.

The book shop owner was standing in his doorway, frown lines furrowing his forehead. Noah nodded at him as Grace swept past him and climbed into the shop window. He, the shop owner and two customers watched in silence as she rebuilt a pyramid of books.

'Oh, my God, it's you! It's him, Julie!'

Noah closed his eyes and waited for the ground to open. Of all the times…

'Will you sign my book for me?'

Grace emerged from the window display and stood, arms folded across her chest next to the door. 'Yes, Noah. Why don't you sign the lady's book for her?'

He couldn't really do anything else, could he? The shop owner hurried round the other side of the counter and produced a pen. Noah took it from him and scribbled his standard best-wishes-hope-you-enjoy-the-book thing.

'Can you put "To Julie, with love"?'

Noah compromised and put "To Julie".

'I haven't got a book,' the other woman said. 'Could you sign something else for me?' She hunted around in her handbag as Noah handed Julie her signed copy.

'Aren't you tall,' Julie said, shuffling a little closer. 'Were you really a spy?'

'No,' Noah said, resisting the urge to clench his teeth. 'I make it up. It's fiction.'

'I bet no one's told you this before, but I reckon you'd make a fabulous James Bond.'

Actually, he'd heard that line so many times he couldn't count. Next she'd be telling him he looked like—

'You remind me a bit of Pierce Brosnan,' the other women chimed in.

Noah looked over at Grace, whom he expected was billowing smoke by now. She was just standing there, her arms by her sides, her quick eyes taking the whole situation in. That was it. He was never going to get any further with her now.

'I can't find a bit of paper,' Julie's friend said with a giggle. 'How about this?'

And she leaned forward and parted her blouse to reveal an expanse of crêpey décolletage. Noah dropped the pen. When he stood up, Grace handed him one of his hardbacks that she'd nabbed from the window display. Again.

'How about I just sign this one for you?' he said quickly and started writing before she had a chance to disagree.

'Don't worry, Martin,' Grace whispered to the man behind the counter. 'He's paying. Full whack too. None of this 'special offer' nonsense.'

Martin nodded and busied himself with a pot of rubber bands.

The two women left in a flurry of good wishes and 'hope to bump into you again's. Noah turned to look at Grace.

'Okay,' she said, her face unusually expressionless. 'I get it.'

Blinddatebrides.com is running 12 chat rooms, 27 private IM conferences, and 5212 members are online.

Englishcrumpet: You'll never believe what I've got to tell you about Noah! You know I said he was a writer?
Sanfrandani: Yes.
Englishcrumpet: Well, it turns out he's rather famous.
Sanfrandani: I knew it!
Englishcrumpet: Couldn't you have told me?
Sanfrandani: I wasn't sure. I just suspected.
Kangagirl: Hey, girls? Care to fill me in. I don't know anything about anything, it seems.
Englishcrumpet: Have you heard of Noah Frost?
Kangagirl: !!!!!!!!!!
Kangagirl: Really? That's him?

Sanfrandani: He's hot.

Englishcrumpet: Hands off, Dani!

Kangagirl: Thought you were just good friends, Grace.

Englishcrumpet: Sort of. We are. It's just...Oh, this is getting so complicated!

Sanfrandani: That's what we're here for, to help you out.

Kangagirl: Fill us in and we'll provide virtual hugs and real sympathy.

Englishcrumpet: He's got a big event to go to and he's asked me to go with him.

Kangagirl: I knew you two were more than JGF!

Englishcrumpet: JGF?

Kangagirl: Just Good Friends! You're always mentioning him.

Englishcrumpet: No, I'm not. And, anyway, I see him almost every day. It's not surprising his name pops into the conversation. And he was the very reason I found you two in the first place...

Sanfrandani: It's probably more accurate to say that you found us because of Daisy's prank.

Englishcrumpet: Same thing.

Kangagirl: Not exactly...

Sanfrandani: How is Daisy, anyway? Where is she now?

Englishcrumpet: I had an email from her yesterday. She's in Athens and doing fine. She had this really funny story about a goat and a moped...

Kangagirl: Don't think you're getting away without spilling the beans on your date with Noah! Hunky authors first, goats second!

Englishcrumpet: Honestly, Marissa! Are you this bossy in real life? Poor Rick!

Sanfrandani: Stop evading the issue, Grace. Are you saying that Blinddatebrides.com really did make a good match with you and Noah after all?

Englishcrumpet: We're just date-buddies. That's all.

Kangagirl: Deep down, I don't think you want to love again.

Englishcrumpet: Maybe you're right. I used to think I couldn't love anyone the way that I loved Rob. And part of me still thinks that's true.

Sanfrandani: That's sad, Grace.

Kangagirl: But very sweet.

Englishcrumpet: But recently I've been thinking that I could find a nice man to share things with, but it'll be different. It won't be the same all-consuming thing I felt for Rob. It'll be gentler, calmer.

Sanfrandani: Sounds like you mean safer.

Englishcrumpet: Is love ever safe?

Kangagirl: Are you sure you can't find this gentler, safer love with Noah?

Sanfrandani: Grace?

Englishcrumpet: Stop already with the matchmaking! I'm going before you both attempt to brainwash me. Catch you later!

Kangagirl: Have a great date! Take care!

Sanfrandani: Bye!

Englishcrumpet has left the conversation.

Kangagirl: Hey, Dani? Do you think I'm barking up the wrong tree here? About Grace and Noah?

Sanfrandani: Don't know, Marissa. You're right—she does mention him a lot.

Kangagirl: Guess we'll just have to wait and see!

Sanfrandani: LOL. You're incorrigible, Miss Bride-to-be!

Sanfrandani: And wipe that goofy smile off your face.

Kangagirl: Busted! How did you know?

CHAPTER FIVE

GRACE let out a shaky breath as the car Noah had ordered for them drew up outside the Regent Palace, one of London's swankiest hotels. She turned to Noah.

'Are you sure about this? About me?'

He gave her a look that made her insides melt. 'Of course I'm sure.'

Right. Okay, then. Part of her had been hoping he'd slap his forehead and mutter, *What was I thinking?* She was just going to have to go through with it now.

'Grace?'

'Mm-hmm?'

'Relax. You look stunning.'

She gave him the tiniest of smiles. She'd dipped into her savings and bought a cocktail dress that she'd fallen in love with when walking past one of the exclusive little boutiques that had opened up in the High Street in the last couple of years. The fabric was the most amazing silver-grey silk and the dress had a fifties feel about it, with its wide, scooping Audrey Hepburn neck and a soft, full chiffon skirt. It was looking a little creased after the car journey and she smoothed the ridges away with her palms.

Noah was looking pretty stunning himself. She totally agreed with the mad shopping lady's James Bond comparison, although she didn't think he looked like Pierce Brosnan at all. He had dark hair and matching charisma, but facially they were totally different.

The driver opened the door on her side. She looked down at her legs, wondering if she could remember the way to get out of a car in a dress without showing her knickers. It was something to do with keeping her knees together—or should it be her ankles? She scanned his face carefully as she took his hand and swivelled out of the car. His expression didn't change in the slightest and she thanked heaven that she must have got the manoeuvre right after all.

As she walked onto the red carpet, she felt like a trespasser, her strappy high sandals making little pock marks in the pile. Noah's strong hand clasped hers and tugged her into his side. Grace pulled herself straight and prepared herself to walk without making an idiot of herself.

While the event wasn't in the league of the film premieres in Leicester Square, there was a smattering of photographers and journalists and a small crowd had gathered. Noah walked over to the railing and shook hands and signed a couple of autograph books, all the time making sure she was by his side. People stared at her.

She tried to smile, but it felt so unnatural. A little muscle at the corner of one of her eyes kept twitching.

Oh, Lord. What was she doing here?

She was just a spare part. Window dressing. All fluff and no substance.

Noah signed the last autograph and slid his hand back into hers. She grasped it greedily and he leaned across to whisper something in her ear.

'You have no idea how much I hate this bit. I always feel such a fraud.'

They smiled at each other, just for a few seconds, before moving on.

Grace tried to ignore the crowd, the paparazzi, the fans pushing themselves at the barriers hoping to see a TV star or two. The women, both on and off the red carpet, were looking at Noah as if they'd like to serve him up for supper on a bed of chocolate, garnished with a sprig of mint in his belly button.

If there was anyone fake here, it wasn't him. She'd sneaked into Martin's book shop during the week and bought his first book. It had left her yawning—not because it was bad; far from it! She'd been yawning because she'd stayed up to two in the morning three nights in a row, totally caught up in the clever plot and life-and-death situations. It had left her feeling as if she had discovered a whole extra level to him.

Just a few days ago he'd been Noah Smith, the nice-looking man who came into her café and ate cake. Now he was Noah Frost, the celebrity author, general superstar and stud-muffin. Suddenly, she was a little in awe of him.

He gently tugged on her hand and they were moving again, towards the liveried doormen who were guarding the hotel's front entrance. Grace let him pull her forwards and soon she was carefully placing her sandals on each step of a sweeping staircase, heading for the ballroom where the awards ceremony was being held.

When they reached the threshold to the room, Grace stopped, her eyes wide.

It was like something out of a fairy tale. A very modern fairy tale with glitz and glamour and celebrities instead of kings and nobles. She could see a few TV comedians and a couple of newsreaders just from where she was standing.

Huge marble columns lined the room and vast crystal chandeliers dripped from every part of the ornate plaster ceiling. Flowers were everywhere—enough to give the population of Vinehurst buttonholes three times over.

Wow.

Noah squeezed her hand and she looked up at him. The

smile for the cameras was gone now and his beautiful pale green eyes held such honesty. Her heart did a little pirouette.

'Thank you, Grace,' he said and placed a delicate kiss on her cheek, just in front of her ear. 'I really appreciate you doing this for me.'

Was he kidding? Most women would sell their own shoe collections to be at an event like this, with a man like him. She straightened her spine. She would just have to think of good old Audrey in *My Fair Lady*—without the OTT cut glass accent, of course—and she'd be fine.

It struck her that this was New Grace's first public outing, her 'coming out' ball, if you liked. She squeezed his hand in return.

'Okay, Mr Frost,' she said, winking her mascara-laden eyelashes at him. 'Let's go get 'em!'

'Sorry you didn't get the gong, Noah.'

Noah turned to find one of the other authors from his publishing house standing beside him. Rebecca was the hot new thing in women's fiction at the moment and had won the award for Best Newcomer.

'Ah, you can't get too worked up about these things, can you?' He nodded at Rebecca's award, which she was clutching with one hand while she balanced a glass of champagne in the other. 'Congratulations to you, though.'

'Thanks.' She sipped her drink for a moment and looked across the room.

'And are congratulations supposed to be coming in your direction too?'

Noah laughed. 'Not unless I go and "relieve" Frankie of his award and run very fast indeed.'

Rebecca rolled her eyes. 'Not the award, dummy. Her.' She gestured in Grace's direction with her glass. The liquid sloshed around and glinted under the chandeliers. Rebecca focused on it slowly and then took another glug.

'Grace?'

'There's much crying in the Ladies tonight, now everyone thinks you might be off the market.'

Noah tried to remain the picture of composure. 'And why would they think I might be "off the market" as you so eloquently put it?'

Rebecca licked her lips, blinked and swayed slightly. ''Cos you've hardly taken your eyes off her all evening. She must be pretty amazing if she's finally caught the attention of publishing's most eligible bachelor.'

Noah opened his mouth to pooh-pooh the whole 'eligible bachelor' thing, but suddenly the group around Grace erupted into laughter and he got caught up in watching her smiling and talking. 'She is pretty amazing, isn't she?'

Rebecca, however, was downing the rest of her glass and had obviously lost track of what they were talking about. 'I think it's time I held off the champers, Noah me old darling,' she said and let out a tiny burp.

'I think you're right, Becca.'

Noah ushered her in the direction of the lobby, where she said her boyfriend was waiting for her. Once he'd safely handed her over, he went looking for Grace. They'd got separated a while ago and every time he tried to reach her, someone—

'Noah, me old mate!'

Here we go again, he thought, as he fixed a smile on his face and turned round. He stood chatting to the group for a while, but after the first ten minutes he found it easy enough to just sip his drink and nod. At literary parties, you were never short of someone who was ready to hold court. It just so happened that, this time, it was coming in rather handy.

Noah stood back and just watched Grace sparkle. She was talking to a group from his publishers and they were hanging on her every word. He was so glad she wasn't a carbon copy of everybody else here, that he had gone with his gut instinct.

He exhaled. There was only so much watching from the sidelines that a man could do. He extracted himself from the conversation he'd been having on autopilot and made a beeline for Grace. When he reached her side, he stood close and wrapped an arm around her waist. She didn't flinch. She didn't even scowl. She just finished what she was saying and flicked a glance in his direction, smiling. That smile was his undoing.

It wasn't one of her sassy smiles, or even one of her wide grins. This smile was soft, almost…shy.

His inner Rottweiler, who'd been sleeping nicely all evening, suddenly decided to go in for the kill.

He didn't want to look for anyone else. He didn't want to spend any more time scouring Blinddatebrides.com. He wanted Grace. He wanted to marry her.

As Noah handed Grace her coat, she sighed. 'What a great night!'

'I'm glad you enjoyed yourself.'

She gave him a look of sheer disbelief. 'Enjoyed myself? Did you see him? That guy who was in the latest Sunday night costume drama on telly? He kissed my hand. Twice!'

And Noah would like to punch him. Just once.

Grace put her hand over her mouth to smother a yawn. 'I'm so glad you decided to book hotel rooms for tonight.' It had been one of the sweeteners he'd come up with when trying to persuade her that this was a good idea. 'My feet are killing me and I couldn't face the drive back, not at—oh, my goodness! Is that really the time?'

He nodded. 'Cinderella left quite some time ago.'

She yawned again and set him off.

'Come on, Sleeping Beauty. Time to get a cab. The hotel we're going to is a little bit quieter than this one, thank goodness.'

'And I've got my own room?'

'Yes, for the third time tonight, you've got your own room!
What do you think I am?'

The limousine nipped down side streets and darted round
corners until Grace was hopelessly disoriented. She yawned
again. She'd drunk just enough champagne to leave her
feeling slightly fuzzy. Only about three glasses over the course
of the evening, but she didn't get the opportunity to drink
anything but cheap plonk from the local supermarket, and the
real thing had gone straight to her head.

A head that was feeling rather heavy at present. And there
was a nice warm chest close by, perfect to loll against.

The car swung round another corner and Grace let gravity
take the blame as she landed on Noah. He didn't seem to mind,
prising his arm from his side and resting it round her shoulders.
A delicious bubbly feeling, which had nothing to do with champagne, started in her toes and worked its way up to her ear lobes.

She breathed out, long and steady. This was nice, leaning
against Noah, feeling the warmth of his chest against her
back and the pads of his fingers lightly brushing her upper
arm. He smelled so good…

But they were here as friends, and it really wouldn't do to turn
her head and bury her face in his shirt as she was tempted to do.

The sounds of hooting horns, revving engines and sirens
were just starting to come from far, far away when the car
stopped and Grace found herself being gently shaken.
Everything seemed slightly unreal as she yawned and
walked and yawned and walked, following Noah into lifts
and along corridors.

A bellboy opened the door and she just stared at a fabulous
room, all in cream and gold and ivory.

'There's no bed,' she said, frowning slightly. 'A room this
nice and there's no bed?'

Noah put an arm around her back and ushered her into the room. 'It's a suite. Your room is this way.'

Grace didn't notice much about the room but the vast, squashy-looking bed. She twisted herself around and just fell onto it, her feet lifting off the floor with the force of impact. Heaven. If she could live in this bed for the rest of her life, she would.

Her shoes were being taken off and she wiggled her toes and let out a giant sigh that grew and stretched until it became yet another yawn. A pair of warm lips kissed her temple.

'Goodnight, Grace. Sweet dreams.'

Grace woke from a delicious sleep and stretched, long and hard, right down to the muscles in her toes and right up to the fingertips above her head. She was naked, having peeled off her dress some time in the night and climbed under the covers.

The clock by the bed showed it was eight. A fairly respectable time to rise after such a late night. She snuggled back into the goosedown pillow. It all seemed so decadent, lying in—on Egyptian cotton, no less—and not going into work today.

She had one last stretch and headed for the shower. When she'd finished, she pulled her pyjamas from her bag, which had miraculously appeared in her room, and then wrapped the soft white towelling robe from the back of the door over the top. She opened the door to the sitting room part of the suite and peered out. Noah was sitting at a desk near the window, working away on his laptop and looking as if he'd been conscious for hours.

He finished a series of taps, hit the enter key, then turned in her direction. 'Good morning. How did you sleep?'

Grace stepped into the room. 'Wonderfully, thank you…And thank you for such a great night last ni—oh, bother!' She pulled up the sleeve of her bathrobe and inspected her right hand. 'I wasn't going to wash the hand that Randolph Marks kissed, but I forgot all about that and gave it a good scrub in the shower.'

'Too bad,' Noah said, a smug smile twitching at his lips. 'How about some breakfast?'

He motioned to an open set of French windows and Grace gasped. Outside, on a small terrace that she hadn't even known existed, was a table laden with rolls and croissants, orange juice and fresh fruit platters.

She ran outside to look at it all. And then she leaned over the balcony. They were at least ten storeys up, and big red buses, taxis and cyclists all jostled far away on the street below. People in dark suits carrying briefcases hurried in straight lines. It was a beautiful morning, with the sky so blue it was almost too perfect. The trees lining the street below shimmered in the breeze and the sun was warm on her face and bare feet.

She sat in one of the wrought iron chairs circling the table, her bottom welcomed by a cushion at least five inches thick.

'This looks fabulous! Thank you so much, Noah—for all of this, last night... I feel like I'm on holiday!'

Noah joined her at the table and poured them both cups of coffee from the silver pot.

'No. Thank *you*. Your presence was very effective in keeping the undesirables at bay. I didn't get asked to autograph a cleavage once last night, so I count it a success.'

Grace grinned at him and reached for a croissant and loaded her plate with strawberries, raspberries and blueberries. 'You're welcome.' She broke off a piece of croissant and popped it in her mouth.

Oh, my. She'd died and gone to heaven. It was light, flaky and buttery all at the same time. As she rested in her chair, she idly thought about infiltrating the kitchens to see how the chef did it.

Breakfast was long and leisurely, with gentle banter and

plentiful cups of coffee. When Grace was confident she wouldn't need to eat another thing until at least next Thursday, she propped her feet up on one of the spare chairs, closed her eyes and raised her face to the sun.

'I could get used to this.'

Off in the distance, the traffic roared and the wind lifted the fine hair at the edge of her temples. She sighed.

'Could you? Why don't you, then?'

Grace turned her head and lifted one eyelid. Noah was leaning forward, his chin on one of his fists, giving her a very serious look. A sudden shiver ran up her spine and she tugged her robe tighter around her. 'What do you mean?'

'I mean…'

Grace dropped her feet to the floor and sat up straight. Noah gulped in a breath, not looking at all like a sexy spy for once.

'I mean, you could live like this all the time… if you married me.'

A sudden wave of vertigo hit her. A delayed reaction from hanging over the balcony, probably.

'What did you just say?'

Noah stood up, circled the table and sat down in the chair she had just had her feet on. He took one of her hands in his and looked into her eyes.

'Marry me, Grace?'

The first time in her life, Grace didn't have a witty come-back, a smart reply. 'But…but…we're just friends…you don't love me.'

'I think you're wonderful, Grace. I have a great deal of respect for you. And I have fun when I'm with you. Fun I'd forgotten how to have.'

'But…'

'And there's plenty of chemistry between us.'

She looked down at their intertwined fingers, then back up

at Noah. 'Yes, there is…' A little too much chemistry on occasion. 'But…'

'You said yourself that you weren't looking for Romeo and Juliet. I'm proposing a partnership based on the mutual respect, compatibility—' a small smile kicked the corners of his mouth up '—chemistry…'

Suddenly, he leaned in. She could feel his breath on her lips and, without warning, her heart rate doubled and her eyes slid closed. The kiss that followed was as soft and slow and balmy as the spring sunshine.

Noah pulled back and held her face in his hands, his eyes searching hers, asking questions, finding answers.

She'd missed this.

Not just the kissing—although it was pretty spectacular—but connecting with someone. She knew Noah was telling the truth. They *were* compatible. And he'd meant what he'd said, how he felt about her. No one had said those kinds of things about her for a very long time. Tears clogged the back of her throat.

But it wasn't love.

Could she agree to a marriage on the foundations that Noah had outlined? A couple of months ago she'd have laughed herself silly at the idea, but now…

No more lonely days. No more struggling to do everything on her own. Someone to talk to when she was down. Someone to laugh with when she was happy. Suddenly her soul ached for those things.

She pulled away from him and stood up, pressing trembling fingers to her lips.

'I… I don't know, Noah. I need to think about this. I'd like to go home, please.'

Her heart was pounding so fast that Grace considered collapsing onto the top step and resting against the front door to her flat for a moment before she went inside. In fact, that was a fabulous idea. She turned and slumped against the door, letting gravity pull her into an untidy heap on the landing.

The ride home had been excruciating. She just hadn't known what to say. How could she have chit-chatted after a proposal of marriage? A proposal she hadn't actually turned down. Was she mad?

When the car had pulled up in the alley behind The Coffee Bean, where the back entrance to her flat was, she'd grabbed her overnight bag and bolted. And now she was sitting here, her heart rate returning to normal, and she still didn't know what to do.

Her flat was her space, her sanctuary, but she had absolutely no desire to go inside at the moment. The first thing that would greet her when she opened the door would be the photo of Rob in his uniform, holding Daisy just a few days after she'd been born.

She sighed. When they'd married, she and Rob had felt so grown up. And yet, when she looked back at her photo albums now, they both looked impossibly young, little more than children themselves. For goodness' sake, Daisy was almost the same age as Grace had been when she'd got married. Just the thought of Daisy with a ring on her finger and a bump under her T-shirt was enough to make Grace break out in a cold sweat.

Back then, she and Rob had been so convinced that what they had would last for ever, but what *really* would have happened if he'd still been alive? Would they have been the perfect family of her daydreams, or would they be living in separate houses, fighting over custody arrangements and child support?

How could she walk past that picture of Rob when she was thinking like this? She couldn't block him out and pretend he'd never existed, not when she'd spent all these years keeping him alive by being the Grace he'd fallen in love with.

She'd never doubted any of this before, not even in her

twenties, when she'd dated quite a bit and had still been full of hope that she'd find someone new to fill the void in her life. But none of them had measured up to fun-loving, generous Rob, and twenty-something men had a habit of running scared from a ready-made family.

It had just confirmed what she'd known all along—Rob had been her soulmate and she wasn't going to find another man like him. Just wasn't going to happen. So she'd given up the search.

But now she'd found Noah.

He was nothing like her darling Rob, and any relationship she embarked upon with him would be totally different from her marriage. Noah wanted companionship, a partnership built on mutual respect. Those criteria hadn't even been on her radar when she'd accepted Rob's proposal. It had been about love and destiny and forever. Only forever hadn't come. And now she had to decide what to do with the time she had left, rather than treading water and pretending she had an endless supply of days left to her.

Respect. Compatibility. Support.

It all sounded so logical. Yet the Grace inside her who liked fishnets, tequila and rock concerts was yelling *no* and shaking her head. Was she just being childish?

Grace rubbed her hands over her face.

The scary thing was, part of her wanted to say yes. Part of her wanted all those things. And, if she decided she could move towards this idea of a more mature, balanced view of love, what did that mean for her marriage to Rob? Would she be crossing it out and saying it was a mistake?

She might not know what it meant, but it *felt* like betrayal.

On the other hand, that love-song, only-in-movies kind of thing wasn't the only kind of love. And perhaps, if that was what Noah wanted from her, she would have turned him down flat anyway. Love like that meant one thing—loss. It was as if the universe had to balance out the intensity by taking it away again. Too much perfection could not be good for a soul. And she couldn't survive that again, losing the man she totally adored.

So, on reflection, maybe Noah's idea was the logical choice...

Oh, she was going round in circles!

She sighed, stood up and let herself into the flat, avoiding both the photo and the laptop sitting on the coffee table in the living room. She had no intention of logging in to Blinddatebrides.com tonight to see if Marissa and Dani were hanging out there. They'd want to know about the so-called date.

She needed time to get her head round this before she shared it with anyone. She wasn't even going to tell Daisy yet.

Noah didn't come to The Coffee Bean for a few days, although he sent her a couple of very neutral emails in the meantime. He was such a gentleman, giving her space, knowing she'd freaked out a little. It was such a relief that she didn't have to explain it all to him, that he understood.

She could do a lot worse than Noah Frost.

Grace unpacked a batch of miniature chocolate tarts and pressed a single fresh raspberry into the smooth surface of each one before lining them up in the display case.

Caz would know what to do. She'd been like a surrogate mother to Grace and a surrogate grandmother to Daisy in the last couple of decades. Grace didn't go to her for advice often. Normally, because she didn't like the advice she got and, even more frustrating, it usually turned out to be spot-on.

But as she approached Caz, who was sitting in the corner table poring over a large accounts ledger, she realised that the older woman was staring off into space, not even looking at the web of figures on the page before her. It was the third time today Grace had spotted her doing this, and it just wasn't like her. She was normally so down-to-earth.

She pulled out an old wooden church chair—complete with hymn book holder on the back—and sat down opposite Caz.

'Penny for them?'

Caz sighed. 'I'm not sure they're worth it, but a couple of thousand might be more welcome.'

'Problems?'

Caz nodded and twisted the book round for Grace to have a look. Maths had never been her strong suit, unless it involved pounds and ounces rather than pounds and pence, and Grace was forced to nod without really knowing what she was looking at. She stood up again, walked behind Caz's chair and wrapped her arms around her shoulders, pressing her cheek against the side of Caz's face.

'Don't give up. We'll make it. We've always managed before.'

Caz just patted Grace's arm and stared off into the distance.

Private IM chat between Englishcrumpet, Kangagirl and Sanfrandani:

Englishcrumpet: Okay, girls. I have something to confess.
Kangagirl: Ooh! Juicy!
Sanfrandani: Ready and waiting.

Grace took a deep breath. She'd kept this info to herself for a few days, but now she needed to let it out.

Englishcrumpet: The day after we went to the awards, the date-that-wasn't-a-date? Well, Noah kissed me.
Kangagirl: !!!!!!!!!
Sanfrandani: Wow!
Englishcrumpet: I know.
Sanfrandani: This would explain why, after a severe case of mentionitis *where the author is concerned, you've suddenly gone quiet about him.*

Kangagirl: Grace? Why didn't you tell us before?
Sanfrandani: I can understand the need for a little privacy. Sometimes there are things you just need to keep to yourself. It's not a reflection on our friendship that Grace wouldn't—or couldn't—tell us. Right, Grace?
Englishcrumpet: Right! You know I think the world of you two! You're my sanity in an increasingly crazy existence. I just…couldn't get my head round it.
Kangagirl: So…how was it?
Englishcrumpet: It was…

She bit her lip. *Soul-churning? Firework-inducing? Utterly fabulous?*

Englishcrumpet: It was nice. Different from last time.
Sanfrandani: Grace!
Kangagirl: Last time!!!!!!!! Grace?
Englishcrumpet: Go easy on the !!!, Marissa. You're going to wear your keyboard out.
Kangagirl: (raspberry)
Sanfrandani: I'm guessing that, in your very British, understated way, that you're saying it was pretty great?

Grace covered her face with her hands. Even now, just thinking about the hotel terrace, she went all hot and tingly. She'd never be able to look at a croissant the same way again.

Kangagirl: And last time*!*
Englishcrumpet: Whoops! Forgot to mention that, didn't I? We had a little kiss after the first date.
Kangagirl: Little kiss? Grace, you're holding back. I can tell.
Englishcrumpet: Okay! Okay! He pressed me up against

the coffee shop window and kissed me until I was left
breathless and melting, is that what you want to hear?
Kangagirl: (grin) It's a start!

Grace chuckled, despite herself. Marissa was right. She
had been holding back from her friends. Which was incredibly
daft. She really needed someone to talk to at the moment. Her
head was constantly going round in circles and sleep depri-
vation was setting in.

Sanfrandani: And you said no to a second date? Why?
Englishcrumpet: I was scared.

She hesitated for a moment, then began typing again.

Englishcrumpet: I still am.
Sanfrandani: What's happening now? Are you dating?
Englishcrumpet: Not exactly.
Sanfrandani: What does that mean?
Englishcrumpet: It gets worse.
Sanfrandani: How?

How did she say this? How did she explain all the weird
things she'd been thinking, all the strange things that had been
happening to her since that night? Did she tell them how her
stomach did the high jump every time Noah walked in the
coffee shop? Did she tell them about how, when she was alone
in bed at night, she longed for him to be there with her, holding
her, touching her…

She swallowed. Okay, she might not be ready to voice
those thoughts, but there was something concrete she hadn't
told them yet.

Englishcrumpet: He asked me to marry him.

For the first time in their Internet friendship there were no witty replies or strings of exclamation marks, no probing questions. These girls kept her real, asking the questions she was too scared to ask herself, encouraging her to reach beyond what she thought were her limits. But, right now, they were obviously just as stunned as she was about what she'd just told them.

After dealing with two very shocked friends, Grace logged off Blinddatebrides.com and turned off the laptop. Her brain was whirring far too hard to let her sleep, so she walked over to the bookcase and pulled out one of the photo albums.

Not the wedding one. One of the family ones, full of shots of her and Rob—and later Daisy too. A record of their relationship.

It had all seemed so romantic, marrying a handsome young soldier before he went off on active duty, and he'd come safely home again. That time.

She sighed. Rob had been husband material from the day he was born—kind, dependable, full of determination. Only a fool wouldn't have snapped him up the minute she'd laid eyes on him.

She flicked through the pages…She and Rob hanging out with their friends…The pair of them in front of the Christmas tree with matching Santa hats and silly grins. And then she came to her favourite one. The one she'd taken on their budget honeymoon in Broadstairs—Rob smiling at her as he sat on a wall eating fish and chips.

She almost couldn't bear to look at it.

Even though I haven't said 'yes' to Noah, I feel like I'm leaving you behind. How can I do that after all we were to each other?

She searched his smiling eyes, looking for answers.

Slowly, surely, the words filled her head, just as if he'd been sitting on the sofa with her with his arm round her, speaking to her, stroking the wisps of hair above her ears with his thumb. She knew exactly what Rob would have told her, his generous spirit and common sense shining through.

You have to. You have to leave me behind. You can't freeze-frame yourself and pretend that time hasn't moved on, because it has. A part of me will always be with you, but it's time to let go. Time to become who and what you were always supposed to be.

But did that mean accepting Noah or turning him down? And what was she supposed to be when she grew up, anyway? She gently closed the album and put it back on the shelf. At forty years and three months, she supposed it was high time she found out.

CHAPTER SIX

NOAH highlighted the last three pages he'd typed into his word processing program and hit the delete key with force. Then he highlighted the three pages before that and deleted them too.

His current hero was giving him hell and, no matter which way he tried to write him, he just wasn't working. Something just wasn't clicking.

He pushed himself away from his desk and let his chair roll backwards. What he needed was a change of scenery, a change of atmosphere. What he really needed was to stop thinking about Grace and what answer she'd give him. He didn't want to pressurise her, but the waiting was driving him crazy.

Maybe it would have been better if he'd picked a glamour vixen instead. At least he'd have had an unequivocal answer there and then.

Actually, he needed to walk. It was a great way to clear his head and get the ideas flowing. And if he could walk where other people were, even stop and watch them sometimes, so much the better. Little questions popped into his head as he observed them, and these little questions were often the sparks for some of his best ideas.

Why is that guy wearing a coat in July? What are those two people sitting on the bench *not* saying to each other? Those sorts of things.

He got into his car and drove into Vinehurst and parked near the large common with a swing park at one end. Although the average person wouldn't think a bit of wild grassland was a great place to people-watch for a writer of spy novels, they'd be wrong. He often wrote about characters who looked so domestic, so benign on the surface, but underneath they were sinister, heroic or just plain nasty.

He stuffed his hands in his pockets and moved his feet. It was time to let his brain off the leash and see where it would run.

It was nearing six o'clock in the evening and most of the mums and kids had gone home for tea, leaving the common to dog-walkers and joggers, but as he passed the playground he spotted a lone figure, pushing themself backwards and forwards with a listless movement of one toe.

Why? his brain asked. Why is that person—an adult— sitting here all alone as the sun lowers in the sky? Why are they using one foot, not two?

He looked again, capturing the exact pose, the exact movement of the swing, because he knew this image was going to come in handy some day. But, as he looked again, he realised it was Grace sitting there on the swing and, suddenly, it stopped being an exercise in logic and became urgently personal.

'Grace?'

She almost jumped off the swing she was so surprised to hear his voice. She couldn't disguise the look on her face that said: *Oh, heck. Does it have to be him who finds me like this?* And then he noticed the puffy red patches under her eyes and the way she sniffed quietly, hoping he wouldn't notice.

'What's the matter?'

'Long story,' she said, finally giving in to a good loud blow into a tissue. He sat down on the vacant swing and they both stared out into the distance, rocking in time.

'Good job I like stories,' he said, risking a look at her. She looked back, but didn't smile.

'The Coffee Bean is on its last legs.' Her voice was almost monotone, so unlike her usual animated conversation. 'Java Express has made Caz an offer to buy the shop and I don't think she can afford to refuse it. If she waits until she has to sell, or goes bust, she won't get nearly as much.'

'You'll lose your job,' he said. 'What will you do?'

Grace sighed. 'I would go back to college and finish my training if I could, but I need a roof over my head. I need to work. Actually, I literally need a roof over my head. The flat is part of the deal.'

She shook her head and big fat tears rolled down her cheeks. 'I can't stand the idea that they'll rip out that beautiful counter and pull up the floor. The Coffee Bean will lose all its character. They'll just make it…generic.'

Oh, hell. He never knew what to do when people cried. Really cried. He never let himself do it, so he couldn't even mimic what other people did when he was in the same situation. He didn't do huggy stuff and there-theres. Didn't know how.

What did Grace like? What would make her feel better?

Food.

Grace liked cooking. And she certainly enjoyed eating.

'Come on,' he said. 'I'm taking you to dinner.' He wondered if Barruci's would have a table free.

Grace looked up at him, her eyes hollow. He was about to pull his mobile phone out of his pocket and make a reservation when his inner Rottweiler growled at him. She stood, and didn't even bother trying to argue with him.

'Where are we going?'

'The Mandarin Moon.'

He didn't know why. He just knew it was the right choice.

Grace poked at her roast pork chow mein with a chopstick. She must really be in a bad way, Noah thought, if she couldn't polish this lot off. He offered her some more sweet and sour chicken and she just curled her lip.

'What are your options?' he said, putting the bowl back down on the table.

'I don't seem to have many options. I do okay working for Caz, but going to one of the large coffee shop chains would earn me virtually nothing. I'd have to move out of the area to find somewhere to live. But where the property is cheaper, the jobs are scarcer. Vicious circle.'

'And there's nothing you can do to save The Coffee Bean?'

She shook her head. 'Nope. I offered Caz my savings, but she said it would just be a drop in the ocean. It's a sad day when ten grand is a drop in the ocean.'

Ten grand. Not a lot to him, but Grace must have worked really hard to save that amount of money. Every day he knew her, there was more to marvel about her.

'In a month's time, I'll have no job, no home. No Daisy, even. It's worse than being back at square one. It's square *minus ten*.'

He had told himself he wouldn't push it. That he'd leave the whole marriage thing off the table tonight, but his mouth ran away with him.

'My offer still stands. Marry me.'

Grace looked as if she was going to put her head face down in her noodles and cry.

'Not only do I think we can make it work, but I can give you financial security, Grace. You won't have to worry about a house. You could even go back to college or we'd look at investing in a shop, if you wanted. I always liked the idea of opening a shop myself. Of course I always thought it would be a book shop but, hey, I can be flexible. I like cake as much as the next guy.'

She bit her lip.

'And Daisy's college fees would be taken care of. No worries.'

'Noah, I can't—'

'I know it sounds like I'm trying to buy you, but I'm not. Honestly. I need things from you too.'

Her eyes narrowed. 'Such as?'

'Well, there's all the travelling all over the world, staying at nice hotels—Paris, Rome, Sydney—'

Grace sat up straighter. 'Sydney? Do you ever get to visit San Francisco?'

'We could, if you wanted. The other part of the deal is promising to protect me from the scary women with autograph books. Scary women in general, really.'

That was supposed to be a joke. She was supposed to laugh.

'And, of course, there's the all-important bonus...'

She folded her arms. 'Which is?'

He grinned at her. 'Nice teeth,' he said, holding the pose. 'Don't forget the teeth.'

Despite herself, Grace let out a little laugh. 'You're as crazy as a box of frogs.'

'I know,' he said, suddenly sobering. 'This does seem mad—or at least it would if it didn't seem like the sanest idea I've had in a long time.'

Grace's thumbnail made its way to her mouth. The weird thing was he was right. It did sound sane, logical even. Noah was offering her everything she'd ever dreamed of. And she didn't feel guilty about wanting to take it. The situation she was in now wasn't down to lack of hard work, it was merely fate pulling the rug out from under her feet. And, while she would never want to be accused of marrying for money, she had to admit that not having to struggle any more, to be able to enjoy the finer things in life was a real pull.

Oh, what was she going to do?

Noah pushed his plate away. 'If you'd said yes to my original proposal, I'd have expected a longer engagement, time to get used to each other, but if you need somewhere to stay, you can move in with me. Of if you don't like the idea of living together, we'll get married sooner. Whatever works for you, Grace. Just let me know.'

He was being so sweet. And she was on the verge of agreeing with him. She liked Noah. Really liked him. She could maybe even love him—in a growing-old-and-wrinkly-together kind of way. Was that going to be enough?

She'd been paying lip service to the idea of growing up, moving on. Now was her chance to make a mature decision about the rest of her life. Was she going to run away like a frightened child, or was she going to reach out and seize the day?

She exhaled long and hard and looked Noah in the eye.

'I need to talk to Daisy. It wouldn't be fair to make a decision without at least asking her how she feels about the changes this is going to make to her life.'

With a heart rate of at least a hundred and seventy five, Grace dialled Daisy's mobile number. They'd mainly stuck to emails while she'd been away because of the cost of the calls, but this was one thing that couldn't be typed out and sent with the click of a button.

Her stomach went cold and crampy when the dialling tone disappeared and she heard it ringing. A few seconds later a surprisingly crackle-free voice said, 'Mum?'

All at once, Grace began to cry. She missed her girl so much. If only Daisy were here and they could sit round the kitchen table with a pot of tea and a stack of bacon sandwiches and they could hammer this all out.

'Mum! What's happened?'

Grace swallowed the lump in her throat and wiped the tears away with a flat palm. 'Nothing's happened. Well, not nothing—but I mean it's not an emergency—nobody died or anything. I'm just so happy to hear your voice.'

'Oh, Mum, me too!'

And then they were both in tears.

Grace pulled herself together first. There was more purpose to this call than just making her phone wet.

'I've got some news…some good news, I think.'

Daisy sniffed and her voice was sunny through the tears. 'Oh, yes?'

Grace nodded. Stupid, because Daisy couldn't see her. 'You know that man you set me up with…on the blind-date?'

'I thought you weren't dating him.'

'I'm not…well, not really…but we've become very close.' She took a deep breath and the words tumbled out when she released it. 'He's asked me to marry him.'

If Grace thought her heart rate was bad before, it was fit to leap out of her chest now. Not so much the high jump, but hurdling.

'Daisy? Are you still there?'

Silence.

'I'm still here. Flipping hell, Mum. You work fast!'

'It's a long story…'

And Grace filled Daisy in on all the details of The Coffee Bean, who Noah was and how quickly things were likely to happen. When, at last, she'd run out of things to say, she waited.

'I don't care who he is or what he does for a living. Although I have to say I've read a couple of his books and they're really rather good…Anyway, that's beside the point. What really matters is: do you love him?'

Grace dragged her top teeth across her bottom lip. *Not yet, but almost…*

'Not the same way I loved your dad, but I'm older now. I'm looking for something different this time around.'

'And you think you can be happy with him?'

Grace stood still and shut her eyes, trying to picture a future—a long one—with Noah in it.

'Yes. Yes, I think I can.'

She could almost imagine the determined expression on Daisy's face as she said, 'Then I think you should go for it.'

Noah had insisted he pay for Daisy to fly home from Greece for a week and then fly back out again to join her friends. In the days before the wedding they sorted through the flat, packing some things, donating other things to charity shops, just falling about laughing at some of their possessions.

Whose idea had it been to buy the light-up Santa that whistled a tune and dropped his trousers to display a bare bottom when you pushed a button? Grace swore it hadn't been hers. As did Daisy.

It was nice to be back into their old home together, laughing, eating stacks of bacon sandwiches as they worked, but sad too. This truly was goodbye to her old life, the old Grace. Still, she packed a couple of pairs of fishnets, just in case.

Daisy looked up from the box she was packing. 'Mum?'

'Yes, sweetheart?'

'I've also got some news.'

She grabbed her daughter by the shoulders. 'Dear Lord, Daisy! Please tell me you're not getting married or are pregnant!'

Daisy did an eye-roll thing that was totally her. 'Mu-um! Don't be so melodramatic! It's nothing like that. It's big...but it's not bad—at least I don't think it is.'

Grace's heart was pumping. 'Well, get on with it before your poor mother has a heart attack!'

Daisy looked at the floor. 'Being away from home has given me time to think about what I want from life. I've decided I don't want to study history at Durham uni any more.'

'But you're going to do it in London somewhere? That's what you're saying. That's what you're telling me, isn't it?'

She shook her head. 'Sorry, Mum. It's just...not my passion, you know.' She looked up, very earnest, and Grace was reminded of a seven-year-old Daisy who had announced, very seriously, that she would run away if she was made to go to any more of the ballet lessons that Grandma had booked and paid for.

Grace's voice came out soft. 'Then…what is your passion?'

Please don't let her say pole-dancing. Please don't let it be that.

'I missed the café, Mum. I missed the cooking and the smells. I know it's gone now, but I realised I want to learn to cook like you do—to make things, beautiful things that make people happy, even if only for a few minutes.' She looked hopefully at Grace. 'I want to go to catering college like you did.'

Grace's face crumpled into a watery smile. 'Come here, you daft girl!'

Daisy ran into her arms and hugged tight. Grace had resisted the urge to sniff her head, as she'd done when Daisy had been a baby, but now she allowed herself the luxury.

'If that's what you want to do, then it's fine by me. Honest! And if I end up going back to college too, we could end up studying together!'

Daisy stepped back and cocked her head to one side.

'Okay, okay. I get it. You don't want Mum cramping your style at college…But think! One day we could open our own little patisserie together. If you want that, that is.'

Daisy grinned. 'I was hoping you'd say that!'

Grace grinned back at her. 'It's a plan.'

This was wonderful. Perhaps Noah's plan for the future was going to turn out even better than expected. For the first time in weeks, Grace felt hope surge within her.

Grace finished packing her belongings from the flat the night before the wedding. The last thing to go into the last box was the photo of Rob and Daisy that sat in the hallway, keeping guard all these years. Daisy walked up to her mother and hugged her from behind.

Grace's eyes stung. She couldn't quite bring herself to put the frame into the box, so she and Daisy just stared at it for a few wordless minutes.

'It's okay,' Daisy whispered into Grace's ear. 'Dad would have wanted this for you.'

Grace looked down at the photo, at Rob's smiling eyes. They seem to be looking straight at her, connecting with her soul. There wasn't a hint of anger, jealousy or betrayal in them. She knew Daisy was right. But part of her ached for what she'd had with him, that wonderful mix of friendship and passion, completeness and freedom. It felt as if, by marrying Noah, she was saying goodbye to the hope of that in her future, even if, deep down, she hadn't really believed it was possible.

Daisy took the picture from her and laid it in the box. 'It'll be okay, Mum. I promise you. I see the two of you together, and Noah's right for you. Besides… I've told him that if he ever hurts you, I met a couple of interesting characters in Sicily who would "deal" with him if I asked them.'

Grace burst out laughing and turned to squeeze her daughter to her. 'I love you, Crazy Daisy. And I'll miss you when you go back to Greece and join your friends.'

'But I'm here now, and everything is perfect.'

'Yes, it is,' Grace said and then she folded the flaps of the last box and taped them into place.

The wedding was an uncomplicated affair. Grace and Noah arranged a civil ceremony in the local town hall before a small group of friends and family. Nobody noticed the colour drain from the bride's face as she joined hands with the groom and prepared to say her vows or, if they did, they just put it down to normal wedding jitters.

No one could have known that, at the exact moment of no return, Grace had a premonition so real, so strong, that it left her feeling cold for hours afterwards.

Noah kissed his bride and didn't spot the hint of wariness in her eyes. But Noah wasn't very good at looking below the surface of other people's emotions. And heaven forbid he ever open the trapdoor to the cellar of his own.

The crowd of well-wishers sighed collectively when the groom announced a surprise honeymoon in Paris and whisked an unusually mute Grace away to the station so they could catch Eurostar. By early evening they were in the centre of Paris, the city of lights. The city of love.

Although there were far more expensive hotels on the north side of the river, in the Louvre and Marais *arrondisements*, Noah told Grace he really liked the atmosphere of St Germain, close to the vibrant Latin quarter and full of cafés where philosophers, politicians and great writers of the last few centuries had come to clash minds and share ideas.

'I can't believe I'm really here,' Grace said as they wandered down the Boulevard St Germain, hand in hand. 'All these quaint little cafés with their wicker chairs and awnings and waiters in long white aprons. It's exactly how I imagined it would be.'

Noah just smiled and ushered her down a cobbled side street, round a couple of corners and then into a rather unique-looking restaurant. 'Everyone has to eat at Le Procope at least once,' he explained as the waiter showed them to a table. 'Even if the guidebooks say it's a tourist trap these days. The food is still spectacular.'

Grace stared around the room, one of many which seem to be arranged over several floors in the tall Parisian house. Old paintings of men in dusty wigs covered the walls and ornate glass display cases held china and champagne flutes, giving the impression they were dining in somebody's best parlour.

The food *was* spectacular, from the marinated leek salad to the famous coq au vin, dished up in its very own miniature copper pot. But, after half of her main course, Grace suddenly lost her appetite.

It wasn't long before Noah put down his cutlery and looked at her. In the month since she'd accepted his proposal, she'd come to see this same expression in his eyes over and over again, as if he could reach into her mind and pluck out her thoughts. It was a little unnerving. Extremely unnerving, considering her current train of thought.

'I know this all happened a lot quicker than either of us anticipated, Grace.'

Oh, heck. He knew. She flushed a deep red.

'Tonight… I know it's traditionally our…wedding night, but if you're not ready, if you want to wait a while, that's no problem. We've got the rest of our lives. There's no rush.'

He was being so sweet that Grace wanted to cry. But she didn't think the ever-so-suave French waiters would be impressed if she dissolved into tears and blew her nose on one of the starched white napkins afterwards.

'Thank you, Noah.'

Her heart swelled and, for the first time in the surreal event that had been her second wedding day, she realised with startling clarity that she really was lucky to have found him.

'The truth is… I just don't know how I feel at the moment. It's all been so…'

He reached over the table and took her hand, stroking the ridge of her knuckles with the pad of his thumb. 'I know. Don't worry. We'll both work out how we feel as we go along.'

It was late by the time they got back to the hotel. Grace got dressed for bed in the bathroom, silently cursing the filmy, strappy white thing that Daisy had egged her into buying. After washing her face and brushing her teeth twice, she put the lid on the toilet seat down and sat on it. Her left leg jiggled all on its own.

Deep breathing. That was it. This was no big deal. It was just—

Who was she kidding? She was terrified, the nerves even worse than her *actual* first time. What was wrong with her? Noah was gorgeous and seriously sexy. Didn't she want to sleep with him?

Hell, *yeah*! her ageing hormones chorused.

But still her left leg jiggled.

She pressed down on it with both hands until it stopped, then stood up. When she emerged into the bedroom, Noah was standing, dressed only in dark pyjama bottoms, staring out of one of the long elegant windows.

He turned slowly and she couldn't help noticing the darkening of his pupils, a little *frisson* of electricity that passed between them. He walked over to her, ran a hand across her cheek, down her neck and along her collarbone. Grace stopped breathing. And then he kissed her, long and slow. A perfect kiss. The kind of kiss that certainly should be a prelude to *something*.

But Grace seemed to be standing outside of herself, watching herself, second-guessing what she should do with her hands, where to touch him.

Noah broke the kiss and rested his forehead against hers.

'I'm sorry,' she whispered.

He shook his head and made a soothing noise.

'Really, I am. It's been a long time since it's been my… you know… first time with someone. I'm being stupid, aren't I? It's no big deal. I should… we should… just do it. You know, like ripping the plaster off—'

Noah said nothing, but pressed a finger to her lips. Grace just stared at him. He was doing that thing again—looking inside her. She wanted to screw her eyes up, but she didn't.

He led her to the bed and pulled her down onto it so she was facing away from him and then spooned in behind her.

'Go to sleep, Grace,' he said and pulled her to him with a strong arm.

'But—'

'Go to sleep, Grace.'

Now it seemed her nerves were for nothing, part of her screamed out in frustration. The other part gave a huge sigh of relief. Even though, in their short engagement, they'd spent plenty of time kissing, touching, it still felt a little artificial, a forced situation. And Noah had been travelling some of that time while Grace had needed to stay behind and help wind things up at The Coffee Bean. They really hadn't had a chance to relax with each other, physically or emotionally.

She did it now, letting the tension seep out of her muscles, enjoying the solid feel of him behind her. And, bless him, tucked in as close together as they were, she could tell he was ready for action, even if she wasn't. She pulled his hand into hers and kissed his knuckles, tears in her eyes.

'Night, Noah,' she said in a croaky whisper.

Grace woke in the morning to find Noah still wrapped around her. She twisted so she could look at him. She'd never seen him sleep before. He looked younger, almost boyish—even with the deep creases at the edges of his eyes and the tiny speckling of grey hairs near his temples.

As if he sensed she was watching him, he shifted then opened his eyes. She smiled.

'What's so funny?' he said and pulled a hand from underneath her to rub his eyelids with his fingertips.

'You always look so in control, so self-contained. I kind of like it when you're all groggy and confused.'

He yawned. 'What's the time?'

She leaned over and looked at her watch on the bedside table. 'Nine.'

'Nine!' He jumped out of bed and ran to the bathroom. 'I never sleep in until nine. Seven at the most. You—' he pointed a finger at Grace before disappearing into the bathroom '—must be a bad influence on me.'

Grace lay back on the bed and stretched. He was being lovely. No guilt trip. No tiny reminders that she had chickened out of their wedding night. She decided to play along. 'I do my best to live up to my reputation. Anyway, what's the hurry?'

His head appeared from around the bathroom door. 'Paris. We've only got three days before we go home and I want to show you everything.'

Grace sat up in bed. 'Everything?'

'Well, lots. I need to come back here in around three months' time for a book launch, so anything we miss now, we can do then.' He looked her up and down. 'What are you waiting for?'

Grace folded her arms across her chest. 'Coffee. I'm not going anywhere until I've had coffee.'

They went out for breakfast and had warm croissants and strong black coffee at Les Deux Magots. They climbed the Eiffel Tower, marvelled at Monet's waterlilies and ate ham baguettes and cold Belgian beer sitting under bright red canopies in an outdoor café in the Jardin Tuileries.

Noah had done all these things before, but doing them with Grace brought a freshness to the experience. She flung herself headlong into every sight, every sound, every taste. There was one place he was desperate to take her, but he was saving it for last.

Since they were close by, they wandered round the Louvre, even braving the crowds to remark on how much smaller than expected the Mona Lisa was and wondering what the Venus de Milo's arms really would have been doing had they not been lost, and if anyone had actually found them and not realised what they were.

But, even in the face of such a wonderful day, Noah felt a little sad for Grace. She really ought to be here with someone who could give her the romance he feared she secretly craved. But he was selfish. She may have settled for second best with him, but he didn't want to let her go so she could find it with someone else.

By three o'clock, Grace went on sightseeing strike. They were back in the Jardin Tulieries, the vast building of the Louvre behind them, and she sat down on a low backless bench amidst the trees and refused to budge.

He tugged at her hand until she consented to stand up. 'One more stop.'

'Do we have to?' she said, her voice muffled by his jacket as she leaned against him.

'We do. Come on, it's just across the Rue de Rivoli.'

Under the large stone façaded arcades of the Rue de Rivoli was a place that was as close to heaven on earth as Grace could get. Angelina. The café famous for the best hot chocolate in Paris, and the pastries! Oh, the pastries!

It was all Noah could do to get her off the street and in through the door. But she found the inside was just as fabulous, with an ornate curved counter filled with works of art. Pink macaroons, stuffed with raspberries and topped with delicate flecks of silver leaf, pistachio bombes the colour of fresh green shoots with contrasting pink icing, éclairs, mille feuille, tartes…It was almost criminal that anyone should think of eating them.

When they were seated at a small round table beside a square ivory column, Grace had no problem in deciding what she should order. It had to be their signature dish, Mont Blanc, accompanied by Chocolat Chaud des Africains. When it arrived, she spent a good minute memorising every swirl in the chestnut purée covering the fluffy white meringue before daring to break into it with her fork. The hot chocolate was just as good: thick gloopy melted chocolate—none of this powdered nonsense—infused with spices and served in individual jugs accompanied by glasses of whipped cream to dollop into it. She didn't understand the reason for the glass of cold water the waiter served her. But then she tasted the hot chocolate. It had a wonderfully thick bitter taste, but a sip of cool water was definitely needed every now and then to clear her palate.

Noah had been going to order just coffee, complaining he'd eaten enough sweet stuff already in the last few months, but she wouldn't let him off the hook. He smiled at her, and she knew he liked it when she got bossy, so she grinned back at him.

He'd done this for her, had planned it all out. A trip to Angelina was all the wedding present she could have wished for. Just like that, all her fears about the future melted away and the anchors holding her in the past let go. This was her life now. This was her husband. And he was funny and caring and sexy enough to eat with a dollop of whipped cream.

She couldn't stop looking at him as he paid the bill and they made their way through the crowded café to the front of the shop. She didn't even break her stride to look at the cakes behind the counter again. She was totally focused on him.

The cool spring breeze was welcome on her face when they stepped back out into the street. She stopped him by tugging his hand, making him come back to her. Now it was her turn to call the shots, to bestow the gift. She leaned in close and kissed his ear before whispering, 'Take me back to the hotel, Noah.'

'But—'

'Take me back to the hotel.'

* * *

All the way back in the taxi, they held hands, played with each other's fingers, unable to stop touching, caressing, stroking. For most of the journey they just smiled and stared out of the window, but they saw nothing, their whole attention given to the tips of their bodies that were intertwined.

It was the same in the lift at the hotel. They stood at the back, behind the other guests, and shared a secret with each other.

Once in the hotel room, there was no place for nerves. Grace didn't even remember she'd had any as they began to kiss and peel layer upon layer of clothing from each other. Sometimes they were hungry and impatient, sometimes slow and teasing.

She was lost. Lost somewhere where there was only Noah. Noah's hands, Noah's lips.

When the last of the barriers between them had been stripped away, he slid his hands down her naked torso and she shivered with delight. Then he scooped her up in his arms so she was cradled against his heartbeat and carried her to the bed.

CHAPTER SEVEN

MAKING love with Noah was like nothing else Grace had ever experienced. It was like handling raw fire, but without getting scorched—well, only in a good way. He was so strong, so totally focused, yet so devastatingly good that, for a few moments, she was incoherent with pleasure. Her whole body thrummed.

She could feel his breath against her shoulder as he lay half-draped over her. His ribs moved up and down, up and down, in a deep, even rhythm. Grace lay still, taking comfort from it, and let her eyes wander over her surroundings. Light from a street lamp somewhere shone on the ceiling and wall, creating a strip of distorted light, and she stared at it, wondering why she'd woken and why she couldn't snuggle back into him and sleep.

With Rob, sex had been good—fun, energetic, playful—but this…Noah…

A different league.

She couldn't kid herself any more. This was no platonic, mutual partnership. This was the real thing. With honest-to-goodness violins playing and birds singing, even though it was nowhere near dawn yet.

She loved Noah.

And so much for it being safe. It was grown up, all right. Big and scary and very, very dangerous with sharp teeth. No wonder she'd made excuses to avoid getting close to it all these years. She should have listened to her instincts and stayed the hell away.

But then Noah made a sound that was half-snuffle, half-snore and pulled her tighter against him and she couldn't help but smile, even as her eyes filled with tears. Why did the good things in life have to come with a dark opposite? Life and death. Love and hate. Fear and faith. Why couldn't she love Noah without the threat of losing him? It would always be there, hanging in the background like an unexploded bomb, waiting to detonate when she finally relaxed and believed it had all been a bluff.

Losing Rob had been bad enough. For months, she'd only dragged herself out of bed in the mornings because Daisy had needed her cereal. Daisy had saved her life back then without even knowing it. Any moments of imbalance on her mother's part had been quickly countered by a ponytail of dark waves and a cheeky smile.

Grace wriggled herself backwards so she was as close to Noah as she could get, not even a millimetre of air between them. His chest was warm against her back and beating a reassuring rhythm.

Not yet. Not tonight. But the loss would come. One day. It always did.

And she was a coward, too scared to face it.

She gently kissed the forearm wrapped around her and pulled it close so she could lay her cheek against it.

You should have seen it coming, Grace. You do love and marriage and babies, remember? What did you think was going to happen?

Her only hope was that Noah was taking the same journey she was, that they were going to do as he'd said and work out how they felt together.

* * *

The next couple of days were exactly what a honeymoon in Paris should be. Grace and Noah stayed in bed and ordered room service quite a lot, making love whenever the mood took them, which seemed to be pretty often. Even Daisy would have been shocked that her old fogey of a mother could have such an appetite for nothing but Noah. Not that she was going to talk to Daisy about this. In Daisy's own words, that would be TMI—too much information. For both of them.

On their last morning, after breakfast in bed, which had turned into *we might as well stay here for lunch too*, Grace snuggled into Noah, her head on his chest and his arm tucked round her.

Even though they were married, there was so much she didn't know about him. It had all happened so quickly that they'd bypassed a lot of the getting-to-know-you process. And she wanted to know everything about him, to understand him. Partly because she was hoping he was feeling the same way she was, but it was more than that. She loved him. And that meant every new thing she learned about him was a treasure, something precious to be stored away in her mind and wondered at.

'You know all about me now—my history with Rob, my disastrous dates between then and now—but you haven't told me anything about you.' She poked him in the ribs. 'That's the problem with being such a nosy parker. You're too good a listener. And I'm too good a talker.'

Noah stroked her arm and kissed the top of her head. 'Seems we've found the perfect balance.'

She shook her head against his chest. 'You must have had a couple of serious relationships in your life. I can't be the first one. And, anyway, I don't really count yet, do I?'

A pair of hands reached round her waist and hoisted her up so she was lying on top of him. A wicked gleam was in his eye. 'Believe me, you count.' And then he started to trail his fingers up the backs of her legs, higher, higher…

'That's not what I meant, Noah. You're avoiding the issue.'

His fingers stopped moving. 'Maybe there's nothing to avoid.'

But the gleam in his eye had been replaced by a shuttered hardness. She slid off him. 'Maybe there is,' she said quietly.

Noah pushed himself on to one elbow and launched himself out of bed. 'I don't want to talk about it, Grace. Subject closed.'

She gathered the rumpled sheet around her as he disappeared into the bathroom and slammed the door. Well, there was her answer. Now she knew exactly how Noah felt.

The face staring back at him from the bathroom mirror was not a pretty sight. His brows were slanted together and his jaw was square and hard.

It had started already.

The probing. The questions.

He just hadn't thought it would happen so soon. Grace had taken him completely by surprise. They'd been having such a good time, just enjoying the moment, and she'd had to go and spoil it with deep and meaningful stuff. Although he knew he shouldn't be—she was just doing what women did— he was angry with her.

It had taken Sara much longer to start trying to unravel him but, after a while, the innocent-sounding enquiries had come. What are you thinking, Noah? What are you *feeling*, Noah? It was like being one giant scab that women couldn't resist picking at.

At first, he'd tried really hard with Sara. He'd tried to dig deep, had tried to come up with answers she'd like. But it hadn't been real. He'd invented a version of himself—fictional Noah—whom he'd analysed like one of the characters he created in his books. The real Noah was just as much a mystery to himself as he was to Sara.

So he'd thought hard about fictional Noah's motivation and

what he wanted out of life. He'd prepared pretty speeches to say in case she caught him unawares. Things that Sara wanted to hear, things that would make her happy. After a while he'd got fed up with fictional Noah. The guy had been just too annoyingly perfect.

Maybe that was why his smokescreen had failed after a couple of years. He'd just got sick of the sound of his own voice and he couldn't stand to regurgitate all that soppy stuff any longer. Then Sara had started talking about glass walls and needing more. She'd picked and picked and picked at him. And when she'd finished gouging away at him, when the scab had finally lifted, she'd discovered the truth. Underneath, there was nothing. And then she'd left.

He really didn't want Grace to leave.

The last couple of days had been amazing and, despite his glass wall, he'd felt closer to the love thing than he'd ever felt before. But still there was something stopping him. He just wasn't that deep. There was nothing there to give.

So, he'd just have to distract her or, like Sara, she'd pick, pick, pick and discover what was under the scab that had reformed itself into a hard little shell. No healthy new skin. Just an empty space.

He took a shower to give himself and Grace a few minutes to calm down. As he towel-dried himself he hoped to God she wasn't crying. Anything he said to crying women just sounded trite. He normally made things worse.

But Grace wasn't crying when he re-entered the bedroom. She was getting dressed—noisily. She was banging doors and stomping from wardrobe to bed and back. He intercepted her.

'I'm sorry, Grace. I didn't mean to snap at you.'

See? Even though the words weren't over-the-top and gushy, they still sounded fake to his ears, like lines in a play. It wasn't that he didn't mean them, just…that he didn't feel anything when he said them.

She stopped and looked at him, a shoe in one hand. He suddenly felt as if he'd been sliced up, put on a slide and shoved under a microscope.

'I appreciate the apology. I wasn't trying to pry. I just think we need to get to know each other better.'

He nodded.

He'd thought he'd be safe from that with Grace. Safe, because a marriage based on nothing to do with love shouldn't require all the painful scab-picking. He'd been wrong. The thought niggled him. He didn't like being wrong on a general level, but also about this specific thing. If he'd got this wrong, what else was he mistaken about?

Time to distract.

'Let's go for a walk,' he said.

They ended up wandering up to the Seine and onto Les Pont Des Arts. Grace leaned on the railing and watched the slate-grey water rushing below the bridge. Then she raised her head and looked towards the Ille de la Cite, the spires of Notre Dame and Sainte-Chapelle poking into the sky. It was so beautiful here, all this pale grey stone, the deep blue of the sky, the vibrant green of the trees that lined the river.

Noah came up beside her and they stared at the water in silence.

He seemed so relaxed, so charming. And she'd not seen anything beneath that until today. It was like the river. She'd been too blinded by the ripples and light bouncing off the surface to see what nasty stuff was lurking at the bottom. There were huge parts of himself that Noah kept hidden and she wanted to know why. She wanted to know why he camou-flaged himself so well.

Noah reached out and took her hand.

She didn't pull away, even though she was still smarting from his remark that morning. She accepted his hand, curling her fingers around his warm skin. He was trying, and that was good enough for now.

They walked to the end of the bridge and down a flight of stone steps so they were walking on the grey stone quay right next to the Seine. Other couples passed them, hands caught just like theirs, and Grace knew she should feel a sense of comradeship with them.

I'm in Paris and in love too.

But it wasn't quite the same, was it? Those other couples were in love with each other.

Now they were close to the silver birches lining the bank she could see that their markings were not just the normal black slits in the pearly bark. Up the entire trunks of every tree, covering every possible square inch, were names and declarations of love in many different languages and scripts. She recognised some English and French and Japanese, but others she just couldn't put a name to. She'd bet Noah would know. But Noah wasn't looking at the trees; he was looking at the river and muttering something about Napoleonic architecture.

An echo of the premonition from her wedding day turned her toes to ice.

Noah didn't love her.

He might never love her.

And he would never carve her name on a tree in Paris.

Back in London, things improved—at least on the surface. Noah and Grace began their lives together. They ate at nice restaurants, attended parties and other functions up in town, and generally stuck to the plan they'd had when they'd married. Noah wrote and Grace started looking at prospectuses for catering colleges, even though she wasn't sure any more that she wanted to go back to being a student, but it seemed she should explore the option, even if she didn't pursue it.

And they made love.

For Grace, it was the only thing that kept the creeping cold feeling at bay. Unfortunately, it wasn't helping with the head-over-heels, desperately in love with Noah thing. It was all such a cliché. Every time he looked at her now, her heart did a triple flip. When he smiled, she just wanted to melt. And when he took her in his arms and touched her with such tenderness, she thought her heart would break with the beauty of it.

In other words, she was up the creek without a paddle. And she was just crazy enough in love with him to want to jump out of the boat and drown in him. She just didn't care.

But they never spoke of love. It was an unwritten rule. Not part of their agreement.

One morning, almost a month after their return from Paris, Grace decided there was only so much mooching around a big old house that a woman could do. Noah was hidden away inside his study, as he often was in the mornings, wrestling with some character problem that was making him a huge grouch, and she knocked on the door and let him know she was going into town. He just waved with his left hand and continued scribbling in a notebook with his right. She didn't take offence. She was starting to get used to the Noah who retreated into his imaginary world for hours every day.

Walking up the cobbles in the High Street made her sad now. The Coffee Bean and Martin's book shop, which had also been snapped up, were now boarded up. It wouldn't be long before the Java Express logos appeared on them. It felt as if a part of the village's soul had died.

Without warning, tears filled Grace's eyes and she began to sob.

What was happening to her? Yes, she was an emotional kind of person, but she wasn't normally given to weeping in the street. Maybe it was all getting too much for her—the pain of seeing Noah, blithely going about his business, never realising for a second that she wasn't totally happy, despite his best efforts to give her all the things he'd promised her. She wouldn't want to be without him. She loved him too much to leave him and still held out hope that, given a few years, he would soften and come to love her too. But she was starting to think that her grown-up decision to marry Noah for companionship and security hadn't been her most sensible moment. After all, even grown-ups made mistakes.

A yawn crept up on her. She was tired, that was all. And, she had to face it, there was plenty in her life at the moment that was contributing to her general weariness. It was probably just PMT making her all emotional. She'd been through a major upheaval in the last couple of months—losing her job, moving house, getting married. No wonder she was wiped out and falling into bed before ten in the evening.

Grace walked down the High Street in the clear fresh sunshine that only came with a gentle English summer's day. It was too nice to spend the morning cooped up in little boutiques, looking for ever more cocktail dresses to wear to Noah's writing bashes, so she kept walking and made for the common. The wind was blowing the long grass flat, first this direction and then that. She chose one of the paths of short grass that had probably marked the common for hundreds of years and followed it.

The school holidays were still a couple of weeks away and it was relatively quiet, with only the playground a source of noise. She chose a bench on the far side of the common, with a view of the pretty little church, far enough away from both the Tiger's Head pub and the playground to be quiet and to have very little traffic. The sun was just peeping over the tops of the houses, sending vanilla rays to warm everything, and she just sat back and closed her eyes, drinking it in.

Despite the practically idyllic surroundings, tears gathered beneath her lids and pushed their way between her lashes to trickle down her cheeks. She smudged them away with her palms. Damn this PMT. It wasn't helping things at all, it really wasn't.

Since relaxing seemed to be beyond her, she decided to look in her diary and check when this hormone-induced dementia was likely to be relieved. She pulled the little book out of her handbag on the seat beside her and flicked through the pages until she found the current week. Then she went back a week and stared at that page. No, that couldn't be right. And then she flipped back another week.

According to her diary, she was—she counted the days with her finger, flipping over onto the current page—thirteen days late.

Late. And not one or two days—thirteen!

Still, she'd never been like clockwork. It was probably just stress. There'd been times when she'd been so stressed that her cycle had gone completely out of whack. However, in recent years, she'd never had a reason to worry that it had been anything *but* stress.

Stop being so overdramatic! There weren't any other symptoms—such as the overwhelming urge for anything starchy like she'd had when she'd been expecting Daisy. This was just panic talking. Any time now, her period would start and she'd laugh at herself for even considering that…

She flipped back to the pages to when she'd been in Paris. Okay, so that would have been slap-bang in the middle of her cycle, but it didn't mean anything. They'd been careful. Okay, considering she'd been very *careless* with her heart, careful probably wasn't a good word to use in connection with Noah, but they'd used protection. She was just worrying over nothing.

Grace put the diary back in her bag and stood up. There was a late-opening chemist three doors down from The Coffee Bean. No, where The Coffee Bean had once been. She'd just pop in. Not that she really needed to. It was just that, with everything else in her life at the moment, she really didn't need one more thing to keep her tossing and turning at night.

Grace sneaked into the kitchen late that night, Daisy's laptop under her arm. Noah had dozed off in front of a war film on telly. She logged onto Blinddatebrides.com and sent up a prayer that, even though it wasn't their usual day to chat, Dani and Marissa would be online.

Blinddatebrides.com is running 12 chat rooms, 26 private IM conferences, and 5216 members are online.

Grace looked at the little header she normally glossed over and laughed out loud. Blinddatebrides.com, indeed! Not only had she found a groom, but she'd come away from one of their set-ups with a little more than she'd bargained for.

She sent an email SOS out to the girls and waited.

Englishcrumpet invites Kangagirl and Sanfrandani to a private IM conference.
Englishcrumpet: Anybody out there?

Grace inhaled, breathed out and waited. By the time she was just starting to run out of oxygen, there was a ping from the laptop.

Kangagirl: What's the emergency? Grace?
Englishcrumpet: We'd better wait and see if Dani shows up. I'm not sure I can do this twice.
Kangagirl: Now you're scaring me.
Englishcrumpet: I'm a little freaked out myself.

A second ping announced Dani's arrival.

Sanfrandani: Hi, guys!

Kangagirl: Grace is just about to drop a bombshell. She's gone all mysterious and dramatic.
Sanfrandani: Bigger than the I'm-getting-married-to-Noah bombshell?
Englishcrumpet: Way bigger. But kind of related.
Kangagirl: Don't leave us in suspense, Grace!

Grace looked down at her stomach. There was another thing that would be getting bigger shortly. Here goes, she thought.

Englishcrumpet: I'm pregnant.

Once again, she'd stunned them into silence. If there were awards for that kind of thing, Grace was sure she'd get a medal.

Englishcrumpet: Say something!
Sanfrandani: Congratulations?
Kangagirl: How? I mean…oh, you know what I mean.
Englishcrumpet: Kinda relieved you're not asking for a blow-by-blow account there, Marissa!
Sanfrandani: You're not taking this well, are you? The more flippant you get, the worse things are, usually.

Grace stared at the home pregnancy test she'd propped up by the laptop screen, just to make sure she hadn't been seeing things. Tests had moved on quite a lot since she'd last taken one and now they were practically idiot-proof, no faint little blue or pink lines to count, just a big digital screen reading: PREGNANT. It might as well have added, *You, Dummy!* The pregnancy tests might be idiot-proof, but the people who needed them obviously weren't. Why else would a forty-year-old woman have got herself into a situation better suited to a reckless teenager?

Englishcrumpet: I'm trying to get my head round it, to be honest. Humour seems to be the only way to stop myself losing the plot entirely.

Sanfrandani: Have you told Noah?

Englishcrumpet: I haven't told anyone! Not even Daisy! What if she doesn't want a little brother or sister stealing her limelight?

Kangagirl: If Daisy is half the girl you've brought her up to be, she'll be wonderful!

Sanfrandani: And Noah?

Englishcrumpet: Dani, do you have to be the voice of reason all the time?

Englishcrumpet: Sorry, that was meant to be a joke, but it just came across snippy.

Sanfrandani: No offence taken. I can tell you're scared witless.

Kangagirl: You can't not tell your husband, Grace. He's going to notice eventually.

Grace sagged. She had no idea if Noah had ever had any thoughts about becoming a parent. They'd both just assumed it wouldn't be part of the package. And that had been fine with her, but now—even though Dani was right, she was scared witless—part of her was desperate to make it part of the package and hope that Noah would agree. Maybe a baby would help. He couldn't help but break out of his cold, tight little shell with a son or a daughter to love.

Englishcrumpet: I'm not sure how he's going to feel about this.

Sanfrandani: Don't be too hard on him if he's a little shocked. After all, you're feeling the same way yourself. But think, what a wonderful way to start your new life together!

Kangagirl: Oh, Grace! I'm so happy for you! The man of your dreams and a new little baby on the way.

God bless Marissa and Dani. Perhaps they were right. Perhaps her dreams could come true.

But then reality slapped her round the face and made her sit up.

Dreams. She'd just got used to thinking about having some of those. A new career. Time to herself. They were just going to have to go on hold for another eighteen years or so. If she wasn't so confused about how to tell Noah, about what to tell Noah, she'd be in fits of laughter. Oh, the irony of it—the empty-nester who'd finally gathered up the courage to find her wings suddenly had another chick to hatch.

Noah woke the next morning to find Grace stroking his thigh, a naughty little smile on her face. He grinned back at her. This was better. In recent weeks Grace had been less and less like herself, and the last few days she'd been positively testy. Whatever had been bothering her was obviously dealt with.

He didn't mind forgoing his morning run for a little bit of exercise with Grace, not one little bit.

Afterwards, when they were wrapped round each other and he was starting to doze, she lifted her head from his chest and looked at him.

'Are you happy, Noah?'

He nodded. Yes, he was. Not just in the afterglow of great sex, but with his life generally. There'd been a few hiccups at the beginning of their marriage—teething problems, he supposed—but now it looked as if things were back on track.

She sat up a little so she could focus on his face properly and he rolled over a little to face her. She licked her lower lip and then stuck her thumbnail in her mouth. After nibbling it for a few seconds, a tiny frown deepening between her eyebrows, she pulled it out again.

'I have some news,' she finally said.

His eyebrows raised. 'Good news or bad news?'

'Um…Depends very much on how you feel about it.'

'Well, why don't you tell me what it is and I will tell you how I feel about it?' he said in a voice as smooth as clotted cream.

'You'll tell me how you really feel?'

'Yes.' Or at least he'd tell her what he thought. That would just have to do.

She took a deep breath. 'I'm pregnant.'

The world seemed to freeze for a second and, when it got going again, he was sure it was revolving in the wrong direction.

'I'm sorry?'

Grace pulled the sheet up over her chest and held it with clenched fists. 'We're going to have a baby. I'm pregnant.'

A baby? How was that…? When had they…?

'But…how could you be? We used—'

Grace lost her forlorn expression and became a bit more like the sassy woman he'd gone on a blind date with. 'Only ninety-eight per cent effective. It says so on the box.'

'But…'

'You said you were going to tell me how you feel.'

He blinked. Something instinctive rushed through Noah. Something primal, fierce and protective. But he didn't know what to call it. And it terrified the life out of him. She didn't really want to know that, did she? That he was feeling strange things—especially fear. That wouldn't help at all.

And that wasn't actually what she'd been asking. She'd be cross with him if he was brutally honest. Just like Sara always had been. Damn these women and their subtexts.

He got out of bed and put on his robe, tying the knot just a little too tightly for comfort. So he retied it, looser this time. He needed to process this, to understand this strange tug inside him. Anchoring it in something real, in facts and figures, might help.

'Do you know when we got…erm…?'

'Pregnant is the word you're looking for, Noah.'

Grace gathered the sheet around her and stood up too. That was the first time she'd done that. She'd never bothered hiding her body from him before, not even right at the beginning.

'Paris, I think. What difference does it make?'

Somehow it helped to know, to analyse. To work out where the turning point had been, the moment at which everything had changed, even if he hadn't realised it at the time. It was the way he looked at his characters, understood what was happening to them. Perhaps it would help him to understand what he was feeling, this new thing that made his eyes prickle and his heart pump. Was he going to cry? He never cried.

A look of exquisite pain passed across Grace's features.

'Come here,' he said, opening his arms.

Grace looked wary but she shuffled over to him, the sheet tangling in her feet, and let him hold her. He could feel her breath moist against his chest.

'Don't worry.' He smoothed her hair with the flat of his hand, long strokes that travelled down her shoulders and onto her back. 'We can deal with this. We'll work through this.'

And then he laid a kiss on the top of her head and stepped back.

'I need to…I think I'll…I'm going for a run.'

We'll work through this?

Grace stared at the bedroom door with her mouth open. He'd made it sound as if this was a problem with their taxes or a lost passport. She'd told him they were going to have a baby and he'd gone for a run? Unbelievable!

She sat down on the edge of the bed and folded the sheet around her.

What a difference from when she'd told Rob they were expecting Daisy. It had been only days before their first wedding anniversary, and Rob had whooped with joy when she'd told him. He'd picked her up and swung her round, only to stop and place her on the sofa as if she were delicate porcelain. He'd apologised a dozen times and kissed her twenty more before phoning everyone he knew to brag.

Grace twisted the sheet between her fists. What was it with her new husband? What was he afraid of? That she'd have less time for him? Was he jealous? She just didn't get it.

Her hands wandered to her stomach. Not exactly flat, but as flat as a woman her age was likely to have. Almost twenty years would separate her two children, but she was as connected now to the tiny life inside her that was only a bundle of promise as she was to the one outside her who was fulfilling that promise by exploring her potential. And it was an even greater joy finding out this time, because she knew all the wonderful times waiting for her in the future.

This was her baby.

Well, at least Noah's reaction had an upside.

Now she knew how she felt about being pregnant. She wanted this baby more than anything. She wanted to feel its kick, to feel it moving inside her. She wanted to hear its first cry and feel that total rush of love when they first met.

She stood up and went in search of underwear. Noah would show his excitement sooner or later, wouldn't he? Perhaps Dani was right and he was just poleaxed by her announcement. Whatever the problem was, she hoped he would be in a better state of mind when he came back from his run.

Noah's feet pounded on the hard paving slabs. He glanced up the road, saw there was a gap in the traffic and sprinted across and onto the cricket pitch. Grace was pregnant. With a baby.

His baby. He wasn't sure if he wanted to jump up a tree and do a Tarzan yell or go and buy cigars.

At least you're feeling something.

Shut up.

But this changed everything. What about the trips all over the world? The parties and awards ceremonies? He hadn't ever envisioned doing that with a pushchair in one hand and a nappy bag over his shoulder.

You're being selfish.

I know. Shut up.

He ran faster, harder, until the breath sliced cold in his lungs and his thigh muscles burned. He'd never considered becoming a father. Although his own had been a poor example, at least the comparison with friends' dads had given him an idea of what a father *should* be. He should be able to interact with his son, praise him, talk to him, teach him about life. Not freeze him out and act as if he didn't exist most of the time, even when the boy did his very best to make him proud.

Noah stopped running and rested his hands on his thighs, panting. But the feeling that he was pounding, churning, moving stayed with him. It was as if darkness were coming up from the inside of him, threatening to overtake him. He didn't like it. He didn't like it at all. This feeling was darker than the one he'd felt when Grace had told him she was expecting his child. Whatever this feeling was, he'd better outrun it.

Fear. What you're feeling is fear.

Well, he had good reason to be afraid. When that baby was born and Grace expected him to be all those things a father should be, she was going to find out. He wouldn't be able to disguise the emptiness any longer. She'd know. And then she wouldn't want him any more. Neither of them would.

And, with that thought ringing in his ears, Noah started sprinting again, even though he hadn't really caught his breath.

* * *

Blinddatebrides.com is running 16 chat rooms, 28 private IM conferences, and 6217 members are online.

Sanfrandani: So what happened after he got back from his run?

Englishcrumpet: He apologised and he was really lovely to me. He took me into town and bought me lunch. This morning he appeared with a little toy bunny for the baby's cot.

Kangagirl: Awwww! It sounds as if he's really coming round to the idea.

It did, didn't it? Then why didn't it *feel* right? Why were her alarm bells clanging? Why had the cold spread from her toes up to her knees?

Englishcrumpet: I know. But it's not that simple. You didn't see his face when I told him.

Sanfrandani: He was bound to be surprised. You were.

Englishcrumpet: How can I explain this? It's like there's…a wall. Between him and me. He's doing all the right things, saying all the right things, but it feels as if he's just going through the motions. As if he's…I don't know…papering over the cracks.

Kangagirl: Give him time, Grace! He sounds like he's doing his best.

Oh, flip! Tears were dropping on the keyboard of the laptop. Daisy would kill her if she fritzed this thing.

Kangagirl: Grace, if anyone can melt his heart back, it's you.

Sanfrandani: And you know we're here for you night and day, whenever you need to talk.

Englishcrumpet: Thanks, girls! You've got me in tears here!
Sanfrandani: Snap!
Kangagirl: Me too!!!!!!
Englishcrumpet: One day I'm going to meet up with you two and give you the biggest hug ever. You'll have to peel me off and restrain me before I crush you to death like a python.
Kangagirl: Sounds fab!
Sanfrandani: It's a date!

Grace logged off and wiped her eyes. She would just have to give Noah some room. She knew without a doubt that if she pushed him to open up he would just push back harder. So she'd wait. They had over seven months until the baby came. Surely they'd make some progress by then.

CHAPTER EIGHT

OVER the next few weeks a truce developed. Grace stayed on the fringes, gave Noah room. Noah took the room she offered, but it never seemed that he came any closer to making a step in her direction. Not really.

The hormones really started to kick in, though. Her pregnancy with Daisy had been a bit of a breeze, but her body was older and crabbier now and it protested loudly at being stretched and changed and fed upon by an invader. Noah tried hard, but he was struggling to keep up with the mood swings, his new wife one minute sweet and affectionate, the next snarling and crying. The waists of some of her trousers and skirts were already tight and she'd woken up one morning to discover she'd gone up a cup size—one change that hadn't flummoxed Noah, quite the opposite, actually.

It was just as well she didn't have to go to work, because even getting out of bed before ten made her want to heave. It got better in the afternoons, but she was suddenly so picky about her food. One minute she wanted something with a ravenous craving, the next thing she'd go green at the sight of it.

She crawled down to the kitchen one morning and slumped on the big oak table Noah had told her they'd had to hoist in through the windows when he'd bought it. It wasn't long before Noah appeared from his study, looking disgustingly well-groomed, even if he did have the largest scowl she'd ever seen on his face. He came over and kissed her on the cheek, anyway. She knew it wasn't personal, that his head was trapped somewhere between his book and the real world.

'Problems?' she said, yawning in the middle of the word.

Noah nodded. 'It's my maddening hero. He just won't behave.'

Grace lay her forehead on the table. Know how that feels, she thought. 'What's he up to now?'

Noah sat down at the table. 'Are you feeling okay? Do you want me to get you something?'

She shook her head very slightly and it squeaked on the surface of the table. 'No. Tell me about Karl the rebellious hero. It'll help to have something to distract me. Why can't you get him to work?'

'It's the love sub-plot. You know…where he gets involved with the woman who's a double agent. It's just not convincing. *He's* not convincing.'

Grace sat up slowly. 'Can you take that bit out?'

'No.' Noah shook his head. 'The betrayal aspect, when she turns him over to his enemies, is important to the central plot.'

'I'm no expert at spy novels, Noah. But perhaps you need a woman's perspective.'

He looked so boyishly hopeful she would have run round the table and kissed him if she'd been able to move that fast without throwing up.

'Would you?'

'Of course. I'm no good to anyone at the moment. I might as well curl up on the sofa and read a good book.' And get to see how your mind works before the manuscript has been meticulously polished and made presentable, she silently added.

He jumped up, kissed her cheek and then rushed out of

the room. 'I'll print it off!' he yelled from somewhere down the corridor.

Grace spent the most wonderful day in the high-ceilinged drawing room, lying on the sofa with a throw over her. It was blissfully sunny outside and Noah opened the French windows for her so the warm air blew in the scent of flowers from the garden. She read his whole manuscript—well, apart from a bit in chapter twenty, where it stopped mid-sentence in the middle of a fight scene and then carried on a few days later. Apparently Noah needed to do some more research on a certain gadget before he could write the rest of that.

Noah had been pacing in the doorway too much so she'd shooed him away, sent him in to town to get some food for dinner. She'd discovered he was a much better cook than she'd imagined, but that was hardly surprising. He liked to use all the wonderful fresh organic ingredients. She'd hardly been able to get creative with the food on her budget over the years. There was a limit to the amount of things you could do with baked beans.

By the time Noah returned home with bags of groceries, Grace was sitting in the kitchen sipping tea, feeling considerably perkier.

'What did you think?' he said, looking a little nervous.

'What did you buy?' she replied with a mischievous wink. 'I'm famished.'

'Oh, it's like that, is it?'

'Yes, it is. You tell me what you're cooking me for tea and I'll tell you what I think of Karl the spy.'

'Minx,' he muttered as he opened the fridge and started shoving vegetables inside. But he dived into a carrier bag and produced a whole chicken. 'Yesterday night, you were waxing lyrical about old-fashioned roast dinners…'

Grace screwed her face up and made a gagging noise, which turned out to be a really bad idea, because thinking about the pink, dimpled, slightly cold, slightly pink chicken in its packaging was making her feel queasy.

'Thought so,' Noah said and shoved it back in the bag, out of view. 'That's why I got this…' And, with a flourish, he pulled a bag of fresh pasta and a handful of ripe tomatoes out of a different bag.

Grace jumped up. 'I love you!'

Noah stuttered.

'I mean…I love what you chose for dinner.' She shrugged, the fake smile on her face making her feel just as iffy as the chicken had. What a stupid thing to say. And the look on his face—pure horror—as if she'd jumped up and said, *I want to cut your left leg off!*

She had to pull things back, pretend she hadn't said it and that everything was normal between them. Although normal for them wasn't quite like any other marriage she knew. She made her voice light and breezy.

'It was just what I wanted. How did you know?'

His face relaxed slightly and she breathed out. 'I don't know. I just did.'

'How about you start chopping and I'll tell you my thoughts on your book over dinner?'

'Oh, no. That wasn't the deal.'

'Well, I'm so hungry I'm feeling a little nauseous so, if you want to do this now, you may have to break off to hold my hair back—'

'Okay! It's a deal. That's all I need to know.'

Noah watched as Grace twirled linguine onto her fork.

'I think I know what your hero's problem is.'

'You do?'

She popped the pasta in her mouth and chewed. When she'd swallowed, she said, 'He's too concerned with protecting himself, staying close to what he knows. He's been trained to deal with the situation he faces with the girl, hasn't he? And he always stays within the boundaries of that training, within his comfort zone.'

Noah put down his fork and stared at her. 'But if I make him forget his training, he's bad at his job and that makes him unsympathetic as a hero.'

She shook her head and put her own cutlery down so she could wave her hands. 'I'm not saying he should be bad at his job. I'm saying that he needs to have a good reason to *ignore* his training, make himself vulnerable. You need to dig deeper.'

Noah snorted. 'You sound like my editor.'

'You know I'm right.'

Yeah, yeah. He did. His inner Rottweiler was in a frenzy, trying to get him to listen. Dig deeper. He'd been living with this character for months now. He wasn't sure there was any 'deeper' to go. What did he do if Karl the spy turned out to be just like his creator?

Well, just like him, Karl would be stuffed.

Noah was being ratty with Martine and he knew it. She also knew it, and had no problems letting him know she knew. He snapped at her while she went through the diary for the next couple of weeks with him and reminded him of the details of his speaking engagement that evening in Manchester.

But Noah was too busy playing with Post-it notes stuck to a whiteboard on his office wall. Laying his story out visually on coloured squares of paper helped him get a feel for its shape, its rhythm. He was flexing his mental shovel and trying to dig deeper into his hero. Unfortunately, Karl, who had first appeared in his previous book, *Silent Tundra*, was living up to his heritage and appeared to be frozen solid beneath the surface.

'Both you and Mrs Frost are booked into the Manchester Royal tonight,' Martine said, breaking his concentration.

'Thanks,' he muttered. 'What?'

Martine looked at him cross-eyed. She slapped a folder onto the desk in front of him. 'Since I'm obviously invisible, I'm going to make myself a cup of coffee. All the info you're not absorbing is in that file. Don't lose it!'

Noah mumbled something out of the side of his mouth that sounded very much like, 'Okay.' Then he ripped a pink Post-it note off his board and replaced it with an orange one from further back in the timeline. The key to Karl's character must be in his past. But where? He looked down on the desk to check his notebook and found it obscured by a file. Where had that come from? He shoved the file in a random drawer.

There was a shuffling noise behind him in the doorway. 'Have you booked the hotel yet?' he asked Martine.

'No.' It was Grace's voice that replied. 'Didn't Martine already take care of that?'

He dropped the stack of Post-it notes and turned round. She looked terrible. As if morning sickness had eaten her up and then spat her out. Her skin was a strange shade of grey and there were large purple bags under her eyes. Although she said the sickness was getting better, she looked so tired.

'How are you feeling?'

'Better,' she said, attempting to sound chirpy and just managing to sound conscious. 'All set for your thing tonight?'

He shook his head. 'No.'

'No, what? I'm not ready? You don't want me to go? Noah, make sense, please.'

She looked so lovely, even pale and washed out. He crossed the room and lifted a hand to stroke her cheek. 'I think you should stay here.'

He'd bought a pregnancy book online and had hidden it inside a folder in his study. Why exactly he'd felt the need to be so anonymous about its purchase and so secretive about its existence, he wasn't sure. He just knew he'd feel embarrassed if Grace found him reading it. She knew all this stuff, had done it all before. He felt such an idiot half of the time, asking stupid questions.

And then he thought that if he didn't sound well-informed, if he didn't keep buying baby stuff, she'd think he wasn't interested. Which he was, on a purely logical level—it was all fascinating. No wonder people called it the miracle of birth. But when he stopped to think that the miracle would be living in his house, that strange feeling happened again. And he didn't like it. It made him feel out of control. Helpless. At the mercy of something greater than himself. So, focusing on the right things to do, the right things to say was better. He could measure his success at that.

If Grace looked pale when he showed her his dinner choices, he knew it was a no-go. In the early weeks he'd known he had to bring her dry wholewheat crackers or plain noodles before ten with a glass of water. Nowadays it could be anything from a list of a dozen weird and wonderful foods. He was busy researching state-of-the-art baby monitors. These were all things he could do without messing up.

Anyway, one of the things he did know from all his reading was that his wife would not survive a journey up the motorway. He shook his head. 'You know I'm right.'

'But why? I'm fine. It was part of our deal, remember? Me going to writing-related events with you.'

Ah, yes. The deal. In which stupid universe had that made sense when he'd thought it up? Certainly not this one. Certainly not now.

A shutter fell over his eyes. She'd do it for him, he knew, even if she felt terrible. But she needed to rest. And he needed twenty-four hours where he didn't feel as if he was trying to be what she wanted and failing her all at the same time.

'You go and lie down. Go back to bed. I'll see you tomorrow lunch time when I get back.'

* * *

It was lonely in the manor house that night. Noah's house. Even though she'd been living there for nearly a couple of months, it still felt a bit like a hotel to Grace. Too big. Too smart. Too perfect. It was the house she'd always dreamed of, but it wasn't her home.

Maybe that had more to do with her state of mind—or her state of heart, to be exact—than it did the house. Her first homes with Rob had been small, faceless army quarters, but they'd never seemed that way to her because every one had been filled with happy memories, laughter, passion...

Perhaps that was why Noah's house felt like a show home. Their marriage was legal, of course, but it wasn't real in the sense that her marriage to Rob had been real. She couldn't blame Noah for that. He'd given her exactly what he'd promised her—respect, companionship, more chemistry than she'd expected.

And, in return, she'd foolishly given Noah her heart. It wasn't that he wasn't worthy of it, just that he didn't want it. Try as you might, you just couldn't make someone accept a gift they didn't know existed.

Grace stayed up late, even though it wasn't one of her scheduled nights to chat to Dani and Marissa. It was good to have some time to herself, without her husband in the immediate vicinity, to get some perspective on her situation.

Noah, just like his wayward character, kept himself firmly inside his comfort zone. Oh, not professionally—he was good at pushing the boundaries there—but personally, he was locked up tight. And she knew, just knew, that there was more inside him, that he was selling himself short. But that didn't mean he'd ever let the invisible barrier between them down.

Each sweet gesture, each thoughtful thing he did for her or for their growing baby, rather than filling her with joy, only reminded her that he was always at arm's length, always out of reach. Those things would be lovely if love was the reason behind them, but when that was all there was…

She thought of Rob and how excited he'd been all the way through her pregnancy with Daisy, how he'd kissed her stomach, talked to it, even before the baby could hear. Where Rob had shared himself, Noah brought her things.

She wandered upstairs, barefoot and in her pyjamas, and into the small bedroom they'd discussed turning into a nursery. It was a lovely room, with plenty of space, high ceilings and sash windows. It was all so perfect, but oh-so-empty.

If Noah was incapable of reaching out to her, how would he cope with a child? Would he be as distant with their son or daughter? Her concern turned to anger. It wasn't fair! Her first child had been robbed of a father who'd been devoted to her, and her second child would have a father who was present in body, but…emotionally? Who could tell?

Things had got worse in recent weeks. She had a feeling that Noah knew something was wrong between them but he was running from it. He'd retreated into his book, his fantasy world, rather than face it. Perhaps that was what he always did. Perhaps that was why he'd become a writer in the first place. You couldn't get hurt in a world where you were God and you called the shots, holding everyone's destinies in your hand.

Just once, she'd like to look in his eyes and see the real Noah. She was fed up seeing herself reflected back by the mirror he kept there, the mirror he hid behind.

In the morning Grace rolled over in bed, no Noah to curl up to. She opened her eyes and waited. The urge to be horribly sick was much weaker today. In fact, she was actually very hungry. But working out what she was hungry *for* was another matter.

She scratched the usual suspects—toast, cereal—off her list pretty quick. She wanted something…something salty! Anchovies? No. Not them. Bacon? A shudder ran through her.

Bleuch. And then she decided that salty was so last minute and started thinking of spicy things. Chilli sauce? Curry? Ginger-snaps?

Nothing appealed. The only thing she could think of doing was fridge-surfing—sticking her face inside it and seeing what appealed. She lolloped downstairs and into the kitchen and looked at the closed cupboards, hoping for inspiration. Nope.

Noah had a fridge the size of her old bathroom and she yanked the door open as it always seemed to suck itself closed extra hard when she approached it. There, sitting on the middle shelf, with a note propped up against it, was a waxy carton.

Dear Grace,
Thought you might like this for breakfast,
Noah

No love, no kisses, just *Noah*. Before she'd even opened the lid, she knew what it was.

Cold roast pork chow mein.

Her stomach gurgled in anticipation.

See? This was how he broke her heart into tinier and tinier pieces each day. Grace slid onto the floor by the open fridge door and began to cry.

Noah couldn't be doing with all this have-to-be-chauffeur-driven-everywhere-I-go nonsense. He'd taken his car to Manchester, the one admission to his James Bond fixation as a boy. His Aston Martin.

Anyway, motorways were good thinking places. Mile after mile of the same white lines, the same hedgerows and fields, the same crash barriers. The trick was to disengage the creative part of the brain, the right brain, from the driving process and leave it to the left half.

What was he going to do with the troublesome Karl, the spy who refused to love anybody?

Dig deeper. Dig deeper. How do I do that? How do I know if there's anything more inside? I've been digging—mining, even—for weeks and I've come up empty. All I've got is a big hole.

As he drove, Noah rolled Karl's character round in his head, looking at him from every conceivable angle. Eventually, and quite unexpectedly, at Junction Four on the M1, his metaphorical shovel hit something solid. Something resembling a flap or a trapdoor.

He hadn't even begun unpacking when he arrived home. It was mid-afternoon and he found Grace in the garden, staring out across the fields. He walked over to her and kissed her on the cheek. 'How are you doing today?'

He daredn't ask if she'd missed him, just in case she said no.

'Fine,' she said, turning to smile at him, but without using her eyes. 'How was your thing?'

Awful without you beside me. Miserable. It was unbearable not being able to see you, to touch you.

It suddenly hit him that he didn't want to use the smoke-screen with Grace any more. He wanted to let her see through it. Great in principle, but the stupid thing had been in place for so many years, he didn't know how to dismantle it.

'Fine,' he finally said. It had been fine. Gone like clockwork. He'd been a roaring success.

That misty look stayed in Grace's eyes all that afternoon, through dinner and into the next week. The only time it faded was when they made love and then she looked as if she was going to cry instead. He wanted to tell her to just let it all out, to drench him with her tears if she wanted, but he didn't know how to make it sound real.

Grace was pulling away. He was losing her.

Maybe she knew. Maybe, without all the picking, she knew. The urge to tell her he'd take the pain away, that it'd be okay, was so strong that he had to bite his tongue. Nice words, but they were a lie. He couldn't tell her that, because he very much feared that everything she was thinking was true.

His brain jumped into action. He had to do something to make her happy.

And he knew just the thing. Her wedding present. A little delayed, to be sure, but she'd understand why when she saw it. It wasn't going to be truly ready for another month, but now was the time to reveal the surprise.

He started making plans immediately and, all the while, his inner Rottweiler was strangely silent.

Noah was behaving most strangely today, Grace thought as she munched her way through a slice of dry toast covered in mango chutney and chocolate sprinkles. He'd been up even earlier than usual. She'd just opened one eye, grunted at the clock and gone back to sleep. But that wasn't all, not by a long shot. After days of scowling at bare patches of wall and muttering to himself, his book filling all his consciousness, suddenly he was back in the real world, smiling, joking and talking.

She had the feeling that this was significant, something important. A turning point.

He bounded into the kitchen and surprised her with a long sweet kiss on the lips, completely ignoring the toast crumbs down her front and the fact that she looked like she'd just escaped from a sci-fi B movie.

'When you've finished that, I think you should get dressed.'

She raised an eyebrow. 'You're getting a bit bossy all of a sudden.'

He tapped his nose. 'You'll see. I've got a surprise for you.'

And then he rushed out of the kitchen again like a mini tornado. Grace put her toast down and smiled. Something was different. He seemed…unguarded, almost open. Her heart quivered at the thought. Was it finally happening? Was he finally ready to stop giving her *things* and give her a piece of himself?

Suddenly, she wasn't hungry any more. Mango chutney and chocolate? Really?

She cleared her breakfast things away and headed upstairs. The morning sickness was definitely fading now she was reaching ten weeks, which was earlier than she'd expected, but a huge relief. And she could get all the way to the top of the staircase at normal speed, without having to lean on the banister for support. Perhaps she was going to start blooming, rather than looking like some weed the dog had dug up.

Jeans and a T-shirt would just have to do, and it was a step up from pyjamas and slobby tracksuits. So much for Noah-the-sexy-author's glamorous wife. When she'd got dressed and run a brush through her hair, she went in search of Noah. She found him in the study, whispering on the phone. He put it down as soon as she crossed the threshold.

'Right. Before we go anywhere, I insist you wear this.' He pulled a woolly scarf out of a drawer and waved it in the air.

'But it's July.'

Noah just grinned. 'Only just. And it's not going round your neck. You need to put it over your eyes.'

His enthusiasm was infectious and she started to laugh. 'Kinky! But…okay.'

He looped the scarf round her head and tied it tight at the back. 'You can save that thought for later, Mrs Frost,' he whispered in her ear. Then he led her out to the car and sat her down in the passenger seat. Her heart started beating fast, partly with nerves, partly with anticipation.

The car journey was not her finest hour, the blindfold making motion sickness a real possibility. Thankfully, the journey was short and it wasn't long before the car stopped and he turned the engine off. Seconds later he opened her door and helped her to stand.

The traffic was loud and she could hear a pedestrian crossing beeping. People were talking and she recognised the sound of shoes on hard ground—on cobbles, if she'd guessed right. They were in the High Street?

'This way…' Noah took hold of her arm under her elbow and steered her round the car. 'There's a step…and another…' A bell jangled and he guided her through a door. 'Just a bit further…There. You can take off your blindfold now.'

Grace blinked as she pulled the scarf down so it hung loosely round her neck. They were in a shop. She looked round, trying to work out where they were. Dark wood shelves lined the walls. The floor had recently had some very old carpet ripped up because pieces of perished green underlay had collected in the corners. It looked familiar, but…

Suddenly Grace gasped, 'You bought Martin's book shop? Really?'

Noah grinned even wider and nodded. 'I outbid the original buyer, saved it from becoming an extension of Java Express.'

She didn't know what to say. She just left her mouth hanging open and waved her hands around. 'And Martin?'

'Martin is going to run it for me—for the next couple of years, anyway. After that, apparently, Mrs Martin will have my hide. Welcome to Love and Bullets.'

Grace frowned. *'Bullets?'*

'It's going to be a specialist crime and thriller book shop. Shops for niche markets are doing well round here nowadays.'

'And the *love* bit?'

Noah looked a little sheepish. 'Well, in recent months I realised that not everybody lives on a steady literary diet of blood, espionage and murder, so I made room for a romance section too.'

Grace blinked slowly, thinking that when she opened her eyes again it might all vanish and prove to have been a mirage. 'I think you're barking mad. Wonderful, but barking mad.'

'There's more.'

Grace suddenly felt like sitting down, but there were no chairs so she just leant against an empty shelf. 'More?'

'This way.' He grabbed her hand and pulled her through an archway that was covered in thick plastic sheeting. Grace stumbled through and, when she saw where she was, she said words that her developing baby really ought not to hear.

She was standing in The Coffee Bean, or what once had been The Coffee Bean and was now a completely updated, buffed and polished café. The fantastic Victorian counter had been waxed. It fairly gleamed. The glass had been cleaned and the missing etched panels replaced with good reproductions. And the floor! The broken tiles had been mended. And in the bay window was a vast display case with glass shelves.

Oh, my! What had he done? What had her stupid husband decided to get her now?

Noah had got her a patisserie, that was what. He'd collected all her dreams together and delivered them to her, wrapped in a pink bow. And she hated him for it.

She turned to face him, her hands on her hips. 'When did you buy this?'

The smile slid from Noah's face. 'A few months ago. Java Express had almost sealed the deal, but I went to Caz with a better offer.'

She shook her head, tears filling her eyes. 'Caz let you do this? Why?'

'I…I thought this was what you wanted.'

Grace let out a long sarcastic laugh. 'Why didn't you tell me? Why did you keep all of this a secret from me, Noah?'

The bemused expression he was wearing solidified into irritation. 'It was supposed to be a surprise. Your wedding present. Okay, it's a little late, but I thought you'd understand.'

Anger contorted her features. 'Oh, I understand all right. You can't treat me like one of your characters and plot my life out for me! I'm going to have a baby! How am I going to run a patisserie? Tell me that!'

Noah's forehead creased. 'Babies sleep a lot, don't they?'

Now Grace's laughter became hysterical. 'You have no idea, do you? Absolutely no idea.'

'You don't like it.'

The hormones were ganging up on her again, filling her eyes with tears. Little monsters. 'Noah,' she said in a wavery voice that got quieter and quieter. 'It's beautiful. It's perfect. It's all I ever wanted. But it's just another *thing*.'

He came and stood close to her, face to face. 'And that's wrong?'

Now the tears really fell. 'No. No, it's not wrong. It's just that, when it's the only thing, when there's nothing else…' She gulped in oxygen. 'I can't do this any more. I thought I could, but I can't. I need more.' Her hands wandered to her slightly rounded belly. 'We both do.'

She had to tell him, so she took a really deep breath and drew all her courage into her mouth.

'I…I love you.' If she'd expected some but-I've-always-loved-you-too declaration, like they did in the movies, now was the time. Now was the moment she'd see his face change, his lips move…

He did nothing but take a step backwards and look blankly at her.

'I'm talking about proper love, Noah. To have and to hold love. Yes, we said those words, we said we'd love and cherish, but we didn't mean them that way at the time. But I love you like that now. And I know it's against the rules and not what we agreed, but I can't help it and you can't do anything to change that, even if you want to.'

The pity in his eyes was more than she could handle. 'Grace, I—'

'Don't. Unless you're going to say you feel the same way, just…don't.'

He turned away and walked over to the display cabinet in the window and ran his hands through his hair. 'What do we do now?'

She folded her hands in front of her. 'I'm not going to stop you seeing the baby. In fact, I'll actively encourage it, but…but I don't think I can live with you any more. I don't think I can stay married to you. Not like this. You understand, don't you?'

He stared out of the window and nodded. If she'd have thought him capable of it, she'd have said his heart was breaking. 'I understand.'

It was better this way, it really was. She could raise a child on her own. She'd done it before when she'd been young and clueless, so she could do it again now she was older and clueless. But she couldn't be the mum she needed to be if she spent every day living with Noah, knowing he didn't love her, not even knowing if he *really* wanted this baby.

Suddenly, he spun around to face her and her breath hitched.

'Don't…don't be in a rush, Grace. I don't want to lose you and the baby. We've got that Paris trip, the book launch in a fortnight. Don't go anywhere until after that. Please?'

Oh, yes. The book launch! Better not spoil that.

'If you still feel the same way when we come home, then we'll sit down and talk about it.'

Oh, he was being far too reasonable. She wanted him to shout, to tell her she was being ridiculous. She'd even settle for relief. Anything would be better than this *non*-reaction. Now was the time to tell him about his stupid spy character, see if she couldn't hit him where it hurt.

'I know what's wrong with Karl.'

He looked momentarily off-balance. 'Huh?'

'Karl. Your super-spy? The reason you can't make him work is *you*.'

'What do you mean?'

She shook her head. Half of her had been hoping he'd tell her not to bother with this now, but he was like a donkey with a carrot dangling in front of his nose.

'I mean, the reason you can't get down to a deeper level with him is because *you* won't go there. Karl is you, Noah. I'm surprised you can't see it. He came out of your subconscious and he's got your weaknesses.'

A look of sudden revelation passed across his face. Good. She hoped something positive would come out of this whole fiasco.

'Until you break through that barrier you use to protect yourself from the world, you are never going to make Karl a convincing hero.'

Grace moved into the spare bedroom that night. Noah tried to insist she stay in the master suite, but she refused, telling him it had never really been her bedroom. She couldn't face rattling round the house knowing Noah was doing the same, so she took herself—and Daisy's laptop—off to bed early. She needed Dani and Marissa more now than ever. When it hit a time that she knew they might be online she sent out a distress call.

Englishcrumpet invites Kangagirl and Sanfrandani to a private IM conference.

Englishcrumpet: Girls?

Sanfrandani: I'm here!

Englishcrumpet: Oh, Dani! I'm so glad you're there!

Sanfrandani: Let me guess...another Noah-related emergency.

Englishcrumpet: You don't know the half of it! First he

blindfolded me and then there was the book shop and then
he gave me all my dreams on a plate and I said no and—
Sanfrandani: Grace! Slow down!

Grace make herself breathe deep and slow. Okay, here
goes again. Stick to the relevant points. And after she'd
filled them in…

Kangagirl: Oh, Grace, I was so sure you two were
going to last.
Englishcrumpet: Well, you know what they say about the
best laid plans…
Kangagirl: What exactly do they say? Everyone just
seems to trail off at that point.
Englishcrumpet: Well, neither do I, actually. What I
mean is, it was a bad idea from the start.
Sanfrandani: Are you totally sure there's no way to
salvage the marriage?

Grace sat back and stared at the screen for a moment. If Noah
could connect with his feelings…If she could accept what he
offered and not want more…If she could be sure their child
would be brought up in a loving and nurturing environment…

Englishcrumpet: I wish there was. But I really
don't think so.

CHAPTER NINE

NOAH stood on the doorstep of Caz's little cottage and rapped on the oversized lion's head knocker. A short time passed and then a voice called, 'It's open!' He pushed the glossy red door and discovered that it swung smoothly, despite its weight.

She was in the kitchen, cooking something odd-smelling. And that wasn't the only thing that was odd. Caz was wearing cowboy boots, a long floaty hippy dress and had a feather stuck in her swept-up hair.

'About time,' was all she said when she saw it was him.

'You know why I'm here, then?'

She nodded and motioned for him to sit down in a sturdy chair next to the bowed pine table. He did as he was told, but had to evict a large ginger cat from the spot first.

The small kitchen was filled with pots, pans, vases. Bits of free-standing furniture and bright hand-painted pottery on the walls. Half-dead herbs hung from an airer hoisted high over his head.

'How can I make her stay?'

Caz stopped stirring what he now thought might be soup and looked at him. 'Noah, you can't make her stay. You have to give her a reason to stay.'

Damn. He was all out of reasons. And, on his own, he wasn't *reason* enough.

'I don't know what to do, Caz. I want her to stay, but I can't give her what she wants. I don't *do* love. Never have. I have no idea how to explain how I feel about her because I don't even know how to define it. Would *you* stay for that?'

She pressed her lips together and thought for a moment.

'Love is more than words, Noah.'

'I know that.'

'Do you?' she said, looking him up and down. 'Really?'

The ginger cat made a reappearance and started rubbing itself on his calf. He tried to shoo it away, not by kicking, more by just nudging with his leg. Caz returned her attention to her soup and, after she'd flung in a few herbs, she nodded to herself, turned down the heat and covered it with a lid. Then she stood with her large bottom cushioning her as she leaned against the kitchen cabinet and folded her arms.

'What's one of the most important things an aspiring writer needs to learn?'

He racked his brain. What had been his weaknesses?

'Spelling?' he said hopefully.

Caz threw her head back and laughed. He'd expected a witch's cackle but it was light and melodious. 'Dig deeper.'

Why was everybody so fixated on digging? It was driving him mad. He was about to ask her as much when one of his hunches hit him and he blurted a phrase out before his conscious brain had even had a chance to give it the once-over.

'Show, don't tell.'

Caz nodded and beamed at him the way a proud teacher would reward her star pupil. 'Exactly. You think about that.'

She turned and put the kettle on and, while she made them both a cup of tea, Noah tried to think about *show, don't tell*. He came up with exactly nothing.

As if she could tell he was struggling, Caz took a different tack.

'Now you're going to be a daddy, you need to think about how a parent loves their child.'

He thought of his parents and also came up blank. Then he thought about Grace and how she would sacrifice everything for Daisy. And, finally, he thought about his own child, the one growing inside Grace, the one he may only get to see on alternate weekends if his wife decided to leave. That pounding, primal, protective thing surged through him again.

Oh.

He looked up at Caz, his mouth open. 'I love that baby already. Even though I haven't met it. Even though I don't know what it will be like.'

She smiled and nodded. 'Of course you do. It won't matter what that child does or says. You will always love it. Always.'

Of course. Unconditional love.

And then another zap hit him. Boy, those hunches were coming thick and fast today.

That was Karl's problem. The girl—the double agent— Karl loves her like that. And he lets her do what she does, even though he knows she'll betray him.

The ginger cat suddenly bounded onto his lap, purred and curled itself up into a ball.

'Yes. That's it,' Caz said. 'Even when it hurts. Even when you lose a little piece of yourself in the loving.'

He understood that much, but...

He looked up at Caz as she peeked into her soup pot. 'But how does this relate to Grace? How can I stop her leaving?'

The feather in her hair fluttered to the floor as she shook her head. 'That's for you to work out. But I'll tell you this...There was a reason I let you buy my coffee shop. And it wasn't so you could hurt Grace.'

Grace wasn't in when Noah got back that afternoon and he found a note letting him know she'd gone for a walk. She seemed to be doing a lot of that lately. Walking. Leaving the house to get away from him. He chucked his jacket over the back of the sofa and headed for his study.

Once there, he pulled a large pad of paper out of the drawer in his football-pitch-sized desk. It was time to make all these thoughts running round his head physical. Then they couldn't shift and change, one second seeming one thing, the next another. And once he could see his thoughts in stark black ink, maybe he'd be able to make sense of them.

He flipped the pad open and stared at the vast white page. Plain paper had been a deliberate choice—no constricting lines or squares. His thoughts could flow where they needed, unhampered. When he'd finished, the page would be full of scribbled phrases and roughly drawn boxes with arrows sprouting out of them and words. Lots of words. Then he'd sit back and stare at it until he saw the pattern.

But the paper stayed blank. Empty.

Realising that he actually had feelings rather than just instincts had been a major breakthrough for him. But putting those feelings into vowels and consonants was still beyond him. He let out a dry laugh. He made his living creating something out of nothing, with words as his only tool. Why couldn't he turn that skill on himself?

Maybe he could.

Maybe he just needed to take a step back and look at himself as he would one of his characters. Maybe he needed Post-it notes and coloured pens and index cards…He stood up and reached for the shelf that held all his supplies.

No.

That was just time-wasting. Procrastinating. Pen and paper would be enough.

He sat down again and wrote his name in the middle of the white space. Then he underlined it and drew a box round it, waiting for the ideas to start. When they did, he'd hardly be able to scrawl fast enough to keep up, but there was always a moment like this when he sat in the silence and he feared they would never bulge over the lip of his subconscious and begin to flow.

The moment stretched and elongated. Noah's heart began to race. What if they never came, what if—

His pen began to move.

Like he had done with Karl, he started with his past. But, instead of building a history to explain who his character was today, he deconstructed. He pulled the layers away, using his pen as a scalpel, until he could see what had made him this way.

He saw his parents—people who abhorred emotional displays of any kind, who valued stoicism. And he saw the boy who had tried so desperately to win their approval by squashing himself into that mould, even if it was a painful fit. A boy who grew up to go into the army at nineteen, who literally saw friends die in front of him. A young man who couldn't let himself grieve because, if he'd let it out there and then, he'd have been no use at all to his regiment. So he'd shoved it all in a big hole and built a trapdoor over it.

His hand flew over the paper now, his usually neat writing becoming more angular, less uniform.

He'd carried all of that with him into his post-army life, into his relationship with Sara. Wow. He saw it now. What she'd said. Why she'd left. His glass wall wasn't a barrier keeping him out, stopping him feeling what everybody else felt. It was a shell. A glass shell. His method of self-protection had been the cause of a lot of his unhappiness. It was still causing Grace's.

Grace. How did this all relate to Grace? Because that was what was important now, not his own self-knowledge.

Show, don't tell.

Had his actions communicated more than his words, even his own thoughts?

How had he treated Grace in the last few months? He

pushed his pad away and bit the end of his pen. Well, he'd practically manipulated her into marrying him for a start. It hadn't been a conscious plan, but when he looked back on his actions now, it made him uncomfortable. Would she still have married him if she hadn't been backed into a corner? What would she have done if she'd known, at the eleventh hour, he'd decided to try and negotiate for The Coffee Bean? He'd told himself he was doing it for her but, really, he'd done it for himself. Because he wanted Grace to marry him so badly he'd thought he needed a sweetener, something to keep her with him when the honeymoon was over—literally.

And what had he done after she'd pledged to join her life to his? He'd starved her of love and he'd drained her dry.

What else? What else have you done?

He'd tried to be a good husband, the best he knew how to be. It was a pity his knowledge on the subject had been so lacking. He'd only done stupid little things like bringing her dry toast in the mornings when she felt sick, or always making sure he came home with a choice of three different dinners every night. If he'd heard a song on the radio he thought she'd like, he'd bought her the CD.

These were all little things, but in the world of *show, don't tell* they added up to something bigger. Noah's spirits began to lift.

For goodness' sake, he'd bought her a patisserie! Not his brightest idea, it turned out, but you couldn't fault him for trying to give her everything she'd ever dreamed of.

What did all those things say?

He still didn't know. And it was all churning around inside his head, making him feel claustrophobic. He left the study and headed for the garden. As he passed through the kitchen, he was shocked to see it was almost six o'clock and that he'd been holed up in his study for hours.

It was one of those balmy summer evenings that the

London suburbs did really well. The horizon was a gentle peach colour and a warm breeze made the trees whisper. His garden was large and rather beautiful, all clipped lawns and leafy trees. No credit to him; he'd inherited them from the previous owner—along with a rather cantankerous gardener who seemed to work different hours every week and had a habit of popping up unexpectedly and scaring the life out of him.

Noah walked across the patio and onto the lawn. There was a beautiful little bench just out of sight, tucked behind a large rhododendron, and he liked to sit there and stare out across the surrounding fields. However, when he got to the spot, he discovered the bench was occupied.

Grace was sitting in one corner. Not sprawled out, relaxing in the early evening sunshine, but hunched into an awkward shape, as if she was trying to physically keep herself together.

In that moment, before she turned and saw him, while a look of unbearable sadness passed across her features, Noah had the strongest hunch of his life. It hit him like an express train going full speed, and he stumbled with the impact of it.

He loved Grace.

With all his heart. With everything he had and everything he was.

That wasn't a hunch, you dummy! It was a feeling. Just like all the other feelings you've been having, but your subconscious dressed them up in disguise and gave them another name so they were safe, so they were acceptable.

And, just like that, the trapdoor sprang open.

Memories and images and everything he'd pressed down and refused to feel for so many years tumbled into his brain. He ignored most of it and rummaged for things labelled *Grace* and *marriage*.

It wasn't just a today thing either, this loving Grace. He'd loved her right from the moment he'd known she was going to be his wife. Maybe even before that. The realisation made him gasp.

Grace, who had apparently been unaware of his presence, jumped up and spun around. 'Noah!'

She was looking at him and he couldn't say a thing. This was the face of the woman he loved. He needed to explore it afresh with his eyes, each familiar curve and line. God, she was beautiful. Of course he'd always thought that, but now…it wasn't just about cheekbones and lashes and lips. It was three-dimensional.

She knew something was different, he could tell. Her eyes held a question. And, since words were still nowhere to be found, he answered it the only way he knew how. He closed the distance between them, pulled her into his arms and kissed her. At first she hesitated, but it wasn't long before the old chemistry started to fizz and she joined him in a deep, hungry, searching kiss.

They made it as far as the conservatory before their patience ran out and the clothes started to come off. A blouse on the wicker chair, a shoe in the kitchen, her skirt left on the stairs, his shirt on the landing…

It was as if he'd been making love in the dark for years and somebody had just turned the light on. No longer was it just about pure physical sensation and muffled feelings he refused to set free.

Afterwards, he lay back and stared at the ceiling. If he'd known it could be like this, that he could feel like this, he'd have started searching for Grace twenty years earlier. Why, oh, why had he wasted all this time?

Even then he couldn't bear any distance between them. He curled round her, dragging her to him, and she intertwined her arms with his and pulled them into her body and kissed his knuckles, his fingers, his palms. At first he was jubilant, ready to leap up and down on the bed and declare his love for her, but then he started wondering why she'd let him make love to her in the first place, why she hadn't shied away from him as she had done in recent days. There had been a poignant sweetness in her lovemaking today, almost a sadness.

As the truth struck home a small pearl of moisture appeared at the corner of his eye. This time together had not been about reconciliation, as he had hoped.

Grace had been saying goodbye.

For the next week, Noah almost buried himself in his study. He didn't know how to fix what had happened between them. He did, however, know how to fix Karl. So he spent his time doing just that. And, as he did, he started to see what Grace had been talking about. He started to see himself, not Karl.

But now Karl loved his double agent girlfriend with true abandon, was willing to die rather than betray her, even if it meant letting her betray him. And, as he wove all of this into the story, the answers started to come to him.

Just telling Grace would not be enough. He was breaking her heart and sounds and syllables would not mend it. Suddenly, he could see so clearly what Caz had been talking about.

The night before they left for Paris, the plan finally clicked into place in his head. He hadn't wanted to jump the gun, to try something and send her running away for ever if he got it wrong, but he was also aware that time was running out and that the hourglass was almost empty.

Paris was just as beautiful. Too beautiful, in fact. Last time she'd been here it had all been new and exciting, her relationship with Noah blossoming. Even she hadn't guessed that in three short months it would all come to an end.

Reminders were everywhere. Places they'd eaten, streets they'd walked down. Noah had even brought them back to the same hotel, although—thank goodness—they occupied a different suite.

Noah was making it hard to let him go.

Harder since they'd made love that day. Every time he looked at her now, her heart did a silly little skip. One better suited to a fourteen-year-old at the beginning of a relationship. It had no place here as they untangled themselves from each other and prepared to go their separate ways.

Grace lay awake in bed early on their second morning there. Her alarm clock showed it was five-thirty but she refused to believe it.

She wished she had Daisy's laptop with her so she could see if Marissa and Dani were online. It would be late in San Francisco, but probably only early evening in Sydney.

Hang on a minute. She could use Noah's laptop. It was sitting in the lounge of their suite, all set up and ready to go. He'd shown her how to use it weeks ago, scoffing at Daisy's outmoded bit of kit. He'd even offered to buy her a new one, but she'd got used to Daisy's scruffy pink laptop and it felt homely, comfortably shabby in the midst of all Noah's high-tech gadgets.

Noah was breathing softly on his side of the bed. He hadn't even made an attempt to touch her again since they'd last made love. As if he'd silently agreed that they couldn't top what had happened and should leave it as their last sweet memory of the one thing that had always worked in their relationship.

It was almost a relief not to have to wriggle out of his embrace. Almost. She threw the covers back, slid her feet onto the floor and stood up quietly and carefully. Being an early bird, Noah tended to sleep lightly at this time of the morning and it wouldn't take much to rouse him to full consciousness. And she didn't want that. She needed this time on her own.

When she was standing, she crept to the door, walking through the soles of her feet like a dancer. Even she could hardly hear her own footsteps.

Noah's breathing stopped for a moment and she instantly became a statue. But then he started again and he didn't sit up or make any sudden movements, so she finally made it to the door and released the breath that had been trapped in her chest.

Noah stared at the wall. He'd woken, having heard Grace—no, it was more as if he'd sensed her—creeping out of the room.

Every second of every day she was moving further and further away from him, retreating into herself. He knew he had to put his plan into action soon. But, at the same time, he didn't want to manipulate her. When he asked her to stay it truly had to be her choice and not because he'd carefully and silently removed all her other options.

'Shh!' Grace clapped her hands over the laptop speaker as it merrily chimed, announcing with some self-satisfaction that it was booting up. She glanced at the bedroom door but no light came on and, after a few seconds, she relaxed.

Her fingers rapped out a familiar pattern on the keyboard as she logged onto Blinddatebrides.com, not even having to think about it. She sent out the invitation:

Englishcrumpet invites Kangagirl and Sanfrandani to a private IM conference.

Nothing happened. Oh, well. She'd known it was a long shot, but she'd been desperately hoping that one of them would be online. She was just about to creep back into the bedroom when the laptop pinged.

Kangagirl: Grace?
Englishcrumpet: Oh, thank goodness! I'm so glad you're here.

Kangagirl: I was just about to leave the office. You just caught me.

Englishcrumpet: Have you got a few minutes?

Kangagirl: Always. Is this a Noah-related emergency?

Englishcrumpet: When isn't it? If I ever get my love life sorted out we'll have nothing left to talk about.

Kangagirl: (grin) We'll just have to start on Dani's, then!

Englishcrumpet: Won't she love that?

Kangagirl: What's up?

Englishcrumpet: I'm regretting saying I'd wait until after the Paris trip to leave. It's just so hard!

Kangagirl: (((hugs))) I'm so sad it didn't work out for you two. I was sure it would.

Englishcrumpet: Me too, or I wouldn't have said yes to him. He's been so quiet the last few days, hardly said a thing to me.

Kangagirl: He's ignoring you?

Englishcrumpet: No. It's not that he's just…not saying much, which is odd in itself.

Kangagirl: Any idea why?

Englishcrumpet: Again, no. And there's this look he gets in his eyes—it's so sad. It makes my heart break. But I can't stay because of a look. I just feel so guilty.

Kangagirl: You believe you're doing the right thing. I know you do.

Grace stretched her fingers and nodded to herself. Other people might not understand, might say she ought to stick it out for the sake of the baby, but she truly wasn't being selfish. She couldn't bring up a child in that kind of emotional atmosphere. It just wasn't healthy.

Englishcrumpet: I do. I really do. Part of me wishes that Noah would just wake up—

She glanced towards the bedroom door.

Englishcrumpet: Not literally. I mean I wish that he'd make an effort to at least try to change.
Kangagirl: You don't think he will?
Englishcrumpet: I don't think he can. *I'd stay if I thought he would. No. All the silence can only mean one thing—he's given up.*

'Grace?'

On a complete reflex, Grace snapped the laptop closed and jumped away from it. Her heart was pounding so hard it felt as if it would pogo stick right past her throat and out of her mouth.

'Noah! You scared the life out of me!'

No trademark sexy smile. No crinkle round the eyes.

'Sorry.'

She looked at the laptop. 'I was just… chatting to Marissa—you know, the girl in Australia. A wedding crisis or something…'

Why was she lying? This was stupid.

He shrugged. 'You know I don't mind.'

'Thanks.'

'No problem.'

'Well…I'm going for a shower. You carry on.'

But when she opened up the laptop she discovered that closing it had put it on power save and terminated the Internet connection. By the time she'd logged on again, Marissa was nowhere to be found.

It was a couple of hours until breakfast and she and Noah moved around each other like chess pieces, every move designed to keep maximum distance between them. Every move planned ahead.

They didn't bother with room service like last time. Too personal. It was much better in the hotel dining room where they could take comfort from the other people filling up the silences. Where they could breathe out.

'I'll be out all morning,' he told her, even though they'd already discussed it. 'Would you do me a favour?'

'Of course.'

'On the laptop…my book…'

She raised her eyebrows. 'You want me to print it out?'

'No.' He shook his head. 'I think I fixed Karl. I'd be really grateful if you'd read it and tell me what you think.'

'Oh. Okay.'

They were so civilised, weren't they?

He nodded his goodbye and disappeared out of the restaurant.

So civilised it made her want to scream.

Grace didn't feel like sightseeing on her own, so she took Noah's laptop into the terrace café on the roof of the hotel and read his book. At first it seemed to follow the same path, but it was still interesting as, now she had a better idea of the plot, she saw little hints of upcoming problems, had time to appreciate the details.

However, by the time she'd got halfway through she'd forgotten all about being cerebral about it. The plot whizzed along, keeping her hitting the Page Down key pretty quickly, but it was the love story between Karl and Irina that really got her. Where had this come from?

Before, they'd been fine doing all the gun-toting, baddie-busting stuff but, as soon as they'd been alone together they'd gone all two-dimensional. But now…now Noah had a living, breathing love affair on the pages, one that made her gasp and shed a couple of tears.

It was wonderful. The whole book was wonderful.

It was fiendishly clever, exciting, page-turning—all the things he was known for—but it also made her laugh, cry, put her hand over her mouth in horror and snort in anger. In short, it made her *feel*. If this wasn't his biggest selling novel yet, she'd eat his laptop.

She was so proud of him. And when he got back she was going to tell him.

On a whim, she picked up the phone and asked for room service.

The hotel suite door loomed before him. Noah stared at it and stroked the smooth surface of the hotel key card that sat in his pocket. Grace was alone in there. With his book. With Karl and Irina. And if she didn't believe in them, she'd never believe what he had to say. It had been his way of laying the foundations, testing the waters.

He was scared. Good and scared. And it felt good to be scared. His heart tap danced with it. His brain swirled with it. He hated every single sensation, but he welcomed them because he knew what they signalled. He was ready to give Grace what she wanted, what she needed, what she truly deserved. In six months that little baby would be born and he would be the best father in the goddam world, because now he had the tools. He had the heart.

He pulled the key from his pocket and dipped it in the lock.

Grace was waiting for him, sitting on one of the sofas with a chick-lit paperback in her hands. Had she even read his book? Had he left it too late?

She put the book down and stood up. 'Hi.'

'Hi.'

Her face turned a slightly darker shade of pink and she looked at the floor.

'My book—'

'Your book—'

They both spoke at once and then broke off.

'You read it?'

Her face softened and she tipped her head to one side. 'Of course I did. You asked me to.'

Pure Grace. If he'd been thinking straight he'd have known that he didn't need to ask. That was just how she was. Always giving. She was going to be a wonderful mother to their child. Another wave of feeling crashed in, breaking the fear into pieces and tumbling it like pebbles in the surf. He loved her so much. It was time to show her.

It didn't matter what she thought of the book. He was going to tell her anyway.

'Grace, will you come for a walk with me?'

She folded her arms. 'But I…I ordered champagne.' She gestured to an ice bucket on a stand that he could have sworn had just appeared from nowhere. Then she smiled. The first one he'd seen in days. 'To celebrate the book. It really was wonderful—'

He held out his hand. 'Come for a walk. I need to tell you something…show you something.'

She stared at him for a second, her hand half-raised to meet his, half-ready to tuck back into the crook of her opposite elbow.

'Okay.'

CHAPTER TEN

THE sun was behind the high-pitched roof tops, slanting through the gaps between tall houses. Where the light hit the quays flanking the Seine, the pale grey stone was transformed with a golden, rosy glow. Grace and Noah walked through these pockets of light and shade silently, their hands joined, on the surface looking like any other pair of visiting lovers who'd decided to finally emerge from their hotel room.

Noah tried to keep his shoulders loose, his jaw relaxed but, whenever he didn't concentrate on doing just that, the muscles just contracted again. This was it. His moment of truth. He thought he was quite possibly going to die.

They'd started walking near Notre Dame, on the right bank, and now they neared the section near the Louvre.

Grace was staring at the river, steadfastly ignoring the birch trees on the bank—almost as if she couldn't bear to look at them. But he needed her to look at them. He took a deep breath and stopped by the first one.

Gently now. Let it come to her slowly.

'Have you seen all these carvings on the trees?'

She nodded. 'Mmm,' she said in a faraway voice, still watching the waves slap against their stone barriers.

'I would imagine that if someone took the time to leave

a message, then the person it was for must mean a great deal to them.'

Now she looked with dull eyes. He stood back. Hoping. Wishing. Praying she'd notice.

Her eyes ran over the bark of the tree and then she sighed and started to turn away. Noah's heart plummeted. But she took one last look and something caught her attention.

'Up there, at the top. What is that?'

He shrugged.

'I didn't notice that before. It's new, carved in a circle round the tree, above all the other messages…'

He followed her eyes, willing her to start reading.

'It's more than just something like *M + D*, isn't it? It's words. It says something.'

Noah held his breath. It said everything.

Grace circled the tree, frowning, then she began to read. *'She is more than her name*— What on earth does that mean? Is that supposed to be romantic?'

He didn't say anything, just put his hands in his pockets and started walking towards the next tree, hoping she'd take the hint. She did. But she kept frowning and looking back at the first tree. His poor quivering heart began to steady itself.

They reached the next one and, just as he'd known she would, she stopped and inspected this one without any prompting.

'There's more…listen! *Free and unearned favour*. This just gets weirder and weirder.'

Now she walked more quickly to the next tree, he walked behind her, trying to regulate his breathing.

'And, despite my current fame…'

She ran back to him, her eyes now bright and alert, totally caught up in the puzzle.

'Noah, it's…Wait. I've just got to—'

She didn't finish her sentence, but ran back to the first tree, circled it, ran to the second, did the same…

'It's a poem!' she said when she'd joined him again. 'Come on. There must be more.'

Good. She liked the poem. Well, a sonnet—of sorts. Clumsy and inelegant by Shakespeare's standards, but he had it on good authority that it came straight from the author's heart, and that had to count for something, didn't it? Finally, he'd come up with a way of *showing* her. Caz had been right. Love was more than words, but words were the best tool at his disposal, so he'd hoped he'd found a way to make them count.

He caught her up at the next tree.

'Read it,' she said, smiling.

He didn't need to look at the scratchings in the bark. In the last few days, while Grace had been sleeping heavily, he'd spent the few hours before dawn shaping them into what he wanted to say. But he played along with her. For now.

He took a deep breath. *'I am humbled to have known her.'* The words sounded strange in his ears. He'd never said them out loud before and it was a bit like going out in public in just his underwear.

Grace sighed. 'It's so beautiful. I wonder if there will be a name at the end, a clue to who wrote it.'

He shrugged again. No. No name. Not his, anyway. But there was a clue.

He was scared of the clue.

Once she'd read it, his life would split in one of two ways—one heaven, one hell. And only she could decide.

She jogged from tree to tree, calling out the lines, chattering about what it meant, pondering the mystery. Noah tried to keep his façade calm and collected, but it was difficult without his glass shell. Everything kept floating to the surface and he had to shove it down again, saying, *Wait. Not yet.*

Three more trees to go. Was it possible for a man of his age and build to just pass out? Grace came back and grabbed his hand, dragging him on.

'*Joined with me, she makes my soul complete.* Only two more trees now. This must be near the end!'

Oh, that her smile would stay, that the joy in her eyes would not flicker out when she reached the last tree.

'*And I will die if I cannot always look upon her face.*' Tears sprang to her eyes and she clapped a hand to her chest. 'Oh, my word…'

No. His words. His heart. For her to accept or reject.

Before she reached the last tree, Noah let go of her hand and stopped as she ran ahead, his heart pounding so loudly in his ears that he could no longer hear the river. She circled the last silver birch in the row. This time, her mouth moved but no sound came out.

She looked at him and he thought he would melt away into nothing.

He walked towards her and, without looking at the tree, completed the sonnet. 'She is my love, my heart…' here his voice thickened so much it cracked '…my only Grace.'

So many emotions flickered over her face, he didn't have time to read them. She marched back to him and grabbed his upper arms, her fingers shaking as they dug into his muscles.

'Why?' she said, almost angry. 'Why did you write that?'

Then the fierceness evaporated and she looked into his eyes. He looked straight into hers. Confusion, hope, fear and desperation all swirled and mingled there. It was as if he were looking right into her heart. He did his best to drop his own shutters and let her see his. Her eyes flicked rapidly right to left as if she were trying to read him, as if she was scared of what he might be saying. And then the tears fell, her mouth crumpled. She nodded.

He kept looking into her eyes and freed his arms so he could touch her face, wipe her tears with the pads of his thumbs. And then he lowered his lips to hers and the kiss they shared was hot and sweet and perfect. It wasn't just their lips meeting, fusing. Something happened—a new feeling he'd never experienced before and suspected he never would again. It was as if, in the back of his head, he heard a clunk, a click, and everything in the world slotted into its right place. He and Grace might have been married for three months, but now they were joined.

'I love you,' he whispered against her lips, and she just began to cry again.

The only thing better than a honeymoon in Paris was a second honeymoon in Paris, Grace decided as she lay in Noah's arms the day after they returned from their extended trip. It had been fabulous. Even better than the first one. And not many women got to boast about two honeymoons in Paris within a few months. And with such a man. She sighed and looked at him. He'd changed so much and she was horribly proud of him. She had no doubt now that he would be a wonderful father.

He was her soulmate. He was a different fit to Rob, but still it worked. She didn't understand how there could be two people who could match her so completely, especially when they were two very different men. But then love wasn't static. It could cope, she reckoned.

It was six o'clock and she was wide awake. Unusually for Noah, he was not. Thankfully, the morning sickness was much improved and she was happy lying in bed watching Noah breathe and feeling the weight of the arm draped across her midriff. She knew she shouldn't, but she couldn't help trailing her fingers across his arm, feeling the soft hair there.

Suddenly, he sniffed and twitched. He opened his eyes, dozy and unfocused at first, but then he saw her and a huge sexy smile broke across his face.

'Good morning, Mrs Frost.'

She smiled back. 'Good morning, Mr Frost.'

Then he dived under the sheet and kissed the slight round

of her tummy. 'Good morning, Little Frost.' Then he reappeared and kissed her on the nose. 'I love you, Grace.'

'I love you too, Noah. My Noah.' She ran her fingers through his hair as she gave him an indulgent look. 'You must have said that a thousand times in the last week. I get it now. You can stop if you like.'

He looked wounded. 'Never! If I only say it nine hundred and ninety-nine times in the next week, you have permission to slap me.'

'I'll keep count,' she said, giggling.

'You'd better.'

They dragged themselves out of bed and down into the kitchen. Grace had a yearning for a full English breakfast now the morning sickness seemed to have waned almost completely. And, as Noah cooked, they discussed the future of the book shop with its attached patisserie, an easy flow from one to the other. If she hadn't been so angry the first time she'd seen it, she'd have realised what a wonderful idea it was.

Grace jumped up to sit on the counter and watched Noah fry her eggs. 'Daisy is thrilled at the idea of helping out while she studies and Caz has been moaning she needs something to keep her occupied. She also felt really bad about laying off all the old Coffee Bean staff and she's begging me to consider re-hiring them. Between all of us, I reckon we can make it work.'

Later that morning the doorbell rang and Noah answered it, then returned to the kitchen, where Grace was sitting, with a small square package in his hand.

'What's that?' she asked and walked over to look at it.

'Don't know.' He turned it over and read the return address. 'It's addressed to me from an Internet company based in Devon. Ceramics or something.' He shook his head.

'It's not *another* thing for the baby, is it?'

Noah had been filling the nursery with books and toys and all sorts of strange gadgets with alarming speed. She really must encourage him to get on with the third draft of his book. That would keep him out of trouble and curb the Internet shopping spree.

'No. Or nothing I've bought.'

She narrowed her eyes, but he stared back at her, the picture of innocence.

'We'll see,' she said, holding out her hand. He gave the package to her and she peeled back the parcel tape and looked inside. Something—an irregular something—was rolled in bubble wrap. And there was a piece of paper. She put the box on the kitchen table and pulled the scrap out.

'It's a message from…Daisy,' she said, one eyebrow shooting heavenwards. 'It's definitely for you. Listen…

> *Dear Noah, here's a little gift to say thanks, I'm happy*
> *I picked you, and I'm glad you've joined our family.'*

She passed the scrap of printed paper to Noah, who examined it.

'It's just a short message she must have typed in on the website when she ordered the…whatever it is.'

'I think you'd better open it.'

Noah shrugged and pulled the box across the table to him. Then he removed the *thing* and started to unwrap it. As he revealed what it was, Grace began to laugh uncontrollably. 'Oh, that girl! She's priceless!'

It was so funny. Noah was just staring at it, completely lost for words.

It was an electric-blue mug with the words 'Hot Papa' written on it in navy glitter. She took it from him and placed it on the shelf next to her pink mug.

Finally, Noah began to chuckle. 'A matching pair. But… *Hot Papa*?'

Grace walked over to him and looped her arms around his

neck. 'She's not wrong, you know,' she said. And then she drew him into a lingering kiss and let him show her just how right his stepdaughter had been.

EPILOGUE

Private IM conference between Kangagirl and Sanfrandani:

Kangagirl: I knew it! I told you right from the start that Grace and Noah were going to end up together, didn't I?
Sanfrandani: Yes, Marissa. You did.
Kangagirl: I've got a sixth sense about these things.
Sanfrandani: Of course you have.
Kangagirl: I have! And you know what, Dani?
Sanfrandani: Uh-oh.
Kangagirl: My 'sense' tells me you're next.
Sanfrandani: LOL!!!! That's so funny, Marissa.
Kangagirl: You'll see.
Sanfrandani: No way. And, Marissa?
Kangagirl: Yes?
Sanfrandani: Wipe that goofy smile off your face!
Kangagirl: !!!!!!!!!!!!

* * * * *

DREAM DATE
WITH THE MILLIONAIRE

BY
MELISSA McCLONE

Welcome to the www.blinddatebrides.com member profile of:
Sanfrandani (aka Danica Bennett)

My ideal partner...

Probably doesn't exist outside the covers of my Jane Austen collection. I'm independent. I don't want a guy to be the centre of my world and I'm not sure I want to be any part of his. Getting my career back on track is my number one priority.

My details...

- **Age:** twenty-six
- **I live:** in San Francisco
- **Marital status**: single
- **Occupation**: sales (don't ask)

You'll match if you...

- Are between twenty-four and thirty-five
- Don't leave your heart here
- Are single and want to stay that way
- Are employed

With a degree in mechanical engineering from Stanford University, the last thing **Melissa McClone** ever thought she would be doing was writing romance novels. But analysing engines for a major US airline just couldn't compete with her 'happily-ever-afters'. When she isn't writing, caring for her three young children or doing laundry, Melissa loves to curl up on the couch with a cup of tea, her cats and a good book. She enjoys watching home decorating shows to get ideas for her house —a 1939 cottage that is *slowly* being renovated. Melissa lives in Lake Oswego, Oregon, with her own real-life hero husband, two daughters, a son, two loveable but oh-so-spoiled indoor cats and a no-longer-stray outdoor kitty that decided to call the garage home. Melissa loves to hear from her readers. You can write to her at PO Box 63, Lake Oswego, OR 97034, USA, or contact her via her website: www.melissamcclone.com

To Jennie Adams and Fiona Harper,
my blinddatebrides.com cohorts
and new chat buddies
Special thanks to:
Markus Frind with plentyoffish.com,
Virginia Kantra and Gary Yngve

CHAPTER ONE

Blinddatebrides.com is running thirteen chat rooms, fifty-six private IM conferences, and 7828 members are online. Chat with your dating prospects now!

Private IM conference #25 (3 participants)…

Englishcrumpet: Who would have thought I'd meet the man of my dreams at an online dating site? I still can't believe it!

DANICA BENNETT blew out a puff of air. She couldn't believe it either.

Alone in her neatly organized cubicle in the otherwise cluttered and messy San Francisco office of Hookamate.com, she reread the purple words written in a funky font on her computer screen. Englishcrumpet, aka Grace Marlowe from London, deserved to be happy. Dani sincerely hoped her friend would find happiness and wedded bliss with her new husband, Noah. Especially with a baby on the way.

But Dani wasn't so sure living happily ever after was possible. She glanced at the photograph of her family—her mother, her three younger sisters and herself. Winning the lottery seemed more likely. Though she'd never say those words to her newly wed friend. Dani typed, the letters appearing in green—the color of money. Too bad her life couldn't be as rich and bold as her computer font.

Sanfrandani: It is pretty amazing.

Grace had only known Noah a short time before marrying the bestselling thriller author and then found out she was pregnant.

More words, rust-brown in a plain but strong font, appeared on screen. Kangagirl, their friend Marissa Warren, from Australia.

Kangagirl: Amazing, yes, but not that rare. Apparently one in eight people meet their spouses online.

Dani almost laughed. Marissa sounded like a commercial for online dating. Or like a happy bride. Which she would be in a few months. She'd fallen in love with her temporary boss, not someone she met on Blinddatebrides.com like Grace. Though it wasn't for Marissa's lack of trying to meet a guy online.

Sanfrandani: Well, it's a good thing for me. Or I'd be out of another job.

Even this crappy job, she thought to herself and stabbed her fork at her lunch, a limp chicken Caesar salad leftover from last night's dinner.

Englishcrumpet: What do you mean?
Kangagirl: You've lost me.

The two messages popped up on Dani's screen at almost the same moment.

Oh, no. She dropped her fork. Distracted by her friends' happiness and her own bleak prospects, she'd revealed more than she intended. The three of them had grown so close over the past six months she'd almost let her secret slip out.

Time for damage control.

Sanfrandani: Nothing. I'm just so glad you guys joined Blinddatebrides.com. I don't know how I would have survived these months without your support and friendship.

But typing the words gave Dani a funny feeling in her stomach. What kind of friend was she? Keeping the truth about what she was doing at Blinddatebrides.com from Marissa and Grace.

Englishcrumpet: You've been through a lot, Dani. Losing your dream job and getting used to your new one. Things will turn around. Just watch.
Kangagirl: And then, when you least expect it, you're going to meet him. That one special man.

Dani hoped not.

Snores drifted from the engineers' cubicle a few feet away. Someone must have pulled an all-nighter.

She needed to get her career back on track first. She'd spent the last six months trying to find another job with no success. Distractions, especially men, weren't allowed right now.

Kangagirl: The only question is…how do we make it happen?

We. Unexpected tears stung Dani's eyes. She ran her fingertips over the bracelet—silver with crystal beads—Marissa had sent her after a trip to Hong Kong. These women, even though they'd never met in person, truly cared about her.

Sanfrandani: Please. No one needs to make anything happen. I'm doing fine. No worries.

Englishcrumpet: We're not really worrying. We just want to help. You joined this site for a reason, Dani.

But not the same reason as Marissa and Grace.

Guilt welled up inside Dani.

It was time to come clean. To stop lying.

Her fingers flew across the keyboard with lightning speed, in case nerves and fear got the best of her. Or her boss showed up.

Sanfrandani: I didn't join Blinddatebrides.com to meet men.

Kangagirl: Then why did you join?

Sanfrandani: Because

The cursor blinked, waiting for her to finish. Dani swallowed hard. Her online friendship with Marissa and Grace was the only thing in her life going well these days. Did she want to risk that?

But what kind of relationship did they have, really, if she couldn't be honest?

Dani took a deep breath and typed.

Sanfrandani: I was forced to.

She stared at the screen, her heart racing, her hands sweating.

Englishcrumpet: Did someone sign you up like my daughter did with me?

Oh dear. Dani snuck another look around the office before ?ing her trembling hands to the keyboard.

Sanfrandani: No, I signed up myself.
Kangagirl: ???

Dani felt sick, but the truth had to be said. Er, typed.

Sanfrandani: I'm a spy.

"There's something you should see."

Bryce Delaney heard his assistant's voice, but didn't glance up from his computer monitor and the database query he was writing. He didn't have to.

Joelle Chang would be standing two feet from the edge of his walnut-stained desk holding a manila file folder with a pen—blue ink only so she could tell the difference on photocopies—tucked behind her ear. Despite her college-girl long hair and trendy clothes, forty-one-year-old Joelle was dedicated, thorough and one-hundred-percent predictable. Exactly the way he liked things. And people. "I pay you enough to see for me."

"You said you wanted to be kept in the loop about possible security issues."

Security. A top priority at his Web site Blinddate-brides.com. Bryce looked up. "Possible or probable?"

Joelle's almond-shaped eyes grew dark. "Two red flags."

Damn. He didn't need this on top of the other problems they'd been dealing with. Scammers, spammers, hackers, marrieds, the list went on.

"It might not mean anything," she added.

In the last year, there had been a handful of false alarms. "But it could mean we have a troublemaker on board."

It wouldn't be the first time. He'd dealt with escorts, cheats, thieves and liars. Had charges brought against them when possible, too.

Bryce wasn't about to let anyone take advantage of his cus

tomers. Too many people pretended to be something they weren't, both in real life and online. He had experience with that. His sister, too. But she was more trusting than him. That was why he'd started a dating—make that a relationship—Web site: to protect good people like Caitlin.

"What do you have?" he asked.

Joelle handed him a file. "This particular client has been a member of the site for over six months. Everything about her looks good, including her background check."

"Her?"

"Yes," Joelle answered. "None of the e-mail filters have picked up anything to suggest she's an escort."

Those were usually easy to detect since they asked for money in almost every e-mail.

"But the chat filter picked up something so we did a little investigating," Joelle said. "The subject spends hours logged on to the site each day, but she has not accepted a date yet, even though her profile has been marked highly compatible with several men."

Bryce had worked with a psychologist to create an algorithm to match clients based on their interests, backgrounds and personalities. Chats, based on compatibility, were also arranged with groups of well-matched people, too, since many people preferred group interactions to one-on-one. Some clients, though, preferred to peruse the profiles themselves and pick matches that way.

He opened the file and studied the photo of a woman. The messy blond hair piled on top of her head and secured with a—was that a red bandana?—caught his eye first. Not the most appealing hairstyle. The picture itself was far from flat-tering. She wasn't smiling or looking at the camera. Shadows ??? what he could see of her face, though she looked ??? unless her skin was always red like that. Her profile stated blue eyes, but he couldn't distinguish the color, really anything about her. "She's been matched?"

"Yes. The compatibility program has matched her with seventeen clients so far. Five of those contacted her. Others must have seen something they liked in her profile because they e-mailed her, too. She replied back to each one, but that was it. No additional correspondence. No chat invites. Nothing."

"At least she's following the guidelines about replying to others even if you're not interested in them."

"Yes."

He read more in the file. Turning down potential dates wasn't unusual. Bryce remembered one shy female client in particular, but others in the past had misrepresented themselves. Better to err on the side of caution. "You've taken the usual steps?"

Joelle nodded. "Customer service called to discuss her experience so far. She asked as many questions as they did, and they were on the phone for two hours."

"Two hours?"

Another nod. "I called her myself after that. She came across as highly intelligent and very friendly, but remember that identity thief? Never assume anyone who is nice is also harmless."

"That's for sure." Bryce flipped through the pages in the file. He noticed a familiar zip code. She lived here in San Francisco. Many of the scammers he'd dealt with lived overseas. But this was on his home turf. He could follow the prosecution to the end if she were guilty. "Where does she go on the site?"

"Chat rooms, particularly the Ladies Lounge, and private IM conferences. She spends most of her time exploring the Web site. Not client profiles, but the content itself."

Most people, whether they wanted to date or not, liked checking out the profiles of people in their area. On some Internet relationship sites that earned revenue through advertising; anyone could register and search profiles for free. Not on Blinddatebrides.com. Only paying members, who'd filled out a detailed questionnaire and agreed to a background check if they lived in the United States, were allowed to search the database, read profiles and contact members.

Joelle continued. "She's online during normal work hours as well as late at night. Two different IP addresses have been linked to her account name, depending on the time of day."

Nothing unusual about that. "Work and home."

"Seems likely, but I don't know many employers who would encourage their employees to spend that much time each day at a dating site while at work."

"Unless the boss doesn't know." Bryce skimmed the rest of the pages and saw one of the red flags. She'd said she was a spy during a chat. "Or she has an employer who wants her checking us out."

The online dating world was cutthroat. The competition stole from each other regularly, but pretending to want to meet dates went against the terms of service users agreed to when they joined Blinddatebrides.com. But she hadn't mentioned anything about her job prior to her saying she was a spy.

"What does she do for a living?" Bryce asked.

"She listed sales as her occupation," Joelle said.

"That's too vague, given the list of options she could have chosen."

"Red flag number three?" Joelle asked.

Bryce nodded. He prided himself on making his Web site a safe and secure place to meet and fall in love. His sister had had her heart broken, as well as her bank account drained, thanks to the "love" she'd found on a competitor's site. The guy had turned out to be the exact opposite of what he'd claimed to be. No one was going to pull a stunt like that on Bryce's site, during his watch. "I'll get right on it."

Joelle smiled. "I almost feel sorry for her."

"Why is that?" he asked.

"Because, once you get started, you don't stop."

He shrugged. "Just doing my job."

"Remember, it's just a job." She pulled the pen from behind her ear. "Grant is e-mailing you a file with additional information you might need."

"Thanks." As she left the office and closed the door behind her, Bryce stared at the picture in the folder. He glanced at the user name. "Who are you, Sanfrandani? And what are you doing on my site?"

At three o'clock, Dani sat at the rectangular table that functioned as the "conference room" as well as the "break room" with her five coworkers at the fledgling Internet dating site Hookamate.com. Pacing back and forth across the floor of the converted warehouse was their boss, James Richardson.

James wore ripped-at-the-knee jeans and a black T-shirt. He had long, straggly blond hair. He spoke fast and loud, as if fueled by caffeine and junk food. He reminded her of a stereotypical computer science graduate student in desperate need of a balanced meal, sunshine and a girlfriend, but his first two Internet ventures had made him tons of money. He'd sold them, and now wanted to replicate that success with a new online dating site.

Succeed at any cost, Dani had finally figured out.

During her interview, James had seemed more captivated with her double-D bra cup sized breasts than the qualifications on her résumé. Yet he'd surprised her by asking detailed questions about her schooling and work experience. He'd known exactly what he wanted in a marketing person.

She had the skills so she'd made the most of what nature had given her, just as her mother had taught her to do, and secured the job. Which meant she only had herself to blame for where she found herself today. She wanted to bang her head on the table for her stupidity.

"The good news is we had an increase in traffic thanks to Danica's marketing efforts." James winked at her. No one at the company except him knew she was undercover, so to speak, spying on the local competition, Blinddatebrides.com. "Unfortunately the traffic exceeded our capacity so we've been having to add machines. But that's not a bad problem. Traffic will drive our advertising revenue. That means more money for us. Anyone have other ideas to generate more users?"

No one said anything.

"Rethinking our branding might help," she suggested. "Taglines, image, ads, name."

James clenched his jaw. "Our Web site name rocks."

"Totally."

"Yeah."

Dani listened to the men in the room support their boss who they held in almost cult leader esteem. The only other woman at the table, Shelley, the office manager, shook her head and mouthed the word *sorry* to Dani.

The responses didn't deter her. She had to do something. Say something.

"Look at Blinddatebrides.com." The name of the fastest-growing competitor brought groans from the three engineers at the table, but Dani kept going. "When people hear Blinddatebrides.com, they can't help but think about brides. That word connotes weddings, which makes people think relationships, marriage, permanence. That's appealing to users."

"Only if you want to end up with a ball and chain," a Ruby on Rails developer named Andrew murmured.

Dani ignored him. "Granted, your…I mean our…site's name does have 'mate', but 'hook' makes people think of…"

"What?" James asked.

"One-night stands," a PHP programmer, who probably hadn't showered let alone had a date in a month, said.

People—okay, guys—laughed.

"Yeah, sex," the interface hacker offered. "Sex appeals to a lot of people, too."

The two men gave each other high fives.

Dani sighed. "I worry the name brings about images of hookups, not serious relationships."

No one spoke.

"There's such a thing as a niche market," Andrew said. "Hookups can be our niche."

She stared at all the nodding heads. Male heads. No wonder women had a hard time finding good men to date these days. Not that she was interested in anything to do with dating.

"I appreciate you bringing this up, Danica," James said finally. "I'll have to think about what you said."

Which meant he would never mention it again. That was how things worked around here. James's way or the highway. He'd given her a choice—join Blinddatebrides.com or quit. She needed the paycheck so did as he'd requested. Up until that point, she'd really liked the challenges of being in on the ground floor of a start-up again. Now she hated getting up in the morning.

"Anything else?" he asked.

No one said a word. No one ever did. Except her. She didn't know why she bothered.

"Get to work, people." James clapped his hands together. "We don't want anyone to be lonely tonight. They need to hook a mate!"

Dani trudged back to her cubicle, frustrated and tired. She'd stayed up late last night sending out another batch of résumés. Speaking of which, she'd better check her e-mail in case someone had replied. She clicked on her in-box. There, at the top, was a new message, but not from a potential employer. This was one was from bigbrother@blinddatebrides.com with the subject header "I read your profile."

Oh, no. She squeezed her eyes shut. Another guy who wanted to get to know her.

Her stomach churned. She hated this. Sure, she could just hit "delete"—that was par for the course on many dating sites—but Blinddatebrides.com was different. The site touted itself as a community where politeness and manners mattered. Users were requested to reply, even if the intent was to give someone a brush-off. Still, the thought of telling another guy she wasn't interested in getting to know him better made her feel physically ill.

But what else could she do?

Leading a guy on when she was on the site under false pretenses ranked right up there with corporate spying in her book. She massaged her forehead to stop a full-on headache from erupting. Okay, one rejection wasn't going to send some guy scampering back to his mommy in tears, but…

Why did this keep happening?

Dani had taken steps to ensure it wouldn't. What sense of honor she had left had made her fill out the profile questionnaire truthfully so she understood when the compatibility program deemed her a match with someone. But Dani had hedged against the computer algorithms by uploading the most unattractive photo of herself she could find. She looked downright ugly. While other women uploaded more than one picture to their profile page, she hadn't.

She'd also downplayed her interests to make herself sound…well…about as exciting as a slug inching across a driveway at dawn. She'd listed the library as her favorite place to spend a Saturday night and a collection of Jane Austen novels as her must-have item if stranded on a desert island.

No man should want to date her.

Maybe this one didn't. Maybe he was one of those guys, the players, who only wanted to have sex. If that were the case, she wouldn't mind telling him to get lost.

Dani opened her eyes and read the entire e-mail.

To: "Sanfrandani" <sanfrandani@blinddatebrides.com>
From: "Bigbrother" <bigbrother@blinddatebrides.com>
Subject: I read your profile
Who are you searching for? Mr. Darcy? Or Mr. Knightley?
-bb

Dani reread the message. Twice.

Okay, she was impressed this guy knew the names of two
Jane Austen heroes, but who did he take her for? Intelligent,
impulsive Lizzy or smug, interfering Emma?

Still, his message intrigued Dani. She typed a reply and hit
"send." With a satisfied smile on her face, she leaned back in
her chair. And almost fell over backward.

Uh-oh. What had she done?

She shouldn't have replied. Dani grimaced. She wasn't
supposed to engage Bigbrother in more e-mails. She was
supposed to tell him she wasn't interested. To. Go. Away.
Politely, of course.

Only she hadn't wanted to do that.

Not when his e-mail had been unlike any of the others she'd
received. He'd obviously read her profile and asked his
question based on what she'd written. Not on her photo or bra
size. Maybe he was genuinely interested.

Or maybe he was ugly.

Her eyes locked on the link to his profile that would transport her to a page all about him, a page with his picture.

Curiosity trickled down the length of her arm to her fingertip, hovering above the laptop's trackpad. She wanted to
know more about Bigbrother. Read what he'd written about
himself. See what he looked like.

Temptation flared. She moved the cursor to the link. All
she had to do was click, but she couldn't.

The less Dani knew about Bigbrother, the better.

She wasn't looking to meet a guy. She didn't want to meet
a guy. Especially one from Blinddatebrides.com.

Not under these circumstances.

Ignoring the twinge of regret, she closed his e-mail.

Goodbye, Bigbrother.

CHAPTER TWO

As BRYCE sipped his coffee, hoping the caffeine would get him through the rest of the day, he stared at the four hundred unread e-mails in his in-box. No way could he get through all of them in the next fifteen minutes, but there was one reply he hoped to find.

He skimmed the list of senders and found the name he was looking for...

Sanfrandani.

That didn't take long.

He couldn't curb his suspicions and wanted to see what she had to say. Which would it be? A polite brush-off or a straight-to-the-point-please-don't-contact-me-again? Curious, he opened the message.

To: "Bigbrother" <bigbrother@blinddatebrides.com>
From: "Sanfrandani" <sanfrandani@blinddatebrides.com>
Subject: RE: I read your profile
Desperately seeking...Colonel Brandon.
-sfd

Bryce frowned and reread the e-mail. He called Joelle into his office. "Who is Colonel Brandon?"

"Didn't he kill Miss Scarlet in the library with the—"

"No. That's a game. This one is in a book. Jane Austen."

Joelle stared blankly at him.

"Come on," he said. "You have to know this."

She raised a finely arched brow. "Because I'm female?"

"Because…" Oh, hell, she had him there. "Yeah."

"I majored in Economics, not English Lit."

Bryce had majored in Computer Science. He pressed his lips together, still staring at the screen. "Wasn't there a movie?"

"Not that I saw. Not with a Colonel Brandon. Colin Firth, now… Yum."

"Spare me."

Joelle shrugged. "Guess you'll have to Google this Colonel guy, then. Or call your sister."

Caitlin.

Thinking of his younger sister brought a smile to Bryce's face. Of course, Caitlin would know the answer. She was a font of movie trivia, especially chick flicks, but a call to her would lead to a lengthy discussion about wedding preparations. Bryce was happy she'd found the love she'd been hoping for on Blinddatebrides.com. Keeping her safe had been his main reason for creating the Web site, but he didn't have time to discuss whether champagne-pink or midnight-blue would be the better choice for bridesmaids' dresses. And he didn't want her probing him about whether he'd found a date for her upcoming engagement party yet.

His search query resulted in 336,000 documents. The Colonel was a character in Jane Austen's *Sense and Sensibility*, but the descriptions Bryce read didn't make sense. One article called the Colonel "sad and reserved." Another said he was a "dull older man."

Nothing, however, explained why Sanfrandani was desperately seeking the Colonel. She was twenty-six, according to her profile—too young for such an old, boring guy. Unless she was a gold-digger.

Bryce stared at Sanfrandani's picture. Even though he couldn't make out any of her facial features, she seemed to have a graceful neck. And that red bandana was starting to grow on him. Still, a woman after a rich husband would have uploaded a better photograph.

But why had she responded to him so mysteriously, almost playfully, instead of telling him to get lost? She'd brushed off the other guys who had contacted her. Was she leading Bryce on? Or not?

He was annoyed. Intrigued.

Attracted.

Not attracted, he corrected. This was an investigation, not a flirtation.

Bryce needed more information so he could figure out where she was coming from and what kind of game she was playing. Then he would know what to do. As he hit "reply", he heard a commotion outside.

He hastily typed a response. He would have rather taken his time, but that wasn't an option right now.

"Look at this," someone yelled outside his office. "Am I really seeing this?"

A low hum buzzed.

Not a good kind of noise either.

Bryce hit "send" with a twinge of regret, but he needed to find out what was going on out there.

"SQL injection."

The words stopped him cold.

"No way."

"It can't be."

He understood the disbelief in the voices. The denial.

"It is."

Damn. Bryce bolted to the door. Someone had entered an executable code disguised as data into the site. No doubt trying to steal credit card and other personal information from the database.

Outside his office, the noise level increased exponentially, his team springing into action like an Emergency Room staff with multiple casualties coming in. Except these injuries weren't as easily diagnosed, and the damage unknown.

"Run forensics on the logs," Bryce ordered.

"Already on it," Christopher, a rock-star caliber software engineer, said.

Bryce nodded his approval. "We need a snapshot of the database right now."

"I'll do it," someone said from across the room.

"Let's patch the hole, people. Compromised data?" he asked Grant, his number two employee.

Compromised data—the stealing or copying of customers' personal information—would be a PR nightmare. Even if credit card account numbers hadn't been captured, there was the issue of privacy. Online dating may have become an accepted way to find love, but some people would be embarrassed to have their anonymous use of the Web site become public knowledge.

Grant rubbed his hand over his face. "We don't know yet."

"Okay." Bryce projected calm. "Then let's find out."

He wanted to jump into the trenches and dig his fingers in. Bryce was a techie at heart, but he was also the boss. Sometimes the two didn't mesh well together. Today he would make sure things worked. He couldn't afford for them not to.

"Should we shut down the site?" Grant asked.

Bryce shook his head. "Not unless we have to."

"Don't want to lose the revenue?"

The money didn't matter to Bryce right now. This was personal. "I don't want to tip off the hackers. Not if we can nail them."

"It's a mess in here," someone murmured from a few desks away.

Bryce imagined himself as one of the Jane Austen heroes Sanfrandani liked to read about, ready to clean up the mess and save the day. Yeah, right.

He sat at an empty desk, one being set up for a new hire, and logged on to the system to double-check the database. Bryce wanted to see that personal information—everything from names and passwords to credit card numbers—was encrypted. The data was. "How strong is the encryption?"

"Strong enough to keep a 100,000-computer botnet busy for years," a security specialist answered.

Good news. But Bryce was still going to have to call their lawyer as soon as he had a better handle on things. It was going to be a long day. And most likely an even longer night.

Talk about a long day.

Dani stretched her arms above her head. She needed a nap but would settle for more caffeine. She'd spent her afternoon working on search engine optimization aka SEO. Increasing traffic to the site was a big part of her marketing job. The more hits, the more clicks. And that meant more money— advertising revenue. But turning visitors into repeat users was important, too, and sometimes harder to do. Especially when the site lacked the type of content it needed to draw people back. Content she'd found on Blinddatebrides.com. Content she now had to create for Hookamate.com.

Too bad she was more interested in checking her e-mail every five minutes to see if Bigbrother had replied. She'd never been like this before, waiting for some strange guy to e-mail her, disappointed when he hadn't.

Pathetic.

That was what she was.

And distracted ever since she'd checked out Bigbrother's profile. Talk about making a big mistake with a single click.

He lived in San Francisco and was cute in a geeky sort of

way. In his picture, he wore a San Francisco Giants baseball cap pulled low on his brow. Dark hair stuck out from the sides. He was dressed casually in a Boston Red Sox shirt and a pair of faded jeans. The photo wasn't a close-up, but she caught a hint of a smile on his face. He almost looked…shy. She liked that.

A beep sounded. Dani checked her e-mail again.

Jackpot.

Bigbrother had replied. Anticipation unleashed the butterflies in her stomach. She couldn't wait to see what he'd written. She opened the message.

To: "Sanfrandani" <sanfrandani@blinddatebrides.com>
From: "Bigbrother" <bigbrother@blinddatebrides.com>
Subject: Colonel Brandon
You're searching for a dull old guy who wears a uniform?

The oh-so-romantic-loves-unconditionally Colonel was near perfect in her mind, but she could see how some might see him as a dull old guy. Especially a man who, based on his attire in his profile picture, preferred baseball to Jane Austen. Dani laughed.

"Care to share the joke?" James asked.

She turned in her chair. Her boss stood at the entrance to her cubicle.

Her cheeks warmed, but then she realized she had nothing to be embarrassed about. James was the one who wanted her checking out the site. "It's an e-mail from someone on Blinddatebrides.com."

James's eyes narrowed. "A male someone?"

She nodded. "Just doing my job."

"A good job at that." He beamed. "So when are you going out with him?"

"I'm not," Dani said with a twinge of regret. Bigbrother

was the only one of the men who had contacted her that she wanted to meet.

"Too many other fish to fry?"

Oh, boy. He had that all wrong. "Uh…no."

"So he must be a loser, then. How many other guys have you met from bdb?" James never called their local competitor by their full name. He seemed to have it in for them, but she didn't know why and was too afraid to ask.

"None," she admitted.

He gave her the once-over. "It can't be from a lack of offers. None of them meet your standards?"

"Nothing like that." She peered over the cubicle walls to see if anyone was around or listening. "I can't accept any dates," she whispered.

"Why not?" he asked. "And why are you whispering?"

"Because of the…you know."

"I don't know."

She lowered her voice more. "The spying."

James sighed. "It's called market research, Danica. Every company does it, so please get over your aversion to your job responsibilities."

Checking out a competitor was one thing, but market research had never made her feel so tacky or dirty, as if she were doing something she wouldn't want her mother to know about. In fact she hadn't told her mother about it. Or her sisters. The only people who knew besides James were Marissa and Grace. Dani wanted to keep it that way.

"I need to know everything about bdb," he continued. "That includes their clients."

The expectant look in his eyes sent a shiver down her spine. "You're not suggesting I—"

"Go out with them," he said at the same time. "Meet whoever contacts you. Dates are the perfect opportunity to check out whether bdb customer expectations are being met or not. You can put together a profile of their users for me, too."

Her shoulders slumped.

When James had told her she would have to get her hands dirty with all facets of Internet marketing she had no idea this was what he meant.

"I can't do this," she said. "I won't lead guys on."

James grinned. "They won't mind. Any guy would be thrilled to date a woman like you. Trust me."

Her boss was the last person she trusted, but she knew what he meant. Most men never saw past her curves to her personality. Or even the color of her eyes. But this felt… "It's still wrong."

"What's the big deal, Danica?" James sounded irritated, as if she'd told him the Web site needed to be patched again to work on Internet Explorer 6. "Meet them for coffee. Cupcakes. Conversation. You don't have to sleep with them unless you want to."

Dani's stomach roiled. "This is a—"

"Start with the guy who made you laugh," he interrupted.

Excitement shot through her. Okay, she liked the idea of meeting Bigbrother, especially with her boss giving her permission, but that wouldn't be fair. "I really don't think—"

"It's not your call." James read the e-mail on her screen. "Bigbrother, huh? I wonder what's big about him."

She cringed. The guy did not look like a player. Far from it. She was worried she might hurt him.

"Hit 'reply'," James ordered.

Dani didn't. She couldn't.

A part of her wanted to quit. Right now. But, with her student loans and family obligations, she couldn't afford to be without a decent paycheck. That was the one thing she had to say about her boss—he paid well.

James reached around and hit "reply". "Tell him you want to meet him for coffee."

"But I don't want to meet him for coffee. I have no idea who he is. I know absolutely nothing about him."

Nothing except he intrigued her. The way he'd approached her. His brief e-mail. His quick reply. His picture.

"If you don't ask him out," James said with a steely glint in his eyes, "I will."

Dani gulped. She knew he would follow through on the threat. "I'll do it myself."

James didn't move. A muscle flicked at his jaw.

"I can reply right now," she added.

Dani started typing an invite to coffee, aware and annoyed that James was peering over her shoulder.

"Make sure you tell him the meeting is your treat," he said. "That can make a difference to some guys."

Darn James anyway. Her exchanges with Bigbrother had been fun and flirty, but her boss was ruining it. "Do I get to expense it?"

James tossed a twenty on her desk. "No expense form needed."

Dani hit the "send" button, lobbing the ball back over the net to Bigbrother's side of the court. The next move was up to him. She was torn over how she wanted him to respond. She hoped he ignored her request or said no because she didn't want to mislead him, but a part—a large part—wanted him to agree to meet her.

Just then another e-mail from Blinddatebrides.com appeared in her in-box. Maybe she'd lucked out and the system had kicked her reply for some reason. And then she saw the sender's name. Gymguy. Oh, no. Not another one. She shook her head.

"Woo-hoo," James said. "Looks like you're Miss Popular. Want some help replying to Gymguy?"

Dani sighed. "I know what to do."

Unfortunately.

"Thanks, Danica," James said, backing out of the cubicle, much to her relief. "I won't forget all that you're doing for the site."

She stared at the twenty. Neither would she.

"How's it going?" Joelle entered Bryce's office carrying a pizza box with a paper bag sitting on top.

The scents of oregano and freshly baked crust made his stomach growl. He glanced at the clock. Eight o'clock? He'd lost track of time, but wasn't surprised with everything going on.

"Trying to stay a step ahead of the scammers isn't easy. They may have found a hole, but they couldn't crack the encrypted format." That unfortunately wouldn't stop them from trying to steal information again. Every time Bryce's engineers changed something, the hackers would modify their programs to try and get around the new security. It didn't help matters that they used stolen credit cards to register and pay for membership. If only he could run background checks on everyone who wanted to join, not just U.S. citizens. That would crack down on foreign scammers. "Talk about a cat and mouse game. It's never ending."

"Just remember to eat," Joelle said.

"The team—"

"I ordered enough food for everyone."

Always thinking. Always one step ahead. Sometimes Bryce thought Joelle could read his mind. "Thanks."

She opened the bag and pulled out a Styrofoam box and packets of Parmesan cheese and chili peppers. "Start with the salad, please."

He grabbed a slice of sausage and mushroom pizza from the box and bit into it. "You're sounding a lot like my mother."

"You think?" Joelle's mouth quirked. "Well, then, as soon

as you fix this problem, why don't you reward yourself by seeing if those matchmaking algorithms you developed can find you a few dates?"

An image of Sanfrandani with her red bandana around her head popped into his mind. Bryce nearly choked. He swallowed and wiped his mouth with the napkin. "You've been talking to my mother. Those words are straight out of her playbook."

Joelle's cheeks reddened. After six months of his mother's lectures about his dating more, he'd finally told her no more. She'd stopped. Now he knew why. She was trying to have Joelle take up the cause.

"You have a profile set up," Joelle said. "You should keep it public all the time, not just when you're investigating clients or trying to flush out scammers."

"I'll tell you what I told my mother," Bryce explained. "I spend all my time working on Blinddatebrides.com. It's a win-win situation. Others find love. I make a whole bunch of money. I can't handle a relationship of my own right now."

He thought about his e-mail exchange with Sanfrandani. That was the closest he'd come to flirting in…weeks. Or was it months?

"Can't or won't?" Joelle challenged.

"You know I can fire you."

She tilted her chin. "Yes, but you'd never be able to replace me."

True. One of the most successful online dating Web sites was a one-man show, but Bryce needed help. Joelle handled everything from finances to human resources. She didn't mind answering the phones, either. Her title of Business Manager was far too bland for all she did. Business Goddess would be a more apt description. He couldn't run Blinddatebrides.com without her. He knew it, and so did she. "Are you this hard on Connor?"

"Harder," she admitted. "But my husband knew what he was getting into when he married me. You, however, had no idea when you hired me."

"No regrets." Bryce winked. "At least none yet."

She smiled. "You have to admit, it would be excellent PR if you married someone you met at your own site. Just look at the interest in your sister's engagement."

"Stop. Now."

"Okay. I'll stop. Only because I know you have more important things to do right now, but tomorrow—"

"Out."

"I'm going." With a grin, Joelle walked out of his office.

As Bryce waited to hear from one of the engineers, he ate dinner. He'd forgotten everything that didn't involve the SQL injection, but now he couldn't stop thinking about one thing. One person really. Sanfrandani. Had she replied yet? He hoped so.

Checking his in-box, Bryce found a message from her. The corners of his mouth curved. The thrill of the catch, he told himself, and opened the e-mail.

To: "Bigbrother" <bigbrother@blinddatebrides.com>
From:"Sanfrandani" <sanfrandani@blinddatebrides.com>
Subject: RE: Colonel Brandon
Wrong on all counts except the uniform. Could go either way there. The Colonel was always there for Marianne. That's what makes him a true hero.
But I won't hold it against you if you meet me for coffee tomorrow morning. Eight o'clock. Crossroads on Delancey. My treat.
-sfd

So she was…assertive. Interesting. And she'd picked a great place to meet—a café that hired people who had hit rock bottom and were trying to turn their lives around. But he was wary.

Why would she make a date with him when she'd rejected everyone else?

It obviously wasn't his knowledge of Austen. He looked again at the screen. *Wrong on all counts.*

So…was Sanfrandani a spy? A scammer? Worse?

He pulled up her profile on the Web site and ran a compatibility match with his questionnaire. The program deemed them highly compatible, possible soul mates. That surprised him.

He stared at her picture. The lighting was a little better than on the print version he had, but not by much.

Bryce didn't like being caught off guard, but it had happened more than once today. Flushing out the scammers who probably used hacked computers to do their dirty work with the SQL injection was near impossible, but catching Sanfrandani might actually be…fun.

What did she want?

Only one way to find out.

Coffee tomorrow morning. My treat.

Bryce smiled. He was looking forward to it.

Remember, Dani. Proposals made after one cup of coffee are rare. Have fun!

Marissa's instant message delivered while Dani had slept brought a needed smile to her face. She'd been a bundle of nerves ever since Bigbrother accepted her invitation to coffee.

Stop thinking about that. Him.

Don't think of the meeting as a date. Consider it market research.

Grace's instant message echoed what James had said. Good advice Dani intended to follow. She wasn't going to let

Bigbrother's profile picture or information blind her to her purpose. Okay, so she'd really liked what he'd written about the importance of family. But she knew from experience most guys would say anything to get what they wanted. Bigbrother was probably misrepresenting himself at least a little.

She winced. And she was misrepresenting herself a lot.

Face it, getting to know Bigbrother wasn't possible under these circumstances. Thinking about him as anything other than market research would be a mistake. Downright wrong. He was not a potential date. He couldn't be.

And neither could she be one for him.

Dani liked what she'd seen about Bigbrother. He looked like a nice guy, the type who might be a little shy and easily hurt.

She would not be responsible for leading him on.

Time to scare him off.

She walked into her closet.

Fortunately, most guys never looked past the surface. All she had to do was keep the packaging relatively unattractive and her breasts covered, and he'd lose interest.

Her hand wavered over the fitted jeans and sharp jackets hanging on the rod and settled instead on an ex-boyfriend's pair of sweats and an oversized hoodie from her college days. She braided her blond hair into a single plait and tied a bandana around her head. She didn't put on any makeup, but stuck on a pair of sunglasses.

She squinted at the results in the full-length mirror hanging on the back of the closet door. Perfect.

Perfectly awful. She grimaced.

Dani took the bus to an area locally referred to as SoMa, south of Market, filled with loft warehouses, galleries and restaurants. As she walked toward South Beach and the café, a place known for giving second chances—something she desperately wanted herself—her breath hung on the air. Mornings in San Francisco were usually cold and foggy, no matter what the time of year.

As she stepped inside the café, warm air blasted her. The scent of freshly brewed coffee and pastries filled the loftlike open space and made her mouth water. A good thing. She planned on spending every cent of James's money this morning.

Hearing the din of the other customers, Dani glanced around. She'd stared at Bigbrother's picture enough last night she should be able to recognize him, but none of the people sitting on the couches and chairs looked familiar. Maybe she'd beat him here. Or maybe her darkened sunglasses kept her from seeing clearly. She moved toward an empty table.

"Sanfrandani?" a male voice asked.

Dani turned. A man, sitting at a table back against the wall near the bookstore portion of the café, was staring at her. She took a closer look, resisting the urge to push her sunglasses up above her forehead.

Thick dark lashes framed clear, warm eyes. Brown, maybe black, hair carelessly styled, as if he'd run his fingers through it, not a comb, fell past his collar in the back. His hair hadn't looked like this in his picture or maybe the cap had hid it. Either way, his hair changed his looks completely. But she wasn't complaining. In fact, Dani wouldn't mind running her fingers through his hair. "Big…brother?"

He nodded.

Heaven help her. The contrast between his dark hair and lighter complexion and eyes was, in a word, stunning. Talk about a picture not doing someone justice. His photo made him look cute, but didn't show his true appearance at all.

Was he hiding something, like her?

Dani was willing to take that chance.

As she walked toward him, he stood. Wowsa. He was tall, over six feet. Fit, trim, perfect. Men who looked like him only existed in magazines or the movies or her dreams. Yet she was having coffee with him. Her pulse quickened.

Pull yourself together.

Dani extended her arm. His large warm hand engulfed hers, his shake solid. She cleared her throat. "Nice to meet you."

He pulled a chair out for her. Good manners. "Thanks for suggesting this."

She wanted to thank his parents for having him and James for forcing her to ask Bigbrother out. Intelligent, handsome, polite. A blind date couldn't get much better than this. Or him.

Dani took the seat he offered. "You're welcome."

He sat across from her. Their gazes met.

Her heart bumped.

Oh, boy. She crossed her legs, tilted her head and gave him her best buy-me-a-drink smile.

He looked faintly startled.

Why…?

"I'm sorry I didn't recognize you." She leaned forward just a little.

"It's an old photo," he admitted. "Good thing I had no trouble recognizing you from your picture."

Dani frowned. "My…"

And then she realized. That picture. No wonder he looked taken aback.

Bigbrother was totally hot.

And she looked totally…not.

CHAPTER THREE

BRYCE watched Sanfrandani tug surreptitiously on the waistband of her baggy sweats and bit back a smile. Nice hips. But the clothes… She looked like a kid who'd dressed with her eyes closed or a coed slumming in her boyfriend's clothes.

Obviously she didn't care what kind of impression she made on him.

He could find her confidence attractive.

Or insulting.

"What will you have?" she asked, standing in line to order.

"Two shots Americano."

She pushed her sunglasses on top of her head to read the menu. "Breakfast?"

"No, thanks."

She turned her head. "Sure?"

He stared into her sparkling blue eyes and suddenly wasn't sure about anything. Where had those beauties come from? "I'm not hungry."

She stepped up to the counter to order. "A two shot Americano, a white mocha and one lemon-poppy seed waffle."

Bryce pulled out his wallet as the barista, a young man with pierced ears and a tattoo on his forearm, pulled the shots.

Sanfrandani handed the bright-eyed girl behind the counter a twenty. "My treat, remember."

Confident, he thought again. And it was attractive.

"You pay," he said. "I'll carry."

A beat passed. And another. "Fine with me."

As she put her change into her wallet, Bryce gave her the once-over. Okay, all was not lost. He could see raw material there, hidden under the bulky sweats. With those pretty baby blues and full lips most women would pay big bucks to have, Sanfrandani wasn't so bad.

She raised an eyebrow. "See something you like after all?"

Bryce broke into a reluctant grin. "I'll stick to coffee."

"Suit yourself."

He picked up their drinks from the counter, followed her past a leather couch to their table against the wall.

Sitting across from him, she took a sip of her white mocha and licked foam off her upper lip. "Just what I needed."

A strand of blond hair had fallen out of her braid and threatened to slip into her drink. Without thinking, he reached forward and tucked it behind her ear. Her hair was smooth, her cheek warm.

She narrowed her eyes at him.

Bryce sat back, feeling foolish. "Your hair…it was about to fall into your whipped cream."

"Oh." She flushed. "The curse of long hair, I guess."

"Is that why you wear the bandana?" he asked.

She touched the cloth, as if to remind herself she was still wearing it. The simple gesture reminded him of Caitlin, when she was little and wore a tiara every day.

"I thought you might be some kind of cowgirl or something."

"Ha-ha. Actually…" she leaned her elbows on the table, cradling her drink in both hands "…I used to work in a stable."

Bryce studied her oval nails with their pretty pink polish. She didn't work in a stable now. "Tell me about it."

"It's not that exciting." She smiled and took another sip from her mug. "My mother works on a farm in central

California. I mucked stables there and at a couple of ranches to earn money. I used bandanas to keep my hair out of the way. They also work well as sweat rags and, if you wet them, neck coolers when it's hot outside."

His family had horses—Caitlin wanted to start riding competitively again. He knew what the work involved and was impressed. "That's a hard way to earn money."

"Yes, but it was worth it. Not only did I get stronger cleaning stalls, but I got to exercise the horses when their owners couldn't." The words almost tumbled from her mouth with excitement. Her face became animated, but she seemed to catch herself and calm down. She raised her cup. "So now you know where my attachment to bandanas comes from."

"A worthy attachment, I'd say." His respect for her grew. He recalled her picture. The shadows. Her red face. Something clicked for him. "The photograph in your profile. Was it taken while you worked at one of the stables?"

She nodded. "I still help out at the farm when I visit my mom. One of my sisters took the picture with her cell phone as a joke."

Definitely a horse-lover. No one else would offer to help out with that job. But that didn't explain her using the unflattering picture.

"Why did you use that photo on your profile?" he asked.

She hesitated. "I wanted to make sure men were more interested in who I was as a person rather than my appearance."

"That makes sense." So maybe she was on the up-and-up. Caitlin had done the same with her profile picture. "Have you found any guys who passed the test?"

"You're here."

In spite of his suspicions, he liked her. "I am."

A café employee placed a plate and syrup in front of her. "One lemon-poppy waffle."

Bryce liked that she wasn't one of those women who lived off salads, rice cakes, nuts and seeds in order to stay a size zero. He also liked her self-confidence. "I'm glad I'm here."

She spread butter on the waffle. "The bandana didn't scare you off."

"It would take more than a bandana to scare me," he admitted. "Do you wear it every day?"

"No." She poured syrup on her waffle. "But bandanas come in real handy on those days I'm rushing out the door."

"Were you rushing this morning?"

She stared down her nose at him. "What do you think?"

That no woman would go to such lengths to look less attractive than she really was. "You were either in a rush or prefer comfort over…"

"Style," she offered.

He smiled. "You said it, not me."

The tension seemed to evaporate from around her mouth. "I do like to be comfortable, but I may have taken being comfy to the extreme this morning. Next time I'll take a little more time getting ready."

"Next time, huh?" He watched her take a bite of the waffle. A drop of syrup hung on the corner of her lips. Damn, she had a sexy mouth. "So do you do this a lot?"

She wiped the syrup off with a napkin. "Go out for coffee and have breakfast?"

"Online dating."

"Oh, no." She stared at her plate, then raised her gaze to his. "You're my… This is my first time."

Bryce looked for a sign she might be lying. But she was making eye contact. Her voice pitch hadn't changed. She wasn't fidgeting or blinking. Then again, she might just be a good actress.

He picked up his coffee. "What do you think?"

"Well, so far so good," she said. "The mocha is delicious,

the food tasty. Ask me again when we're finished, and I'll tell you how the company was."

Bryce might not trust her, but she was bright and had a sense of humor. He was enjoying this. Her. He sure hoped Sanfrandani wasn't guilty of anything. "I will."

"What about you?" she asked. "Do you rush getting ready in the morning or take your time?"

He sipped his drink. Strong and hot, the way he liked his coffee. "I'm a guy. Once we're out of high school, it's pretty much shower and go."

"Mm." She looked him over, taking her time but keeping her opinion to herself. "Well, at least no one could accuse you of being metro."

"Thank you." The amusement in her eyes brought a smile to his face. "I think."

"So I'm a newbie at this online dating thing. What about you?" she asked. "Have you gone on a lot of dates with people you met through Blinddatebrides.com?"

"Not a lot, much to the chagrin of my mother and sister."

"Why is that?" she asked.

"Both of them think it's time I settle down."

Dani raised her mug. "Do you think it's time to settle down?"

"No." Bryce found her easy to talk to. Strange, considering his reasons for wanting to meet her. "But my opinion doesn't matter much where my mother is concerned. She has been lecturing me about being over thirty and single. She wants grandchildren to spoil. My sister, who is a member of the site, has jumped on my mother's bandwagon and sends me links to the profiles of women she thinks I should contact."

"Your younger sister, right?"

"Yeah. How did you know?"

"Your user name is Bigbrother."

He nodded. "Caitlin picked the name for me."

"That's so sweet."

"She's a sweet girl. Woman," he corrected. "Sometimes I forget she's all grown up."

"And how does she feel about that?"

"She thinks I'm overprotective. Overbearing and a bully, too."

Sanfrandani's smile lit up her face. "The two of you are close."

It wasn't a question. "Yeah, but Caitlin drove me crazy when we were kids. Following me everywhere. I wanted to trade her in for a brother, but I couldn't help but watch out for her back then, too."

"That sounds so familiar. I watched out for my three little sisters, even though there were days I wanted to kill them. But I knew if I did that it would destroy my mother so I controlled myself."

He grinned. "I'm sure three younger sisters were much worse than one."

"Especially trying to get ready for school with only one bathroom for the four of us."

"Catfights?"

"Every day." She laughed. "How about with your sister?"

"She's one of my best friends, even though I still watch out for her."

"Lucky girl."

"She might disagree about that." Though Caitlin's luck had changed for the better. Contentment settled in the center of Bryce's chest. "She recently got engaged to a man she met on Blinddatebrides.com."

"That's exciting news."

"Very." He smiled, thinking about Caitlin, all bubbly and glowing, showing off her diamond engagement ring. She'd thanked him for creating the Web site where she'd met her fiancé. That moment had made all his work, the sleepless nights and constant fires needing dousing, worth it. "My sister and her fiancé prove the matchmaking algorithm works, since that's how they found each other."

Sanfrandani set her fork on the plate. "You believe the algorithm actually works?"

He understood the doubt in her voice. Turning matters of the heart over to a machine wasn't easy. "I do. Relying on the program is the easiest and smartest way to find a compatible date."

"It's difficult for me to accept a computer could do a better job picking a date for me than I could."

"Is that why you haven't gone out with anyone before?" he asked.

"It didn't seem right."

Her response set off warning bells in Bryce's head. "Right?"

"The right time," she clarified. "But the compatibility program did work for a friend of mine who lives in London. They are married and expecting a baby."

"I'll have to tell my sister. She wants everyone to be as happy as she is."

"I have two friends like that. The one with the baby on the way and another who is engaged. I met both on the Web site," Sanfrandani said. "They're always pushing me to go out more. They mean well, but the…"

"Pressure."

"Exactly." She drank her coffee, seeming completely at ease. "Luckily, my mother doesn't care if I get married or not."

"She's not on the grandma track, then."

"Not at all. The only thing she wants is for me and my three sisters to pursue our passions and follow our dreams, whatever they may be."

Bryce wondered what her dreams entailed. "She sounds like a great mom."

"My mom's the best. My hero." Sanfrandani's eyes softened, as did the tone of her voice. "She raised us on her own. We didn't always have a place to sleep at night, but we always had food to eat and we knew we were loved. No matter what was going on, there was always more than enough love."

Her words squeezed Bryce's heart. No place to sleep sounded like she'd been homeless at times. No one should have to go through that, especially an innocent child. Maybe her background explained the way she acted and her ambivalence about dressing nice for their date.

He thought about his silver spoon upbringing—the overabundance of toys and clothes, the mansion and vacation homes, the revolving door of stepparents and the trust fund he'd never touched. His parents loved him, but they were so busy with their own lives and marriages, they'd often left him and Caitlin in the care of nannies. He couldn't say more than enough love existed at his house. Houses. "Sounds like you still had everything you needed in spite of the tough times."

"I didn't think so then, but growing up like that made me stronger, more determined."

"To do what?"

"Succeed. Make it on my own. Show the world I'm more than what they think I am." She raised her chin, then looked down. "Sorry, that probably sounds arrogant."

"No. Not at all." Even though the two of them came from different worlds, Bryce understood because he felt the same way. That was why he'd taken a job as a Web developer. He'd wanted to make it on his own terms. Not live off the rewards of his great-grandfather's real estate foresight over a hundred years ago. "It's important to make it on your own, especially if people said you couldn't."

She reached across the table and touched his hand. "You get it."

He nodded, trying not to stare at her hand. Dani's gesture was friendly, not sexual, but he enjoyed the feel of her soft skin against his. She pulled her hand back. He missed her warmth.

"I want to buy my mom a house. Nothing fancy, maybe a white picket fence. Just someplace that belongs to her. We never really had that. A home of our own."

"A worthy goal."

She nodded. "Something to work toward, that's for sure."

Sanfrandani seemed nice. She was close to her family, funny and intelligent. A guy could do a lot worse. But he couldn't forget why he was here.

I'm a spy.

Bryce straightened. He needed to figure out what she'd meant by that. Spying didn't always mean espionage. She might have joined the site to spy on a crush, a boyfriend or an ex.

"Why haven't you gone on more dates?" He wanted some answers. "Did you try using the compatibility matching program? The questionnaire seems thorough enough."

"Oh, it was thorough all right." Her mouth quirked. "That stupid thing took forever to fill out, with all its nitpicky and redundant questions."

He'd heard the criticism before, but the questionnaire was far from stupid. "The time you spend pays out in the end."

"Let's be real." She leaned toward him. "How do you know someone else is going to fill it out as carefully as you did? They might choose an answer they think someone might want to hear."

"That's built into the algorithm and the reason for so many questions, even redundant ones. To get to the bottom of what a person needs in a relationship and a mate. Not what they think they need."

"You seem to know a lot about it."

"I work with computers," he admitted, waiting for questions to follow. So many people worked with computers in the Bay Area, yet some women wanted to know more—where do you work, what's your title, do you get stock options?—in order to gauge future earning potential.

"Poor you." She poked her fork into her waffle and swallowed a bite.

Was Sanfrandani really disinterested in him or playing hard to get? Maybe she was just hungry. That waffle looked good.

"I like computers," he said. "And with anything Internet based, there's an element of trust involved."

"Not everyone plays fair."

Bryce wasn't exactly playing fair with her. But then again, she might be guilty of the same. He was here protecting his company and his customers. He doubted her reasons would be considered honorable if she'd come under false pretenses. "Did you have a bad experience?"

"You're my first experience."

At least she was keeping her story straight. "You don't seem the shy type."

Her gaze met his. Unwavering and strong. "I'm not."

"You just haven't wanted to date anyone."

She nodded once.

Why pay the monthly membership fee then? Something with her story didn't add up. "So why did you join the site in the first place?"

"I…" She opened her mouth. Closed it. An attractive pink tinged her cheeks. "Curiosity?"

He didn't buy her answer. "Don't you want to meet somebody?"

She leaned back in her chair, eyeing him warily. "For a first date, you're awfully interested in my sex life."

Bryce grinned ruefully. "You caught me."

"Sorry."

"No, I like it."

"Like what?" Two lines formed over her nose. "That I'm abrasive?"

"Not abrasive. Confident. Willing to speak your mind and challenge me without getting all flustered." Bryce might be keeping his identity secret, but he could be honest about what he liked about her. "I find you very…"

Sanfrandani raised her chin and boldly met his gaze. "What?"

"Interesting."

She drew her brows together. "Even looking like this?"

"Yes."

"Be still my heart. That's almost as good as saying I have a great personality."

She was a tough nut to crack. Then again, he always loved a challenge. "You do have a great personality."

"Oh, boy."

"What did I say?"

"Great personality." Her eyes danced with mischief. "That's what guys say right before they say let's be friends."

"Nothing wrong with starting out as friends and seeing where things go."

She drank her mocha, feigning disinterest. Unless her indifference was real.

He found her charming in a curious sort of way. "So let's see, we've talked about dating and our families. What's next?"

"The weather?"

Bryce laughed. "Tell me about your job. Your profile says you're in sales."

"Yes, I am." She pushed up the sleeve of her sweatshirt and checked her watch. "Oh. Would you look at the time? This has been great, but I really need to be going."

"So soon?" Without answering his question. He shouldn't have been surprised.

"Yes." But the regret flickering in her eyes appeared genuine. "I'm sorry."

"Me, too." He didn't know what to make of her odd contradictions. "I don't even know your real name. I'm guessing it might be Dani, based on your user name."

She bit her lip. "Does it matter?"

Yes. No. "Not really, but I'm Bryce."

He didn't say his last name. He couldn't. One visit to Google, and she'd know exactly who he was.

Her face clouded with uneasiness. "I'm Dani."

"Thanks, Dani." He might like her, but her evasiveness had raised his suspicions. Bryce knew better than to trust her, but he wasn't ready to say goodbye just yet. He wanted to learn more about her. Who was he kidding? He wanted to see her again. "Would you like to have dinner with me? Tomorrow night?"

"I'd like that," Dani said. "But tomorrow doesn't work for me."

"Got a date?" he teased.

She wet her lips. "Actually, I do."

Blinddatebrides.com is running sixteen chat rooms, fifty-three private IM conferences, and 9289 members are online. Chat with your dating prospects now!
Private IM conference #42 (3 participants)…
Engishcrumpet: So he's attractive?
Sanfrandani: Yes. His profile picture doesn't do him justice. You can't tell how green his eyes are. Or how nice his smile is. Or see the slight bump on his nose that makes him look a little rugged.
Kangagirl: Bryce sounds yummy.
Sanfrandani: I wouldn't mind a taste.

Who was she kidding? She wouldn't mind gobbling him all up. But he appealed to her on a variety of levels, both physical as well as emotional. She'd felt a connection with him. One she wanted to explore further. If only she could…

Kangagirl: Go for it!
Engishcrumpet: Unless you already have.

Sanfrandani: I haven't. We only had coffee. I hardly know him.
Kangagirl: Sounds like you should get to know him better.
Englishcrumpet: When do you see him again?
Sanfrandani: He said he'd be in touch. But after I told him I had another date, I doubt I'll hear back from him.

And that bothered Dani. More than she wanted to admit. He'd had a funny look on his face when she'd told him about her upcoming date. Maybe she shouldn't have told him the truth, but his dinner invitation had taken her by surprise. The entire meeting had, really. She kept replaying their conversation in her mind. Not that it mattered with her job and all.

Sanfrandani: It's no big deal. Remember, this is market research.

At least that was what Dani kept reminding herself as she had checked her in-box for the umpteenth time. Not that she expected Bryce to contact her after saying goodbye to her this morning, but on the off chance he had…

Kangagirl: You could always ask him out.
Englishcrumpet: That's a brilliant idea, Marissa.
Sanfrandani: I can't. Not unless I wanted to lie to him or tell him the truth about why I joined the site and risk losing my job. And now, with my boss wanting me to go out with any guy who contacts me, it's just too complicated.
Kangagirl: Maybe, but look at Rick and me. That was complicated. You have to remember, if it's meant to be, it'll work out.
Englishcrumpet: That's right. I never expected to fall in

love again, let alone get married and have another baby.
You never know how things will work out, Dani.
Kangagirl: So don't give up hope.

Dani wanted to believe her friends, yet she had her doubts.
And the guilt kept building. Her life had felt like a lie for half
a year now. The job, the spying, now the dating.

She thought about the man she was meeting tomorrow
night for dinner. Gymguy seemed pleasant enough, but his
e-mail had been more of a sales pitch about himself. He didn't
mention anything about her. Nothing like…

She sighed.

Bryce.

Bryce didn't know what to do.

He tapped his pencil against his desk. The rapid tattoo on
the wood matched the throbbing at his temples. He had work
issues to deal with, but only one thing was on his mind—Dani.

Actually, I do.

She had another date. A date, he'd discovered when he
probed deeper, with another guy from Blinddatebrides.com.

He shouldn't care. He didn't care. He should be glad she
was proving herself to be an ordinary client.

Except there was nothing ordinary about Dani.

Bryce couldn't stop thinking about her.

Why would she suddenly decide to go on dates after
months of turning men down?

Not knowing the answer bugged him. He needed to find
out what was going on. Not for his sake, but for the Web site.

And he knew how to do that.

Bryce was the founder and CEO of Blinddatebrides.com.
The terms of use customers agreed to when they joined the Web
site gave him permission to read whatever he wanted. He had
administrative access to everything, from chat logs to messages

sent between users on the site. Viewing a user's account wasn't unheard of for debugging or monitoring metrics for site usage.

Or tracking down abusers.

Or possible abusers, such as Dani.

Checking her user account made perfect sense, Bryce rationalized. Reading private e-mails for personal reasons was unethical, but as part of an ongoing investigation…

That was all he was doing. Investigating.

It wasn't as if he'd asked Grant to pull all her chat logs. He'd let the filtering system deal with those.

She'd made the date before she'd met him. Bryce had figured out that much from what she would tell him. Now he just wanted—make that needed—to know a little more.

He logged into the admin system.

Time to do a little poking around in her e-mails to see exactly what was going on with Sanfrandani.

CHAPTER FOUR

"SEE anything you like?" asked Dani's date.

She looked over her menu at Gymguy aka Gregg.

He smiled back smugly.

Most women would like *him*, Dani supposed. His blond corporate hairstyle, tanned skin and bleached teeth reminded her of a weekend news anchor. Nice-looking, but easily forgettable once you changed the channel. Though she wasn't sure where his user name came from because he looked more on the thin and weak side than fit and strong from working out at a gym.

She glanced at her menu. "There's quite a selection."

He'd chosen a popular restaurant in Cow Hollow for dinner, although she'd suggested they meet for coffee instead. He'd even ordered an expensive wine, a bottle of Cabernet, over her objections. Maybe he wanted to impress her. Maybe he had control issues.

Maybe he was trying to get her drunk.

"The salmon with the cranberry chutney looks interesting." Her budget didn't allow splurging on expensive meals, but James had given her enough cash to cover the entire tab, including tip, so she could order whatever she wanted. One good thing about her boss—he wasn't a cheapskate. If he developed some ethics, morals and a heart, she might even like working for him. "Though the Macadamia nut-crusted halibut sounds delicious."

"I noticed that one myself." Gregg lowered his menu. "And just so there's no tug of war over the bill later, tonight is on me."

Maybe Dani had misjudged his ordering the wine and everything else. He was probably just being polite.

And she wasn't.

She couldn't blame Gregg for her not wanting to be here. It wasn't his fault she'd accepted the date under false pretenses and was feeling guilty.

How could she not when the ambience of the restaurant he'd selected oozed romance, with white linen tablecloths, candles and flowers and soft classical music playing? A tad much for a blind date, perhaps, but his choice showed he'd put some thought into where to take her.

Too bad she would rather be out with Bryce. Remembering his bright, warm eyes brought a sigh to Dani's lips. She pressed them together.

No sighing or swooning allowed. Especially over a man who hadn't e-mailed her since their coffee date. At least Gregg wanted to be with her.

"Thanks." She placed her menu on the table. "But I was planning on treating you to dinner."

Gregg's beaming smile showed two rows of perfectly white, straight teeth, but he had nothing on Bryce's easy grin. "Good thing I beat you to it."

Not really.

Dani wanted to pay. She had to pay. Or the mounting guilt might do her in.

Once upon a time, she had a great job, a new car and a one-bedroom apartment with a peek of the San Francisco Bay out her living room window and a reserved parking spot.

How had she gotten…here? Dating strangers to get information her boss wanted?

She reached past her wineglass to her water and drank.

Dani didn't want to be dating. Not Bryce or Gregg or any man. Relationships were like flesh-eating viruses that destroyed dreams and gnawed away at life plans. And when they ended you were left with nothing. She was better off without one.

"So…" Gregg raised his wineglass "…you're a lot better-looking than your profile picture."

"I hoped guys might read my profile instead of going by a photo."

"That's exactly what I did." His gaze dropped from her face to her breasts. "Smart move on your part, that's for sure."

Darn it. Dani had worn loose-fitting clothes—a skirt, blouse and sweater—to hide her curves, but he'd somehow seen enough to capture his attention. She should have worn the baggy sweats instead.

Gregg stared at her chest, focusing on her breasts as if he had see-through clothing vision. "Though you'd probably get more takers if you mentioned you had such nice melons in your profile."

Dani choked. Coughed. Wiped her mouth with her napkin.

O-kay. So much for him being polite.

But she knew how to deal with men like Gregg. Knew all too well.

With her napkin back on her lap, she straightened. "Stick to the Macadamia nuts, Gregg. You can't handle the melons."

His mouth gaped. He closed it.

"I sure would like to if you'll give me the chance." Gregg leaned over the table toward her, and she noticed how his eyes looked beady like a sewer rat's. "My place is walking distance from here. Why don't we skip dinner, head over there and go straight to dessert?"

She bit back a sigh. So typical.

And to think she'd been feeling guilty for using him to get

information when he wanted to use her for sex. At least Bryce had been a gentleman when he was out with her.

Gregg raised an eyebrow and puckered his lips slightly. "You know you want to go back to my apartment with me."

Jerk. She bypassed the water and sipped from her wineglass. No sense wasting an expensive bottle.

Or the opportunity. Although lowering herself to his level left a bitter taste in her mouth.

Consider it market research, she told herself. Or morbid curiosity. "Do you do this a lot?"

"Depends on your definition of a lot, but I'm sure I could squeeze you in with my busy schedule." He sipped his wine. "We will be so good together."

She should have gone out with Bryce instead of this wannabe who gave players a bad name. "In bed, you mean?"

"Where else?" Gregg took another drink. "Women might say they are looking for a long-term commitment on their profiles, but secretly they're looking for an adventure. All they need is the right man to lead the way."

"You've figured this out on your own?"

"All by myself." That smug smile of his returned. "Are you ready for an adventure, Dani?"

Gregg reached across the table, past the flickering votive candle, past the bud vase containing a Gerbera daisy, past her hand, to stroke the juncture of her breasts with his fingertip.

Disgust sent her flying back. She nearly fell. As she jerked to her feet, her chair crashed to the floor.

The restaurant was dead quiet. Customers stared. The waitstaff, too.

She didn't care. "What are you doing?"

"Giving you what you want," he said.

"What I want?" Dani's blood pressure soared. His words took her straight back to high school, where the boys had elbowed each other and propositioned her when she'd walked by. She'd ignored their taunts even though it hurt because she'd wanted to be part of the popular crowd. She was older, wiser now. No need to try and fit in with people she'd never liked in the first place. "What I want is for you to crawl back into the hole you slithered out of."

"You're a feisty one, aren't you?" He raised his eyebrows up and down, as if performing a bizarre mating call. "Women who play hard to get are usually good in bed."

"You'll never know." She picked up her glass of water and tossed the contents on his lap. "That should cool you off."

Gregg jumped up, grabbed a napkin and patted himself. "Why, you little—"

"Is there a problem?"

The male voice came from behind. She turned.

Bryce.

Surprise skittered through Dani, along with a flash of joy. Her mouth went dry. She'd been thinking about Bryce all evening and wanting to see him. Now he was here, looking all gorgeous in a brown suit, and concerned about her, as if she'd summoned him from those same thoughts.

Dani gloried in the moment, a wide grin on her face.

And then she remembered.

She wasn't alone. Her cheeks burned.

Dani glanced at a red-faced Gregg, frantically drying the front of his pants and muttering to himself.

"Are you okay?" Bryce asked.

The tenderness of his voice alleviated some of her humiliation. She stared up at him. So handsome. So strong.

He had a looking-for-a-fight gleam in his eyes. His wanting to protect pleased her. Feminine power surged. And then she remembered the brawl scene from *Bridget Jones's Diary*.

Oh, no. All she needed was two yuppies who didn't know how to fight duking it out over her in a nice restaurant to top off the night. No way could she allow that to happen.

Sure, she appreciated Bryce wanting to come to her assistance, except this wasn't a dark alley or the backseat of some guy's car. She had this situation under control. "I'm fine."

"Well, I'm not." Gregg frowned. The water stain on his pants made him look as if he'd wet himself. "I should have known a chick with such a nice rack would be nothing but a tease."

A vein throbbed at Bryce's jaw. "Why don't we step outside?"

Okay, she might not need rescuing and she sure didn't want anyone fighting over her, but the way he'd challenged Gregg was totally romantic. Totally Austen hero-worthy, too.

Dani bit back a sigh.

Gregg must have agreed because he seemed to shrink before her eyes. He took two steps backward. "You want to fight me?"

"No," Bryce said. "I want her to have more room when she kicks your scrawny wet ass."

Her heart melted.

Gregg's startled gaze darted between Bryce and her. A second later, he bolted from the restaurant.

She laughed. "I never realized I was that terrifying."

"You have no idea."

Outside the restaurant, streetlamps illuminated the crowded sidewalk. A breeze carried the salty scent of the bay. Dani stood next to Bryce.

A foghorn sounded. The cyclical blares reminded her she was no longer the dirt-poor girl she'd once been, the housekeeper's daughter with boobs too big and hips too round. The girl no boy respected, but every boy wanted.

The memory sent a shiver down her spine. Dani crossed her arms over her.

Bryce shrugged off his jacket and placed it around her shoulders. "This will keep you warm."

He was doing a good enough job heating her up himself.

Standing there with shadows cast on his face, he looked dangerous and sexy, but acted more like a knight than a rake.

Smiling, she buttoned his coat. Not only because of the cold, but because she wanted to feel closer to him. This might be her only chance. She wasn't going to miss out. "Thanks."

"You're welcome."

"I can't believe you were at the restaurant." Dani breathed in his soap and water scent on the jacket. Funny, but for some reason she thought he would wear cologne. "What a coincidence."

Bryce stared at a yellow cab driving by. "Yeah, I ordered takeout, but decided to eat here instead of going home alone."

Hope fluttered. He wasn't on a date. She shouldn't care. She didn't care. Okay, maybe a little.

"But you had it covered," Bryce continued. "You didn't need my help with that guy."

"It was nice to have backup."

He bowed. "Big brother at your service."

She gave a quick curtsy. "We made a good team."

"We did." Bryce glanced back at the restaurant. "But what went on in there should have never happened."

She waited for the familiar litany to begin. That she was the one to blame when guys got carried away. That it was her fault. That she had been asking for it.

"The guy was a total jerk. You deserve to be treated so much better than that. He should be kicked off Blinddatebrides.com for his actions."

Dani felt a familiar melting of her heart, the same way she'd felt when he'd stuck up for her a few minutes ago. His anger seemed so sincere, so real. And though he had bad things, valid criticisms, to say about Gregg, Bryce wasn't using her experience to talk himself up. She respected that.

Him.

She wanted to hug Bryce. To thank him. To hold him.

He was different, a gentleman.

Someone who looked beyond the surface to see the person underneath.

Someone who wasn't afraid to step forward.

Someone who cared.

About her.

Her pulse raced as if she'd just completed a competition round in the ring. "I'm going to file a complaint with the site."

"Do," he encouraged. "His account can be suspended."

"Unfortunately, he'll go to another dating site and do the same thing with other women," she said. "What we've experienced is the dark side of online dating. Some people, and not just men, only want sex and are willing to do or say anything to get it."

"Blinddatebrides.com is for those people wanting a serious relationship." Bryce sounded frustrated, annoyed.

"Players and liars are everywhere. Even on Blinddate-brides.com."

"It shouldn't be like that." Bryce sounded so idealistic. "Those people should sign up for one of the casual sex sites like Hookamate.com instead."

Dani winced. His words were like a slap to the face. Hearing Bryce say the truth embarrassed her. Worse, she agreed with him. But nothing could change about that until she found a new job. She only wondered whether he would want to see her again if he knew the truth about where she worked and what she did.

"Not everyone reads the terms of use," Dani said. "Or cares."

"They should care." His eyes practically caressed her, and she sucked in a breath. "I care."

Uh-oh. Her mouth went dry. Her heart beat faster.

Bryce was someone she could maybe care about. Maybe have something real with, but not this way.

She swallowed around the lump of emotion lodged in her throat.

Not under these circumstances.

She had to get away from him. Now. Before she messed up having any chance with him in the future. "I should be going home so you can get back to your dinner."

"I finished eating."

His gaze locked with hers. Hypnotic.

A connection seemed to draw him to her.

They stood there, silent, staring at each other as if entranced. The noise of the city disappeared, consumed by the night. It was only her and Bryce.

And that felt…right.

No, not right.

Dani fought hard to break his spell. She didn't know enough about him. And he didn't know the truth about her, which made it nowhere close to being right.

She looked away.

"It didn't look as if you ate dinner in there," Bryce said. "Would you like to get something to eat?"

Yes. No. Life wasn't fair.

Why had she met him now?

She found Bryce to be intelligent, nice and totally hot. He was exactly the kind of man she wanted to meet in, say, five years, when she had her career established and was ready to make a commitment. She wasn't ready for that at the moment, with her life in such disarray.

"Thanks, but I need to go home."

Far, far away from the sexy and attractive Bryce.

"I'll walk you to your car."

She'd had to sell her car after she'd got laid off. "I took the bus."

He swept his hand through his hair. "Would you like a ride home?"

* * *

What a stupid move.

Some idiot had accosted Dani, and Bryce had asked her to get into a car with him, someone she barely knew. He wanted to kick himself. That was what he got for acting impulsively.

But he hadn't been able to help himself.

Dani brought out his impatience. Bryce didn't like that.

Nor did he like how she had been constantly on his mind since having coffee and how he couldn't stop staring at her now.

But damn, she cleaned up well, even if her clothes still looked a couple of sizes too big. If he weren't careful, he was going to blow this.

The investigation, he meant.

"I can call you a cab," Bryce offered.

"I take the bus all the time."

"It's late," he countered. "My treat."

"I'm a big girl."

"I know you can handle situations after seeing you in action. But you shouldn't have to deal with anything else tonight."

The determined set of her jaw reminded him of his sister when she wasn't going to take no for an answer. Bryce knew when to surrender.

"If your heart is set on riding the bus home, I'll walk you to the stop."

That was the least Bryce could do. He felt guilty for using information from her e-mails. She'd called his being at the restaurant a coincidence. Good thing she didn't know that no chance or luck had been involved in his witnessing her date-gone-bad.

Frustration gnawed at him. Bryce hated how guys like Gregg could slip through the system without being weeded out. He felt protective over Dani, the way he did with all his customers, and right now a part of him wanted to hold her. Though he normally didn't hug clients.

A hug would probably go over as well as his offer of a ride home had so he kept his hands to himself.

"I'm sure the last thing you want to do is get into the car with a total stranger. Or a player or a liar." Bryce remembered what she'd said. "Not that I'm strange or any of those other things. But you wouldn't know that."

"I wouldn't," she admitted. "It's hard to separate the good guys from the psychos these days."

He fell in step with her. "Unless one happens to be carrying around an axe or a chainsaw."

"That would give them away." She walked toward the street corner. "Still, I can't imagine you wielding a knife with a crazed look in your eyes."

"Once you get to know me, you'll realize I'm harmless."

Dani stopped at the corner and hit the crosswalk button. Traffic zipped across the intersection. "When I get to know you?"

Bryce nodded. "That's the only way I won't be a stranger to you. You never know when you might need another ride home."

"You've got this all figured out."

"I'm working on it."

"What did you have in mind?" she asked.

She was tempted. He could hear it in her voice. Good.

"Dinner and conversation," he said.

The light changed. The walk sign illuminated. She stepped off the curb. "As long as nothing else happening will be assumed."

"I never assume anything." Bryce didn't want to let her go without getting a commitment from her. He wanted to know when he would see her again. "How does Friday sound?"

"This Friday?" she asked.

He nodded. Waited. Reminded himself that patience was a virtue.

"Okay," she said after what seemed like hours but was only minutes. Probably seconds. "That sounds good."

They reached the other side of the street. "Great."

A bus pulled to the curb, the brakes squealing as it rolled to a stop. The door opened.

"Are you sure you don't want to take a taxi?" he asked.

"Thanks, but I'm comfortable taking the bus." She started removing his coat. "Your jacket—"

"Keep it," he said. "You don't want to get cold. Give it back to me on Friday."

She stepped onto the bus and glanced back at him. "Thanks for everything."

Bryce hated to see her go. "You never know who you'll run into on Muni. E-mail me when you get home, if you get the chance."

"Will do." She smiled down at him. "Bye."

A disturbing feeling settled in the bottom of his stomach. "Goodnight, Dani."

An hour later, Bryce stared at his laptop monitor. No e-mail from Dani yet. He'd even checked to see if she'd logged into the Web site. She hadn't.

His fingers tensed over the keyboard.

Maybe he should call her. She'd listed her phone number when she'd registered for the site. And then he remembered. Blinddatebrides.com had her number. Not him.

He glanced at the clock.

What was taking Dani so long to get home?

Worry seemed premature. Still…

Bryce should have called a cab for her, but he hadn't been thinking straight. Not since he'd met Dani for coffee…

Had it only been yesterday?

He felt as if he'd known her longer.

Still, his interest in her made zero sense given what he knew about her and what he didn't.

Yes, Dani was pretty, but she wasn't the most beautiful woman he'd ever met. Tonight she'd worn her hair in a ponytail, but had bypassed the makeup again. He liked the fresh-faced natural look. And that subtle perfume of hers—vanilla with a hint of something else, something exotic—smelled so good. He wouldn't mind waking up to that scent on his pillow.

But cyberspace was full of players and liars. Dani had said so herself. And thieves and spies, he reminded himself. Was she one of them?

Bryce didn't think so.

He recalled her look of surprise when she'd first seen him at the restaurant. Her smile had told him she'd been relieved and happy. Not even an award-winning actress could fake the kind of sincerity she'd shown tonight.

Dani was probably a timid dater. Okay, she had been able to take care of Gymguy on her own, but he couldn't imagine her as a scammer or spy, in spite of what she'd said. Taken out of context, almost anything could sound suspicious. And that made his motives for following her seem suspect.

Still, he would remain cautious.

He couldn't forget his responsibility in all this—make sure no one caused trouble on the Web site. Blinddatebrides.com was his priority. No getting sidetracked allowed.

The phone rang. The only person he wanted to talk to didn't have his number. Bryce noticed the name on the caller I.D. Caitlin. She wouldn't call at this hour without a reason.

Bryce snatched up the receiver. "Hey, sis. What's going on?"

"Mother doesn't want Father to bring his newest girlfriend to the engagement party." Caitlin sniffled as if she'd been crying. "And she wants me to be the one to tell him. If I do that, he might not come. He might not win any father of the year awards, but I want him there, Bryce."

The crack in his sister's voice squeezed his heart. The ripples from their parents' divorce hadn't lessened over the years. He still remembered the years of yelling, screaming and breaking things that had led up to their split. "Don't worry. By the time the party rolls around, the girlfriend will probably be his new wife."

"That's what I told Mother," Caitlin said. "She got even more upset. You'd think, after twenty-some years apart, with almost a dozen marriages between them, they'd be able to get over it."

Bryce stepped around a stack of newspapers he needed to take out to the recycling bin and sat on the couch. "I'll talk to her."

"Thanks." Gratitude filled her voice. "I knew I could count on you."

"That's what big brothers are for."

"Are you okay?" Caitlin asked. "You sound…I don't know…different."

He glanced at his laptop, sitting on the coffee table. "I'm waiting for something."

"You've never been good at waiting. Remember on Christmas Eve when you woke up in the middle of the night and wanted to open presents?"

"I was ten."

"And now you're thirty-two. Not too much has changed."

"Thanks, sis."

"Anytime," Caitlin said. "So what are you waiting for at this hour?"

"An e-mail."

"I was hoping it was a woman," she admitted.

He wasn't about to go there. "Sorry."

"Don't forget, you need to find a date to the engagement party or you'll be fighting off all the single women there. And a few of the married ones, too."

"I can handle them—" he thought about Dani "—though I may have a lead on a possible date."

"Who?"

"A woman."

"Give me a name. Something." Caitlin sighed, but he would guess she was smiling now. "Come on, Bryce. You saying 'date' without making it sound like a four-letter word is huge."

"There isn't anything to tell right now." Inviting Dani to the party probably wasn't a good idea given the circumstances. "But if the situation changes I'll let you know."

"Promise?" Caitlin sounded more like a little girl than a bride-to-be.

Bryce knew his sister would call their mother about his potential "date." Maybe that would take some pressure off Caitlin and whether their father and his girlfriend could attend the party. "I promise I'll let you know if I ask someone, but don't get your hopes up."

"Are you kidding? Hope is already overflowing."

"It's not that big a deal."

"Oh, yes, it is," Caitlin countered. "The fact you're actually considering getting away from your computer long enough to meet and go out with a woman is almost miraculous."

Bryce frowned. "You make me sound like a total geek."

"If the pocket protector fits…"

His computer dinged. He glanced at his in-box and saw an e-mail from Dani. Finally. "I gotta go."

"That e-mail you're waiting for is from her, isn't it?"

He clicked on the message. "Goodnight, sis."

"It is." Caitlin laughed. "Goodnight, big brother. Keep me posted on what's going on. And don't forget. You promised."

The line disconnected. Bryce turned off the phone. The e-mail appeared on his screen. He pulled his computer onto his lap and read.

To: "Bigbrother" <bigbrother@blinddatebrides.com>
From: "Sanfrandani" <sanfrandani@blinddatebrides.com>

Subject: Made it
I'm in my apartment though there were moments I doubted whether I'd make it back or not. A group of mimes boarded at Divisadero and decided I needed to be entertained. Not a smart decision on their part. I would rather face a psychopath wielding an axe than a clown. -d

To: "Sanfrandani" <sanfrandani@blinddatebrides.com>
From: "Bigbrother" <bigbrother@blinddatebrides.com>
Subject: RE: Made it
Glad to hear you survived the trip in spite of the mischievous mimes. Sorry I wasn't there to see it.
Note to self: leave face paint at home on Friday night.

To: "Bigbrother" <bigbrother@blinddatebrides.com>
From: "Sanfrandani" <sanfrandani@blinddatebrides.com>
Subject: RE: RE: Made it
You didn't miss much except for seeing a grown mime cry. Good call on the face paint or you'd be spending the evening alone and in tears.

To: "Sanfrandani" <sanfrandani@blinddatebrides.com>
From: "Bigbrother" <bigbrother@blinddatebrides.com>
Subject: RE: RE: RE: Made it
Wouldn't want that.
Meet me under the rotunda of the Palace of Fine Arts at six-thirty on Friday. I'll bring dinner and we can have a picnic.

To: "Bigbrother" <bigbrother@blinddatebrides.com>
From: "Sanfrandani" <sanfrandani@blinddatebrides.com>
Subject: RE: RE: RE: RE: Made it
What can I bring?

To: "Sanfrandani" <sanfrandani@blinddatebrides.com>
From: "Bigbrother" <bigbrother@blinddatebrides.com>
Subject: RE: RE: RE: RE: RE: Made it
I won't suggest dessert.

To: "Bigbrother" <bigbrother@blinddatebrides.com>
From: "Sanfrandani" <sanfrandani@blinddatebrides.com
Subject: RE: RE: RE: RE: RE: RE: Made it
I have no problem providing dessert as long as it's not assumed to be me.
P.S. Looking forward to Friday.

Bryce smiled. So was he.

CHAPTER FIVE

NOT a date, Dani reminded herself as she adjusted the shoulder strap of her bag and walked along a path at the Palace of Fine Arts. That was all she had to remember tonight and she'd be fine.

Marissa had e-mailed, calling the not-a-date with Bryce strictly another information-gathering meeting. Grace had agreed in an e-mail of her own, suggesting Dani keep the conversation tonight focused on Blinddatebrides.com and his online dating experiences.

Good advice from both her friends, except for one thing…

Dani wanted this to be a real date.

Not that she wanted a boyfriend per se, but she wanted to see Bryce, to spend time with him. And, to be honest, she couldn't care less if Blinddatebrides.com even came up in the conversation.

On her right, two swans swam across the lake. Elegant and graceful, a pair mated for life.

She watched them, feeling a little envious. Not that she wanted a husband in the near future, if ever, but the idea of something lasting a lifetime was beginning to appeal to her heart and soul. Nothing in her life had ever lasted long.

Was it so horrible to want forever? Or to want to go on a date with Bryce?

He was a really nice guy. She enjoyed his company. No sense pretending she didn't because of what might happen.

One date wouldn't stop her from finding a new job or moving forward with her life. One date wouldn't make her dependent on someone. One date wouldn't change anything.

Dani walked to the exact center of the Romanesque rotunda and looked up at the top of the dome.

The vastness of the structure made her feel so small, so inconsequential. The way she'd felt ever since being laid off from her dream job. She hated feeling this way, floundering and frustrated and living a lie. That wasn't the kind of person she'd strived to be all these years. Dani wanted to make something of herself, make a difference, but she felt as if she were standing on a playground merry-go-round being spun around by a group of mean kids with no way to get off.

She wanted off. Out.

Dani was tired of things being out of her control, of struggling to check the next item off her to-do list. She needed to lighten up and have fun. Tonight with Bryce would be a good start.

So might something else. She remembered a piece of trivia she'd read about this place on a San Francisco tourist Web site.

Dani clapped her hands together once. The sound echoed perfectly through the dome.

"I used to do that when I was a kid."

She jumped, startled by Bryce's voice. He looked handsome in a green polo shirt and khaki pants. With his casually styled hair and steady grin, he reminded her more of a fashion model than a computer geek. Except for the paper bag he held.

"You don't have to be a kid to do it," she challenged.

His gaze, intense and unwavering, met hers. "Step aside." She did.

Bryce handed her the bag. The scent of rosemary wafted out. He positioned himself at the center, looked up at the dome's ceiling and clapped. The sharp sound echoed through the rotunda. "Satisfied?"

"Very."

"Me, too."

The way he studied her made her think she'd gotten a smudge of dirt on her face. "What?"

"You wore your hair down."

She tucked her hair behind her ears. "I couldn't find my bandana."

"Your hair's longer than I thought it would be."

Dani couldn't tell if her hair length was a good thing. Not that his opinion mattered. Much. "I keep thinking I should cut it and go for one of those trendy new styles."

"Your hair looks great the way it is," he said. "You shouldn't change it unless you really want to."

He sounded as if he'd had this conversation before. And then she remembered. Caitlin. "Spoken like a true big brother."

Bryce shrugged, looking a little embarrassed and a lot more like his profile picture—that shy, easy to hurt guy Dani had imagined.

"It's sound advice," she added. "Thanks."

"Just don't ask me to braid your hair." He shivered. "I still have nightmares over that one. Caitlin, too."

Dani laughed. "Don't worry, I can braid my hair myself."

He made an exaggerated swipe at his brow. "Good, I was worried for a minute."

She was a little worried herself.

Bryce was too cute, the kind of guy you wanted to take home. Intelligent, nice, attractive, funny. Her friends would like him. Her mother and sisters, too.

Not a date, she reminded herself.

"Nice outfit," he said.

"Thanks." She'd chosen a nice pair of brown pants, a blue blouse and a cropped lightweight jacket. Not super-fitted clothes, but these showed a few curves. She'd considered wearing her baggy sweats or another of the loose-fitting outfits hanging in the back of her closet and forgoing makeup again, but something inside of her had revolted at the thought of playing the role of ugly duckling again. She wanted Bryce to see her for who she was.

Inside and out.

His gaze, slow and appreciative, didn't stop at her breasts, but ran the length of her and back up again. "Your shirt brings out the blue of your eyes."

She drew back. "You know what color my eyes are?"

"You sound surprised."

"I am. Most guys…"

"Most guys," he prompted.

She might as well be honest. "Most guys never see beyond my bra cup size."

He shrugged. "Their loss."

Dani was used to men liking her body, not her. She was always seen as a trophy, a piece of arm candy. She bit her lip, not sure what to make of Bryce.

"Close your eyes," he ordered.

She did.

"What color are my eyes?"

"Green."

"Correct," he said as she opened her eyes. "Guess you're not just interested in my cup size, either. So we're even."

Dani wasn't sure about that. She felt off balance, as if her not-so-neat little world had been spun in yet another direction by him. She didn't like the feeling.

"Ready to eat?" he asked.

"Please. I worked through lunch and am starving," she said. "Whatever you brought smells delicious."

"It does smell good, but I can't take credit for the food. I picked up dinner at a little place on Chestnut."

Bryce led her from the rotunda to a path leading around the lake. "I put down a blanket to claim a spot. With nice weather like this, I didn't want to take any chances."

"It is a beautiful day." She tilted her head toward the sky so the sun's rays could kiss her cheeks. "Though I'm not sure there are any bad picnic spots here."

"True," he admitted. "That's why I like this place. Even with the tourists snapping pictures like crazy, it's still peaceful."

"I know." His words echoed how she felt and made her feel warm and fuzzy inside. "I've always thought of this place as somewhere to escape from the hectic pulse of life in the city. And you never know what you'll see. One time they were filming a television show."

He stopped at a grassy area where a blue blanket was spread out. "Here we are."

Dani stared across the water. The two swans she'd seen earlier were still floating on the lake, but this time they had the "palace" as the backdrop behind them. "A veritable feast for the eyes with the lake, plants and architecture."

"It's kind of like stepping back to ancient times with the Corinthian Columns."

"And the Roman-inspired rotunda. All that's missing are gladiators and deities." She looked at Bryce. "Thanks for choosing such a lovely location for a picnic."

"You're welcome," he said. "This spot actually has a lot of sentimental value to me."

Warning bells sounded in her head. Dani bit back a sigh. She had a feeling what was going to come next—a story about Bryce's ex-girlfriend who he used to bring here before she'd done him wrong. Dani didn't have much experience with that but, to be honest, she'd rather listen to him talk about an ex than deal with the I-want-you-for-your-body dates who usually asked her out.

She plopped onto the blanket, ready to hear his woeful tale. "Sentimental how?"

"I had a nanny who claimed bluebird days demanded picnics. She would have our cook make us a picnic, sometimes two, if she planned on keeping us outside the entire time." Bryce patted the blanket. "This was one of her favorite picnic spots."

The affection in his voice brought a smile to Dani's face. "Sounds like you had fun with her."

"We did." He pulled white boxes from the sack. "She was one Caitlin and I were sad to lose."

"You had a lot of nannies?" Dani asked.

Nodding, he pulled out plates and utensils. "My parents paid them well, but the nannies earned every penny of their salary dealing with my mother and father, not us."

Dani toyed with a blade of grass. "Leaving your kids with someone for an extended period has to be hard on parents."

"I wouldn't do it."

His adamant tone surprised her, but didn't seem to affect him in the slightest. He placed asparagus spears with salad on one side of the plate and a scoop of couscous on the other. A chicken breast covered with mushrooms in a light sauce went in the center.

"Do you plan on being a stay-at-home dad or having your wife give up her career?" she asked, thinking about her mother and all she'd given up for her marriage and children.

"I haven't given much thought to marriage or having a family. It's not something I'm interested in right now." Bryce handed her a plate. "But I do know when I was a kid and got hurt or was upset, I wanted my mother or father. Not my nanny. I'd rather not have to go that route with children of my own."

"Some people have no choice." Dani stared at her plate, overflowing with food, and remembered the times when she didn't have as much. "When I was in sixth grade, we moved to Los Angeles. My sisters and I would go to day care—they called it after-care, when school got out until about six o'clock. We were there in the morning before school started, too. It was hard on all of us, but I think most especially my mom. She didn't want to have to put us there for so long each day, but she had no choice because of her job."

"Sounds like you all did what you had to do."

She nodded, scooping up a forkful of couscous. "That was the first time any of us started and finished a grade at the same school."

"Did you live in Los Angeles a long time?"

"Just a year." Dani shook her head as she swallowed. "The company downsized and my mom lost her job so we moved on."

"I've lived in San Francisco my entire life. Well, except for college. My mother still lives in the same house where I grew up."

"Wow. I can only imagine how wonderful that must be." She inhaled deeply, caught up in her dream of home owner-ship. "I would love to put down roots like that and never have to move again."

"Aren't you a little young for wanting that?"

Oops. She didn't want him to get the wrong idea. "I should have added someday. That's not in the plan right now. But still, you are so lucky."

His gaze locked on hers. "I feel…fortunate."

Dani was used to male attention, but Bryce wasn't focused on her chest. If anything, his watchful eyes seemed to pierce straight into her soul, to see not only her dreams, but her heart and her secrets.

She shifted position on the blanket, angling away from him slightly. "Dinner is delicious. Excellent choice of food."

"Thanks, but I just realized I haven't been a good host," he said. "I forgot to offer you a drink. I have white wine, a Chardonnay or sparkling mineral water, lime-flavored."

Her favorites. "Did you check my profile page before going shopping?"

"Of course." He grinned. "If you'd been vegan, this dinner menu would have been a flop. So what's your poison tonight?"

Water was the smart choice, but she didn't care. "Wine, please."

He uncorked the bottle. "Did you read my profile?"

Over and over again, the same way she had obsessively been checking her e-mail since he'd first contacted her, but she didn't want to tell Bryce that. "I may have skimmed your profile a couple of times. I noticed baseball seemed to be a common theme to yours."

"And Jane Austen yours." He poured the wine into glasses. "I thought about wearing a flowing white shirt."

"How long did you consider that? A second?"

"Try a nanosecond." He handed her a glass. "Cheers."

"Cheers." Dani tapped her glass against his. The chime hung in the air. She took a sip. "Great. But I thought you preferred red wine."

"Red doesn't go as well with chicken," he explained. "You must have done a little more than skim my profile if you remember what kind of wine I liked."

She ate another piece of chicken. "Yum."

"Trying to change the subject?"

"Yes." She wiped her mouth with a napkin. "Do you mind?"

A devilish gleam flashed in his eyes. "Not this time."

Did that mean he wanted to see her again?

Excitement shot through her at the possibility. She forced herself to calm down. One date. That was all this could be even if her heart might disagree. "Looking at our profiles, hearing how we grew up, we're very different."

He shrugged. "Everybody is different. But the compatibility program says we're a match."

It was her turn to shrug.

"That's right." Bryce raised his glass to his lips. "You don't believe in the matching program."

She remembered the "match" page where you could check to see who the computer thought you were most compatible with. She had visited there once to capture screen shots, analyze the information and present a report to James. "I didn't realize that's how you found me."

She cringed. Her words made it sound as if she'd been lost and needed a man—Bryce—to find her.

He didn't seem to notice. "There are lots of ways to find people on the Web site."

No kidding. Just look at her.

Dani swirled her glass. She felt like the wine spinning around inside. Everything happening in her life was out of her control. Waiting for James to tell her she could stop spying and going out on dates. Hoping another company would want to hire her so she could start afresh. Wishing things could be different right this moment.

She wanted to take action, change things now, but had no idea how to start.

Bryce refilled their glasses.

If only she could tell him the truth about working for Hookamate.com and what her job required her to do.

But she couldn't.

She couldn't risk losing her job.

Dani's family counted on her financial support. Her youngest sister's fall tuition would be due soon as well as her mother's health insurance premium. Nothing had changed since lack of money six months ago had forced Dani to take the position at Hookamate.com.

But the least she could give Bryce was her gratitude.

"Tonight has been wonderful," Dani said. "Thanks for going to so much trouble."

"It wasn't any trouble."

A comfortable silence descended as they finished their dinner. A breeze rustled the leaves of nearby trees. An older couple strolled hand in hand along the path. They glanced her way and smiled.

Dani wondered if they thought she and Bryce were a romantic couple or if they could tell this was the first dinner they'd shared together. Probably the only dinner they'd ever share. She sipped her wine.

As Bryce put things back into the bag, three white limousines pulled up to the curb. The doors opened and laughter filled the air. Members of a wedding party piled out of the cars. Eight, nine… They kept coming. Bridesmaids dressed in lavender full-length gowns and groomsmen in black tuxedos with tails. Fourteen in total. Not counting the bride and groom.

Dani stared in disbelief. "That's a huge wedding party."

"Either they come from a big family or have money to burn."

"Or both."

The bride's gown was a billowy confection of tulle and silk. Three of the bridesmaids held up the dress to keep the hem from touching the floor. Dani thought about Marissa and Grace.

"They should get some nice photos with this lighting," Dani said. The sun shone high in the sky, even though it had to be past eight by now.

She removed her cell phone from her bag and snapped a picture of the wedding party as they posed for the photographer.

"You know," Bryce said, "a guy could get the wrong idea of his date snapping pictures of wedding parties."

"Nothing nefarious. I'm not a wedding junkie or a bride wannabe," she admitted. "The photo is for my two online friends Grace and Marissa. We met in the newcomers chat on Blinddatebrides.com and have stayed in touch ever since."

"They are the ones you mentioned before."

She was pleased he remembered. "Yes. I've been trying to talk them into coming to visit me, but they are so busy with their own lives—and now loves—I don't think it's going to happen anytime soon. Maybe this picture will whet their appetite for a personal tour of San Francisco."

"My sister plans to have wedding pictures taken here."

Dani wasn't surprised. This place was popular with bridal parties for a reason. "Wedding photos here would be lovely."

"Agree, but the logistics are turning into a nightmare and causing arguments between my mother and sister, even though the wedding isn't until next year." He sipped his wine. "Caitlin wants to have photos taken before the ceremony so the wedding party can go to the reception without delay, but my mother says it's bad luck for a groom to see the bride before the wedding so they must do the pictures afterward."

Dani knew nothing about wedding planning except for what she'd picked up from Marissa and Grace. "Couldn't they do pictures the day before?"

"My mother doesn't think Mark should see Caitlin in her wedding gown. Period."

"Google it."

"Excuse me?" Bryce asked.

"Find out in what percentage of divorces did the groom see the bride before the wedding ceremony. That will either prove your sister's point or your mother's and they won't have to argue anymore."

"That's…brilliant."

"More like common sense, but thanks. It's not often I'm called brilliant."

"Then you're hanging with the wrong crowd."

Being with Bryce was so easy. Conversation flowed as easily as the wine. Being quiet didn't feel awkward or uncomfortable. He felt like an old friend, not a stranger she'd met only a few days ago online.

As he packed away the food, she handed him her plate.

"Relax," he said. "I've got it."

Dani couldn't remember the last time she'd felt so…pampered. She watched a row of turtles, a mother and her babies, swim across the lake. Bryce definitely knew what he was doing. But he didn't act like a player. Still, she couldn't help but wonder if he took every woman he went out with here. "Do you take all your dates on picnics?"

Not exactly subtle, but she wanted to know the answer.

"I don't," he admitted. "The last one was…maybe four years ago. But a woman who wears a bandana seemed like the type who might enjoy a picnic."

He sounded genuine. Dani wanted to believe him. Just because she wasn't being truthful didn't mean he was dishonest. "I do like picnics, though I haven't been on a real one like this since college. The other times were just brown bagging it and sitting on the grass."

"Then it was time for both of us to do this the right way."

Hair fell over Bryce's eyes as he finished cleaning up. Dani longed to push the strands back into place, to touch his face, to kiss him.

Maybe it was time. And not only for a picnic.

She smiled. "Are you ready for dessert?"

"These are sinfully good."

"Not sinful." Dani's smile reached her eyes, raising Bryce's temperature a degree or two. "Criminal, maybe."

No way could a woman who looked as hot as Dani did tonight and cooked delicious candies be a spy. Bryce picked up another one of her homemade bonbons. "I need more evidence before I can make a final verdict."

Lying on the blanket and resting on his elbows, he bit through the bittersweet chocolate covering to the softer Tiramisu inside. The flavors exploded in his mouth.

Sweet, moist, rich.

Like the cook herself? Bryce wouldn't mind finding out.

She watched him. "What's the verdict?"

"The calories are criminal, but worth it."

Dani beamed.

Bryce liked how a simple comment or compliment pleased her so much. She wasn't like other women he'd dated, who wanted to eat at the newest restaurants and go to the hippest clubs. Dani seemed content to be with him, no matter where that might be—a park, sidewalk, café. And when he was with her everything cluttering his brain seemed to magically disappear.

He wasn't in the market for a girlfriend, but he could get used to this. Her.

As she picked up a bonbon, her hair shifted forward. With a flip of her head, she sent the hair back behind her shoulder. The movement was subtle yet sexy, especially with the slight bounce of her breasts.

He reached for his wineglass.

"I haven't made bonbons in a while," Dani said. "I forgot how good they are."

She raised the white chocolate-covered candy to her mouth. Her pink lips parted, then closed around the bonbon.

Heat rushed through Bryce's veins. He jerked his gaze away from her and focused on the lake. He'd rather stare at her full lips or sensuous curves, but he didn't want her to compare him to the other men she'd dated. Guys like that jerk from the other night or the ones who didn't remember her eyes were a spectacular shade of blue.

"My compliments to the chef."

She bowed her head.

He picked up another. "Bet you have to know how to boil water to make these."

"That skill might come in handy, but it's not necessary," she explained. "They are easy to make unless you mind getting dirty. By the time you're finished, your fingers will be covered in chocolate sauce."

Bryce grinned. "I don't mind dirty, especially if chocolate is involved."

"If you're interested in learning how to make them, I'll show you."

"Sure." Dani and chocolate together. That was a no-brainer combination. "But I'll warn you now, I'm not much of a cook. I grill but that's the extent of my cooking talent. It's kind of a family joke."

"So you weren't kidding about boiling water?"

"I can do a little more that that, but I avoid recipes requiring oil and frying."

"Were flames involved?" Dani asked.

"Fire, smoke, a call to 9-1-1," he admitted.

Her eyes widened. "What happened?"

He gave a half-shrug, still embarrassed after all these years. "I tried to make French fries one day when the cook was sick. Unfortunately, I made two critical errors. I took the telephone to my mother, who was in another room, while frying. I also left the bag of potatoes sitting on the counter right next to the gas stove top."

"Uh-oh."

"The fire investigator wasn't sure which caught fire first, the oil or the plastic. By the time I returned to the kitchen, both were fully engaged in flames and the room covered in thick smoke. My mother and sister ran in while I was trying to put out the fire. I kept trying to remember what I'd learned about fires. One phrase kept running through my mind so I yelled it, 'Stop, drop and roll.' My mother dragged us outside and called 9-1-1. I wanted to go back in and use the fire extinguisher, but she wouldn't let me. She said kitchens could be replaced. Children couldn't. So I stayed outside, watching the flames grow and the smoke billow out."

"What happened to the house?" Dani asked.

"The kitchen had to be gutted and redone. The rest of the

house had some smoke damage, but was okay." He smiled. "As soon as the damage was repaired, my mother had our cook fill the freezer with bags of frozen French fries. Sometimes, my mother still brings me a bag when she comes over."

"That's cute."

"Try embarrassing."

"That, too." She smiled. "But now that I know about your cooking abilities, do you mind if we make the bonbons at your place? Just in case there's another fire. I don't have renter's insurance at my apartment."

Dani winked.

"Very funny. And smart." Bryce laughed. "I don't mind at all."

He'd be willing to give a soufflé or a crème brûlée a try if it meant spending more time with Dani. He hadn't enjoyed being with a woman this much in years. Yes, he dated, but only casually. He didn't have time for anything more. Besides, finding a woman intriguing enough to put his work second probably wasn't going to happen.

"So where do you live?" she asked.

"Not too far away."

Bryce saw the expectant look in her eyes, but he preferred keeping his personal life private and didn't open up to just anyone. Except…he realized he hadn't been as guarded with Dani for some reason. Still, he wasn't ready to tell her his house in one of the more "exclusive" neighborhoods in San Francisco had been a gift. Each Delaney received a house when they graduated college. A family tradition.

He'd thought about donating the house to charity, but practicality had overcome his objections. So he'd taken the house and rented it, donating the profits to a local charity, until he'd tired of apartment living this spring and decided to move in himself. "I used to live in Cow Hollow, but recently moved to Presidio Heights."

If the neighborhood surprised her, Dani didn't show it, but

she glanced at the row of elegant, pristine houses on the opposite side of the street. Mentally comparing the Marina to Presidio Heights, he wondered.

"That's a lovely neighborhood," she said. "There's a great consignment shop on Sacramento and I love that old theater, too. Not that I get to too many movies these days."

"What about you? Where do you live?"

"Inner Sunset," she said. "Not as trendy as around here, but there are some great places to eat and it's easy to get where I need to go taking public transportation."

"Except when you run into a band of menacing mimes."

Her smile lit up her face. "Except then."

She had a pretty smile. Pretty face. Pretty everything.

"Before I forget." She reached into her large bag and pulled out his jacket, neatly rolled. "Thanks for letting me borrow your coat the other night and saving me from a cold walk home from the bus stop."

"Anytime." Bryce glanced at the sun, sinking toward the horizon. Soon it would be dark and the temperature cooler. Almost time to say goodbye. Or maybe not.

"It's not that late. How does seeing a movie tonight sound?" he asked. "I can use my BlackBerry to see what's playing."

Her brows drew together, making it appear as if she were considering the offer. Good. That was better than a straight-out no.

"Okay." She placed the remaining candies into a yellow insulated lunch box. "We can sneak what's left of the bonbons into the theater and finish them off during the movie."

"Bringing outside food in is usually against theater rules."

"Do you always follow the rules?" she asked.

"I don't suppose you do," he countered.

"Not always."

He appreciated honesty, but her answer only brought the suspicions he'd pushed to the back of his mind front and center. Instead of trying to flush out the truth, he'd spent the evening flirting and having fun.

What was going on?

Bryce never lost sight of where he was going, what he was supposed to be doing. He had never allowed his personal life to interfere with work.

Until now.

The line between investigating her and dating her was blurring to the point of being unrecognizable. He'd never met a woman who made him want to forget everything except her.

Bryce had no idea if Dani was being honest with him or not. Yet he hadn't cared. Being around her made him feel good. He liked feeling that way. Still, he couldn't forget he didn't have time for a girlfriend. He didn't want to lead Dani on. Though she might be the one leading him on.

Face it. Something out of the ordinary was going on. Here she was, dressed nicely and showing off her real looks like tonight was a real date. Not one where she'd dressed down, acting suspicious, like on their first meeting. Why the difference? Maybe it was time to say goodbye.

"If you're tired or would rather not go…" he offered.

"I want to go, but on one condition."

A condition would give him an out. A way to get some much-needed distance from her. He interacted daily with women at work, but not with this kind of relaxed interaction and flirting going on.

The switch in her from the other day bugged him. He didn't get it. Was the change because of what had happened with Gymguy and she now knew she could trust Bryce? Or the elusive something else?

"What's the condition?" Bryce asked.

"I pay for the movie."

That wasn't what he'd expected to hear. He stretched out his legs in front of him.

Having her pay for breakfast the other day had been an anomaly. Women, especially those who recognized the Delaney name, assumed he would pick up the tab and never offered to pay. Of course, Dani didn't know his last name. "I'm the one who asked you out."

"So?" She stared down her nose at him. "You picked up dinner. I get the movie. What's the big deal?"

"Not a big deal." He wasn't old-fashioned or chauvinistic, but he had more money than he knew what to do with. Based on what she'd said so far, her taking the bus and shopping at a consignment shop, Bryce guessed she didn't have a lot of money. He didn't want her spending what little she had on him. Especially given the circumstances. Like it or not, he had to get to the bottom of what she was doing on his Web site. "But what if I want popcorn? And a soda?"

"No problem." Amusement danced in her eyes. "Feel free to order a box of candy, too."

After her bonbons? He better say no.

"Are you always so—?"

"Difficult?" she offered.

"Easy."

Her eyebrows shot up. "Excuse me?"

"Not easy as in sex. But in dating." The way her eyes narrowed told Bryce he was digging his own grave here. "Easy as in making things more equal."

She tilted her chin. "Why should one person have to foot the bill every time because past generations did it that way? Having things, especially finances, so lopsided doesn't bode well if a couple ever wants to have an equal partnership in the future."

"That's smart thinking."

"I wish I could take credit for it, but I found it on the Web site."

"Web site?" he asked.

"Blinddatebrides.com. The site has good advice on how to have a successful relationship."

Bryce's team put up new content all the time, but he'd been so busy putting out fires and thinking about Dani this week he hadn't read any of the new additions to the site. "Sounds like you've been studying up on the subject."

"Not really, since I'm not in the market for a serious relationship."

Ouch. He wasn't looking for any kind of commitment, either, but the way she dismissed one with him so easily stung. Dani might not know who he was, but several women considered him a catch.

"My friend Marissa e-mailed me the link a couple of days ago."

His suspicions shot up like a radio antenna.

Had Dani mentioned him to her online friends? Maybe they'd provided that link to help her plot how to snag a guy. That might explain why she was on the site and had started dating after so many months. And wanted to continue their date at the movies.

"Did the article say what to do if a man wouldn't let you pay?" he asked.

"Drop him like a hot potato because a man like that probably has control issues," she teased.

He didn't consider himself a control freak. "Or an unlimited supply of money," Bryce offered.

"Even the richest man in the world probably would like to be treated to a meal or movie sometime." She stared up at him, her eyes full of warmth and anticipation. "So will you let me pay for the movie?"

The hopeful tone shot straight to his heart and doused some of his suspicions. Okay, maybe she wasn't on a husband hunt. Dani might be self-reliant, tough and evasive, but at this moment she wore her emotions for the world to see. He liked seeing this side of her. "I'd be honored."

She placed the yellow insulated lunch box into her bag. "The theater will never know they are here."

But Bryce knew.

And that made him wonder…

What were the other rules that Dani didn't mind breaking?

CHAPTER SIX

Blinddatebrides.com is running sixteen chat rooms, sixty-three private IM conferences, and 5134 members are online. Chat with your dating prospects now!
Private IM conference #59 (3 participants)…
Englishcrumpet: What happened next?
Kangagirl: Don't leave us in suspense.

DANI sat on her bed, placed her glass on the nightstand and caught up on the messages she'd missed.

Her friends cracked her up. They had been waiting for her to log on when she got home from her date and tell them all the details. She could imagine the silly grin on Marissa's face, too.

Not that Dani minded. She'd been as curious about their dating lives. She remembered the first time Marissa wrote about her temporary boss Rick, even though she'd been dating men she'd met through Blinddatebrides.com at the time. And Dani would never forget Grace's panic before her first date with Noah that her nineteen-year-old daughter Daisy had set up.

Funny how the three of them had grown closer since then, even though they'd never met in person, but Dani really wished they could. She couldn't afford to go anywhere. So far neither Marissa, with her upcoming wedding, or Grace, with her pregnancy, had time to fly to San Francisco. Maybe someday.

Sanfrandani: Sorry, I was getting a glass of water.

Kangagirl: I thought you lost your connection.

Sanfrandani: Nope, thirsty. So, the movie turned out to be one of these epic battle guy flicks. No plot. Lots of special effects and death.

Englishcrumpet: Forget the bloody movie. Tell us about you and Bryce.

Sanfrandani: LOL! I am!

Sanfrandani: The movie was so bad all we could do, other than leave, was make fun of it as we watched. Bryce has the best sense of humor. We couldn't stop laughing. People must have thought we were drunk or something.

Kangagirl: Were you drunk?

Sanfrandani: No, we drank wine with dinner, but we were just having fun at the theater.

Englishcrumpet: Tell us what happened next.

Kangagirl: And don't leave anything out.

Dani imagined her two friends, oceans away, with their gazes glued to their monitors, waiting for her to finish telling them about the date. She knew what they wanted to hear—details describing a romantic evening for two, complete with tender gazes and passionate kisses. Too bad nothing like that had happened.

Sanfrandani: The rest of the evening was pretty uneventful. He drove me home, walked me to the door and said goodnight.

Englishcrumpet: Did he kiss you?

Sanfrandani: No.

Kangagirl: Did you kiss him?

Sanfrandani: No.

As she stared at the "no" on her screen, regret and disappointment gnawed at her. She knew better than to have expectations for a not-a-real-date, but still… Dani wasn't used to a guy not staring at her body or trying to steal a kiss. Especially when she wanted him to kiss her.

Sanfrandani: There was the almost kiss during the movie, but that's it.

Kangagirl: You didn't mention an almost kiss. What happened there?

Sanfrandani: Oh, sorry. It's almost one in the morning here. Past my bedtime.

Englishcrumpet: We can wait to hear the rest if you're tired.

Sanfrandani: I'm not sure I could sleep right now.

Kangagirl: Good, because I'd rather not wait!

Sanfrandani: Well, we were sharing a bag of popcorn. Bryce leaned over to whisper something. We both reached into the bag at the same time, and our hands touched. Really our fingers. They sort of intertwined. I looked at him. His face was so close to mine. He was staring at me.

Kangagirl: Sounds romantic.

Englishcrumpet: Very.

Sanfrandani: It was the perfect moment for a kiss. Even the music soundtrack was right for it. My heart was pounding. I wanted to kiss him, but then I turned my face away.

Englishcrumpet: Why?

Sanfrandani: I didn't feel right, kissing him without him knowing the truth about me.

Kangagirl: This is serious.

Englishcrumpet: No kidding. You must really like him or you wouldn't have worried about what he would think if he found out the truth.

Kangagirl: Did you make plans to get together again?

Sanfrandani: We didn't, but…

Englishcrumpet: You like him.

Sanfrandani: More than I thought I would. But we only just met so I'm not sure why I feel this way. I mean he's gorgeous and all that, but still it's a bit disconcerting.

Kangagirl: Been there, done that.

Englishcrumpet: Welcome to the club!

Sanfrandani: I said LIKE not LOVE.

Kangagirl: We know.

Sanfrandani: I just wish I could be honest with him.

Kangagirl: If that's what you want to do, then tell him the truth.

Englishcrumpet: He's going to find out at some point if you keep seeing him.

But Dani didn't know if she should keep seeing him. Being honest with Bryce could jeopardize her job. She couldn't afford to be without a paycheck or she would have quit. She'd already wasted over six months of her life at Hookamate.com.

Kangagirl: If you're not sure what to do, then wait. You'll know when the time is right.

Dani hoped so.

But, after hearing what Bryce had to say about where she worked, she wasn't sure he'd understand anything she had to say. And that realization tied her insides up into a knotted jumble.

Englishcrumpet: Think about what you might want to do, Dani. After all, what do you really have to lose?

My job. My heart.

Dani wasn't sure which she wanted to keep safer. Both

were at stake and that scared her. Maybe it would be better if she never saw Bryce again.

She thought about his green eyes and his beautiful smile that warmed her heart.

Maybe not.

On Saturday morning, Bryce crawled out of bed. A sleepless night left him longing for extra shut-eye, but he couldn't fall back to sleep. Caitlin wanted to meet him for brunch in an hour, but he wasn't that hungry.

Not exactly true.

He wanted something. Someone. Dani.

Why hadn't he kissed her last night?

He'd had plenty of opportunity, but he'd been trying to be a gentleman. To make up for her experience with other men. Bryce had wanted her to feel safe and comfortable with him, but he needed to remember that a gentleman still kissed his date goodnight.

Bryce walked to the French doors leading to a balcony and looked down at his yard.

Below, a hummingbird hovered near a blooming bougain-villea. The rapid wing motion and the way the bird flitted from one flower to the next, feeding off nectar, reminded him of Dani. Even though she'd sat with him during the picnic and at the movie, she never seemed to slow down or relax or simply be in the moment.

Was that her personality or nervousness or perhaps her age? She was only twenty-six. Six years younger than him.

He wanted the chance to find out which.

The hummingbird flew off in search of another flower. Bryce wasn't about to let Dani get away so easily. He went downstairs to his computer and typed an e-mail.

To: "Sanfrandani" <sanfrandani@blinddatebrides.com>
From: "Bigbrother" <bigbrother@blinddatebrides.com>
Subject: Today?
Had a great time last night. Any chance you are free for lunch today?

To: "Bigbrother" <bigbrother@blinddatebrides.com>
From: "Sanfrandani" <sanfrandani@blinddatebrides.com>
Subject: RE: Today?
Not unless it's a late lunch. I'm working today.

To: "Sanfrandani" <sanfrandani@blinddatebrides.com>
From: "Bigbrother" <bigbrother@blinddatebrides.com>
Subject: RE: RE: Today?
A late lunch won't work for me. I have a family thing. Tomorrow I need to check out a horse my sister is thinking of purchasing over in Danville. Want to come?

To: "Bigbrother" <bigbrother@blinddatebrides.com>
From: "Sanfrandani" <sanfrandani@blinddatebrides.com>
Subject: Yes!
I love horses. I need to finish up a project at work tomorrow, but can be done by one if that works for you.

To: "Sanfrandani" <sanfrandani@blinddatebrides.com>
From: "Bigbrother" <bigbrother@blinddatebrides.com>
Subject: RE: Yes!
One o'clock works fine. Where do you want me to pick you up?

To: "Bigbrother" <bigbrother@blinddatebrides.com>
From: "Sanfrandani" <sanfrandani@blinddatebrides.com>
Subject: RE: RE: Yes!
Pick me up at the corner of Howard and Beale. Near

Starbucks. If you're running late just give me a call 555-2328. See you tomorrow :-)

Yes! A date and a phone number.

Bryce reread Dani's replies, noting the exclamation marks and the smiley face on her last e-mail. He grinned.

Many women liked flowers, others preferred chocolate, some favored sparkly jewelry.

But who would have known the way to Dani's heart was with a…horse?

"How was it?"

"The best ride of my life." Dani sat atop a gorgeous fourteen-hand bay gelding. Giddy with excitement, she smiled down at Bryce. "He's a great horse. Fabulous gait, compliant, good attitude."

"How does he handle?"

"Wonderfully. I think I'm in love." She knew Bryce had only asked her to ride the horse because she was close to Caitlin's size and hadn't ridden in months. Dani didn't care about the reasons. She leaned forward in the saddle to pat the horse's hot neck. "Did you see those lead changes? They were great."

He smiled up at her. "You were great."

She sat taller in the saddle. "Thanks. I've always felt comfortable with horses."

"It shows," he said. "You're fun to watch."

He was, too, with his dark hair gleaming in the sun and a wide smile brightening his face. "Thanks for letting me ride him."

And thank goodness she'd thought to bring her paddock boots or she might have missed the chance. What an opportunity.

With a final reluctant pat, she dismounted. She'd taken the horse through his paces and showed Bryce what he needed to know. Her job was finished.

Her feet hit the ground. She held the reins in her left hand and removed the helmet she'd borrowed from the stable with her right. "I forgot how much I enjoyed riding."

"That's what Caitlin said." Bryce took the helmet from Dani and fell in step beside her. "Her fiancé, Mark, could tell she missed riding and told her to buy a horse. She used to be really competitive and he's encouraging her to go for it again."

As Dani led the horse around the ring to cool, she glanced toward the entrance to the indoor riding arena where the owners, a man and woman in their mid-fifties, spoke to a male rider.

Dani wiped her sweaty palms on her jeans.

The couple had kept their distance from her and Bryce once they'd realized Dani knew what she was doing. She appreciated the vote of confidence. "Caitlin will be able to do whatever she wants with this handsome fellow."

"Good to hear." Bryce moved with the grace and agility of an athlete. Dani would love to see him ride. "The vet's already done an examination. He looks like a winner. I'm going to tell Caitlin to buy him."

The horse snorted.

Dani didn't blame him one bit. She wrinkled her nose. "Is that really your job?"

"Who else's job would it be?"

"Caitlin's."

His grin crinkled the corner of his eyes. "That's one of the things I admire about you, Dani. You say exactly what's on your mind."

"If I didn't, you wouldn't know what I was thinking."

"It works both ways," Bryce said. "So you know, I'm not trying to make Caitlin's decision for her. She asked me to come out here and give my opinion. That's all. There's also something you don't know about my sister. Something you should know."

His eyes darkened.

"What?"

Bryce paused. His lips thinned into a narrow line.

His serious expression worried Dani. "What is it?"

He took a deep breath. "Caitlin fell in love with a man who wasn't what he claimed to be. He stole her money and broke her heart. I don't want her to be hurt like that again so I look out for her, whether it's with love or horses."

Dani respected how he looked after his sister, yet... "That's admirable, but what about your father? Isn't he the one who's supposed to do that?"

"My father's into his own thing. He was never around much when he and my mother were married and it's gotten worse over the years." Bryce's jaw thrust forward. "He spends his time seeking young wives."

"How young?"

Bryce grimaced. "His current girlfriend is the same age as Caitlin. He's not exactly big on being a parent these days."

He acted nonchalant about the whole thing, but an edge of bitterness in Bryce's voice made her want to reach out to him.

The horse butted her with his nose.

Okay, she could take a hint.

Dani touched Bryce's arm. His muscles rippled under her hand.

"At least your dad's still around. That counts for a lot. He could have just..."

Bryce's brows slanted. "What?"

She pulled her arm away from him. "Left."

As she led the horse toward the gate, Bryce followed.

"My dad took off when I was six," she explained. "My youngest sister was only a couple of months old. He said he loved us and would be back, but we never heard from or saw him again."

Bryce's eyes clouded with sympathy. "I'm sorry."

She didn't want his pity. "Thanks, but my mom said he

wasn't cut out to be a husband and father and we're better off without him."

"You must miss him."

Dani shrugged. "I don't remember him. I have some of his DNA and his last name. That's all I ever want from him. I think what I miss is the idea of having a dad, but my sisters and I have done great, thanks to my mom."

Bryce shook his head. "I don't see how a man could desert his family like that."

Neither did she. Especially since her father had left them with nothing. But Dani wasn't about to let his selfish actions years ago ruin this beautiful day. She looked up at Bryce, the sun warming her already heated face. "Not all men are like you."

"Me?"

"Yes, you." A welcome breeze blew through her sweaty hair. "I can tell when you get married you'll be a great husband and father because of the things you do for your sister."

"I can't help being protective over the things I care about."

Would he ever care about her? Dani wasn't sure she wanted to know the answer.

As she led the horse out of the ring, his hooves kicked up dirt.

"Being protective is an honorable trait, but not many guys would spend a weekend afternoon driving to the other side of the Bay and checking out a horse their sister wanted to buy."

"Well, spending twenty-two thousand dollars on an animal deserves some checking into."

Dani stumbled. She clutched the reins. "Twenty-two—"

The price was so ridiculous she couldn't even say the amount.

Bryce nodded. "Caitlin thinks he's worth it."

Of course, she would. Dani had cleaned the stalls and exercised horses for rich little girls like Caitlin. "The question is, do you think the horse is worth it?"

"Now that I've seen you ride him, yes."

The words came out strong and sure. His certainty made

her feel good about her riding abilities, but she was having trouble coming to terms with the cost.

"Doesn't that price seem a tad…" she searched for the right word—*indulgent* and *ridiculous* probably wouldn't go down well "…excessive?"

He shrugged. "It is expensive for a horse, but you get what you pay for."

"Twenty-two thousand would pay for a lot."

Her mother didn't make that much money after taxes in a year.

A teenaged boy wearing jeans, a long-sleeved shirt and paddock boots approached them. "I'll take him from you."

Dani stared at the kid with acne on his face and a love of horses shining in his eyes. She'd been like him, mucking stalls so she could be around the animals she loved and exercise them when their owners didn't have as much time.

Bryce stood waiting, hands in his pockets.

Giving the kid the horse felt wrong though, until she remembered that was his job. Dani didn't want to get him into trouble. She handed over the reins. "I put him through his paces."

The teenager smiled. "I'll take care of him."

"Thank you." Dani watched him lead the horse away. She noticed his boots. A lot like hers. Scuffed and creased after years of use. She never could afford new ones so kept cleaning the leather with Murphy's Oil and Saddle Soap. Bryce's boots were the opposite of hers—newer and very expensive.

Uneasiness crept down her spine.

Dani knew she and Bryce were from totally different worlds, but being out here with him drove the point home. He was a horse owner; she was a stable hand.

She'd spent her high school years surrounded by people who'd treated their animals with more respect than they'd treated her. She'd lived in apartments, a car and a single-wide trailer.

He'd grown up in a world of nannies and chefs and chauffeurs. Where his father dated women young enough to be his daughter. Where paying an obscene amount for a horse was considered normal.

Her heart twisted.

"Thanks for helping me out today," he said.

"It was my pleasure."

And it was. In spite of the jolt of reality, she'd enjoyed being with him today. Truth be told, she didn't want the day to end. She didn't want their differences to come between them. She wanted to focus on the good things, not what gave her pause.

For the first time in a long while, Dani wanted to believe in happy endings, that obstacles, no matter how big, could be overcome. That just because people came from opposite worlds, things could still work out. That loving someone didn't mean you'd eventually be left with nothing but a broken heart.

"Being out here has been like a dream come true," she admitted.

"I know." The intensity of his eyes made her feel as if she were the only woman in the world. "I wouldn't want to be here with anyone but you."

Her breath caught in her throat. Dani wanted to be the only one for him. She forced herself to breathe.

Dani didn't want to care. A lifetime of being disappointed, of struggling, of simply surviving didn't want her to care. But, heaven help her, she did care. About what he'd said. About him. She couldn't help herself.

"Me, either," she said.

Desire flared in Bryce's eyes, but his attention didn't make her feel cheap, like some man's possession or plaything *du jour*. He made her feel beautiful, sexy, wanted. A way she hadn't felt in…forever.

She wanted him to kiss her. Her lips parted in hope.

He lowered his head and covered her mouth with his. The

touch of his lips brought a jolt of electricity crackling through her.

His lips ran over hers with such tenderness tears stung Dani's eyes. His kiss flowed through her, a current of affection, filling all the empty spaces inside with warmth.

He tasted like the coffee they'd drunk on the drive—warm, strong and rich. But there was more—salt, heat, male.

She drank up his kiss as if she'd never taste another drop.

As he increased the pressure of his mouth, her knees went weak. She'd heard the phrase "being kissed senseless." She finally understood what those words meant.

She wrapped her arms around his shoulders to keep from falling.

If he kept kissing her this way, she'd be a puddle on the ground.

Dani didn't think she would mind.

The familiar scents of dirt, hay and horse reminded her of the farm, but here in Bryce's kiss she'd found the only home she needed.

His arms wrapped around her, pulling her against his chest. Dani wanted to get closer. Body pressed against body. She hadn't realized he was so strong, so solid before.

All the while his lips caressed, his tongue explored.

Sensation pulsated through her. She hadn't known it was possible to feel this way.

Every nerve ending sizzled. Her stomach quivered. Her heart melted.

This was how she'd dreamed of being kissed someday. Dani couldn't believe it was happening now. Here. With Bryce.

She might not have been looking for a boyfriend, but somehow she'd found him. And, even though she didn't want a relationship, she might need one.

The realization should have scared her more than it did.

As Dani ran her hands through his hair, he trailed kisses along her jawline. She arched back, wanting…

More.

He returned to her mouth, stealing her breath and her heart…

Warning bells sounded. Rational thought returned. With her hands on his shoulders, she pulled her lips away from his.

The emotion in his eyes and the smile on his face made her want to start kissing him all over again.

But that would be too dangerous. She didn't want to lose herself in him. She couldn't.

Dani tried to catch her breath, regain control.

He pushed a strand of her hair off her face. "That was amazing."

Awesome was more like it. She stared up at him, wanting to memorize everything about him, from the faint lines at the corner of his eyes to the way he smoothed her hair with his hand. "Yes, amazing."

Somewhere a horse neighed.

"Ready to head back to the city?" Bryce asked.

No. A sense of inadequacy swept over her. She wanted to go somewhere else—a neutral place, where they could just be themselves and not have to worry about their jobs, their families, their lives. Their differences.

"Not really," she admitted.

Bryce laced his fingers with hers and gave a squeeze. "We can come back."

We.

Hope surged. Dani didn't want to let go. She didn't want to say goodbye.

Not today. Not ever.

She looked up at him. The tenderness in his expression brought a sigh to her lips.

Happiness bubbled, threatening to spill from her heart. She wanted this feeling to last.

Today, tomorrow, always.
That couldn't happen unless she did one thing…
Tell Bryce the truth.
About her job. About everything.

CHAPTER SEVEN

"WOULD you like something to drink?" Standing in the doorway to her kitchen, Dani wrung her hands. "Eat?"

Bryce wanted to put her at ease, not make her wait on him. "No, thanks."

Her nervousness disturbed him. Especially after the great time they'd had at the stable.

He understood how she felt though. They were alone in her studio apartment after some really hot kisses. He was a bit on edge himself. Maybe a little conversation would help.

"Nice place." Bryce noticed the futon sofa that probably doubled as her bed. He looked away. "Comfortable."

"Thanks." Her voice sounded shaky. "It's small, but I don't need a lot of space."

A photograph of her riding a large black horse caught his attention. Even in the still frame, he could see the fluidity of her body as she and the animal made a jump. "Where was this picture taken?"

Her faint smile seemed to relax the rest of her face. "A stable near the farm where I worked during high school."

He noticed she was wearing the same old paddock boots in the photo as she'd worn today. Functional and well-worn. She deserved new ones. "You should come out to my family's stable and ride."

Uncertainty crept into her eyes. "You have a stable?"

Darn, he'd wanted to put a smile on her pretty face, not make her feel worse. "Not me, my family."

She paced in front of the doorway to the kitchen. She reminded him, not of a hummingbird, intent on reaching its next destination, but of a cat, trying to decide whether to chase after a mouse or not. The indecision seemed out of character for Dani.

Something must be on her mind. Bryce hoped she wasn't thinking he wanted to take their kiss further. Okay, he did, but not if it made her act like this. He wished he could go back and change things because, even though he liked Dani, he didn't like the complications relationships often brought with them.

Not that kissing her meant he was in a relationship.

Yet…she'd gotten under his skin.

Her friendliness, her sense of humor, even her evasiveness intrigued him. And he couldn't deny he wanted to kiss her again.

Bryce crossed the room and held her hands. "Today has been great, but since we got here you seem a little tense. Don't be. There's no rush. The only thing I want is to see you smile."

"I want to smile, except…"

He led her over to the futon and pulled her down so she was seated next to him. He kept hold of her hand. "Tell me what's going on."

She took a breath. And another. "Well, you know I've told you how I grew up."

Bryce nodded. "You didn't have it easy. No father. No place to live at times."

"We're very different."

She'd mentioned that before. Maybe he could ease her concerns. "In some ways, we are. No matter whether someone's family has money or not, I believe a person has to make their own way in life. I've done that. And so have you. I respect how much you've overcome, Dani. I just wish you didn't have it so tough, but look at the person you are now. Where you are. That's what counts."

Dani looked at the floor. "I'm not very happy with where I am now. I mean I'm happy I'm with you, but not…my job situation."

The sadness in her voice squeezed his heart. He'd been wrong about what she was worried about. He rubbed her hand with his thumb.

"When I graduated with an MBA, I thought I'd finally made it. Put the past behind me." She got a faraway look in her eyes. "I was sure I had everything I needed. A dream job, a cool apartment, a new car, enough money to more than cover my expenses, student loans and still be able to help my family out each month and then…

"I was laid off from my marketing position at Clickznos at the beginning of the year."

"One of the buyout casualties."

She nodded.

He squeezed her hand.

"I'd recently been promoted and gotten a big raise." Her voice sounded almost wistful. "I suppose the signals were there, but we were working too hard to notice them. We assumed things were okay, that we'd be taken care of, but all but a handful of us soon found ourselves on the street with a 'thanks for your hard work' goodbye and a pitiful, almost insulting severance package."

He placed his arm around her. "That had to be tough."

She nodded. "I had a savings account, but I also help my youngest sister pay for college and my mother with her medical insurance so the money didn't last long. I had college and grad school loans to pay for. Bills started piling up fast. I did what I could while I searched for a comparable job. I downsized and moved into this place. I sold my car. But I couldn't wait any longer for the perfect position to material-ize. I needed a paycheck so I took a job that under normal cir-cumstances I would have never considered."

Her worried eyes watched him. Waiting.

So this was what she'd been keeping from him. Relief flooded him. That explained why she didn't mind him not dis-cussing his work. She hadn't wanted to discuss hers either.

He remembered what he'd checked on her profile. "You're in sales?"

"Kind of…sort of…but not really." She blew out a puff of air. "It's complicated."

"Life is complicated," he said. "We can work through anything if you believe we can."

A beat passed. A clock ticked.

"I have a job." She cleared her throat. "It's just not a job I'm particularly proud of."

"Nothing wrong with flipping burgers."

"Except when it doesn't pay."

He stared at her. "Then what…"

She stared at her lap.

Lap dancer? Okay, that was a leap from fast food, but she had the looks and the body. Plus the money was good.

Bryce smiled. Not exactly the job he'd imagined his girl-friend doing, but he wasn't about to judge her, especially under these circumstances. "You found a job that worked at the time. I could never hold what you do against you."

"Sure?"

"You're more than your job, Dani. More than what's on the outside. I like your tenacity, your character. I care for you."

Relief filled her eyes. The tightness disappeared from around her mouth. "I really needed to hear you say that."

He kissed the top of her hand. "So what do you do?"

She straightened and took another breath. "I'm marketing director for Hookamate.com."

Bryce flinched. He let go of her hand as if it were a grenade with a missing pin.

Lines creased her forehead. "Bryce…"

He looked away, trying to come to terms with what he'd just heard.

I'm a spy.

Hookamate.com.

Everything clicked into place.

He swallowed. "I don't believe this."

Her gaze implored him. "You said my job didn't matter."

"That was when I thought you might be a stripper."

She stiffened. "A stripper?"

"Or lap dancer."

"That's so insulting." Her chin jutted forward. "I really thought you were different from other guys, but you aren't. You think I can only use my body to make a living, not my brain."

"You really think James Richardson hired you to be one of his lackeys because of your IQ?"

Her mouth tightened. "I've made a difference at Hookamate.com."

"Oh, yeah, I'd be real proud of the results of your spying on me."

"You?"

Bryce ignored the confusion in Dani's eyes. He pretended not to see her lower lip tremble. He focused on all the problems Blinddatebrides.com had been having with scammers. Problems he should have been investigating instead of wasting his time with her. "I used to work with the guy. He's had some sort of vendetta against me since I left."

"You worked with him, so that means you're…?"

"Bryce Delaney."

Her face paled. "The founder and CEO of Blinddatebrides.com."

He nodded once.

She slumped against the futon. The hurt in her eyes told him that she'd had no idea who he was. At least she hadn't been using him to get information. The realization didn't make him feel any less betrayed.

"You knew about me this entire time." Disbelief and anger dripped from each word.

"I didn't know why you were on the site, but a chat filter picked up the words *I'm a spy*." He kept his voice cool, calm. "We've been trying to figure out what that meant ever since."

"We?"

"My security team and me."

She winced. "So all of…um…our dates…"

"An investigation."

Who was the one who was lying now? Bryce didn't care.

Dani bit her lip. "So while I was spying on Blinddate-brides.com, you were spying on me."

"Investigating you," he countered.

"Without my knowledge."

"Yes."

She sat only two feet away from him, but the space felt insurmountable. He liked her. Or had liked her. He wasn't sure what he felt now.

She glared at him. "Guess that gives new meaning to your user name."

"Don't put this on me." He stood, not wanting to be drawn into an argument. "You're the one who broke the terms of service. Everyone's wondered why Hookamate.com's traffic ranking has been up for the past four months. Now I know the answer. Were you there to steal content or was hacking and sabotaging the site part of your job description, too?"

"None of the above." She rose and walked to the opposite side of the room. "I gave James screen shots, but I never stole anything. I used the site to get ideas and create new content for ours. Traffic is up because I was doing my job. And a damn good job at that."

She placed her hands on her hips. "And I never did anything else on your site. No hacking. No sabotage. I might have broken your TOS, but I followed every other rule, especially when another user contacted me. That's why I turned down dates. It wasn't fair to lead them on when I had no interest in dating."

"I find it very hard to believe you." His words sounded harsh to his own ears. Suddenly, he didn't care about remaining in control. "What did you say that night after your date with Gymguy? 'Players and liars are everywhere.' Guess you spoke from experience."

"You, too." She drew her lips into a thin line. "You admitted following Hookamate's traffic rankings. Every company checks out their competitors. It's irresponsible not to. Yes, I crossed the line when I joined the site, but I was only doing my job."

"Your job?" Bryce's temper flared. "Joining a community, making friends, going on dates so you could spy. Having men fall…"

Damn her. He'd known about the red flags, yet he'd wanted to believe she was on the level.

So much for taking care of his Web site, customers and company. He was no smarter than those suckers who got conned out of their hard-earned money by responding to foreign spammers' e-mails asking for money to be wired overseas.

Still curiosity got the better of him. "Why did you go out with me?"

"James wanted me to put together a clientele profile and see what clients really thought of Blinddatebrides.com. I only went out with you and Gymguy. No one else contacted me after that."

"I turned off your participation in the compatibility matching program and site search engine."

"Why?"

"The investigation," Bryce admitted. "I wanted to make sure you weren't a troublemaker and trying to cause problems with clients."

She pursed her lips. "You didn't want me going out with any other guys."

A beat passed, and another. "Maybe not."

Definitely not. And, from the expression on her face, she knew it.

"That night at the restaurant. You knew I'd be there with Gymguy."

Bryce nodded once.

"How?" she asked.

"Your e-mail."

"And you're upset over what I was doing?" Her eyes darkened to a midnight-blue. "Reading e-mail is an invasion of privacy. It's—"

"Part of the terms of service you agreed to when you signed onto Blinddatebrides.com."

"It's still not right," she said. "We've both been keeping secrets but, except for telling you about my job and why I joined the site, I was open and honest about everything. I never lied to you or invaded your privacy."

"I was doing my job."

"And, as I said, I was doing mine," she countered. "I had misgivings over doing it, but it's still part of doing business on the Internet. I'm sure there are other competitors who signed up at Blinddatebrides.com, too."

But he hadn't just kissed them passionately or wanted to kiss them again. "If I find out about them, I'll kick them off. I want Blinddatebrides.com to be a safe place."

"Safe doesn't exist, Bryce. You just proved that to me by saying my job didn't matter when it does. At least I was honest about my feelings for you, unlike you."

"I've been honest."

"If that's your version of honesty, I'd hate to see you being dishonest." She pressed her lips together. "I'll admit what I did wasn't right, but neither was what you just did to me.

"And, just so you know, I didn't want to join your site or go on dates, but James threatened to fire me if I didn't. I couldn't afford to quit."

"You've thought about quitting?" Bryce asked.

"Every single day since I signed up for an account on Blinddatebrides.com over six months ago."

The sincerity in her voice clawed at his heart. Everything he believed people capable of—misrepresenting themselves and lying—was right here in the room. He was guilty of it himself which made this all the more confusing.

He didn't know what to say or do.

Everything they'd experienced, everything they could share together in the future, was unraveling. The way they were arguing reminded him of his parents fighting. A part of him wanted to walk away and not look back. Yet another part couldn't imagine never seeing her again. Never kissing her.

Blood pounded at his temples. A headache threatened to erupt. He squeezed his eyes shut.

When he opened them, she was staring at him.

"I never wanted to hurt anyone. That's why I wrote the profile I did. So guys wouldn't want to go out with me. I'm sorry if I hurt you. That wasn't my intention." Her eyes glistened. "I'll cancel my account tonight."

Bryce hated feeling the way he did, but he also hated seeing Dani so upset. "What about your friends?"

"We know each other's personal e-mail addresses. There are other places on the Internet where we can chat and send IMs from."

"What about your job?"

The truth was clear in her eyes. She expected to be fired. "Why do you care?"

He shouldn't care. "Because you told me what drove you to take the job in the first place. I'm not the bad guy here."

"No, you're just the hypocrite telling me one thing and doing another. I trusted you. I believed what you said. But you used my falling for you to set a trap."

She'd fallen for him? Bryce wasn't sure what to think or believe right now.

"I just wonder what your reaction would have been if I'd been a stripper. I doubt you'd have been so understanding then, either."

Her criticism stung. The disapproval in her voice made him feel like a jerk. "Don't cancel your account until you find another job."

Her shoulders sagged for a moment, then she straightened. "I've been trying to find a job for months with no luck so that might take a while."

"As long as you work for James, you can use my site for e-mailing and chatting with your two friends. Nothing else."

"Will you be checking up on me?"

Bryce's jaw clenched. "What do you think?"

Blinddatebrides.com is running sixteen chat rooms, forty-seven private IM conferences, and 7305 members are online. Chat with your dating prospects now!
Private IM conference #28 (3 participants)…
Sanfrandani: I feel so bad.
Englishcrumpet: Don't worry, Dani. We can find another place to chat if we need to. The main thing is we don't lose touch.
Sanfrandani: I agree. At least he didn't kick me off the site right away, but I'm sure that's coming.
Kangagirl: Have you heard anything from Bryce?

Anger surged. Granted, Dani was the one who'd joined the Web site under false pretenses, but Bryce had had no reason to set her up so she'd spill her soul to him and then have him turn on her the way he had.

Whatever they'd shared before no longer existed. She wondered if a connection ever had.

Sanfrandani: Nope. It's been a week.

At least she'd apologized for her part in the mess. Telling her she could stay on the site didn't count as an apology in her book.

Englishcrumpet: What about your job search?
Sanfrandani: Still nothing. It's like my résumé disappears into a black hole every time I send one out. It's really frustrating. James keeps asking about my dates. I've been putting him off, but I'm going to have to say something to him soon.
Englishcrumpet: A job will turn up.
Kangagirl: Fingers crossed.
Englishcrumpet: Are you going to contact Bryce?
Sanfrandani: There's no need. We're over.
Englishcrumpet: I'm sorry.
Kangagirl: Me, too. I know you liked him.
Sanfrandani: Thanks, but I'm more angry than sad. I'll survive.

And she would.

She'd just wanted to believe there was a man out there she could trust and love. She'd wanted that man to be Bryce.

"Check this out."

In his office, Bryce turned the monitor on his desk so his coworkers could see what he'd spent his days and nights working on this week. He'd needed something to focus his attention on so he wouldn't think about…

Dani.

Grant stared at the HTML page displayed on the monitor. His smile widened. "That is one sweet honeypot."

"Where?" Peering over Grant's shoulder, Joelle adjusted her plastic-rimmed glasses. "I don't see anything except code."

Grant continued reading the screen. "That's because you're a non-techie, Joelle."

"A non-techie who makes sure you receive a paycheck."

"Look right here." Bryce highlighted lines of commented-out code that gave clues of how the internals of the site were implemented. "When a hacker tries to exploit the code he's found, he'll think he's hit gold, except what he's really found is fake user info on an isolated network. We can then hunt him down. It would feel good to actually catch one of these losers trying to mess with the site."

"And if you can't catch them?" Joelle asked.

"The data we get can help mitigate our risk," Grant said.

Bryce leaned back in his chair. "I just hope someone takes the bait."

"I'm sure they will," Joelle said. "You're really good at setting traps, boss."

She'd meant the words as a compliment, but they echoed Dani's a little too closely.

I trusted you. I believed what you said. But you used my falling for you to set a trap.

And that was exactly what he'd done.

He'd misled Dani by saying one thing, then doing another.

The same way he'd built the honeypot into the code to catch hackers.

Dani hadn't been honest about who she was. Neither had he.

His intentions had been good. Hers hadn't.

But she'd been honest about her feelings. And he…

Bryce sighed. He owed her an apology.

The only question was, after their fight, would Dani even want to listen to one?

To: "Sanfrandani" <sanfrandani@blinddatebrides.com>
From: "Bigbrother" <bigbrother@blinddatebrides.com>
Subject: Pot. Kettle. Black.
I'm not Colonel Brandon, but I'm not Willoughby, either.
I owe you an apology for setting you up the way I did. It wasn't intentional.
How does meeting at Crossroads before work tomorrow to discuss sound? My treat.
-b

To: "Bigbrother" <bigbrother@blinddatebrides.com>
From: "Sanfrandani" <sanfrandani@blinddatebrides.com>
Subject: RE: Pot. Kettle. Black.
Well, no one would ever mistake me for Marianne Dashwood.
Open to discussion, but busy in the morning. Free for lunch. Anytime from 11:30 to 1:30. Let me know.
-d

To: "Sanfrandani" <sanfrandani@blinddatebrides.com>
From: "Bigbrother" <bigbrother@blinddatebrides.com>
Subject: Lunch
See you at noon. Just look for the black pot.
-b

Uncertainty filled Dani as she sat in her lonely cubicle re-reading Bryce's e-mails. She stirred in her chair, unsure what meeting him would bring. Still a kernel of hope remained.

Hope that Bryce meant what he said about apologizing for his part in their fight.

Hope that he forgave her for her part in all this.

Hope that maybe he was different from other men and things between them might not be totally over.

At twelve o'clock, Dani entered the café. Lunch customers packed the place. Conversations from the crowd filled the air.

She spotted Bryce sitting at a table not far from the one they'd occupied the first time they'd met. He wore a gray suit with a white dress shirt and a yellow tie.

Dani was still angry over what had happened in her apartment, but the butterflies flapping and wreaking havoc in her stomach had nothing to do with her being upset and everything to do with attraction. He seemed to have gotten better-looking over the last week. Darn him.

A glass crashed to the floor.

An omen, perhaps? She wasn't sure whether to move forward or retreat. Maybe he hadn't seen her…

Bryce's gaze caught her. His face brightened.

Maybe he was happy to see her. Maybe he wanted to get this over with.

Dani inhaled deeply to muster her courage. She could do this. She had no choice really since she'd said she was open for discussion. Unlike him, she wasn't going to renege on her word.

He offered her a forgiving smile and raised a small black pot in the air.

She half laughed. He hadn't been kidding about the pot.

Okay, maybe she was overreacting a little. The least she could do was have lunch with him and hear what he had to say.

She wove her way to his table, taking advantage of the time to prepare herself. All she wanted from him was an apology. Not a handshake or hug or kiss…

Bryce stood. "Miss Kettle?"

"Mr. Pot, I presume?"

He nodded.

Tension simmered between them, a strong mix of anxiety and attraction. She stood across from him like a total stranger.

Dani swallowed. Agreeing to meet him was a really bad idea.

A cell phone rang somewhere near the bookshelves.

"Do you want to order lunch before we sit?" Bryce asked finally.

"Sure," Dani said, even though she didn't have much of an appetite at the moment.

She followed him to the counter, where they ordered sandwiches and drinks. Bryce paid as he'd said he would.

Back at the table, Dani sat across from him. She heard the typing of keys on a laptop. She squeezed a slice of lemon into her iced tea and stole a glance at his face.

He was staring at her.

"I'm sorry." Bryce's voice cut through the silence at their table and the noise around them. "You took responsibility for your actions. I didn't. I apologize for not being honest with you, for setting you up like that and everything else I said and did. It wasn't fair of me."

Those were the words Dani needed to hear. "Thank you. I know you feel betrayed over something very important to you. I appreciate and accept your apology."

"Good, because I don't like how things are between us."

She stirred her iced tea. "There isn't anything between us."

"But I want there to be again," he said with such heartfelt honesty she dropped her spoon. "After everything that's happened, I miss what we had. I miss you, Dani. I might have started to see you under false pretenses, but my feelings for you were never faked. The things I said on our dates, the kissing, all that was true and not part of my checking up on you."

She stared at him, transfixed by the emotion in his eyes and his voice.

"I know you said you weren't interested in dating, but I want to keep seeing you. If you're game, we could start over."

"Start over," she repeated, fighting the tumble of confused thoughts and emotions in her head.

"Yes, we could wipe the slate clean," he explained. "Knowing what we know about each other now, we put what happened behind us and start fresh. This could be our first date."

The unexpected proposition had her heart dancing a two-step, but doubts swirled. Dani wasn't about to step onto the dance floor just yet. "What about my job? I still haven't found another one."

"Did you sign a non-disclosure agreement?"

She nodded.

"What about a non-compete clause?"

Another nod.

"Then I can't offer you a job."

"Nothing personal, but I wouldn't want to work for you," she admitted. "I learned from my mother that it's best to take charge of your own life and not rely on others to give you what you need."

That was something her mother hadn't done after she married and paid the price when Dani's father left. She would not make the same mistake.

A woman with a short asymmetric haircut delivered their sandwiches and walked away.

"I understand that, but what if I send your résumés out to some people I know?" Bryce offered. "I have a lot of connections that could come in handy."

"I…" Dani knew former coworkers had found jobs through contacts. That was how most people found new positions. And she couldn't pretend her own job search had yielded anything except feelings of futility. "As long as you only give them my résumé and promise to do nothing else. I don't want something just handed to me because I know you."

"Getting the job will be up to you."

"That's what I needed to hear." Satisfied, she smiled. "Thanks."

"Are you always so independent?"

"Yes."

"E-mail your résumé when you get home tonight."

"Thanks." Except a question niggled at her. "You talked about starting over. How does that work? Do we wait until I get a new job or…"

"I don't want to wait," Bryce said without any hesitation. "I want to see you as much as I can."

"I'd like that, too," she admitted. "But we have to be honest with each other from now on. You have work and so do I. Plus I need to find a new job. Given the circumstances, we might want to take things…slow."

Bryce smiled back. "Slow works for me."

CHAPTER EIGHT

Instant Message from Dani to Grace and Marissa: *Trying 2 work things out with Bryce. Cross ur fingers! TTYL!*
Instant Message from Grace to Dani: *Good luck! Keep us posted. But please be careful.*
Instant Message from Marissa to Dani: *Fingers crossed! Watch out for yourself, okay?*
Instant Message from Marissa to Grace: *Do you know what's going on with Dani and Bryce? I'm a little worried.*
Instant Message from Grace to Marissa: *No idea! But it sounds like we might not have to find a new place to chat!!!*

OVER the next two weeks, Bryce's work and travel schedule kept him busy. He only saw Dani twice, but kept in touch with her via phone calls, texting and e-mails. She didn't mind his work taking up so much of his time. She had things to do herself.

By the time Friday rolled around, he couldn't wait to see her. Thoughts of this evening had kept him going today, through an interview with a technology blogger, a phone call from his father and a meeting with his attorney.

Rain pelted Bryce as he ran from his car to the Palace of Fine Arts, where he was supposed to have met her twenty minutes ago.

Helluva time to be late.

The relentless storm had flooded roads, turning the city streets into gridlock with backed-up drains and fender benders.

He lengthened his stride, his feet pounding against the wet pavement. Water beaded on his jacket and dripped from his hair.

The entire park was deserted. A foghorn blared in the distance. Not the ideal conditions for a romantic picnic beneath the stars.

He should have checked the weather forecast before leaving the office. He'd tried to call Dani, but gotten her voice mail. Not that he would have canceled. Storm or not, he wanted to see her. He only hoped she hadn't gotten caught in the downpour, too.

Up ahead, lights illuminated the columns and the interior of the dome. Dani would be underneath the rotunda waiting for him. The way she had been the first time they'd been here.

Anticipation surged. Bryce accelerated.

For once they had nowhere else to go, nothing else to do but be together.

He focused on the rotunda. Almost there.

Cold water shot up his pant leg. His shoe squished against the concrete.

Damn. Bryce glanced down at a big puddle. He shook his foot and continued on. A little more water didn't matter when he was already soaking wet.

He ran underneath the dome, out of the cold rain and into the light. The first thing he saw was…

Dani.

She leaned against a column, looking like a goddess from ancient times except for the small cooler and picnic basket at her feet.

The sight warmed Bryce right up.

Water dripped from the hair plastered against her head and onto her soaking wet pale blue jacket. The thin, wet fabric clung to her like a second skin, accentuating every curve of her body and leaving little to his imagination.

Awareness rippled through him.

He wanted her.

It was as simple and as complicated as that.

"Looks like I'm not the only one who forgot an umbrella," she said.

Her wide smile sent his pulse sprinting through his veins.

"Nope." His gaze raked over her once again. Talk about a feast for the eyes. "But I'm glad you forgot yours."

Dani raised her chin. "Why is that?"

"Because you are totally hot, Miss Bennett."

He walked toward her. She met him halfway with a wry grin on her face.

"You're not so bad yourself, Mr. Delaney."

Bryce stood across from her at the center of the dome. The darker sapphire flecks in her eyes mesmerized him. He hadn't noticed them before. "It's hard to believe we were here only a few weeks ago."

"This does have a bit of a déjà vu feeling."

"Except for the rain."

Her gaze remained locked on his. "The darkness."

"And this…"

Bryce covered her mouth with his. She tensed for a moment, then relaxed, moving her soft lips against his. He didn't know how long they stood there with only their lips touching. He didn't care.

Kissing her like this was what he'd been thinking about, dreaming about, wanting to do, ever since they'd started over. Okay, ever since the kiss at the stable. He wasn't about to rush through the opportunity. He wanted to savor the moment, make it last.

Dani's kiss, full of sweetness and warmth, like the woman herself, was addictive. Intoxicating. A mysterious elixir with a secret ingredient. Bryce wanted more.

He deepened the kiss, wrapping his arms around her.

Sheets of rain fell from the sky, drumming against the dome and the cement beyond the rotunda. The pounding water matched the beat of his heart.

His hand splayed her back, the wet fabric beneath his palm, and he pulled her toward him.

Dani went willingly, eagerly against him. She wrapped her arms around him, running the palms of her hands over his shoulders and back. A ball of need formed low in his stomach, an ache only she could soothe.

He moved his lips away from hers, trailing kisses along her jawline. She arched, giving him access to her neck. He showered kiss after kiss.

She moaned.

Heated blood pulsated through his veins. The hot ache grew inside him.

Dani wove her fingers through his hair. She rose up to kiss him, but bypassed his mouth and went straight to his ear. She nibbled on his earlobe, ran her tongue over it.

Bryce felt himself sinking into her.

He didn't care. The only thing he cared about was…

Her.

The realization jolted him. He pulled away.

She stared up at him with wide eyes filled with desire.

Bryce placed his hand on her flushed face; her normally warm skin was wet and cold. "We said we were starting over and were going slow, but I don't want to go backward, Dani."

"Me, either." She wet her lips and looked around. "I don't think we're going to be able to have much of a picnic here."

"We could have a picnic on my living room floor," he suggested, not caring where they ended up as long as they remained together. "It won't be the same as this place, but it's warm and dry."

"Sounds good."

Very good. Spending time alone at his house with a rain-soaked, sexy, intelligent woman on a dark and stormy night was as good as it got.

A satisfied smile settled on Bryce's face. "Let's make a run for my car."

Playing house as a kid had never been this fun. When Bryce had said he lived in Presidio Heights, she'd thought he meant an apartment not a multimillion-dollar house.

Dani stood in Bryce's gourmet kitchen and rolled up the sleeves of his shirt, which she was wearing. A drawer opened and closed behind her. She pulled up his sweatpants that kept slipping down her hips.

Her lips tingled from the kiss under the rotunda and her body felt cold without Bryce's arms around her.

Face it, she liked him. A lot. The realization didn't terrify her as much as it once would have. But she still needed to be smart about things and move slowly.

A pop sounded behind her—the cork from the wine bottle.

She shot a sideways glance Bryce's way. His damp hair curled at the ends. His casual clothes, a long-sleeved brown T-shirt and green trackpants, made him seem more real and less like some fantasy guy in a designer suit from a glossy magazine. And that made him appeal to her even more. Darn it.

She would have to make sure he didn't kiss her again tonight. Or she didn't kiss him. Otherwise, she might find herself wanting to rush into something with him.

Dani looked away, wrapping her hands around her.

"Your clothes should be dry soon." Bryce handed her a glass of red wine from the bottle she'd brought for their picnic. "I have a bottle of Chardonnay if you prefer."

The hunger in his gaze made her think he wasn't only interested in tasting dinner. Too bad she wouldn't mind another taste of him. Dani gulped.

No more kisses, she reminded herself.

"Thanks." She tried to sound relaxed, even though every single one of her muscles was bunched up in knots. She took a sip of the Pinot Noir. "This will go better with the dinner I made."

"Whatever you brought smells delicious."

He was delicious. Eating dinner ASAP made a whole lot of sense; otherwise she might have to taste him. Dani set her glass on the smooth granite countertop. "I'd better dish up the food before it gets too cold."

"I'll lay out the blanket in front of the fireplace in the living room," he said.

Oh, boy, that sounded romantic. Maybe they should eat here at the kitchen island and sit on stools instead.

Before she could say anything, Bryce disappeared through the butler's pantry, leaving Dani alone in the to-die-for kitchen.

She hadn't wanted a man in her life, but she seemed to have found one. A good one. If she weren't careful, she could find herself in a serious relationship. And that wasn't sounding like such a bad thing at the moment.

With a resigned sigh, she padded barefoot across the wide-planked hardwood floor.

Music played, streaming from speakers she hadn't known were there. He must have turned on a sound system. As she placed a marinated steak and vegetable kebob on each plate, a soft melody filled the kitchen.

"Do you like to dance?" Bryce asked.

Dani realized she was swaying to the music. She stopped, embarrassed. "I don't get much opportunity to dance."

Standing behind her, he placed his hands on her shoulders. "But you like dancing."

It wasn't a question. Still Dani nodded. That was the only response she could manage.

Standing with him like this felt so comfortable and right. She fought the urge to lean back against him. They seemed like a…couple. She straightened and added a scoop of rice pilaf to the plates instead. "What about you?"

"I'm not really into dancing," he admitted. "My mother forced dancing lessons on me when I was a kid."

"Let me guess." Dani placed a salad with fresh strawberries and poppy seed dressing on the plates. "You didn't like the lessons."

"I hated them." Bryce picked up his wineglass. "I'll never forget having to dance in front of all the parents. All those eyes watching me, seeing every mistake. It was a living nightmare. One I don't want to repeat."

She picked up the plates and silverware, wrapped in napkins. "Everything's ready."

He tucked the wine bottle in the nook of his arm and grabbed their glasses. She followed him into the living room.

A blanket lay on the floor in front of the roaring fire. Flickering candles on the built-in shelves and mantel added to the romantic atmosphere.

A mix of emotion welled inside her. His thoughtfulness at making things so special for their "picnic" and her worry that she might find herself caught up in the moment. She sat on the blanket. "This is lovely, Bryce. Thanks for going to so much trouble."

"You're welcome. But you deserve the thanks for going to all the trouble with a home-cooked meal." He took a plate from Dani, sat across from her and swallowed a forkful of rice pilaf. "This is fantastic. Where did you learn to cook?"

"My mother taught me." Dani removed the stick from her kebob. "She cooks at the farm and had us help her sometimes. During college, I worked at a café near campus."

"Is there anything you can't do?"

She drank her wine. "Find a job."

"You will. Your résumé is out there." He reached across the

blanket and touched her hand. "Remember, finding a good job doesn't happen overnight. Give it time."

Staring into his eyes made her think everything—job, life, even love—would work out. Somehow. "Okay."

As they finished eating dinner and he explained where he'd sent her résumé, she noticed the architectural details of the living room. The moldings, the wood-paned windows, French doors. She could imagine herself in the drawing room at Netherfield. Only Bryce was much sharper than Mr. Bingley and more amenable and approachable than Mr. Darcy. "This is a beautiful house."

"Thanks." Bryce placed his fork on his plate. "I've managed to get two rooms remodeled, but there's more to do."

"Are you going to be doing heavy construction or just surface, cosmetic stuff?" she asked.

"No wall moving," he said. "Painting, window coverings and new furniture."

She smiled. "The fun stuff."

"You might think so."

"Come on. You get to decorate your own house. That's—" she searched for the right words "—a dream come true for many people. I'd love to have a house to do that with. I remember…"

"What?" Bryce asked.

"Nothing." She stared into her wineglass, feeling self-conscious. "It's silly."

"No holding back," Bryce urged. "Please tell me what you were going to say."

"When I was younger, I used to draw floor plans for houses. There would be tons of scrap paper with my scribbles on them everywhere. One Christmas, I got a book, one of those thick magazines really, of house plans. It was my favorite present. I still have it somewhere."

"Did you want to be an architect?" he asked.

She watched the flames dancing in the fireplace. "No, I just wanted to have my own house."

"If you have any ideas for mine, I'm open to suggestions."

"Be careful," she warned. "I share my suggestions as much as my opinions."

"I don't mind." Bryce refilled her wineglass. "That will be better than my mother having interior designers call to set up appointments I don't want."

"Echoes of your dancing lessons?"

"Yep." He grinned. "She can't understand why I'm not in any hurry to get the house done right away."

"I'd think you'd want to live here a while and get a feel for the place first."

"That's exactly what I told her, but I'm not holding my breath she'll listen." He leaned back on his elbows. "My mother likes getting her way, but now that Caitlin and I are older that doesn't always happen."

"Most people prefer getting their way," Dani said. "I know I do."

"What would you like right now?" Bryce asked.

A kiss. No, that wouldn't be smart, considering the circumstances. She'd go for second best. "How about dessert?"

"This brownie is the most decadent I've ever tasted and, no doubt, going straight to my hips." Dani's pink tongue darted out and licked her lips. "These have to be homemade, but I thought you said you couldn't cook."

Busted. Bryce couldn't lie. "I never said I made them. Just that I was bringing dessert."

"So the question is, who baked them?" She studied the small piece that remained on her plate as if she were a jeweler examining a flawless diamond. "Let me guess. Either your mother, your mother's cook, your sister or an old nanny baked them."

"Nope."

"Then who?" she asked.

"I have a hot-shot programmer on my team named Christopher. He's a real rock star, but his hobby is baking."

"No way." She straightened. "I can't believe a computer geek baked these tasty morsels."

"It's true."

She snagged another brownie. "You'd better give the guy a raise or some restaurant is going to steal him away."

"I'd set him up with his own bakery before I let that happen."

She sighed.

"The brownies?" Bryce asked.

"No, you." She studied him with observant eyes. "I've never met anyone like you."

"Well, I've never met anyone like you, either." He appreciated her quick thinking and sense of humor. Not to mention her beauty. "I'm happy you're here."

"Me, too."

Bryce kissed her quickly, tasting chocolate and Dani.

The corners of her mouth curved. "Now that's the perfect end to this dinner."

"I suppose it's getting late."

She glanced out the window. "The rain is still coming down pretty hard out there."

"Do you want to wait it out by watching a movie?" he suggested. "There's a home theater and media room upstairs. That's the other room I had redone. Nothing better than playing video games on a large screen."

"Video games?" Interest flashed on her face. "Can we play instead of watching a movie?"

"You like games?"

"I love them."

The more time he spent with Dani, the more perfect she got. She was definitely a woman worth making time in his life for.

"I'd rather play video games than watch a movie any day," she added. "What platform do you have?"

"A Nintendo Wii and Xbox."

She shimmied her shoulders and stood. "I think I'm in heaven."

So was he. The lighting provided an alluring silhouette of her breasts. Bryce swallowed.

"A man after my own heart," she said.

Well, maybe not her heart, but he wouldn't mind a few of her other parts. Except he wasn't just after her body. He wanted Dani.

"So are you ready?" she asked.

Her question jerked his gaze away from her chest.

She squared her shoulders and gave him a pointed look.

Okay, he deserved it. She'd caught him ogling her. But, hey, he was a guy. Men only had so much self-control. "Ready?"

For an apology, another brownie, a kiss…

Dani winked. "Ready to lose."

CHAPTER NINE

WEAPONS blasted. Targets exploded. Pulse-pounding music blared. The button of the game controller toggled beneath Bryce's fingertip. "I am not going to lose."

Dani fired back. "Yes, you are."

He shot her a sideways glance.

Her breasts bounced. Her butt wiggled.

So hot. No wonder he kept losing with those sweet things to distract him. He needed to focus on the game instead.

"How did you get so good at video games?" he asked.

"The break room at my old job had all the different platforms for us to play."

Bryce launched one of his missiles, nearly wiping out Dani.

She sent a challenging look his way. "You are going down, Delaney."

"Think again, Bennett." A surge of adrenaline sent Bryce jumping to his feet. Frustrated, yes. Defeated, no. He tapped faster, trying to fire shots in rapid succession. "You're the one who's going to be history."

"In your dreams." She fired a shot. Direct hit. His character exploded into red, orange and yellow flames. "Yes!"

"Nooooo!" he cried.

She raised her hands in the air. "I am officially the undefeated master—make that mistress—of the galaxies."

The title fit her, in more ways than one. Bryce tossed his controller onto one of the leather game chairs. "If you're expecting me to bow down before you—"

"I wasn't." Mischief gleamed in her eyes. "But now that you mention it…"

"You're a worthy opponent, but I don't get on my knees for anyone."

She winked. "We'll have to work on that."

Desire rocketed through him. "We could start now."

"I…" Dani glanced around the room, her eyes avoiding his. "It might be a little late for that."

Her coyness added to her sex appeal.

"Late is a relative term." He glanced at his watch and did a double take. "Though one o'clock in the morning is late by anyone's standards."

"It can't be that late."

"It is." He turned off the game console and sound system, ready for whatever would come next. "We totally lost track of time. Do you know what this means?"

"Yes." She plopped into a chair and buried her face in her hands. "I've turned into a gamer geek."

"Then what does that make me?" he asked.

A grin replaced her look of despair. "With a choice setup like this, you're a gaming guru."

"I kind of like that, but not as much as I like having you here."

Dani blushed. Not exactly the reaction he was expecting from a gaming goddess but, then again, he never knew what to expect from her. At first that had bugged him, but now he could accept her unpredictable nature as just part of who she was.

She stood, lifted one of the blackout shades and peeked out. "It's still raining."

Bryce noticed the dark circles under her eyes and the wary lines around her mouth. He wanted her to stay, but only if she wanted to. "You're tired. I'll drive you home."

"Not in this rain. This late." She wrung her hands. "I'll call a cab."

"No cab," he said. "I drive you home or you spend the night."

She bit her lip.

"You don't have to sleep in my room. Unless you want." No way would Bryce rush things. Her. She should know that by now. He dragged his hand through his hair. "There's a guest room. You can borrow a pair of my pajamas. Heck, you can lock the door if that makes you more comfortable."

The corners of her mouth curved. "I don't mean to be difficult."

"And I'm not going to push you into anything you're not ready for."

Even if he might be ready for more.

The gratitude in her eyes made Dani's decision clear and, honestly, he was okay with that. Disappointed, but okay. He could see the two of them being together…a while.

"Not that I could make the mistress of the galaxies do anything she didn't want to do."

Dani laughed; the sound floated on the air and smacked him right in the gut.

"Smart man." Her tone sounded less tense. "So where's this guest room of yours?"

Bryce led her down the hall, making a quick stop at his room to grab her a pair of pajamas. "These are brand-new. Washed, never worn. I sleep in shorts and a T-shirt, but no matter how many times I tell my mother this she always buys me a pair of pajamas every Christmas."

"Thanks." Dani rubbed her fingers over the flannel fabric. "I usually wear a T-shirt to bed, but these are so soft they'll be a treat to sleep in."

The image of her wearing only a T-shirt sent his temperature up and made him wish she'd opted to sleep in his room instead.

"So which door…?" she asked.

Her words jostled him from the fantasy forming in his head.

"Right here." Bryce motioned to the closed door across from his. "In the bathroom drawer, you'll find toothbrushes and other stuff."

"Get a lot of overnight visitors?" she asked, her tone icy.

"Nope." He liked the idea she might be concerned about female visitors. And jealous. "I get a lot of freebies."

Her eyebrows raised.

He grinned. "From hotels and airlines. Help yourself to whatever you need."

"Thank you." She placed her hand on the doorknob. "Tonight has been so much fun."

Too bad the fun had to end. "Sleep well."

"You, too." She stared up through her lashes at him, her eyes full of affection. "Sweet dreams."

Bryce really wanted to kiss her goodnight, but she didn't want to rush things and he didn't trust himself not to. If she would only open the door and get away from him...

"Goodnight, Dani."

She rose on tiptoe and kissed his cheek. A chaste peck, really.

Not at all close to what Bryce wanted, but he'd take it.

Dani opened the door and stepped into the guest room. "Goodnight."

The shy, sweet smile on her face hit him like an arrow to his heart. He almost stumbled back.

She closed the door.

A good thing. Bryce leaned against the wall in the hallway. He blew out the breath he'd been holding.

Another second with her and he would have been on his knees.

Sunlight stole through cracks in the wooden blinds. Dani stretched her arms over her head. She couldn't believe how rested she felt. No doubt sleeping on a real mattress, complete with a pillow top, and not her hard futon, made the difference. She'd never known what sleeping on a cloud would feel like until last night. She could get used to this.

And Bryce.

Thinking about him brought a smile to her face. Dani owed him a home-cooked breakfast this morning for his hospitality. She was sure Bryce would have preferred a different sleeping arrangement last night. Yet he hadn't pushed her into something she wasn't comfortable with or ready for. She appreciated that. And him.

For all her talk of not wanting a boyfriend, she had to admit Bryce had quickly changed her mind. Funny, the thought of not being with him bothered her more than the realization she was dating someone.

Dani threw back the duvet-covered comforter. She wanted to see Bryce.

A quick stop in the bathroom, and she headed out of the room. Seeing Bryce's bedroom door closed, Dani walked softly down the stairs and into the kitchen. She didn't want to wake him.

"Good morning," a female voice greeted her.

Dani looked over at the kitchen table and saw a pretty young woman sitting there. She had dark hair and green eyes like Bryce. "Caitlin?"

"You know who I am, but I haven't a clue about you." A smile, complete with dimples on either side of her mouth, lit up the woman's face. "My brother is good at keeping secrets."

The word *secret* prickled the hair at the back of Dani's neck, but only warmth flowed from Caitlin.

"Not really a secret," Dani said. "I'm Dani Bennett."

An older woman with the same green eyes as Caitlin and Bryce but lighter hair strode into the kitchen with a cloud of expensive-smelling perfume in her wake. She carried a bag of frozen French fries. "His car is in the garage. He must have forgotten and slept…"

The woman's surprised gaze flicked over Dani with curiosity. "Who are you?"

"This is Dani Bennett," Caitlin said. "Dani, this is my mother, Maeve."

With expertly highlighted hair, porcelain skin and designer clothing, Bryce's mother radiated beauty and wealth. She studied Dani with sharp eyes, as if she were trying to decide if she'd found a masterpiece or a forgery.

Talk about intimidating. Awkward. Humiliating.

But Dani wasn't about to let nerves get the best of her. She owed it to Bryce and herself not to act overwhelmed. "It's nice to meet you, Mrs. Delaney."

"I haven't been a Delaney in decades." The woman's friendly smile caught Dani off guard and made her seem more like a mother than a matriarch. She placed the bag of fries in the freezer. "Call me Maeve, please."

"Thanks, Maeve," Dani said, trying out the name. "I'm a friend of Bryce's."

Maeve raised a finely arched brow. "More than a friend, I'd say, since you're wearing the pajamas I gave him for Christmas."

Embarrassed, Dani cringed. She could only imagine what Bryce's family thought she was doing here on a Saturday morning, wearing his pajamas. "This isn't what you think. I mean, Bryce and I aren't… We didn't…"

Maeve laughed. "Then my son's not as smart a man as I thought he was. You're absolutely gorgeous."

An unwelcome heat crept into Dani's cheeks. She wished the ground would open up and swallow her. "Thank you."

"And modest, too," Caitlin said.

"Wherever did he find you, Dani?" Maeve asked.

Dani shifted her weight between her feet. "Blinddate-brides.com."

The two Delaney women smiled like a pair of Cheshire cats. They seemed happy over what they'd learned, not concerned.

Caitlin clapped her hands together. "Well, it's about time."

"I'll have to give Joelle a call," Maeve added.

Dani stood there, feeling as if they were speaking a foreign language.

"We've been telling Bryce to use his own site for dating since he founded it," Maeve explained. "But he says he's always working too much."

"Bryce does work hard," Dani said.

"We know," Caitlin said. "But he's always looking out for everyone else. It's nice to see that he's finally doing something for himself."

Maeve walked to the kitchen table and pulled out a chair. "Come over here and sit down for a little chat, Dani. I want to hear all about you and my son."

"Uh…sure." Dani sat, making a silent cry for help. She might have handled Gymguy on her own and the mimes on the bus, but the two Delaney women, who looked as if they'd stepped from a window display at Neiman Marcus, absolutely terrified her.

Where was her backup when she really needed him?

Bryce hopped out of bed. Dani was in his house, in his guest bedroom. No reason to stay in his room alone. Not when he could see her and maybe snag a good-morning kiss.

He opened the door to his bedroom. Her door was ajar.

Bryce peeked inside. "Dani?"

No reply. Just an empty bed with the covers turned back. He made a beeline for the stairs.

Halfway down the steps, the sound of feminine laughter drifted up. Not just Dani, either.

His heart plummeted to his feet.

Today was Saturday. He was supposed to go out to breakfast with Caitlin and…

His mother.

Bryce sprinted down the stairs, taking them three at a time. Poor Dani. He loved his mother, but she wasn't known for her subtlety. He skidded into the kitchen.

The three women sat at the kitchen table with steaming coffee cups in front of them. Uh-oh, they'd been there a while.

"Good morning, ladies," he said.

Three heads turned toward him at the exact same time like a trio of synchronized swimmers. But one person wasn't wearing the same uniform as the other two.

His gaze focused on Dani, trying to assess any damage already afflicted upon her. At least she was smiling. And he didn't see any blood or bruises. Though her cheeks had more of a pink tinge than normal.

"Did you sleep well?" he asked.

"I did. Thanks." She looked into her coffee cup as if she could see the secrets to the universe inside. "I was coming down to get my clothes out of the dryer—"

"And she found us," Caitlin interrupted.

"I used my key," Maeve added. "I see you forgot about our breakfast date this morning."

The warmth in Dani's gaze made his senses reel. "I've been busy."

"I can see that." Maeve smiled. "But, this time, I understand why. We've enjoyed chatting with your...friend."

His mother emphasized the last word.

"Dani is my friend." Bryce didn't want Dani to feel uncomfortable, but that seemed impossible under the circumstances. "She and I are dating."

"You might have mentioned it," Maeve said. "Her."

"He hinted, Mother," Caitlin added. "Remember what I told you, but I'm sure he just wanted to keep Dani all to himself."

As the color on Dani's cheeks deepened to a bright red, Bryce's chest tightened. His sister was right. He did want to keep Dani for himself. He wanted to pull her away from his family and spend the morning with her. The afternoon and evening, too.

Caitlin leaned forward. "Dani, I don't know if Bryce has talked to you about—"

"Later," he interrupted.

"But—"

"I promise."

His sister nodded, her face glowing as if she were walking down the aisle today, not in nine months. "I have a great idea. What if the four of us go to breakfast and then Mother and I can take Dani shopping?"

"That would be a lovely way to spend the day," Maeve said. "We could stop in at the Fairmont afterward. The Laurel Court puts on a nice afternoon tea."

"Oh, afternoon tea would be perfect." Caitlin clasped her hands together. "We could always go to the Garden Court at the Palace Hotel. I love the harpist there."

Dani sat still, not saying a word. A smile remained frozen on her face, but her eyes reminded him of a deer caught in the headlights of two semitrucks approaching from opposite directions. No matter which way she went, she was going to get hit head-on.

Bryce wasn't about to let that happen.

He placed his hands on her shoulders and gave a reassuring squeeze.

"Of course, there's always the Ritz-Carlton," Maeve said. "What do you think, Dani?"

"Well, there's always Lovejoy's Tea Room in Noe Valley," she said before he could put a stop to the nonsense. "It has more of a cozy, eclectic feel, but they have a high tea on the menu and the most delicious scones."

Pride filled Bryce. Dani didn't need his help at all.

"I've been to Lovejoy's," Maeve said. "It's a charming teahouse."

Caitlin nodded. "One of my sorority sisters had her baby shower there. It was so much fun. I can call for reservations."

"Another time." Bryce rubbed Dani's shoulders. "We have plans for today."

With the wind on her face, Dani hung off the side of the cable car later that day. She was enjoying Bryce's "plans." Who was she kidding? She couldn't have cared what they did as long as they were together.

The driver clanged the bell. And, like the old song her mother used to sing, zing went her heartstrings.

For Bryce.

She couldn't help herself. And that was…okay.

As she leaned farther away from the car, he tightened his hand around her waist.

Always the protector.

Dani didn't mind today. She glanced back at him. "I can't believe you were born in San Francisco and have never ridden a cable car. That's downright criminal."

He shrugged. "What can I say? I've never played tourist in my own town."

"You don't know what you're missing."

"I'm getting an idea."

So was she. Dani grinned, looking up at the overcast sky. More rain might be predicted, but she didn't care. The day was perfect, no matter what the forecast. The only thing missing—a rainbow.

The cable car stopped. Passengers disembarked. Bryce jumped off and extended his hand. Her fingers clasped his as he helped her down.

Pleasurable sensations of wanting tingled through her.

"Thank you for showing me San Francisco." He raised her hand to his mouth and kissed it. The beat of her heart quadrupled. "Fisherman's wharf, North Beach, Chinatown—"

"And now Union Square," she finished for him. "Though this is more your part of town so it's your turn to show me around."

Bryce took over as tour guide, leading her across Union Square. He stopped in front of a tall winged statue. "This is the goddess Victory. You and she have a lot in common."

Dani raised a brow. "Trying to soften me up with compliments?"

"It's either that or I'll have to buy you some chocolate."

"You've got me figured out pretty well."

He smiled. "I'm working on it."

And she knew he was. That pleased her.

The sounds of cars, trucks and buses on the four streets surrounding the square were loud, but Dani heard music. The haunting sounds of a lone violin filled the air. She looked around. A violinist stood on the corner. She smiled. That was one thing she loved about the city—the unexpected.

"There's something I've been wondering," Bryce said.

She focused her attention on him. "What?"

"How does an evening of mayhem with my crazy family and over two hundred of my mother's most intimate acquaintances sound?"

"Is this a trick question?" she asked.

"No. My mother is throwing Caitlin and Mark an engagement party next Saturday. Would you like to go?"

A family event? Dani quivered with excitement. "Yes, I'd like that very much. Thanks."

"Thank you." Relief filled his eyes. "If you'd said no, I don't think Caitlin would have forgiven me."

"Then it's a good thing I said yes."

With a nod, he led her to a crosswalk in the city's downtown shopping district. They stood on the corner waiting for the lights to change.

"You've got to promise me you won't hold my family against me, though. The Delaneys are an odd cast of characters. I come from a line of men who foresaw what land in San Francisco and the surrounding Bay Area would be worth someday. They bought as much as they could, whenever they could and held on to it. Thanks to their real estate acumen, my relatives now live off trust funds."

"Not you."

"I've never touched mine and my family can't understand why," he admitted. "I did accept my house. A graduation present from the family trust. But, like you, I want to make it on my own."

Her respect for Bryce shot off the scale. "You really do understand what I want to do."

"I told you we weren't so different."

She was beginning to think he was right. Dani smiled. "You did."

"And, as I've said before, I admire your determination."

His compliment sent a welcome shot of confidence flowing through her.

The light turned green. She stepped off the curb into the street. She jogged around a woman pushing a baby stroller and drinking from a Starbucks cup as they crossed the intersection.

Dani followed him through a white iron gate to a pedestrian-only narrow street dotted with umbrella-shaded tables.

"Maiden Lane used to be the red light district during the Barbary Coast era so I'm not sure where the 'Maiden' part came from," Bryce said, as tourists in baseball caps and sunglasses snapped pictures. He clasped his hand with hers. "But the street has become more upscale since then."

As she strolled with Bryce, Dani noticed the signs of the expensive boutiques and salons. Women dressed as if they were going to a fancy party and loaded down with shopping bags darted in and out of the shops. Even when Dani had earned more money at her last job, she hadn't shopped here. "It's nice."

"This is nice." Bryce rubbed her hand with his thumb. "I never thought I'd find someone I wanted to date using my own Web site."

"Me, either," she admitted. "I was pretty anti-dating."

"And now?"

A man in a fluorescent orange warm-up suit walked a tiny black dog.

"Not so much."

He smiled. "I'm happy we met, Dani Bennett."

"Me, too."

She noticed a pretty green dress displayed on a mannequin in the window of a boutique. She stopped to take a closer look. Now, that would be something to wear to the engagement party if she wanted to make a good impression.

"That's a pretty dress."

Dani nodded.

He pulled her over to the window. "Do you want to try it on?"

She shook her head. "New clothing isn't in my budget right now."

"You can still try the dress on," he said.

She shot him a look.

He made a face. "Don't tell me you've never window-shopped. Caitlin dragged me along on one of her arduous excursions and she said trying on clothes is half the fun, whether you buy them or not."

"I don't know." She stepped back. "There's no chance of me buying anything in there."

Bryce pulled her to the door. "Come on."

"I—"

"Trust me. It'll be fun."

Dani found herself inside an elegant boutique with pale green walls and gilded fixtures. Cheerful music from a string quartet played. The air smelled of flowers and money. All the women were dressed to the nines. She couldn't tell who was a customer or who worked there and felt out of place wearing her work clothes from yesterday. A tall, thin woman with long red hair walked toward them.

"Pick a few things to try on," he encouraged.

Dani selected two dresses, neither of which had price tags attached.

Bryce handed her a third. "I want to see how the color looks on you."

She shrugged. "Why not?"

"That's the spirit." He sat in a big overstuffed chair.

Gabrielle, the redhead, who looked more like a supermodel than a clothing salesperson, handed him a drink. "Fashion show time."

In the dressing room, Dani found matching shoes, compliments of Gabrielle, to try on with each of the dresses and changed into the green dress from the window.

"Come out here so I can see," Bryce called.

Dani studied herself in a full-length mirror. "It's a little short."

"I'd like to be the judge of that myself."

"Oh, boy." She wedged her feet into the coordinating shoes, heels higher than she normally wore, with more crystals than she could count, and teetered out of the dressing room. "Too short?"

"I was going to say just right." He grinned like a kid turned loose in a Lego store. "No more hiding those long legs of yours, okay?"

"I usually wear pants."

Bryce waved her off. "Try on the next dress."

Dani squeezed into a red cocktail dress. The halter neck style really accentuated her breasts, making her look like a hooker who might have worked this street during the city's bygone era. She gulped.

"Do you have it on?" Bryce asked.

"On is relative," she admitted. "There isn't much fabric."

"Out—now," he said, sounding impatient.

She jammed her feet into a pair of stilettos, afraid to look in the mirror, and carefully walked out of the dressing room so she wouldn't topple over.

Bryce's eyes widened. "Wow."

"Don't you think it's a bit…skimpy?" she asked.

"You look hot, but I'm sure there'd be a fight or two if you wore that out in public. But the dress would be great for an intimate dinner for two at home."

"I'd rather wear your sweats," she admitted.

"Comfort over style."

Dani smiled. "You know it."

"Are you having fun yet?" Bryce asked.

She nodded.

Satisfaction gleamed in his eyes. "Let's see the next one."

In the dressing room, she wiggled into the blue cocktail dress Bryce had selected. She stared at herself in the mirror, not recognizing her reflection.

She looked and felt like a princess. A warmth settled in the center of her chest. Was this how Marissa had felt when she'd finally found her wedding dress?

Dani slipped on the pair of silver slingback heels that actually fit and were reasonably comfortable for heels.

Feeling like the heroine from an animated movie, she pirouetted out of the dressing room.

"Stunning." Bryce leaned forward, cradling his drink in his hands. "That's my favorite."

"Mine, too." She touched the soft fabric with her fingertip. "But I'd better put on my own clothes in case someone wants to buy it."

In the changing room, Dani stepped out of the shoes. The other two dresses and shoes had been removed from the changing room.

Gabrielle handed her a glass of sparkling mineral water with a slice of lime. "For you."

The places where Dani shopped limited taking clothing into a dressing room to six items or fewer. The only thing the attendants handed customers were plastic numbers. She placed the drink on the small table in her dressing room. "Thanks."

"May I please have your dress once you have it off so I can put it on the hanger?"

"Sure." Dani closed the curtain and took off the dress. She reluctantly handed it through the slit in the drapes to a waiting Gabrielle.

"Thank you, Dani."

"You're welcome."

This was like no window-shopping expedition she'd ever been on before. Even the dressing room was luxurious, with silk curtains, overstuffed benches and gilded mirrors.

Dani put on her own clothing and walked out to find an empty chair. She looked around the shop. Bryce stood by the door with a glossy bag in his hand.

Her heart fell. "You didn't."

"The blue dress was made for you."

Dani started to speak, but noticed people staring at them. She exited the store. Bryce followed, carrying the bag.

"We were window-shopping, not buying," she said.

"That's before I saw you in the dress."

She stopped in front of the store next door. "I appreciate your thoughtfulness, but I don't feel comfortable with you buying me clothing."

"It's a gift," he said as if he'd bought her a latte at the corner coffee shop and not a designer cocktail dress and, guessing by the box in the bag, the shoes, too. "I'm sure you have something nice you could wear to the engagement party, but I wanted to do something special for you. Is that wrong?"

He looked so pleased with himself. She didn't want to hurt his feelings. "It's very sweet of you, but it's important to me that I do things myself. Buy things myself."

"Do you buy gifts for yourself?"

"No."

"You don't like gifts."

Dani noticed it wasn't a question. "I'm not really used to getting gifts."

"It's time for that to change." Bryce hugged her. His soap and water scent made her heady. "Let's start today."

She loved being in his embrace, with his strong arms wrapped around her. He made her feel safe and secure, as if he'd never let anything happen to her. She'd never felt this way with anyone before. And she liked the feeling. A little too much.

Dani stepped back. "I'm—"

"Not trying to be difficult," he finished for her. "Neither am I."

Stalemate.

She didn't know what to say or do. Her gaze strayed to the shopping bag. She looked away.

"You know, I took your advice and checked out some of those dating articles on the Web site you mentioned," Bryce said. "Compromise is the key to a successful relationship."

"Are we in a relationship?" she asked.

"You've worn my clothes, kissed me until I couldn't see straight, spent the night at my house and charmed my family." He smiled. "If we aren't in a relationship, we're pretty darn close."

The air whooshed from her lungs. This was more than she'd hoped for. She stared up at him. The affection in his eyes matched how she felt about him.

"What do you say now?" Bryce asked.

This was the last thing she'd thought she wanted, but a wellspring of joy flowed through her, settling at the center of her chest. Dani looked back at the shopping bag. "I guess I'd better learn to compromise."

CHAPTER TEN

To: "Englishcrumpet" <englishcrumpet@blinddatebrides.com>
"Kangagirl" <kangagirl@blinddatebrides.com>
From: "Dani" <sanfrandani@blinddatebrides.com>
Subject: You won't believe this!

I got your messages. Sorry I've missed our chats. I've been with Bryce. We're back together and spending all our free time together this week!!! Dinners, movies. I even taught him how to make bonbons. It's been incredible. He's such an amazing person. I know it's a little soon, but I think he might be the one. My one. Can you believe it? I'm attending his sister's engagement party tonight. Cross your fingers I make a good impression on his family. I'm nervous about that. I'll fill you in on all the details later. Hope all is well with you. Miss you! xoxox
-d

"I'M ALMOST ready."

Saturday night, Bryce heard Dani's panicky voice through the closed door to her walk-in closet. He didn't mind waiting. Anything to make things easier on her. "No rush."

To tell the truth, he was nervous, too, and dreading the evening ahead. All his extended family would be there. He felt like an outsider when the whole clan was together so he was glad to be bringing Dani with him. She understood him better than his own family ever had.

"Is the press really going to be there?" she asked from behind the closet door.

"Yes. Delaney events usually bring out the society columnists, but since I founded Blinddatebrides.com because of my sister and now she's met her future husband at the site, the engagement has become a human interest story."

"It's pretty unbelievable."

No kidding. And he didn't only mean Caitlin's engagement.

Bryce hadn't brought home a woman in almost five years. That had been his last "serious" relationship until its daytime talk show worthy breakup. He'd been dating casually—okay, sporadically—since then, but hadn't wanted another relationship. Not until he'd met Dani. And now he kept thinking he might have found more than just a girlfriend on Blinddatebrides.com himself.

The door to the closet opened. Footsteps tapped on the hardwood floor. Dani's heels.

Bryce turned.

Hot! Attraction hit fast and hard, sending his already warm blood into the red zone. "I didn't think you could look more beautiful than you did at the store. I was wrong."

Dani radiated beauty and warmth. He'd picked out the dress because the color matched her eyes. But the style accentuated pretty much every other part of her body. "You are totally captivating and very sexy."

And his.

Dani spun around on the balls of the silver slingback shoes. The fabric of her dress wrapped around her hips and thighs. The asymmetric hem made her legs look even longer. She gave a slight curtsy. "Thank you."

Her shy smile contrasted against her curvaceous body was a total turn-on. "If my father hits on you, I'm going to slug him."

"Don't worry, I'm too old for him."

Bryce's gaze lingered as he went from the top of her shiny blond hair to the V between her breasts to the curve of her hips to her delicate ankles and her hot-pink painted toenails. His heart rate kicked up a notch. No doubt other men's would, too. A protective instinct kicked in. "A couple of extra years won't matter in your case. But he's not the only one I'm worried about."

"Well…" Mischief gleamed in her eyes. "On the farm, parties never got going until a fight happened."

He laughed. "The Delaney crowd is much too civilized for throwing actual punches. They resort to verbal barbs to one's face and gossip behind one's back instead."

"Sounds like high school."

"Pretty close." The look of vulnerability flashing across her face brought him to her side in an instant. Bryce wrapped his arms around her. "But you won't have to worry about a thing. I'll be right there with you to make sure you feel safe and comfortable."

Dani gazed up at him. "I figured you weren't the kind of guy to desert me while he went off to socialize."

"Never. I have everything I need right here." He brushed his lips across the top of her hair. The scent of grapefruit filled his nostrils. "Is it totally sexist of me to say I'm going to like having the sexiest, most beautiful woman at the party on my arm?"

"Yes." A seductive smile spread across her shimmering glossed lips. "But since I'll be on the arm of the hottest man at the soirée, I'll let it slide.

"Soirée?"

She shrugged. "When in Rome…"

"You're going to fit in just fine, Miss Bennett."

Dani fluttered her eyelashes. "Why, thank you, Mr. Delaney."

He extended his arm, no longer dreading the evening ahead. "Shall we?"

Maeve Delaney-Stuart-Whitney-Roya-Mayer's house reminded Dani of Pemberley, with its marble floors, crystal chandeliers and uniformed servants milling about with trays of champagne and hors d'oeuvres. Dani glanced around the mansion, trying to imagine Bryce, an active and inquisitive little boy, growing up among the valuable artwork and antiques.

Tried and failed.

Standing at the doorway to a balcony, she watched Bryce weave his way through the crowded room with two drinks in his hands. He looked suave and debonair in his tailored suit, white shirt and tie. He stood out from the others. It wasn't his height or his looks, but his presence. He exuded power and, though he'd disagree with her, wealth. People followed him, trying to get his attention or catch his eye. Men who wanted his advice. Women who wanted him.

Dani didn't blame them. She wanted him, too.

Bryce said a word to one, nodded to another and continued toward her, his steps never faltering and his gaze never leaving hers.

Outside on the patio, he handed her a Cosmopolitan. "Did the animals leave you alone while I was gone?"

"I had a couple of close calls, but I survived unscathed."

A man with his tie askew yelled Bryce's name from the doorway. Bryce acknowledged him with a wave, then lowered his hand. His fingertips stroked her arm, sending tingles shooting up and down from the point of contact. "What happened?"

"Nothing you need to worry about. It was more funny than awkward."

"I just want to make sure you're comfortable."

"I'm better than comfortable." She raised her glass. "I'm Cinderella at the ball with Prince Charming at my side."

"At least you won't have to worry about the clock striking midnight," he teased. "Your dress and ride home have no expiration time."

"Good to know." She stared up into his concerned eyes. "What?"

"Please tell me what happened while I was gone."

"It was nothing."

Bryce raised a brow.

"If you really want to know, your cousin Simone asked me who did my breast augmentation because she thought they looked so natural."

"She's been redoing herself part by part," he explained. "Breasts are next."

"No wonder she seemed so disappointed to find out mine are real, but I appreciated the compliment."

"You should." He eyed her chest momentarily. "Anything else?"

"I bumped into your great-uncle Edward. Or he bumped into me." Dani grinned. "I think he wanted to cop a feel."

"He's known for that."

She took a sip of the pink-colored drink. The martini was strong. Better limit herself to two tonight. Especially since they'd already drank champagne during a toast to Caitlin and Mark. "See, it was nothing."

"I'm not leaving you again," Bryce said. "I told you I wouldn't desert you."

"I told you I wanted a drink, but didn't feel like pushing my way through the crowd to the bar. It's okay," she said. "I'm doing fine. I was intimidated when we arrived, but everyone has been so welcoming, especially your mother. Things have been much better than I imagined. And Caitlin and Mark are such a cute couple and so nice."

"That's because they, and the rest of my family, like you."

Music played. She couldn't tell if it was a live band or a DJ. "Good, because I like them."

"Even my great-uncle Edward?" Bryce asked.

She nodded. "He's funny. He told me if he were fifty years younger he'd give you a run for your money over me. Then he said if I wanted to fly to Las Vegas and marry him tonight he wouldn't make me sign a prenup."

"What did you tell him?" Bryce asked.

"I told him I couldn't desert my date tonight, but if things didn't work out with you, we could talk later."

Bryce laughed. "No wonder he stopped me on my way back from the bar and asked my intentions toward you."

"Oh, no." She cringed. "I thought he knew I was kidding."

"I'm sure he did, but hope springs eternal, especially when enchanting young women are involved," Bryce said. "His words, not mine."

Dani smiled.

"So is this the woman who Edward called dibs on?" A handsome man with black hair and green eyes approached. Dressed in a tuxedo, he looked like an older, bronzed version of Bryce. "Hello, son."

Bryce's eyes narrowed. He placed his hand on Dani's lower back. "Father, this is Dani Bennett. Dani, my father, Peter."

Peter kissed the top of her hand, holding on to it too long to be considered proper or polite. "Edward wasn't kidding. You are stunning."

The man looked at her as if she were the special of the day he could order off the menu, not his son's date. "Thank you."

A photographer asked them to pose. Dani stood between the two Delaney men, both of whom had an arm around her. The flash of the camera blinded her.

She blinked.

When the spots went away, she noticed Peter checking her out. Bryce might resemble Peter in looks, but that was where the similarities ended. His father exuded charm, but his tone and mannerisms came off as too smooth. Too practiced. Too superficial.

No wonder Peter Delaney went for younger woman. Any older female would see right through his gentlemanly façade to the player underneath. He seemed like the type of guy who would trade in wives along with his cars when their leases expired.

Dani appreciated Bryce's protective, almost possessive hand on her, and inched closer.

"Don't get all territorial on me, son," Peter teased. "I promise not to steal this one away from you."

This one? Dani thought.

"Not that you don't have excellent taste. But your last girl-friend cost me a bundle." Peter laughed. "Of course, she would have cost more if I'd married her."

Ick.

"It's not marriage that cost you, Father. It's the divorces," Bryce said dryly.

"What can I say? I'm a sucker for a beautiful woman. And so, apparently, are you." Peter smiled again at Dani.

His words rankled. "Bryce is no sucker, Mr. Delaney. Not that I would ever try to sucker him in the first place."

Peter's eyes widened. "A woman with a sharp tongue who speaks her mind, eh?"

"Dani's more than beautiful," Bryce said. "She's also smart."

"Then you'll need to watch yourself even more, son." Peter appraised her from head to toe. "Those smart ones are dangerous."

No doubt the history between these two involved more than your typical father/son issues. She wondered if Bryce had gotten over what had happened or if that was why an attractive man like him was still single.

Sipping her drink, Dani stared at the two men.

An undercurrent charged the air.

"I'm not worried," Bryce said finally.

"Maybe you should be." Peter's gaze bounced between her and Bryce. "Well, I'm off to find my fiancée. She's probably gotten herself lost trying to find the restroom."

"Same thing happened when she was here for one of Caitlin's sleepovers in high school." Bryce raised his glass. "Good luck."

"You, too." Peter turned his attention on Dani again. Her breasts, actually. "It was a pleasure meeting you. Catch you two later."

He disappeared into the crowd.

"Sorry about that," Bryce said.

"No worries." She had questions, lots of them, but tonight was neither the time nor place to ask about something that had happened long before she'd entered the picture. "Let's just enjoy the party."

He kissed her cheek. "Come on."

"Are we going to meet more people?"

"Nope." Bryce held her hand and led her inside and through the throng of guests toward the door. "Cinderella should dance at the ball."

She stopped. "You don't like to dance."

He grinned. "But you do."

Later that night, Bryce stood with Dani at the door of her apartment. This was only the beginning for them. "Tonight was…"

"Magical," she finished for him, then rose on tiptoe to kiss him on the lips.

Magical was right. Especially her kiss.

"Thank you so much for inviting me to the engagement

party and dancing with me," she said, her cheeks flushed and her eyes sparkling. "I had the best time."

"Uncle Edward and my father aside."

"Uncle Edward was cute."

"And harmless. My father, however, is the ultimate player," Bryce explained. "He doesn't respect women or treat them well, but he has enough money he's willing to spend that some don't mind."

"Like your girlfriend?"

"Ex-girlfriend," Bryce clarified. "She had her eyes on my father from the beginning and used me to get to him."

"I'm sorry." Dani reached up and caressed his face. "I hope you know I would never…"

"I trust you, Dani."

He kissed her gently, soaking up the feel and taste of her. And then something changed. Something in him ignited, catching fire. He couldn't get enough of her kiss—of her. With his hands in her hair, he backed her up against the door. She pressed against him. His lips moved over hers. Dani tugged at his shirt, impatient. She was with him all the way.

Bryce pulled back to look her in the eyes; her pupils expanded.

Her face flushed, she moistened her swollen lips. "I think we know where this is going."

"I hope so."

That shy smile of hers appeared. "I really like you, Bryce. I want to invite you in, but I don't want to make any mistakes or do something we might regret later if we go too fast."

Not what he wanted to hear, but so what? She was worth waiting for.

He took a deep breath. And another.

"You are a smart one." Bryce looked into her eyes. His affection for Dani grew with each passing second. "We've got plenty of time ahead of us."

"Us," she repeated, her eyes twinkling.

Bryce nodded. He liked the sound of *us*. More than he'd thought he would.

"And, for the record," he said, running his finger along her jawline, "I like you, too."

On Monday, the clock still hadn't struck midnight. Sure, Dani was back in her routine and at work, but she felt as if she were still floating from Saturday night. The entire weekend, really. She'd joined Bryce and his family for brunch on Sunday. All of the Delaneys made her feel so welcome. And Bryce made her feel so…loved.

Forget about falling for him.

She'd fallen, body and soul.

Dani might as well wrap her heart in pretty paper, tie the package with a neat bow and stick a tag with Bryce's name on it.

Could love happen so quickly?

Marissa and Grace thought so. Dani wanted to believe, too. She didn't know what else this all-consuming wonderfulness could be.

An emergency meeting at Blinddatebrides.com meant she couldn't see Bryce tonight, but he'd called, texted and e-mailed her. That had kept a wide smile on her face the rest of the day at work.

At her apartment, Dani found a breathtaking bouquet of stargazer lilies waiting for her with a note:

Thinking of you. Missing you. Can't wait to see you. B.

Happiness consumed her. Definitely love. She held on to the vase and swirled. She couldn't wait to hop onto chat and tell her friends. A happy ending might be in her future after all. She sure hoped so.

Tuesday morning, Dani sat in her cubicle, thinking of ways to build the Hookamate.com community. Even though she had two job interviews, courtesy of Bryce's contacts, lined up for later in the week, she wouldn't allow herself to do a lousy job at Hookamate.com, even if she hated working here. She'd made up for not going on any more dates by writing some killer content for the site that had earned her high fives from the engineers.

But each ping from her e-mail in-box captured her attention. She wanted to hear from Bryce, even though she was meeting him for lunch in less than an hour.

"I knew you were good, Danica," James said from the opening of her cubicle. "I just didn't know how good."

She kept working at her computer. "Is revenue up again this month?"

"Yes, and traffic, too, but that's not what I'm talking about." Paper crinkled. "Way to go, getting on the inside. I've got to hand it to you, Danica. I didn't know you had it in you."

The approval in his voice made her nervous. Made her turn. He held a copy of the *Life* section of the newspaper in his hand. "What are you talking about?"

He showed her the society page, specifically a picture of her with Bryce and his father. The description identified her as the date of Bryce Delaney, CEO of Blinddatebrides.com.

Her stomach roiled. She hadn't wanted James to find out about her and Bryce this way. Not until she had a new job and was ready to quit.

"Congrats on hooking a really big fish," her boss said. "What kind of inside info have you found out?"

Inside info?

And then she realized… James thought she was using Bryce for information, not dating him for real.

"Nothing. I—"

"Take your time." Excitement filled James's voice. "Get him to trust you."

Dani raised her chin. "Bryce already trusts me."

"So soon? You must be good."

She frowned at James's suggestive tone. "I'm not dating Bryce to get information. I really like him. Our jobs have no impact on us."

At least no longer. Thank goodness.

"Perhaps not on him, but you can use this to *our* advantage."

The emphasis on the word *our* made her straighten. "I'm sorry, James, but I can't do that to Bryce or myself. I have more ethics than that."

"Ethics, huh." James's features hardened. His eyes narrowed. He stood, towering above her, boldly intimidating. "Don't forget you signed a non-disclosure agreement and a non-compete clause when you accepted this position."

"So?" Dani asked.

"So if you're not getting info out of Bryce, I will have to assume you're spying on Hookamate for him. And that's a job-terminating offense."

Bryce hated seeing Dani so torn up. He sat next to her on a park bench and put his arm around her. "But James didn't actually fire you."

"No." Dani's voice trembled. She clasped her hands together. No doubt if she hadn't, she'd be wringing them. "Not yet anyway, but his intent was clear. I use my being your new girlfriend to get info or I lose my job."

"That's blackmail." Anger burned. She didn't deserve to be treated this way. "James is using you to get to me. He's had it in for me ever since I quit and founded Blinddatebrides.com. That's the only reason he decided to start his own online dating Web site."

"Did you know he won't even say the name of your Web site? He calls it bdb.com."

"The guy is an idiot." Bryce pulled Dani against him. "Just quit. I'll cover your expenses until you find a new job."

She straightened, drawing away from him. "I appreciate the offer, but I can deal with James on my own."

Her independence was admirable, but unnecessary. "This isn't only about you now. I feel responsible for what's happened. And I know James better than you—"

"Please don't," Dani urged. "You're Caitlin's big brother, not mine."

"My feelings for you aren't at all brotherly."

Dani's hair caught on the wind. Simply beautiful.

Who was Bryce kidding? There was nothing simple about her. She was complex, challenging and even difficult at times. He wouldn't have her any other way.

"I care about you, Dani."

"I care about you, too, but it's my job at stake. You remember how I told you my father left us?"

Bryce nodded.

"Well, my mother had relied on him for everything. When he took off, she was left with nothing except the four of us girls. She'd dropped out of college to get married, never worked a day in her life and didn't even know their checking account number. She learned her lesson and wanted to make sure me and my sisters didn't repeat her mistakes. She taught us to take charge of our own lives and ourselves. That's what I've been trying to do. That's what I need to do with James. I can handle this." Her eyes implored him. "I need to handle this."

He squeezed her hand reassuringly. "You can handle anything."

"Thanks for understanding. That means…a lot to me."

"I do understand, but just know I'm here if you need backup."

"Okay."

But, back in his office, he wasn't so sure. James's behavior had everything to do with Bryce and Blinddatebrides.com, not Dani. He hated seeing her caught in the middle and wanted to keep her from getting hurt.

Bryce knew she was attending an afternoon training class off-site when he arrived at Hookamate.com.

James didn't look surprised to see him. "You're here about Danica."

Bryce seethed with anger, but losing control wouldn't solve anything. The last time he'd lost his temper and argued with Dani, he'd almost lost her. He wasn't about to do that again.

He set his jaw, determined to put an end to James's dirty dealings, once and for all. "Stop taking out your problems with me on Dani. Keep her out of this and stay away from my company or I'll bring legal action against you."

"You have no proof." James glowered. "No prosecutor would touch the case."

"They will if Dani testifies."

"Is that all the wunderkind Bryce Delaney can come up with? A frivolous lawsuit to spend his trust fund on." James cackled. "You think a jury would believe a disgruntled former employee who's sleeping with my top competitor?"

Bryce's blood ran cold. "Former employee?"

"Why, yes." James smirked. "If there was any wrong-doing, Danica's involved. What else can I do, but fire her?"

Fired.

Dani's shoulders sagged and her bottom lip quivered.

Bryce hadn't listened to her. He hadn't trusted her to handle James on her own. Even after she'd explained why she needed to.

Carrying the box containing items from her desk and cubicle, Dani trudged up the stairs of her apartment building.

I thought more of you, Danica. I never expected you would send your lover in to fight your battle.

James's words splintered her heart.

She'd lost everything in one fell swoop.

Because her boss was a jackass.

Because her boyfriend was a control freak.

Because she was a starry-eyed idiot.

How could she let this happen?

Dani had spent her entire life trying to make something of herself. To be someone. To do everything on her own so she'd never be in the same position as her mother had years ago.

Yet she'd trusted Bryce, believed in him and that had cost Dani her job. And…

Her heart.

Tears pricked her eyes. She blinked them away.

Turning the corner, Dani spotted Bryce.

Concern clouded his eyes. "Dani—"

Just for a moment, she longed to sink against him, to have him hold her and make everything better, but that would make James's accusations true. She wasn't going to rely on Bryce. She couldn't.

Dani swallowed around the gigabyte-sized lump clogging her throat. "Go away."

"We have to talk."

Raw pain stabbed her heart. Dani fought against the sting of tears. She was suddenly six years old, standing on the driveway as her dad loaded his suitcases in the trunk. *I love you, Danica. I love all of you. I'll come back. Promise.*

But he hadn't and didn't.

Her dad had said one thing and done another.

Just like Bryce.

Her chest tightened as if being squeezed by an extra-large vice grip. "Why should I believe anything you have to say to me now?"

Bryce's gaze sought hers. "You're upset."

"Damn right I am."

He pressed his lips together in a thin line. "I don't want to argue about this. Fighting won't solve anything."

His coolness and rationality irritated her. Her heart pounded. Her heart ached. Every nerve ending shrieked. And he stood there acting like Mr. Cool. "Neither do I."

"Good. Let's—"

"You don't get it." *Or me.* The unspoken words scorched her throat. "I don't want to talk to you."

"Don't do this, Dani."

Dani fumbled with her keys, opened the door and hurried inside. She dropped the box. It thudded against the floor. Sort of like her heart had done when James told her Bryce had stopped by and she was fired. "You cost me my job."

"James cost you your job." Bryce followed her inside the apartment and closed the door behind him. "That guy is a sleaze."

"That guy is—was—my boss."

"You deserve a better one."

"Maybe. Or maybe I deserve a better boyfriend."

His expression froze for a moment. "I have a lead on a job opening. A great opportunity for you. I talked to a friend this afternoon—"

"You mean you went behind my back. Again."

He frowned. "If you mean James, I did you a favor."

"A favor?" She squared her shoulders. "You did the exact opposite of what I asked you to do."

"Yeah." Bryce exhaled. "I'm sorry. I was trying to protect—"

"Your company?"

"My company, my employees. And you."

She took a deep breath, trying to keep herself together, when all she wanted to do was shout and cry. "I don't need you to protect me."

"Yeah, you do."

"I don't want you to protect me," she clarified.

"What you want and what you need are two different things."

She rubbed her tight neck. "I told you I needed to take care of this myself."

"I told you, I was trying to protect you."

His calm manner sent her temper soaring. "You don't want to protect. You want to control. Me, Caitlin, every single one of your clients on Blinddatebrides.com with that stupid matching program of yours."

His mouth twisted. "That program said we were highly compatible."

"There must be a bug in the code." Dani stared down her nose at him. "I need someone who respects my independence."

His eyes darkened, the green turning into that of a stormy sea. "You care more about your damn independence than our relationship."

"What relationship?" she countered, crossing her apartment to put much-needed distance between them. "You want me to trust your judgment about James and my job, but there's no commitment between us. You've said we're dating, but you've never called me your girlfriend or asked us to be exclusive or said…"

"Those are just words." He took a step toward her, then stopped. "What I do is more important than what I say. I did what I thought was best for you today."

Tears choked Dani. "You have no idea what's best for me."

A muscle throbbed at his temples. "I can fix this."

"You've done enough." She stood in one corner with an ocean of room separating her from Bryce. "I've fallen in love with you, but being with you has never been about what your wealth and influence could do for me. By going to James the way you did, you acted as if it was. As if I were no different than any of the women your father marries and divorces."

Bryce's nostrils flared. "I'm nothing like my father."

"No, you're like mine. Promising one thing and doing another."

He made a fist with his hands, then stretched out his fingers. "You won't let me do anything for you."

"That's because you want to do everything for me."

Dani waited for him to deny it. He didn't.

"I…" Her voice cracked. "I want you to go."

Bryce's jaw clenched. "I know I overstepped, Dani, but is this what you really want?"

No. She wanted him to say he loved her, even though she was angry with him. She wanted him to say he would never leave her, even though she'd told him to go away.

She wanted…the impossible.

Her pounding heart felt as if it might explode.

Dani might want those things from Bryce; she might want him. But she didn't need him; she didn't need anyone.

She raised her chin. "Yes, I want you to go."

CHAPTER ELEVEN

DANI took a deep breath. Her fingers trembled on her laptop keyboard. She typed…

To: "Grace", "Marissa"
From: "Dani"
Subject: Hey!
Thanks for the e-mails and IMs. I knew you guys would understand why I had to cancel my Blinddatebrides account and make a clean break. My landlord found someone who wanted an apartment ASAP so I packed up and rented a truck. I'm now at my mom's trying to regroup. Sorry I can't chat. Dial-up sucks. Hope you both are well. Miss you! TTYS.
Love,
Dani

She hit "send" and logged off so her mom could receive phone calls. No DSL or cable to connect to the Internet at her mom's trailer.

It was strange being back on the farm.

Dani had been here two days. It felt like two years the way time was passing so slowly, and she was hurting so badly.

She'd gone from standing on the edge of forever, of

having the elusive pot of gold at the end of the rainbow within her grasp, to falling into an endless spiral of regrets, heartache and tears.

Lots and lots of tears.

She missed Bryce more than she'd thought possible. And she felt as if she had only herself to blame.

Something clanged outside.

Dani rose from the kitchen table and walked to the window. Outside, the wind chime they'd made out of silverware for their mom on Mother's Day hung on a rusted nail. A fork with missing tines blew into a bended spoon. She laughed.

"Now that's a sound I like to hear." Dolly Bennett spoke with a Southern accent even though she'd only spent the first twenty years of her life in Mississippi. "There hasn't been enough laughter around here since you all moved away."

"I can't believe you kept that old wind chime, Mom."

"That's a masterpiece, darlin'. No way could I get rid of it." Her mom handed Dani a plate with freshly baked choco-late-chip cookies. "I know these are your favorites. Maybe they'll help you find that beautiful smile of yours."

Dani set the plate on the table behind her and took a bite of one. The still warm chocolate chips melted in her mouth. "Thanks, Mom. For the cookies. For letting me come here and stay."

"No thanks are necessary. You always have a place here." Her mother smoothed Dani's hair. "This is your home, no matter where you end up making your mark on the world."

"Home."

Dolly pulled her into a hug. "And it feels a lot more homey when you girls are here with me. That's for sure."

Emotion welled within Dani. For so long, she'd been searching and dreaming about finding a place to call home when, in fact, she'd had one all along.

Home wasn't something you bought, but the place where you

were surrounded by love. Whether a house or a beat-up station wagon or an old two bedroom, one bath single-wide trailer.

She was home.

An unfamiliar contentment filled her.

And this was the perfect place to pull herself together and figure out what she wanted to do next.

"Your father's here," Joelle said from the doorway to Bryce's office. "Do you want me to send him in or tell him you're busy?"

Peter Delaney visited the office when he wanted Bryce to act as a go-between with his mother. The two only spoke when attending the same social event, where they limited their exchanges to polite platitudes. Bryce had assumed the mediator role as a child, but dealing with one of his parents' endless battles when he felt so broken up inside didn't appeal to him in the slightest.

"Did he say why he wants to see me?" Bryce asked.

"Only that it was important," Joelle said.

He stared at the code on his monitor. He'd thrown himself into work for over a week now, but the long hours hadn't made him feel any better over what had happened with Dani. If anything, work made him feel worse. They'd met through the Web site. Every time he logged on, he thought about her.

Dani would never admit she needed anything, not even love, if that meant she had to rely on someone except herself. She hadn't wanted his help. She hadn't wanted him. And there wasn't a damn thing he could do about it. Not unless he wanted to be accused of trying to "control."

"Boss?" Joelle asked.

Maybe talking with his father would take his mind off her. Something had to. Bryce saved and closed the file. "Send him in."

A minute later, his father sauntered in, checking out Joelle's backside as she walked away. "How's it going, son?"

"Fine."

Peter sat. He studied the stacks of papers on the desk, grimaced and looked at Bryce. "Your mother's worried about you."

"Caitlin called you."

"No, Maeve called me herself."

Bryce straightened.

"That's why I'm here," Peter admitted. "She's very concerned about you, Bryce. You haven't returned any of her phone calls."

Bryce wasn't ready to tell his family he was no longer dating Dani. He hadn't wanted the questions or the company. "It's been a hectic week."

"You haven't been home. Your mother and I stopped by your house last night."

"You and Mother together at my place. I hope I still have a house to go home to."

Peter frowned. "We may not be the best parents, but we're adult enough to put aside our differences for our children's sake."

A bitter guilt coated Bryce's mouth. Even he could see his father was here trying to help. "Sorry. Rough week."

"Were you with Dani last night?"

"No, I slept here at the office," Bryce admitted. "I've been putting in more hours lately."

Not that he'd been getting anything done.

The lines on his father's face relaxed. "Your mother will be relieved."

"You seem relieved, too."

"We like Dani, but you haven't been together long. Your mother is worried you might be rushing into something. She thinks you might be thinking about following in Edward's footsteps and eloping to Las Vegas."

Bryce winced. "Not going to happen."

"But if things do get more serious, you have to start thinking about a prenup."

He shook his head. "I don't have to worry about that."

Not now.

"One of these days, you will," Peter counseled. "You have so much to lose, including half of your share of this company."

"I—"

"Hear me out, Bryce," Peter said. "You said Dani was a smart woman."

"She is."

"Her brains match her body."

"They do."

"Your mother is like that." Peter's eyes narrowed. "Women like your mother will take you for everything you've got."

"Dani's not like my mother."

Peter raised a brow. "How do you know?"

"I trust her." And he did, Bryce realized in spite of everything. "Dani wants to be independent. She won't take anything from me."

Not even my heart.

Peter stood. "Just remember, son, a man has every right to protect himself."

You don't want to protect. You want to control.

Dani had been right about his trying to control things with her, but he hadn't known the reason until now.

Being in control was the way Bryce protected himself.

The realization brought a rush of shame and a flash of clarity.

But controlling things hadn't worked. He'd lost what mattered most.

Dani.

Peter walked toward the door. "Call your mother."

"I will," Bryce said. "Thanks for coming by."

His father smiled. "Catch you later, son."

Bryce dialed Dani's cell number. One ring, two rings. The line connected. Every one of his muscles tensed.

"I'm sorry," an automated voice said. "This wireless number is no longer in service."

He grabbed his keys, told Joelle to cancel all his appointments for the day and drove to Dani's apartment. He parked illegally, not caring if he got a ticket or was towed.

He'd known what she'd needed, but done the exact opposite. Sure he'd thought about her, but he'd also been thinking about himself. Just like…her father.

Bryce took the stairs three at a time. He knocked on Dani's door.

Something clicked. The knob turned.

He breathed a sigh of relief.

The door opened.

"What do you want?" asked a man dressed in a pirate costume complete with eye patch and a real parrot on his shoulder.

Bryce's heart fell. "I was looking for the woman who used to live here."

"She's gone."

"Gone," the parrot mimicked. "Long gone."

"Do you know where she went?"

"Nope, but if you find her tell her thanks for cleaning this place so well."

Bryce walked back to his car, trying to figure out what to do next. He had never let anything stand between him and what he wanted and he'd never wanted anything, he'd never needed anyone, as much as he wanted and needed Dani.

Bryce was going to make things right. He would make things work. Somehow.

But first he had to find her.

Dani speared a clump with a pitchfork. She hadn't mucked stalls in over a year and already the muscles in her arms and shoulders ached. Good thing she'd remembered gloves or she'd have blisters on her hands.

Her pitchfork scraped the wheelbarrow.

The smell of horse and hay reminded her of the day at the stable with Bryce. Her mind burned with the memory.

Of her riding.

Of the sexy smile on Bryce's face as he'd watched her.

Of the passionate kiss they'd shared.

Stop thinking about him. Dani squeezed her eyes closed, trying to force the images from her mind.

It was over. She opened her eyes. Over.

She stabbed another clump.

The horse from the next stall neighed.

Her boots crunched beneath the mixture of straw and shavings.

"Just be patient, Penny," Dani said to the pretty little chestnut mare. "Your stall is next."

The horse snorted.

"I know how you feel." She leaned against the pitchfork handle and rolled her shoulders. "It's not easy being patient."

But Dani finally had a plan in place. She wiped her sweaty forehead with her forearm. She'd spent the last three days e-mailing her résumés to more companies. This morning, she'd even had a phone interview for a position in Raleigh, North Carolina. That was on the other side of the country, but nothing was stopping her from taking a job anywhere in the world. No one cared where she ended up except her mom, and she only wanted Dani to be happy wherever that might be.

She sifted through the clumps. The physical work felt good, satisfying.

"I wondered whether you'd be wearing a bandana," a much too familiar voice said.

As Dani clutched the pitchfork handle, she pivoted toward the doorway.

Bryce stood at the entrance to the stall. Her stomach fell to the tips of her paddock boots. He stared at her as if he were seeing her for the first time. And liked what he saw. Dani ground her boot against the floor.

She stole another glance his way. Sweat beaded on his forehead as if he were nervous about something. Not so calm and collected today. That surprised her.

He also looked out of place in his dress pants and Oxford shirt with the sleeves rolled up and the top button undone at his neck.

Out of place, but handsome as ever. Not that she cared what he looked like, Dani reminded herself.

"How did you find me?" she asked.

"Once I figured out you'd moved, I found your two friends' user names on a chat log I had. Unfortunately for me, Kangagirl and Englishcrumpet weren't about to give you up until I'd convinced them I had your best interests in mind. But they were easier to convince than your mother."

Dani's mouth dropped open. She closed it. "My mother?"

Bryce nodded. "I spent the last hour talking to her."

"Whatever you said must have worked."

Another nod.

"You went to a lot of trouble to find me." She eyed him warily. "Why?"

"I wanted to see you."

She noticed the dirt smudges on the sides of his fine leather shoes. "All that just to see me."

"And to explain."

"Go ahead then." Dani wanted to feel indifferent and kept her voice steady, but inside she trembled. Heaven help her, she wanted to hear what he had to say. "I'm listening."

"Before I say anything—" he strode across the stall toward her "—I need to do this first."

"Do—"

Bryce pressed his lips firmly against hers, taking what he wanted and giving back what Dani so desperately needed. His warm, wet kiss filled her up, and she wanted more. She kissed him back with an eagerness of her own. As he pulled her closer, she wrapped her arms around him. The pitchfork crashed to the floor of the stall.

Bryce pulled back, his gaze never leaving hers.

Oh, my. Oh, no. Dani wiped her mouth with the back of her gloved hand, afraid what her response to his kiss might have told him. She raised her chin. "Something else you think I need?"

"Something I needed." His eyes gleamed. Anger or something else, she couldn't tell. "I need you, Dani."

Her breath caught in her throat. She hadn't been expecting that.

"I'm sorry for not trusting you to handle James on your own," he said, his tone genuine and his voice strong. "I thought all this time I only wanted to protect the people I care about, but you're right. I've only been trying to control things. That's my way of protecting myself. My heart."

The sincerity of his words, the honesty in his eyes, brought tears to her eyes. Deep inside, a sliver of hope sparked.

"I've been doing that ever since my parents' divorce to keep from getting hurt, but I didn't realize what I was doing until you pointed it out."

"I appreciate you coming all this way to say that." She cleared her dry throat. "It means…a lot."

"You mean a lot to me," Bryce continued. "You said I was like your father, but I'm not him. I'm here. I'm not going anywhere. Even if you push me away, I will still love you."

His words reverberated through her. The oxygen seemed to evaporate from the air. She might as well be twenty feet underwater, the way she struggled to breathe.

Bryce loved her.

"I've needed to hear you say that," she said. "Even though you said they were just words."

"Words are important, and I can say them as many times as you want."

"Thanks, but saying the words doesn't change things." Dani wanted to ignore the truth, but couldn't. "You like being in control, Bryce. You like protecting people. That's who you are, and I'm afraid I'll lose myself, the way my mother did with my father, if I'm with you."

"I know being independent is important to you, but I love you. I have to be able to protect you. You're strong enough, though, to stand up to me and let me know when you need help or when you don't. And I'm smart enough to learn." He raised her chin with his fingertip. "You're not your mother. You've never been her."

A million thoughts ran through Dani's mind. But only one came to the forefront, as clear as the Golden Gate Bridge on a sunny day.

Bryce.

"You're right. I'm not." She stared up at him. "But I never wanted to be hurt again, the way my father hurt me. I figured if I didn't rely on anyone, it couldn't happen again."

"I never wanted to hurt you, Dani."

"I see that now." Her cheeks warmed. "And I never meant to hurt you, either."

"We've both been protecting ourselves."

She nodded. "I'm sorry, Bryce. I've been using anything I could—your background and your money—the same way I used my baggy clothes, to keep you at a distance. Just like a heroine from a Jane Austen novel."

"That's okay." He smiled. "So long as I don't lose you to the Colonel."

"Don't worry about him." Dani removed her gloves and placed her hand on Bryce's chest. His heart beat beneath her palm. "You might be a Web tycoon, but you're also a caring man who reaches out to others, whether it's me, your family or Blinddatebrides.com users looking for love. You're definitely Colonel Brandon material."

"Even without a uniform?"

Warmth flowed through her veins. She nodded. "You, Bryce Delaney, are my Colonel Brandon."

Bryce's smile widened. "From the moment you entered my life, I needed you. I'll always be here for you. I love you, Dani Bennett."

"Oh, Bryce." Joy overflowed from her heart. "I love you, too."

He pulled her into his arms and kissed her. A kiss of hope. A kiss of promise.

"You decide what you want to do yourself and what you don't. I'll support you either way." He tightened his arms around her. "Together we can make our dreams come true."

She gazed up at him. "That sounds wonderful, but it's not as simple as that."

"No?"

"For this to work and to last, we have to trust each other. Take care of me, but let me take care of you, too. I'll tell you what I'm thinking and feeling and you have to do the same."

"I'm not used to being taken care of, but I want this to work and to last. I'm willing to try," he said.

"You said you're smart enough to learn."

"That I did," Bryce admitted. "Have no worries, Miss Bennett, I am and I will."

Tingles exploded inside of her. "So we're back together, dating again."

"I think we've skipped right on over to serious relationship."

"Fine with me."

"Me, too." He brushed his lips across the top of her head. "Now we just have to figure out what comes next."

"That's easy," she said without any hesitation. "We head back to San Francisco."

"You're sure about that?"

She nodded. "I finally know where home is."

Bryce kissed her gently on the lips. A strange expression crossed his face. "This isn't how I planned things, but hang on."

Confused, Dani watched him run out of the stall and return with a large box that he placed on the ground. "What...?"

He dropped to his knee.

"You'll ruin your pants," she said.

"I can buy a new pair."

He held on to her hand.

A mixture of anticipation and nerves made her hold her breath. She was too stunned to believe, too hopeful to doubt.

He stared up into her eyes as if she were the earth and heaven to him. "Being without you has only made it clearer that I want to be with you always. I don't want you to ever question what I mean by us being in a relationship. Will you marry me, Dani Bennett?"

Her heart soared, but her brain dragged her back to the ground. Was marriage to Bryce what she wanted?

Her heart screamed the answer. It was time to move forward with this man who loved her, a man she loved back.

"Yes." Dani laughed. "Of course I'll marry you. I love you, Bryce."

"I love you."

He stood and sealed the proposal with a kiss.

"Ever since I was a little girl, I never felt like I belonged anywhere. But when I'm with you, I do." Dani smiled up at him through tears of happiness. "I feel safe, secure and loved. Nothing else matters as long as we're together."

"I don't have an engagement ring for you, but I do have these." He removed the top from the box and pulled out a pair of new paddock boots. "I bought these for you after we went to look at the horse. I figured you could use an extra pair. One to wear when you're hanging around the stable and another pair for when you ride."

Dani touched the shiny leather. "These are more practical than any ring."

"You're still getting a ring. I want to put a big one on your finger. Not practical, but you deserve it. And I want the world to know that you're with me."

"Do you plan to carry me off like some caveman, too?" she teased.

He grunted. "If that's what it takes."

Things couldn't get any better. Dani's entire body seemed to be smiling.

"Can I put the boots on you?" he asked.

She stilled. "Just like Cinderella."

"Well, if the shoe fits…" Bryce reached for her left foot. "But they aren't exactly glass slippers."

Dani's heart sang. "They're better."

She leaned against a wall of the stable while he pulled off the old boots and put on the new ones. These were what she wanted, what she needed. Just like him. Bryce really did know her.

This was like a fairy tale come true, but with no fairy godmother required.

"How do they feel?" Bryce asked when he'd finished.

The love in his voice brought a sigh to her lips. She straightened, leaned back on her heels and wiggled her toes. "A perfect fit."

"Perfect fit, huh?"

She nodded. "Just like us."

"I could have told you that."

"Your compatibility program did."

He smiled. "I don't need a computer algorithm to tell me what my heart's known all along."

Dani saw not only her dreams coming, but a lifetime of love in his eyes. "What's that?"

"The two of us are perfect for each other."

EPILOGUE

To: "Englishcrumpet" <englishcrumpet@blinddatebrides.com>
"Kangagirl" <kangagirl@blinddatebrides.com>
From: "Sanfrandani" <sanfrandani@blinddatebrides.com>
Subject: Let's schedule a chat!
I have so much to tell you, but the biggest news is…
I'm engaged! Can you believe it???
We considered eloping for about thirty seconds, but know a long engagement makes smarter sense. Plus then maybe you both can come!
Bryce said you two told him where to find me. Thank you so much! You are the best friends ever!!! xoxox
Love,
Dani
P.S. Bryce reactivated my Blinddatebrides.com account.
P.P.S. Do you think six bridesmaids would be too many? My three sisters, Bryce's and the two of you!!!

* * * * *

So you think you can write?

Mills & Boon® and Harlequin® have joined forces in a global search for new authors.

It's our biggest contest yet—with the prize
of being published by the world's
leader in romance fiction.

In September join us for our unique
Five Day Online Writing Conference
www.soyouthinkyoucanwrite.com

Meet 50+ romance editors who want to
buy your book and get ready to
submit your manuscript!

So you think you can write?
Show us!

HARLEQUIN®
entertain, enrich, inspire™

MILLS & BOON®

SYTYCW_2

A sneaky peek at next month...

By Request

RELIVE THE ROMANCE WITH THE BEST OF THE BEST

My wish list for next month's titles...

In stores from 21st September 2012:

☐ Mistress to the Mediterranean Male
   – Carole Mortimer, Diana Hamilton & Kathryn Ross

☐ The Equalisers – Debra Webb

3 stories in each book - only £5.99!

In stores from 5th October 2012:

☐ The Garrisons: Parker, Brittany & Stephen – Roxanne St. Claire, Sara Orwig & Anna DePalo

Available at WHSmith, Tesco, Asda, Eason, Amazon and Apple

Just can't wait?

Visit us Online
You can buy our books online a month before they hit the shops! **www.millsandboon.co.uk**

Book of the Month

MILLS & BOON

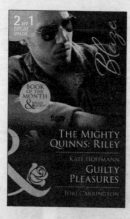

We love this book because...

This irresistible 2-in-1 introduces Kate Hoffmann's latest Quinns trilogy. Set in Ireland; expect rolling green hills...and drop-dead gorgeous Irish men! Songwriter Riley Quinn isn't looking for The One. Of course, that is before he meets the American girl who makes his blood burn like fire. He can't get enough of her. But in a few days, she'll be going home...

On sale 21st September

Visit us Online

Find out more at
www.millsandboon.co.uk/BOTM

0912/BOTM

Special Offers

Every month we put together collections and longer reads written by your favourite authors.

Here are some of next month's highlights— and don't miss our fabulous discount online!

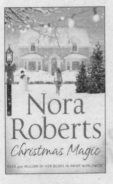

On sale 5th October

On sale 5th October

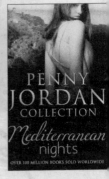

On sale 5th October

Save 20% on all Special Releases

Find out more at
www.millsandboon.co.uk/specialreleases

Visit us Online

1012/ST/MB38